HEAVENLY
ELAINE FOX

"Hurray! There's a vibrant new voice in romance, and her name is Elaine Fox!"

—Patricia Gaffney, Bestselling Author of
To Have and to Hold

"A delightful heroine, a dream of a hero, and a timeless love combine for a charming debut! Elaine Fox's *Traveler* is a winner!"

—Nora Roberts

"Fox hits on a winning combination!"

—*Romantic Times,* on *Traveler*

"Engrossing, compelling, and completely believable...one of the best-written, original, and fun novels to come across my desk in ages!"

—Bestselling author M. L. Gamble, on *Traveler*

RACING HEARTS

Angell shifted so that he faced Ava, both of them leaning one shoulder against the back of the car. Then the train hit a curve and she lurched against him, her hand on his chest.

His hands caught her shoulders and the train steadied, but he did not loosen his grip. She felt her nerves melt beneath his touch, felt the barely concealed longing within her rise up and make her lean into his hands.

His eyes were on her, she could see them despite the darkness, now that they were so close. And they were so close. It was so dark. And they were so alone. On the back of a speeding train that raced through the coal-black midnight of Midwestern farmland. The knowledge of such privacy squelched the protesting voice inside her.

"What do you want, Ava?" he asked, his voice dusky, his hands hot even through the jacket.

She was on the verge of saying it, of asking for what she'd wanted since she'd stepped out on this platform with him. Her breath came rapidly, and she parted her lips to speak.

"Say it," he said, his grip tightening. "You have to say it, Ava."

"Kiss me," she said in a hot, hoarse breath.

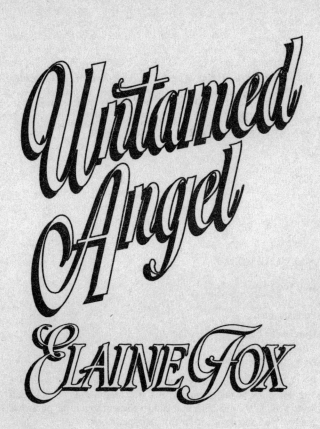

Untamed Angel

Elaine Fox

LEISURE BOOKS **NEW YORK CITY**

*My profound thanks to Marsha Nuccio (aka M. L. Gamble)
for keeping me true to the story and to Angell.*

And thanks to Mary McGowan for a great title!

A LEISURE BOOK®

July 1997

Published by

Dorchester Publishing Co., Inc.
276 Fifth Avenue
New York, NY 10001

Printed in the United States of America.

Prologue

March, 1860
Georgia

The boy sprinted through the trees, wet branches lashing his face and slicing his hands. His good shoes slapped against mud and muck, his feet slipped, caught, and pushed forward again. Behind him, through the mist, the baying of the hounds echoed hollowly. Always the same distance, never tiring.

His lungs burned. His breath rasped loud in his ears. Unconscious tears of terror burned hot on his cheeks. Strong, coltish legs protested every step, yet he could not stop. They would catch him, and if the dogs didn't tear him up, they would take him back to River Oaks and chain him like an animal. He knew what would happen then; he'd seen Seth after the dogs had got to him and he knew the stings suffered from tree branches would be nothing compared to the lash of the driver's whip.

The underbrush grew thick. He stumbled on, pushing aside brambles and prickers, heedless of the blood

9

they drew. Ahead of him, the forest was dense. Tendrils of mist rose up from the ground like specters, ghostly arms wound around trees and beckoned him forward, enveloping him as he plunged onward.

The boy felt his knees falter at the same time his toe caught on a root. Momentum threw him forward, hands outstretched, and he splattered to the ground, sliding hard on soaked leaves and mud.

He lay still, gasping in the gauzy air, and strained to hear the barking of the dogs, the snapping of tree limbs, the shouts of men as they thrashed through the underbrush. But he heard nothing. Nothing.

He didn't move, taking momentary comfort in the feel of the earth on his chest, the mud in his hands. The dank smell of leaf mold thickened the air. He lay his head on one arm, listening, unable to stop the sharp, desperate heave of his own breathing.

All was quiet. Had they reached the creek and lost his scent?

He closed his eyes. The earth warmed quickly to his body, conformed to his shape. He thought if he could just be safe, he would never leave this spot.

Behind his closed eyelids, he saw the dogs again. The horrible moment when the driver had rounded the barn with them straining forward against their leashes. And behind him had stood the overseer, his face still a livid red from the scalding water.

The boy had meant to kill him—had flung the kettle at his head in an attempt to bash in the man's brain. But though the overseer had screamed in pain, he'd leapt up from the broken, bloody body beneath him and lunged for the child.

The last word the boy's mother had spoken had been his name. A terrified appeal to him for help. But he couldn't help her. He couldn't stop the man, nor the words that assaulted her.

Master's toy. Mulatto whore.

Slave.

It didn't matter that she was octoroon, or that her skin was fairer than the overseer's. It didn't matter that her son was the son of the master and tutored by an English governess, or that he carried no brand in deference to his paternity. Now that the master had a legitimate son, the boy and his mother were worthless. The overseer could have her.

The boy raised his head and held his breath. There. One braying hound. He waited, paralyzed. Another joined it.

His heart skipped a beat, and he hauled himself to his knees.

The howling increased, crawling along his skin like bugs.

His legs trembled as he pulled himself upright along the rough bark of a tree. Were they closer? Or farther to the right?

He swallowed hard. How much farther did the forest go? If he were truly heading west, he should have come to the river. If only it weren't so foggy . . .

With a wet burst of rain, something broke out of the trees to his left. A deer with a full rack of antlers bounded deftly past and disappeared into the mist.

He stared after it, heart thrumming. The dogs must be close.

He clutched the tree beside him and rested his cheek against its bark. His lungs struggled for air, and his legs shook. He had a hard time swallowing over the lump in his throat. He couldn't go on. He could never escape them.

From somewhere out of the mist came the whisper of his mother's voice. *Run, angel,* she said, the words suddenly so close to his ear that his hair might have trembled with her breath. *Run as fast and as far as you can. Don't let them kill you, too.*

The boy pushed himself up and ran.

Chapter One

New York City
September, 1882

"You're *what?*" Ava Moreland spun on her younger sister, her mouth dropped open in shock. Her silk skirt swirled about her legs, and she grasped the closest thing to her for balance, a faux marble half-column topped with a huge fern in robust health.

Priscilla Moreland lay on the brocaded davenport, plucking moodily at a box of pralines. With an irritated shake of the wrist, she disentangled the lace sleeve of her negligee from the candies. "Please don't get all dramatic about it, Ava. I just need some advice and, believe me, if I could turn to anyone else, I would."

Ava watched Priscilla's tongue cover her full lower lip while she studied the sweets. The mannerism had been cute on the chubby, curly-haired child her sister had once been, she thought angrily, but on the heels of the news she'd just casually dropped into the conversation, it now smacked of a lewd insolence.

12

At Ava's protracted silence, Priscilla looked up. "All right, if you must have it repeated, I'm expecting. Pregnant. With child." She enunciated the words with schoolroom precision and widened her eyes in mock horror. "I've been sullied, soiled, *ruined*. I am impure—"

Ava winced as if the words were a physical assault. "You have had sexual intercourse with a man," she stated, knowing she sounded stupid and slow but hoping to God her sister would burst out laughing at the awful joke. Her lips were stiff as they formed the unfamiliar words.

Priscilla waved a pale hand. "All right. Say it that way."

Ava stared at her. "With whom?"

Limpid eyes drifted up to Ava's astounded glare. Priscilla raised a brow and her baby-doll mouth curved into a smile. "Come now, Ava, do you think I'm going to tell you as easily as all that?"

The impudence of Priscilla's tone sent irritation sizzling along Ava's nerves. Clearly, her sister, who had always been the darling of the family, the perfect, creamy-skinned, downy-soft debutante of the decade, had now proved beyond a doubt that she was nothing more than a spoiled, self-centered child. This time, Ava thought with a weary, fatalistic outrage, *this time*, she'd gone too far.

"Fine," Ava snapped. "Don't tell me. Don't tell me any of it. I don't want to know." She turned swiftly to the door, half-hoping the movement would force her sister to confess, half-hoping Priscilla would let her go.

"I don't intend to tell you," Priscilla said loudly.

Ava stopped, turning slowly.

Priscilla popped another praline past perfect lips and chewed appreciatively. "Not that part, anyway."

Despite her desire to leave, Ava hesitated. It was incredible, this nonchalance in the face of the most monstrous confession she could have made. A combination of fear and shame for her sister bubbled beneath Ava's breast. Without another thought, she strode to the satin-covered davenport on which Priscilla lounged, grabbed the box of candies and flung them back against the wall.

Priscilla gaped as the little nuts clattered to the floor, some bouncing like marbles.

"Listen to me, Priscilla Moreland," Ava ground out, teeth clenched against a sudden nausea. "*You* are in a lot of trouble. If this cretin who defiled you doesn't stand up and do the right thing, you shall be ostracized from society. We *all* shall be! Neither Mother nor Father, nor all the family's wealth will be able to save you from banishment. *No one* will have you. Do you understand? No one. Do you remember Daphne Carollton?"

At this, Priscilla blanched, and Ava caught the first inkling of fear in her sulky eyes.

"Daphne was not even with child. She was merely caught—in—ah—" Ava struggled for an acceptable euphemism.

"They were caught naked," Priscilla grumbled. "Just say it, for pity's sake."

"They were caught in a *compromising position*," Ava insisted. "Daphne with that odious, middle-class man. And now the whole family has moved somewhere out west. They couldn't stay here in New York, not after that, not with everyone *knowing* what she'd done. Is that what you want for us? Social exile?"

Priscilla watched her petulantly, as if it were Ava's reaction that created the scandal, not her own pregnancy. "Mr. Marks is still here," she said. "It couldn't have been so bad if *he's* still accepted."

Ava shook her head and closed her eyes. "It's different for men. And besides, he's not accepted, not really. The Hendersons won't have him, and neither will the Aldens."

"Pah," Priscilla spat. "The Hendersons. Who couldn't do without them? And their horrid dinner parties! If I never see another swan sculpted out of liver—"

"Pâté," Ava corrected sharply.

"*Whatever*. I can live without it."

Ava's fists clenched by her sides. "What in the world are you thinking? How can you be so indifferent? Do you really think you'll be able to bear this child without repercussions? For the love of God, Cilla, people won't even walk on the same side of the street with you!"

Priscilla narrowed her eyes. "Then perhaps I'll . . . I'll see someone. . . . A doctor," she said, frowning.

Ava gasped and stared at her sister as if she'd grown another head. "You'll do no such thing! Do you know how many women *die* trying something like that?"

Priscilla leaned forward, mouth twisted in anger. "Do you know how many women die in childbirth?" she countered.

Inexplicably, a lump grew in the back of Ava's throat, and she had to swallow hard before speaking. "It's worse, Cilla," she insisted. "Much worse. I won't let you do it."

A long moment passed before Priscilla shrugged and leaned back. "All right. I'll go away."

Hope sprang into Ava's heart. "Yes," she said, thinking. "*Yes*, you can go away. To France! To Aunt Felicity. We can trust her. We'll tell people you've gone to visit your aunt!" Ava's mood swept upward. "It won't even be a lie. And the child can stay there with her."

"No!" Priscilla said.

"Perhaps she knows a good woman in her vill—"

"I said *no*!" Priscilla sat up straight, and her feet hit the floor with a slap.

Ava abruptly closed her mouth.

"I want it," Priscilla stated.

She felt rooted to the spot. "What?" It was breath of a word.

"I won't leave it there. The baby. I want it."

Into Ava's head popped an improbable vision of Priscilla in the parlor with a baby amidst the countless admirers who always congregated around her.

"What would you do with a baby?" Ava asked. But at the same time she had the reluctant thought, *Who could leave a baby behind?*

"I don't know. It could be fun," Priscilla said in a

small voice. Then she smiled, thinking. "Men just *adore* babies, you know. I've seen it. They turn into mush around them."

A hopeless awareness descended on Ava at that moment, a clarity that allowed her to see Priscilla would never understand the magnitude of her problem, nor would she see how it could ruin all of their lives. She had no intention of helping herself. She would simply sit back and allow Ava to come between her and disaster—again.

But this was worse than the time Priscilla had been caught gambling, Ava thought. Worse than the time she'd tried smoking Randolph Peterman's cigar at the Masons' ball. Worse even than that which Ava had previously considered the most heinous crime possible—when Priscilla had posed in a toga for one of Gerard Pelletier's raunchy, trendy oils.

No, this time she'd actually done the unthinkable. This time she'd lain with a man.

The swift stab of an emotion she could not identify penetrated Ava's breast and caused her cheeks to flame. She covered her mouth with her fingers, paralyzed with realization.

She was jealous.

"All right. I won't visit a doctor," Priscilla conceded. "Sit down, would you? Before you faint and knock over one of Mother's Mings." She gestured toward the ornate vase on a nearby table.

Ava gazed at her sister, seeing her now as a possessor of hidden truths, a woman who had crossed the Rubicon and appeared unremorseful. Priscilla knew what it felt like to be kissed. Not pecked in a stolen drawing room moment, but really kissed—open mouths, searching hands—the way she'd once seen a lady of uncertain morals kiss a man on the corner of 39th Street.

Priscilla knew what a man looked like naked. She knew what that bulge actually was, what it meant, what it could do, what it *felt like*.

Ava sat down, stunned by the enormity of her own curiosity.

"What?" Priscilla demanded, irritated. "Why are you staring at me like that?"

Ava chewed her lower lip, then realized what she was doing and stopped. "What was it like?" she asked softly.

Priscilla's eyes grew wary. "What?"

Ava pressed her lips together, appalled at her gross interest. But the persistence of the feeling would not abate. "What did it feel like?"

"What?" Priscilla asked irritably. Then comprehension dawned. She raised her brows and looked at her sister through heavy-lidded eyes. "You mean, *it*? The dreaded *act*?"

Ava could only nod, once.

Her sister's face softened a fraction and a smile, nothing like the sultry one she'd issued earlier, caressed her lips. "Oh Ava. It was *wonderful*," she said breathlessly. "I've never felt so good in all my life."

The words were a shock, and at the same time they were strangely exciting. After years of hearing the disgusted murmurs, quickly hushed, of the married women in her mother's sewing group, and then the sly whispered musings between her own contemporaries, to speak with someone who actually *knew* about the deed and thought it *wonderful* was completely unexpected. And for some reason Ava found it exhilarating.

She lowered herself onto the opposite divan. "It was wonderful?" she repeated breathlessly.

Priscilla closed her eyes and nodded. "Oh, yes."

"*Tell* me who the father is," Ava said, leaning forward in the seat toward her sister, hungry to know the identity of the person who had wrought such pleasure. Someone she knew? How strange that one of the shallow young men who hung around Washington Square was capable of such a mystery. Which of those silly lapdogs was able to transform her sister so?

But at the question Priscilla's face closed up. "No."

"Why not?" Ava blurted.

"Because I don't want you to know." Priscilla toyed with the fringed sash of her morning negligee.

Ava threw up her hands, frustration and embarrassment swallowing her. "All right. Fine. Can you tell me this? Will he marry you? Will he do right by you and own up to his abhorrent behavior?"

Priscilla pursed her pretty lips and stared obstinately off toward the Italian marble fireplace, her fingers braiding and unbraiding the tassel.

She was fabricating a lie, Ava knew. She always got that dazed look on her face when she was making something up.

"He's dead." Priscilla turned her face back to her sister and raised her chin. "How's that? He wanted to marry me and now he's dead. Will you help me now? Will you make people accept that?"

Ava slumped in her chair. "They won't believe it, and neither do I." She ignored her sister's exasperated sigh. "There's only one thing to do."

"What's that?" The stilling of Priscilla's pale hands told Ava more than she wanted to know about her sister's true measure of concern. For Priscilla to turn to her at all should have been evidence enough that her sister was desperate, despite her casual attitude. The two of them had never been close. Ava had always been the smart one, Priscilla the pretty one. While Ava used to think the enmity had originated on Priscilla's side, her own jealous reaction to Priscilla's predicament shed an uneasy light on the subject.

"I'll help you," Ava said finally and looked her sister dead in the eye. "I'll do the only acceptable thing." Ava's fists balled in her lap.

Priscilla licked her dry lips and looked at her, at once defensive and expectant.

Ava swallowed hard. "I'll do the one thing that will allow you to have your baby and keep it, too. I'll find you a husband."

Chapter Two

Himey, Missouri
October, 1882

The group of calico-clad women near the post office caught Joshua Angell's attention as he hefted three twenty-pound bags of flour onto his shoulder in front of the General Store. He slowed to a stop, flipped a lock of dark hair out of his eyes with a jerk of his head, and studied the group a moment.

It was possible, he supposed, that the appearance of the afternoon stage in this backward little town was cause for such excitement, but he hoped it was something more worthy of attention than that. Lord knew, he could use a little excitement right about now. Helping put up supplies for a wagon train heading west was about as much fun as watching an old mule on a hot day. And it was netting him about as much pay.

He caught the eye of a cowhand leaning against the weathered clapboard of the store and moved closer. "What's doin' with the ladies?"

The man turned a beady gaze on him, spat onto the

19

planking of the boardwalk and shrugged. "Stage come in."

Angell raised an eyebrow. "That so?" He shifted his eyes back to the crowd. "Reckon that's the one bringin' them dancin' girls," he mused, squinting at the gathering crowd as if to see better.

The cowhand straightened. "How's that?"

"I say," Angell scratched his cheek awkwardly with one shoulder, shifting the heavy weight of the bags on the other, "I heard they was importin' some dancin' girls for Grandy's Saloon. A passel a eight, maybe ten of 'em. Bet that's them."

The man craned his neck in the direction of the stage and unconsciously tucked a baggy portion of shirt into his pants. "Why's it all women folk gatherin' 'round, then?" He narrowed his eyes at Angell, who shrugged.

"What better time to let 'em know they ain't welcome?" With that Angell stepped off the boardwalk and headed across the dirt road to the boardinghouse, behind which the wagons were being loaded for the trip. Out of the corner of his eye, he noticed the cowhand strolling toward the post office, a low cloud of dust following his shuffling footsteps.

Angell supposed he could join up with this ragtag group heading west, maybe pick himself up some pay for herding cattle or riding shotgun, but he didn't really have an urge to head farther out. Life was lonely on the plains, he'd heard, and he was not interested in being lonely, not anymore. He'd kept his head down and his face out of sight for so long now, he was ready to try something new. Anything new, so long as he wasn't running anymore.

After loading the flour, he headed back to the store, noticing it wasn't just women gathering at the stage now. A few men had stopped to look. *Hell, before long the entire town might be in attendance*, Angell thought, hating the fact that he himself was feeling a mite curious.

A kid in a shabby green vest raced by, and Angell

nabbed him by the scruff of his collar. "Hold up!" he said, laughing, as the boy skidded to a halt in the dirt.

"Hey, git offa me!" The kid squirmed beneath Angell's grip, his collar up around his ears. "Whadya want?"

"What's goin' on?" Angell asked. "Over there, with the stage."

"I don't know. Coupla city folk, is all, duded up real slick. Miz Wiggins told me ta git my ma. Them's fancy riggin' they got on."

Angell set him back on the ground, and the boy shrugged his clothing back into place. "That's it? Fancy clothes and the whole goddamn town flocks to see 'em?"

The boy looked back at the gathering group. "Why not? Ain't much else doin'," he said, then added, "See ya," and was off like a shot.

Angell glanced after him, then back at the gathering, which now seemed to be moving. Whoever it was apparently wanted to get someplace, and the mob was moving with them. He smiled cynically to himself. Bet they were surprised to find themselves celebrities, just for showing up.

Well, it didn't matter any to him, he decided, ducking back into the store, as long as they weren't from anyplace near Georgia.

Half an hour later, Angell could not help but stare at the stunning, honey-haired woman in the dark green traveling suit who entered Miss Howkam's boardinghouse.

He was sitting in an armchair near the front desk, waiting for Old Jem to come back with his pay when she entered, gracing the room with both beauty and a pretty smell. She had to be the one who'd drawn the crowd earlier, he thought, for she was extremely well dressed and was followed by a foppish, bespectacled gentleman whom Angell hoped to heaven was not her husband, if only to maintain his faith in the rightness of things.

Miss Howkam, straightlaced and pickle-faced,

stood tense and inhospitable behind the front desk, somehow exuding both awe and disapproval simultaneously.

"Can I help you?" she barked at the newcomers.

"Are you the proprietress?" the beauty asked in a voice that was as rich and honeyed as her hair. At the sound of it, Angell felt something wither inside himself—his confidence, or his optimism, perhaps both. The lady was class. As fine as silk sheets and twice as smooth. A lady the likes of which he hadn't seen in more years than he could count—and one he could not even engage in conversation without feeling as if he was courting serious danger. And she was just as pretty as a damn picture.

"Yes'm, I am." Miss Howkam's sour air of displeasure looked to have taken a beating in the face of Beauty's obvious breeding, and she attempted a gruesome smile. Up until the moment the lady spoke, there'd been the possibility she was one of those highpriced courtesans, not deserving of respect even though she wore nice clothes. Clearly, that was not the case. Angell wondered what on earth could have brought such a specimen to a filthy little backwater like Himey.

"We require two rooms. The cleanest you have will do." Beauty pulled off her gloves a finger at a time with cool, snapping efficiency.

"Every one of 'em's clean," Miss Howkam said peevishly, taking a card from beneath the desk. "I'll set you up in my best rooms. I run a clean house here." She produced a blackened ink pot and dipped an ancient pen into it.

"I'm sure you do," Beauty concurred, in a tone that to Angell's ears warned the place had better be clean. "Have you a man to take our bags up?"

Miss Howkam finished filling out the check-in card with painstaking slowness and turned it to Beauty for her signature. "I'll get 'em up there," she promised. "Rooms two and three, upstairs to the right. Privy's to the left, first door. You'll find it's clean, too."

"Very good," the cultured voice said, effectively ending the topic of conversation by tone alone.

Angell watched Beauty's hand move in a graceful flourish as she signed her name, then she handed the quill to the little professor by her side. "I'd appreciate your having the bags taken up directly, as I would like to freshen up before supper. Might you recommend a reputable establishment where we could dine?"

Miss Howkam's expression screwed up uncertainly at this statement. "You want to eat?"

Beauty's mouth curved in a forced, though pretty, smile. "That's correct."

Miss Howkam pursed her lips. "There's only one place in town for the likes of you," she pronounced, grabbing the card back from the little professor and holding it protectively to her middle. "Rose's Place, out the door to the left. Food's not grand, but the atmosphere won't offend your ladylike senses the way them other places will."

It was Beauty's turn to look perplexed, Angell noted with a private smile, but she didn't ask what manner of evil her ladylike senses should be on the lookout for.

"Rose's, then," she said with a nod.

"That'll be cash up front, now," Miss Howkam added, as if their fine clothes and upscale demeanor weren't fooling her.

"Now just a—" the professor piped up, but Beauty cut him off.

"Pay her," she instructed.

"But her implication . . ."

Beauty sighed and shook her head. "Just pay her, Harvey. What difference does it make?"

Miss Howkam glanced at the card in her hand. "Thank you, Miz . . . Moreland. I appreciate your understanding."

Miss Moreland waved her hand in dismissal and started for the stairs.

Before he knew what he was about, Angell stood and cleared his throat. Beauty, as he preferred to think of the lady, turned and fixed dark-lashed gray eyes on him. He felt the blood stall in his veins.

Elaine Fox

"Yes?" she inquired.

Though he'd only meant to rise as she passed, he guessed he must have looked as if he were about to speak, so he did. "Rose's ain't the place to eat," he improvised, realizing as he spoke that the bumpkin accent he'd affected for so long sounded especially coarse in the harsh light of the lady's refinement.

She moved not a muscle, just stood there looking at him with those fine, cool eyes. The little professor stepped around her to glare at him with what he considered unwarranted hostility.

Angell held up his hands in a kind of shrug and took one step backward. "I ain't tryin' to be presumptuous," he said, pulling the word out with mild triumph from some long-unused lexicon in the back of his brain. "I'm just thinkin' your *ladylike sensibility* might be more affected if you had to spend the next three days in the privy." Though the words were true, he nearly winced at his own crudeness as they emerged. But, he reminded himself, it wasn't as if this conversation could possibly go anywhere anyway. He might as well play it up, see how much the lady could take.

Miss Moreland's face took on a mild look of disgust. "And where might you recommend we dine, Mister . . . ?"

"Angell," he said and promptly doffed his hat, pushing it under his arm. He could still be polite.

Miss Moreland covered her look of surprise at his name as soon as it appeared, something most people didn't even try to do, and Angell was impressed. With his dark hair and tanned skin, most people just laughed outright at the incongruous name.

"I appreciate yer not laughin' at the name, ma'am. Most people can't resist it. I reckon it's my light-colored eyes with this black hair. One lady told me I looked downright demonic." He laughed briefly. "But she was a whore so I don't suppose her opinion matters much." Neither Beauty nor the professor appeared to have much to say to this, so Angell, masking an amused smile at their identical expressions,

24

cleared his throat and repeated, "Anyway, I'm Joshua Angell, at your service."

He held out his hand, and the two of them looked skeptically at it. With a grim smile, he withdrew it and continued, "Grandy's, across the street, is where you want to eat. It's a saloon and there's girls in there, but it's the best food for a hundred miles."

The little professor started to laugh, or sneer, making some kind of noise that seemed to come primarily from his nose. Angell raised a brow.

"A saloon?" the man asked. "You can't be serious."

Angell eyed him a moment until the man shifted uncomfortably. "I know you folks might be a bit lofty for the settin', but I reckon Rose's'll take more a the shine offa your pride—bein' on the john for the better part of a week and all." He shoved his hands in his pockets and moved his gaze from one to the other of them.

Miss Moreland still wore a faint look of distaste, and the little professor smirked openly.

"You don't honestly expect that I should take someone of Miss Moreland's caliber to a common saloon, Mr. Angell? Surely I've misunderstood you."

Despite his desire to tweak the finer sensibilities of these gloriously out-of-place blue bloods, Angell felt suddenly stupid for ever opening his mouth. Stupid and coarse, in his dusty leather vest, mud-encrusted boots and hefty two-gun rig. He would never have admitted it out loud, but at that moment he envied the pompous little professor. Envied his round intellectual glasses, his fine, dove-gray frock coat and even those ridiculous button-up ankle boots.

"Suit yourself," he said. His gaze swept back to Miss Moreland's face, his eyes taking in her flawless skin, the clear eyes, the amber sheen of her hair. Unexpected desire, like a hunger, roiled deeply in his gut. "I reckon I was just tryin' to help." He took his hat from under his arm and placed it firmly back on his head. He started to turn away when she stopped him.

"Thank you, Mr. Angell." Her voice held the first note of warmth he'd heard. He turned back. Her slim white hand was outstretched toward him. "I appreciate your intervention. We will take your advice."

An unaffected grin tugged at Angell's mouth. He took her hand in his. "Happy to oblige," he murmured, peripherally absorbing the softness of her skin.

With a nod and a sweet smile, she turned and walked up the stairs, followed by the pompous professor. Angell couldn't help but watch her go, admiring the sway of her hips under the fine material of her skirt, the precise set of her shoulders and the vulnerable curve of her neck where tendrils of hair had escaped her braided coil.

She was not the typical haughty belle, he reflected, bringing the fingers of the hand she'd touched toward his nose. *Lilac.* He folded his arms and sighed, gazing after her. What would a man have to do, he wondered, for God to grace him with a woman like that?

He was only taking his own advice, Angell told himself as he pushed through the doors of Grandy's saloon. It wasn't as if *he* wanted to sit on the john for the next week just to avoid the appearance of following her.

His eyes swept the room in search of her and came up empty. She might be like one of those European types who only eat once the sun goes down and the moon is high, he thought, and wondered how long he could stretch out his meal without looking ridiculous—or getting rip-roaring drunk.

Angell frowned, shook his head, and moved forward into the dining room. It wouldn't do any good for him to hang around here waiting to see her anyway. What would he do—engage her in more brilliant conversation as he did earlier? Stupid, he thought. He'd wanted to provoke her and ended up feeling stupid himself. He should have listened to that part of him that said not to talk about privies with a lady. Especially not such a real high-born gem. What in the world had he been thinking?

He'd been thinking about her eyes, that's what, and that cool distant stare. He'd been thinking about her long, vulnerable neck and the arrogant confidence she had that her position would protect her from any passing ruffian. But she'd proved herself human, and he'd ended up thinking of her pearly skin, and how soft that hair might feel if he were to plunge his fingers into it.

The fact is, he reminded himself, a woman like that doesn't eat, she *dines*. She doesn't need a bed and a bath, she *requires a room*. She doesn't rustle up some chow, she asks for a *reputable establishment*. He didn't need a woman like that.

Angell seated himself at a table toward the back of the room, close to the door so that if she came in he could see her without her noticing him. He just wanted to watch her a while, he told himself, let himself imagine talking to her as an equal, like the little professor. He wondered if the two were engaged. Maybe they were brother and sister, he thought brightly, though they didn't look at all alike. Beauty was all spun gold and alabaster white. The little professor had flat brown eyes, dirt brown hair, and a naturally brown expression. Not a laugh line on his face.

Angell opened the newspaper he had brought and scanned the front page.

"Hi there, Angell," a feminine voice cooed.

He looked up from the paper to see Pauline saunter toward him, the end of a bright pink feather boa that looped around her shoulders in each hand.

The redhead had been trying to get him to sample her wares since he'd ridden into town two weeks ago, and he'd come pretty damn close on more than one occasion. But even before Beauty had shown up and spoiled his appetite for common things, he'd been resisting the easy route of paying for satisfaction. He'd even considered seeking out some nice young thing and courting her, though of course he'd never marry. No, that wouldn't be fair. Not to any woman.

"Hey, Pauline," he said. "What's cookin' this fine evenin'?"

Her rouged lips curved upward, displaying a sensuality belied by the childlike gleam in her eyes. "Why,

27

you know I'm always on a slow boil for you, Angell," she purred. She settled one hip on his table and caressed the bare skin just above her low-cut bodice.

He felt his own lips bend in return. She was comely, no doubt about it. "Well, I sure am hungry," he drawled, when a sudden hush filled the room. His eyes strayed from Pauline's pink boa to the door. There, in sudden uncertainty and obvious trepidation, stood Beauty, her hair pinned loosely on the top of her head, her sleek figure clad in a peacock-blue gown.

His impulse was to get up and go to her, try to ease the worried line of her brow, but when she caught sight of him she swiftly averted her eyes. Stung, he leaned back in his chair.

"Who's *that*?" Pauline asked, her young mouth agape. "She sure ain't from around here."

Angell chewed the inside of his lip and studied her. "Nope. She sure ain't."

The professor hadn't noticed him, but it wouldn't have mattered if he had. There would have been no acknowledgment, Angell knew.

"Pauline, honey, get me a whiskey, will ya?" he asked, his eyes not leaving the smooth passage Beauty made from door to table. A host of sorts had materialized from behind the bar and seated them at the best table in the house. Gradually, the noise in the room worked its way back up to normal.

Angell didn't know why he cared about Beauty's rejection. Hell, he'd asked for it. It was just that he'd almost convinced himself she was made of better stuff than the usual highbrow. Why, he wasn't sure. She was beautiful, it was true. But there was something else, something in her look. Something that drew him like a witch's long-lost familiar.

Pauline returned with his whiskey, and he slammed it back in one swig. He ordered another, along with whatever today's special happened to be, and continued to watch Beauty and the professor.

Beauty spread her napkin on her lap and said something low to her companion. As she spoke, her eyes trailed around the room, taking in the motley crew at the bar and the vociferous poker game in the corner. One of the boys at the bar graced her with a yellow-toothed leer and she blanched, then stared rigidly at her hands in her lap.

Angell wished she'd relax, show some curiosity instead of that prudish fear of the unwashed. The man was probably just happy to still *have* teeth and showed them off at every opportunity. But her mouth was pinched into a line, and the stealthy travel of her eyes undermined her pretty face.

As the professor bent toward her and spoke, Angell was sure the little jackanape was filling her head with all the evils represented by the collection of men in Grandy's this evening. He was probably guaranteeing some sort of calamitous molestation unless she stuck right close to him. It was a trick he'd seen done a dozen times by men with unmarried ladies they wanted to keep.

It was what he'd be doing right now if he were sitting with her.

His meal arrived, and he looked down in dismay to see that he'd ordered liver and onions. He glanced up at Pauline and caught her in an ungracious smirk.

"That'll teach ya to pay more 'tention," she said with a flip of her bouncy red hair.

"Where's the whiskey?"

She pouted. "Keep yer pants on, I'll get it." She flopped off again.

Angell sighed and plucked an onion off the plate with his fingers. *This is stupid,* he thought again. Sitting here like a love-starved puppy while the Grand Dame of Aristocracy sat not ten yards away, probably wishing he would disappear. He picked up another onion and chewed it before he noticed it tasted like liver. He pushed the plate away.

Pauline returned with his drink and leaned against his table, pulling one leg up onto it to expose a fish-netted line of calf. "Whadya say, Ange? I got a free couple hours tonight and you know I had my eye on you for a while now." She leaned forward, and Angell noted a light sprinkling of freckles across her chest above the swell of her breasts.

Instead of answering, he took a sip of whiskey, determined to nurse this one. He wasn't making near enough money to start squandering it on liquor.

Setting down the drink, he studied her. "You're a right fine-lookin' girl, Pauline." He pushed his thumbs into the pockets of his vest and leaned back. "What ever made you turn to such a life as this one?"

Confusion floated in her blue eyes. "What's wrong with my life?"

Angell shrugged. "I don't know. Why don't you find some nice guy and settle down, 'stead a selling that pretty little body of yours?"

Instantly, her face cleared and she pushed one end of the feather boa around her neck. "Why, Mr. Angell," she purred and slid adroitly from the table to his lap. She wrapped a slim arm around his neck. Feathers tickled the underside of his chin. "You offerin', honey?"

He settled his big hands on her tiny waist and attempted to push her from her perch. "No, I wasn't talkin' about me, sugar." But, damn, her young body was warm and nice, right there for the taking. "I ain't worth marryin', take my word for it. I was talkin' about some nice boy a little closer to your own age." He glanced around the room in search of someone who might fit the description. But it was woefully clear why a pretty young thing like Pauline had turned to the life she had. None of the men in this room could provide her with the living she earned herself—with the possible exception of the little professor.

Angell's eyes narrowed, and he felt the devil take hold of his soul. He looked sideways at Pauline. "Take that young gent over there." He nodded his head in Beauty's direction. "I heard him talkin' earlier today about some redhead he saw—well, you know how men talk."

Pauline followed his gaze and took in the fancy clothes, the well-stocked table, and the obvious manners of the man in question. *"Him?"* She pointed and wrinkled her nose. "Why, he's sittin' there with his *wife*. You don't expect me to go flirtin' on him now, do you?"

"That ain't his wife, darlin'. I talked to them earlier today. I think she's his sister." He gave another light push, and this time Pauline rose, if only to get a better view. "And I'll tell you something else. I bet if you go on over there right now and start battin' them pretty blues of yours, you'd have him in the palm of your hand before dessert. And at the very least, a man like that's gotta have a right big purse."

"He is kinda cute," she mused, teasing her own cheek now with the tip of the boa.

"Hell, honey, it's worth a try. A swell like that's prob'ly got more money than he knows what to do with."

She licked her lips.

That little jackass wouldn't know what to do with a woman like Pauline, Angell thought, but at least she might keep him busy a minute or two. He wouldn't mind talking a minute with Miss Moreland, getting the ridiculous idea out of his head that she was any different than the rest of her class. And if he was wrong, perhaps she'd invite him to sit a spell with her. Some time spent with a beautiful woman wouldn't do his self-esteem any harm.

"Go on," he encouraged her. "If he gives you a hard time, come on back here and I'll buy you a drink. How's that?"

Pauline turned back with a sly smile. "What's in it for you?" she asked.

"Well," he hedged, "I wouldn't mind gettin' a word in edgewise with the lady, given the chance."

Pauline laughed and pinched his cheek. "My, but you do like to set yer sights high. You don't quite seem her type, Ange."

He snorted a laugh. *That* was the understatement of the century.

She looked at him with something like compassion. "All right. But I'm only doin' it for you. Flash her that pretty grin, slick, and you'll have a chance." With that, she stood and began a slow saunter toward their table.

Angell watched her. The closer Pauline got, the harder time the little professor had ignoring her. It was obvious he knew she was coming. She was right in his line of vision. And it was just as obvious that he was flustered by her perusal, because his color was as high as the stars and stripes and his eyes looked everywhere but her direction. When she was close enough, Pauline leaned her provocative hip on the table, her back to Miss Moreland, and bent toward him.

Angell couldn't hear what she said, but he knew it must be good from the way the professor's complexion took on an almost apoplectic hue. Beauty said something, no doubt some objection so polite Pauline wouldn't recognize it, and Pauline threw a rejoinder over her shoulder as lightly as the end of her boa.

The professor laughed nervously and slid his chair back a few inches as Pauline moved closer. Angell saw her finger the material of his lapel. Then, just when he thought she might be making some headway, Beauty stood up.

He heard her this time, for her voice was raised. "I would appreciate it if you would leave us to our meal in peace, Miss Whoever-You-Are."

Pauline gazed back over her shoulder like a cat with a treat she had no intention of surrendering. "Don't get your bloomers all in a knot, hon," she said. "We's just havin' a conversation here."

The little professor was speechless as he looked from one woman to the other, giving Pauline a weak smile and attempting to roll his eyes at Beauty.

Pauline took advantage of the situation and slid onto the professor's knee. "Why don't you go find yourself somethin' to do for a few minutes," she suggested to Miss Moreland. "We could use a minute or two to get acquainted."

In the same way that Angell's had, the professor's hands encircled her waist in an attempt to prompt her from her seat. But Pauline would have none of it. She raised her forearms to his shoulders, the ends of the boa in each hand.

Angell smiled to himself as he watched those bright pink feathers tickle the professor's scarlet baby face. He would just bet the feel of that corsetless waist beneath his palms would be the undoing of the pompous little man.

"This is outrageous," Beauty said, looking around the room as if for confirmation of the absurdity of the situation.

While every line of her body spoke her indignation, Angell experienced the first inkling that maybe this had been a bad idea. A moment later, when the man with the yellow leer approached her, he knew it was.

"Don't git uppity, now," the man said, every one of his ugly teeth showing. "Let the boy have a little fun. I'll keep ya busy for a while."

It was obvious old Yellow Teeth had had quite a bit to drink, and he had probably gone a mite too long between baths as well. Angell groaned and got to his feet. He'd started this whole mess. Now he was obligated to stop it.

"Thank you, no," Beauty stated. "If all of you would simply leave us alone, we'll be on our way. Harvey?" She snapped the professor's name like a whip, and he looked quickly at her, guilt obvious in his eyes.

Angell nearly chuckled. So the lick-spittle was enjoying Miss Pauline's company. He noted the swift removal of Harvey's hand from Pauline's nearly bare back.

"Oh, don't go, sugar," Pauline cooed, smoothing Harvey's hair with her fingers and leaning in so close her breasts pushed up against his shirt front. "I was just startin' to really like you."

"Jus' a drink," the thug slurred to Miss Moreland, placing a grimy paw on her pristine sleeve. "It'll calm ya right down. Tek my word fer it."

Beauty's eyes scanned the room in panic.

Angell felt a sharp pang of remorse. He cleared his throat. "I believe," he started in his laziest drawl, ambling toward the group, "the lady ain't interested in your company."

Yellow Teeth's yellow eyes slid to Angell. "Who in blazes are you?"

Angell felt regret seep into every pore. If he hadn't been so anxious to speak a few meaningless words to the poor woman, none of them would be in this predicament. He could tell just by Yellow Teeth's syrupy stare that the man was going to cause trouble. He was in the obstinate stage of drunkenness.

Angell sighed. "Consider me a—what's it called?" He deliberately took his time thinking. "A good smarmitan. That's what I am."

"What the devil is that?" Yellow Teeth barked, then looked back at his companions. "What the devil is he talkin' about?"

Beauty nearly swooned at the man's language, so Angell stepped up beside her, ready to catch anything that fell. Unable to resist the opportunity, he laid one hand lightly behind her elbow.

"How in tarnation should we know, Pug?" one of the man's companions said while his eyes rolled around in his head, seemingly without direction. "We don't know no more than you."

"I should think y'all would like to control your language in the presence of a lady," Angell offered. "But iffen you can't, she'll just be leavin' now."

Angell started to pull her back a step when Yellow Teeth, or Pug as his buddy had called him, moved one hand to the holster at his hip.

"I wouldn't go nowhere if I was you, mister," he said ominously.

Beauty gasped and leaned into Angell's side.

For a moment, he could think of nothing outside the sweet warmth of her body's pressure against his. He squeezed her elbow reassuringly.

"What, you gonna shoot me?" Angell inquired. "Right here? In front a all these witnesses?"

Pug looked around. "I don't see no witnesses. You boys see any witnesses?"

A surprising number of the men at the bar and surrounding tables answered with a resounding *"No."* Angell frowned. This idea was getting stupider by the minute. He glanced over to see the little professor struggling to stand despite Pauline's weight on his lap. Before the jackass had time to add to the problem, Angell suggested, "Maybe you and me oughta just settle this outside, just the two of us."

Pug showed his yellow teeth again. Beauty turned thick-lashed eyes at him and said, "You *mustn't*, Mr. Angell."

He flashed her a confident grin. "Don't you worry 'bout me, Miz Moreland. I can take care of myself."

Pug snorted. "I kin take care a myself," he mimicked in a high voice, then wiped the grin off his face and growled, "Why don't we jes go outside and see about that?"

The professor managed to extricate himself from Pauline's clutches and bustled over to Miss Moreland's other side. "This is absurd. This is completely uncalled for. Miss Moreland and I came here to enjoy a simple meal. We have no desire to be party to a *gunfight*," he objected, his voice cracking on the last word.

Pug and his buddies cackled loudly. "You kin stay here with the womenfolk, then," Pug said. "I'll be right back, doll," he added to Miss Moreland with a wink.

Angell rolled his eyes and turned toward the saloon doors. Behind him he heard the scrape and clatter of chairs as what must have been the entire room rose to its feet. He dreaded the scene he knew awaited him.

Another town to get kicked out of, he thought with fatigue. Not that Himey was anything special, but how did he always manage to get himself into these kinds of scrapes? Seemed the more he tried to be inconspicuous, the more he stirred things up. Inevitably, after a scene like this, he was asked to leave town, usually by the sheriff.

The group emerged into the gray light of dusk. Angell made his way to the middle of the road. Pug stumbled down the steps from the boardwalk and moved to a spot a few paces away. Dust kicked up behind his boots, and he checked the barrel of his pistol with a bleary eye.

Angell blew out a slow breath. The man was too

drunk to kill. The question then was which appendage to go for. He thought about shooting the man's hat off, but, generally speaking, when drunks were made to look like that much of a fool, they got ornery and kept shooting until they hit something. He considered shooting the gun out of his hand, but if he was just a little bit off the man could lose a finger, and that would make him really nasty. He could go for a shoulder or a thigh, but that would involve a lot of blood, and he didn't want Beauty collapsing into the dirt.

He opted for a foot. Maybe a little toe. No real damage, but enough pain to stop him from continuing to shoot, and enough blood to remind the fellow of the price of being a pig.

One of Pug's buddies stood off to the side with a red bandanna.

"Soon's I let go a this, start shootin'," the man said, loud enough for the crowd to hear.

Angell spied Miss Moreland off to the side, speaking frantically to the little professor. She pointed toward the jailhouse, probably demanding that he get the sheriff to break it up. Before the man had a chance to follow up on those orders, Angell planted his feet and gave a nod to the man holding the bandanna. No sense waiting for the law to show up.

Pug picked his stance and moved his arms stiffly out over his guns.

Angell narrowed his eyes, allowed his breathing to slow and felt his whole body relax. He nearly smiled with the familiar sensation.

The crowd hushed. Dust spiraled in a soft breeze.

The bandanna dropped.

Angell felt his body go fluid and his focus shrank to nothing but the one spot.

Shots rang out. Pug spun in the dust, jerked to the ground, then howled in agony, holding his foot.

Angell holstered his gun.

Then he noticed the sheriff step out of the crowd.

Chapter Three

"He's *perfect*," said Ava.

"He's *in jail*." Harvey was clearly aghast.

"He's just what we're looking for," she insisted.

"Ava, he's little better than a savage. Have you taken leave of your senses?"

Ava, standing by the window, sent Harvey a frosty glare, the kind she knew reduced otherwise self-composed men to guilty little boys. "*He* got me out of a very precarious situation while *you* were dallying around with that trollop. Father would have been horrified."

Harvey picked up a chunky cigarette lighter from the table next to him and flicked it on and off. He wanted his pipe, she knew, but she abhorred the smell and would not allow it in her presence.

He snorted at her words and shook his head, but he did not meet her eyes. "I daresay your father would be horrified at this whole venture. Picking a husband for your sister from amongst this rabble—it's outlandish, outrageous. It may even be dangerous."

Ava stepped away from the window and came toward him, forcing him to look up at her. "Must I remind you that you agreed with this solution when I presented it to you in New York? Must I remind that we *both* decided Mother and Father should know nothing of it? And must I remind you that you *insisted* on coming along with me instead letting me bring Mrs. Carruthers as I'd originally planned?"

Harvey sniffed and resumed his study of the lighter. "Mrs. Carruthers is not to be relied upon. I didn't like the idea of entrusting your sister's reputation and future to such a stuffy old windbag."

Ava laughed in disbelief. "A stuffy old windbag? I can hardly believe you would say such a thing. Mrs. Carruthers has been a dear friend of my family's for almost half a century. And she has single-handedly saved the reputations of more than one esteemed matron I could name."

"The very fact that you can name them is evidence enough of what I mean." He held her gaze for a significant moment before turning back to the lighter. "*I* am capable of keeping this secret between us. And anyway, she's too old. She couldn't have withstood the trip."

"Which was the only reason I agreed to travel with you." Ava took a deep breath and strode to the the fireplace. It was warm for October, so the logs and kindling sat unlit. She gazed at an appalling landscape that graced the focal point above the mantel. "That, and we needed to leave immediately—which brings up another point. We're nearing the end of our allotted time. We must return with a groom for Cilla before she begins to show. And with enough time for them to make some rudimentary social rounds, just to make it look real. I'd say that gives us another three weeks, four at the outside."

Harvey arched his brows at her. "And would you then still have time to plan and execute a formal wedding? I believe we're out of time right now."

"All the more reason to choose Mr. Angell," Ava snapped, turning to fix him with a speculative look. "Why are you fighting me so on this, Harvey? Have you another idea? Or do you think perhaps no one will notice Cilla becoming increasingly round this winter?"

Harvey groaned and buried his face in his hands. "Oh, for pity's sake, no. Of course not." After a moment, he lifted his head and spoke harshly. "It just makes me so—frustrated. The fact that her foolishness—her imprudence and irresponsibility—have brought us to this . . ." He ran his hands along the sides of his head and muttered, "It's revolting."

She squelched an automatic desire to defend her sister. After all, everything he said was true. "Even so—"

"Even so," Harvey straightened and pointed a finger to emphasize his words, "I can't see someone of your sister's caliber marrying an ill-bred rustic like Mr. Angell. Think for a moment, Ava. Would *you* marry someone like him?"

Ava's cheeks flooded with heat at the question, and she turned away. "Of course not. Our situations are completely different."

But she could not help the image that sprang to mind of the man in question. When he'd approached her at the boardinghouse, she'd barely been able to catch her breath. He was so startlingly handsome, in a rough sort of way. All that dark reckless hair and those light blue eyes. And when he'd smiled—that blinding white, devastating smile—she'd nearly felt the floor dip beneath her feet.

Then he'd spoken. And the repulsion she'd felt had been in direct inverse proportion to her attraction. He might as well have slapped her, so drastic was his unexpected crudeness. How could a man be so physically gifted and so vilely coarse at the same time? An unutterable sadness had filled her, increasing the more he spoke. He was Adonis with a twang and a toothpick. It was almost too cruel to be borne. The more he spoke, the more she expected him to become visually repugnant, but still she could not take her eyes from him. So beautiful, and so unbearable.

"There, you see?" Harvey pressed. "You cannot conceive of marrying him yourself, and yet you propose to marry him to your only sister. It's unthinkably unjust." He set the lighter down with a final *thump* and glared at her. "We'll find someone else. Someone—more suitable."

Ava regained her composure and turned a withering frown on him. "Harvey, no one suitable will have her." She let that sink in a moment before continuing. "Perhaps I cannot conceive of marrying Mr. Angell myself, but neither can I imagine being pregnant before marriage. What you seem to have lost sight of is that Priscilla is out of options. She is with child." Ava enunciated the words clearly, her tone not concealing her frustration. "She will not name, much less marry, the father. And she desires to keep the child."

"Yes. Who would have imagined that?"

"So in order to keep her from ruining both herself and our entire family—which would put *you* out of a job, Mr. Winters—I am taking the only course of action I can think to take."

Harvey seemed to shrink beneath her words. He sat back in his chair and clutched his knees with his palms, his eyes downcast. "It just seems so desperate, so—so unsavory."

"Harvey," she softened her tone just a fraction, "Priscilla has agreed to the scheme. And she only needs to marry the man, stay out of the spotlight for a year or two, and then return. She'll be able to keep her child and she need never see Mr. Angell again."

"Suppose he won't do it, this Angell fellow? Really, what's in it for him, ultimately? A wife he won't see—a life he won't have—what's the point?"

"There's a great deal of money in it for him, which is the point *he's* most likely to appreciate."

"Money isn't everything!" Harvey sputtered, waving a hand. "He'll never be able to marry again, not unless they divorce, which would be equally unthinkable. Suppose one day he decides he wants children of his own? What then?"

"Then he can discuss it with his wife," Ava said implacably.

"*Wha—! Disc—!*" Harvey's face turned crimson as he lurched to his feet. "You would have *Moreland blood* mixed with—with—whatever this Angell person happens to be?"

She folded her hands at her waist and regarded him calmly. "It's common knowledge that breeding outside the direct line produces stronger stock."

"Stronger stock! Breeding!" Harvey's arms gesticulated wildly as he circled the chair on which he'd sat. "We're not talking *horses* here, Ava! For God's sake, *think* of the little brutes that man might produce."

He looked on the verge of physical calamity, Ava thought. "Well, you're the one who brought up blood. In any case, I doubt he'd be able to convince Priscilla to have more children, so we shan't belabor the point. The crux of the matter is this." She paced forward, her hands clasped behind her back, her voice the essence of rationality. "Mr. Angell shall have the choice of marrying a very wealthy woman and claiming her child as his. Or he may choose to spend an indeterminate amount of time—perhaps years—in prison for shooting off a man's toe. I daresay most people would choose marriage over jail."

Harvey stared at her in abject horror, then scoffed and muttered something that sounded like, "*You* wouldn't."

She froze. "I beg your pardon?"

The short stab of pain his comment produced was automatic. True, she told people she didn't care to marry, but it was mostly to disguise the fact that no one had asked her. No one had even come close. She knew she was not as pretty as her flirtatious sister, but her character was beyond reproach, and she knew she was reasonably intelligent. Paramount to all that, she was a *Moreland*. Still, while the gentlemen were always scrupulously polite with her, no one stayed around long enough to want to court her.

Harvey shook his head. "Nothing. I'm sorry. I just— I—This whole plan is starting to get to me." He smoothed his oiled hair back with one hand, shoving the other into his pants pocket.

"You don't wish to save Cilla?" she asked stiffly.

"Of course. Yes, of course." He nodded his head and swallowed hard.

"Then I think we should approach Mr. Angell. I believe he is trainable. With a change of wardrobe and a haircut, he could become quite presentable." She tried to keep her voice even, but felt blood rise again to her cheeks at the image she conjured, so she paced slowly back to the window. "We'll take the next several weeks to teach him manners and improve his speech, then we'll introduce him to New York society as a cattle baron. That's all, no details. We shan't elaborate and muddy up the lie with particulars. Priscilla can get to know him, take him around, introduce him, then they'll marry. A small ceremony, just the family. She can wear something full—it'll be cold enough, and no one will be able to tell." She was lost in thought now. Her plan was a good one; she knew it. "Then they'll go to Europe for an extended stay with Aunt Felicity, who lives in an isolated area. Mr. Angell may go with her for the duration, or he may return to his life here. That shall be his choice. In any case, he'll disappear after the child is born. It's in Europe that Priscilla shall give birth prematurely. We may even be able to fudge the date a little—nobody keeps track in those out-of-the-way places. A month or two will hardly matter." She clapped her hands together once. "It will work."

She turned back to Harvey, who sat miserably on the sofa. "It's a very good plan," she insisted to the top of his bent head. "Can't you see what a good plan it is? Not even our parents will know. Aunt Felicity is *quite* trustworthy, I assure you."

His head moved up and down in a movement she took for a nod.

"It's a good plan," he echoed. He lifted his head, his eyes thoughtful. "It will probably work. It's just—I just don't have a good feeling about this Mr. Angell. I thought we would find someone a little more . . . someone with . . . someone a bit more polished."

Ava shook her head, determined. "Someone more

polished would have other choices. Mr. Angell is perfect. He has nothing to lose and everything to gain. *And* he's already shown himself to be of good character."

Harvey's brows raised. "By shooting a man's foot off?"

She pursed her lips. "It was only a toe."

"Excuse me." Harvey inclined his head.

"By standing up for my honor, he demonstrated a good deal of integrity. I believe we can trust him."

Harvey sighed. "All right. We'll go with Angell. But we'll keep a close eye on him, *at all times*. I'm not quite as trusting of ignorant ruffians as you seem to be."

The jail was a tight, musty-smelling place that was probably ice cold in the winter and sweltering in the summer, Ava reflected. Surely she was doing the poor soul a favor by offering this chance to escape the dead-end life of an outlaw. Though she knew he'd been acting merely to circumvent a more serious crime, a remarkable number of people had recounted to the sheriff a far different scenario. Mr. Angell had picked the fight, one of them said. Another said they'd seen him haranguing Mr. Pug earlier in the day, and at Mr. Angell's denial another corroborated the story.

Ava was not so gullible that she didn't see the plot against him, but she could see no way of foiling it. And since she could not help Mr. Angell in any forthright way, and as it happened that his plight aided her own, she decided that resorting to bribery was not immoral in this instance.

It was a well-known fact of business that desperate times demanded desperate measures, and she could think of nothing more desperate than her sister's situation. She had never been one to back down from responsibility, and she wasn't about to start now. So if bribing a sheriff in an obscure town like Himey, Missouri, was the measure that was called for, Ava Moreland would not shy away from it. The first thing she procured was a visit with the prisoner.

The smell of potatoes and onions was most prominent as Ava and Harvey followed Sheriff Reese into the office of the town jail. Their footsteps rang hollowly on the bare plank flooring, and the startling slam of the door behind them, one of the hazards of building a structure that leaned twenty degrees forward, caused a sorry selection of battered Henry rifles to rattle in a rack on the wall.

"He's right on back here, folks," Sheriff Reese said, his thick leather boots clumping through the tiny office. A metal ring with three keys on it hung from a hook next to a door. The sheriff plucked this off the wall, inserted one into the lock and pushed the heavy wood portal open.

"Right in here." He stepped to the side of the threshold and motioned them through. "You folks just give me a holler when you're through and I'll lock up again." He pounded hard twice on the door. "Git up, Angell. Folks is here to see you."

Harvey twisted a dry look back at Ava before preceding her through the door. Ava followed, expecting to see all manner of cutthroats and brigands behind the bars within, and was vaguely disappointed to find only Mr. Angell lounging on a clean cot in one of two barren cells.

When he caught sight of them, he rose to his feet. Ava was pleased to note that though he was a big man, he moved quite gracefully, and he knew enough to stand and try to straighten his hair and clothing in the presence of a lady.

"Miz Moreland, Mr. Winters," he greeted them in surprise. "What on earth're you doin' here?"

Ava and Harvey exchanged a tense look. Then Ava nodded for Harvey to begin.

Harvey cleared his throat. "Mr. Angell," he began, standing a foot away from the bars and looking down his nose at the man in the cell. "We'd like to ask you a few questions, if you've got the time." He allowed himself a smug smile, and Ava glanced at the prisoner to see how he took it.

"Got nothin' but," Angell said, his eyes cool as he gazed at Harvey.

Harvey chuckled once. "Good, good. Now, Mr. Angell, how would you describe your profession?"

"My what?"

Harvey looked down at his feet a moment, then up. "By profession I mean, what is it that you do? For a living?"

Angell chewed the inside of his lip, the question apparently taking some thought. "Well, now, I do a little a this, and a little a that. Whatever it takes to get a good meal."

"Does any of that which you do involve illegal activities?"

Angell drew back, an exaggerated expression on his face. *"Hell, no."*

Harvey raised one brow and glared at the man. "I'll thank you to remember there's a lady present."

Ava nearly smiled at the blush she thought she saw creep into Angell's face.

"I'm sorry, ma'am," he said with such sincerity that she did smile. "I just don't cotton to bein' called a lawbreaker, ma'am. I'm sure you understand."

"It's all right," she murmured as Harvey continued, obviously wanting to press the point while Angell was upset.

"Are you a gunfighter, Mr. Angell?"

Angell swung on the man so swiftly Ava gasped. "Didn't I just answer that question?"

"Didn't we just witness you gunfighting?" Harvey insisted.

Ava turned surprised eyes on Harvey at the strength and energy of his questioning. She had no idea he could be this self-possessed in the presence of a man as physically imposing as Mr. Angell. Of course, they were separated by iron bars at least an inch thick, but even so, he was acting decidedly courageous.

"What you witnessed," Angell replied icily, "was *me* defendin' *your* woman from a pack a dogs out to do no good, that's what. You'd'a been out there yourself, if you had any—"

"Mr. Angell," Harvey interrupted. He made a half-motion toward Ava, as if he might place his hands over

45

her ears; then he glared at Angell as if he wanted to wrap his hands around his neck.

Ava stepped forward. "Excuse me, gentlemen," she said firmly. "Harvey, perhaps I should continue."

"But—"

She stopped him with one gloved hand upraised. "No, I believe I can be more impartial in this situation."

Harvey rolled his eyes and flung his hands out to his sides. "Fine. Fine." He turned and leaned heavily against the far wall, fuming as Ava addressed the prisoner.

"Mr. Angell." She paused, gathering her thoughts. "Mr. Winters and I had in mind to speak with you about a matter which has caused us great heartache recently."

Angell's brows beetled and he glanced from one to the other of them. It was obvious he was suspicious of their motive, but it was also clear that he was more willing to speak with Ava than with Harvey.

"I'm real sorry to hear that," he said carefully, "and ordinarily I'd love to help you out, but I reckon I'm gonna be a bit tied up for a time here." His arms fanned out to indicate where he stood.

Ava smiled and Mr. Angell smiled back immediately. The grin was disarming and caused a faint fluttering in her stomach. It was, she thought, the trusting smile of a boy. She lowered her gaze.

Ava cleared her throat. "If you were truly of a mind to help us, Mr. Angell, we might be able to help you in return." She winced internally at the bartering sound of the words, then continued, "We may be able to secure your release."

She watched his expression, saw it change from curiosity back to suspicion. "Just what're you proposin', Miz Moreland?" he asked, in such an intimate, almost amused tone that she felt the strange fluttering move along her nerves.

Harvey, from his corner, laughed dryly. "Interesting choice of words, wouldn't you say, Ava?"

She shot him an annoyed look. Taking a deep

breath, she turned back to Mr. Angell. His sky-blue eyes rested on hers, the expression in them reminiscent of a puppy's who wanted to trust but had been kicked one too many times.

"I come from New York City, Mr. Angell. Do you know where that is?"

The beautiful eyes narrowed and his mouth formed a small smile. "Reckon I heard of it."

"My family is there, has been there for generations, and we're generally considered to be quite—respectable." She brushed some road dust from the sleeve of her jacket while she pondered how to continue. "We have a position in society that requires great care and attention to maintain." She moved one or two paces along the side of the cell.

"No offense, Miz Moreland," Angell said, leaning one hand on the bars, "but it's pretty obvious you're rich. You're makin' me nervous, all this pussy-footin' around the subject at hand. What is it you want me to do for you in exchange for my freedom?"

Ava glanced at Harvey, who shrugged his eyebrows and folded his arms across his chest.

She cleared her throat. "I have a younger sister—"

Angell burst out laughing. "Whoa-ho-ho, there." He held up his hands as if in surrender. "I ain't *never* heard a conversation begun like that turned out to be anythin' but trouble for *me*."

Ava was disgusted to hear Harvey chuckling with him from the corner. She pressed her lips together and scorched Angell with a look. His laughter trickled.

"Are you interested in securing help for yourself or not, Mr. Angell?" she demanded.

His eyes widened and his chin sunk toward his chest in exaggerated humility. "Damn, Miz Moreland, I bet you're a schoolteacher. Ain't nothin' can slice a joke outta the air like the tongue of a teacher." His words rang in her ears as he neared where she stood. Large, well-formed hands grasped the bars between them, hands that looked powerful enough to pull the heavy iron asunder. "Here's what I don't understand, though. I don't understand why you and your fancy

47

man are treatin' me like an idiot, even though you came to me, remember? Why don't you try actin' like I might be able to do somethin' *for you?*"

Ava clamped her teeth together and stepped back at the sudden change of mood. His pale blue eyes held hers with none of the uncertainty they'd held before. Perhaps Harvey had been right. Maybe it was foolish to be toying with someone of Mr. Angell's ilk. She was conscious of Harvey's shift to attention.

"Of course you're not an idiot," she said, attempting to keep her voice steady. "But you must admit that now is not the time for levity. You're in a prison cell, and you're likely to stay here."

"Maybe," he conceded, not taking his eyes from her, but relaxing once more. "What've you got for me?"

"An opportunity." She kept her eyes on his, unwilling to let them drift to the broad, tanned hand that gripped the bar of the cell, or the small vee of chest visible at the neck of his homespun shirt. "I have a sister in need of a husband. You have a life in need of rescue."

Angell studied her so intently that Ava felt the soles of her feet and the palms of her hands grow damp.

"You got a reason," he asked finally, "for thinkin' I need a life other'n the fact that I'm sittin' here in this jail cell?"

She resisted the urge to wipe her palms on her skirt. "Isn't that enough?"

A second passed, and then two. Then the smile crept back onto his face, as sweet and natural as a child's. "I reckon so. You know, Miz Moreland, I'd really like to help you. But if you're thinkin' of marryin' me to your sister, you're makin' a bad mistake."

"Why is that?" she asked. Of course he wouldn't jump at the chance, she thought. It's too unexpected. He needs to be sure I'm serious. He needs to know what else he'd be getting besides his freedom.

"Well," he began, "I never did have no plans to marry. I just ain't the marryin' type, you know. And anybody's a sister to you, well now, I can tell she wouldn't be wantin' to marry someone like me." The admission came easily enough, but though she might have imagined it, Ava thought she saw an instant of defeat.

"My sister is pregnant, Mr. Angell, and she is unmarried. She needs a husband who will accept that fact and keep it to himself. If you were that man, you would be expected to claim the child as your own and proclaim it a product of your matrimonial union. In return, we would obviously see that you were released from this cell. We would also confer upon you a large sum of money in advance, as well as endow you with a monthly stipend for the rest of your life."

Angell stared at her, then he backed up and sat heavily on the cot. "How much money?"

She considered a moment. "More than you've got," she said finally. "More than you'll ever be able to make, in jail or out."

"And I'll be living in New York City with you all. In a house. With a family."

Ava glanced down at the floor a second, then over at Harvey. He shook his head with just the slightest of motions.

"For a time," Ava said, looking back into Angell's suddenly shrewd eyes. "We would of course have to present you as someone of—some wealth and social standing. You would have to study rules of etiquette and diction, along with basic poise and carriage. Also," she took a steadying breath, "methods of personal hygiene and grooming. Harvey would help you with that on our return trip."

Angell laughed shortly, without humor, and looked away from her toward the wall. "Sounds to me like you want a completely different person."

Ava felt something pull taut deep inside. She clenched her fists in her skirts. "We want someone we can trust. Someone with integrity . . . a sense of personal honor." She watched Angell's eyes drop, noted the length of the dark lashes against his cheekbones. "Those things can't be taught, Mr. Angell. We needed to find those first."

She saw his lips curve up slightly just before he gave

her a look from the corner of his eye. "That's some real nice words," he said. "I don't even care if you don't mean 'em. So go on, tell me the rest. What's the bad news? Tell me what 'for a time' means."

"Once you've convinced everyone of your respectability and you've married my sister, you would have the choice of leaving with her for Europe, or returning to your home here."

"This ain't my home," Angell said.

"Wherever your home might be, then. In any case, once the child is born and my sister is sufficiently recovered to return home, you would be expected to leave New York and never return." Ava released the death grip she had on her skirts and folded her arms at her waist.

"Never," Angell repeated. "In other words, I wouldn't never be no proper husband to her. I'd just be a—whaddya call it—a figurehead, of sorts. Keep the child from bein' a bastard." He smiled again, but this time the boy was not in it. It was a sad smile . . . a cheated smile.

Ava swallowed. "That's correct." She nodded once.

He sighed. "Good."

"I beg your pardon?"

"I said, good. I ain't lookin' to be a husband. I ain't lookin' to be a father. This'd be just temporary, am I right?"

Ava could barely believe their good fortune. "That's right."

Harvey, apparently, couldn't believe it either. "Let me get this straight," he said, emerging from the shadows. "You don't want children, ever?"

"No," Angell said. "Somethin' wrong with that?"

"You don't ever plan to marry?" Harvey persisted.

"You heard me." Angell looked suspicious once again.

Harvey broke into his first sincere smile of the trip. "That's good. That's perfect." He could barely contain his glee, which Ava found a bit tacky. Then, realizing something, he turned a sober face on the prisoner. "Tell me something, Mr. Angell, and please try to be honest. Isn't there *anything* you want out of life?"

Angell's gaze seemed to bore holes in the man, Ava thought with just a trickle of dread. For a long moment, the two men's eyes locked, and Ava could tell Harvey was more than a little intimidated.

Finally, Angell spoke. In a voice low and sure, he said, "I wanna be like you, Mr. Winters. I wanna walk like you, and talk like you and dress like you." He rose and moved toward Harvey, who despite the bars between them backed up a couple of steps. "I wanna live life the way you do. No—better'n you. I even wanna wear them prissy cocklebur ankle boots you got on."

Ava stifled a nervous laugh as Harvey glanced down at his shoes.

"And then," Angell continued, his eyes skewering Harvey where he stood, "I wanna get the hell away from you and everyone like you. There's other ways to live besides yours, you high-falutin' boot licker." He punctuated this by grabbing the bars with both hands and pulling himself up straight against them, causing Harvey to stumble back in surprise.

Then he beamed that angelic smile at the two of them and said, "Deal?"

Chapter Four

Angell awoke to the stiff clang of iron against iron. Reluctantly, he opened his eyes and squinted against the light of an oil lamp held high by a man too shadowed to identify. He raised himself on one elbow and confirmed what his body told him, that outside was still black as midnight. A key turned in the lock, and the tumblers clicked loud in the midnight stillness.

"What—?" Angell muttered in a voice hoarse with sleep. "Sheriff? That you?"

The door creaked as the sheriff pushed it wide, causing the man holding the lamp to step back or be run over.

"It's me, Angell," the sheriff said. "Get up. You gotta go with this man." The sheriff pushed his hat back on his head, strode into the cell and hauled Angell up and out of the cot with a rough hand. "C'mon, now. I ain't got all night. Get your ass outa bed."

Angell stumbled to his feet and grabbed for his vest and boots, just managing to snag his hat from the bedstead before being pushed from the cell, arms full. The man holding the lamp exited swiftly to the office. Angell caught sight of his face as he passed through the door. It was Harvey Winters, Beauty's traveling companion. So, they were as good as their word, he thought. So far, anyway.

Angell followed the two, trying to project into the future where on earth this adventure would take him. The fact that he had no other prospects, except possibly spending the winter in jail, did not stop him from wondering if he'd done the right thing in agreeing to their scheme.

"Here you are," Winters intoned to the sheriff as the lawman locked the door behind them. "As we agreed." In his outstretched hand lay a pile of bills, new, crisp and numerous from what Angell could see. Winters bestowed them solemnly into the sheriff's palm, as though conferring upon him some kind of benediction. "Thank you for your cooperation, Sheriff. I expect neither of us would like to hear another word about this incident."

"You got it." Sheriff Reese flipped a finger through the pile, more out of glee than any desire to count the money, it seemed.

"Well, damn." Angell applied a jaunty grin. "I didn't know I was worth *that* much to anybody."

Winters glanced at him coldly. "You're not. You were in the right place at the right time, so don't get any inflated ideas of your worth."

Sheriff Reese chuckled as he pocketed the cash. "Don't feel bad, Angell. You're looking pretty valuable to me right now."

"Thank you, Sheriff," Angell said, clapping him on the shoulder, then bent to pull on his boots. "Gotta be cheaper'n buildin' a gallows, wouldn't you say?"

The sheriff shook his head and moved to the desk. "You wouldn't a hung," he said, pulling Angell's guns from a bottom drawer. "Most you'd a got was a year, mebbe two. But you're headin' on to bigger and better things now, huh?"

Angell shrugged into his vest and pushed his hat on his head before taking the holster from Reese's outstretched hand. "Don't rightly know, Sheriff." And he didn't. Could the deal possibly be as easy as it sounded? Learn a few manners, marry some girl for a month or two, then head out of town for a new life. Seemed pretty sweet. He'd even be able to keep the clothes they bought him, he'd made sure of that. Sure, life could be good about six months from now. And in the meantime, he'd be spending his leisure with one Miss Ava Moreland, Beauty Extraordinaire.

Angell strapped on the guns and allowed himself to think optimistically for a minute. The sheriff scouted around outside to be sure no one was watching. Then he followed Winters from the jail to a coach waiting near the edge of town.

The weather had turned chilly in the last day or so, and as the two of them approached the carriage, Angell could make out the frosting breath of the horses in the night air. He shivered lightly beneath his cotton shirt and wondered if they'd let him go back to the boardinghouse to pick up his things.

Winters stopped to speak to the driver before entering the coach, so Angell grabbed the door handle and pulled it open in search of warmth. Inside the lamp-lit cabin sat Miss Moreland, closely swathed in a deep green cape with a fur-lined hood. Her face wore an anxious expression.

He hauled himself into the coach with a big friendly smile. He was greeted by a small, cold one, followed by an alarmed expression and the swift application of a handkerchief to her nose and mouth by one gloved hand.

"Heavens," she said, consternation in her eyes, as Harvey stepped in behind him. "Couldn't they have let him bathe?" she asked the well-heeled man as he deposited himself next to her.

Genuine embarrassment welled up like a balloon in Angell's chest as he realized what she meant. A quelling self-doubt swept over him as the enormity of his agreement to their scheme hit home, making him notice all that was right about the little professor and all that was wrong with himself. He was even suddenly conscious of how the carriage still shook from his entrance, and he mentally compared his large movements to the professor's smooth maneuvering as he delicately pushed aside a corner of Miss Moreland's cape and sat without causing a ripple.

Across from the two impeccable people, Angell felt huge and filthy. He wished he could unfasten the thick leather holster from his waist, something about his pistols seeming suddenly offensive in the presence of Miss Moreland. He insisted to himself, though, that they were about as pretty a set of guns as could be had—pearl-handled, 1873 Colt .45s. *Peacemakers*, as they ironically liked to call them.

Regardless, he sank down in the seat and pushed his hat low on his forehead. He didn't have to impress these people, he thought stubbornly, and hoped no one would notice the flush he could feel to the roots of his hair.

"Beggin' yer pardon, ma'am," he mumbled, "but there weren't any tub—they got nothin' but a pot over there at the jail."

Then, realizing he'd once again brought up the subject of privies, he closed his eyes and muttered, *"Damn."* What on earth had made him think he could do this? he thought with disgust. It had been more years than he could count since he'd had to display any sort of politeness, and though he had memories of what the fine life was like, he was suddenly conscious of the fact that any manners he may once have had were buried deep and possibly long gone. The realization surprised him.

Beneath the brim of his hat, Angell saw Miss Moreland and Winters exchange a worried look. Well, the hell with *them*, he thought irritably. Did they think just because they'd made a deal he'd miraculously turn into some spit-polished dandy? It would serve them right if he turned out to be nothing but an honest-to-God, dyed-in-the-wool hayseed.

Winters rapped harshly on the roof with an ivory-handled cane. Instantly, they heard the sharp whistle of the driver and the short crack of his whip. The cabin swayed as the horses surged forward.

"Mr. Angell," Miss Moreland began, her voice soothing as a balm to his fraying self-confidence, "would you mind if I asked you a few personal questions?"

He eyed her for a moment from beneath his hat, hoping this wasn't the personal interrogation he dreaded. Then he pushed himself up a little and unfolded his arms. "All right."

"Do you know your letters? Can you read and write?" Her eyes beneath lush lashes were impartial, as far as he could tell.

"Yas'm, I can," he answered, noting with a disturbing degree of gratification that she looked glad he was able to give her an affirmative response.

From beneath her cloak, she pulled a thin booklet and handed it to him. "Please read the first paragraph."

He took the book from her, opened it and began reading. A moment later she spoke again. "Aloud, please."

The now-familiar heat stole into his cheeks, and he cleared his throat. He used to like to read, as a child, though it had been a long time since he'd picked up a book. " 'A nation is a—a number of people ass . . . so . . . associated together for common purposes, and no one . . . cue—questions the right of those people to make laws for themselves. Society is also an . . . an organized . . . *association* and has a perfect right to make laws which shall be bending—' "

"Binding," she corrected gently.

" '*Binding* upon all of its members.' " He lifted his head from the paper and smiled, inwardly disgusted with himself. When had he become so ignorant? "There, now, nothin' to worry about, eh?" he said cavalierly.

Beauty smiled back, and a disturbing quiver coursed through his stomach. "Very good. Now." Again, she pulled from beneath her cloak a pen and paper. He was half-tempted to ask her what else she had under there, but decided the joke wasn't worth the sour comment Harvey would no doubt utter.

"Would you sign your name and then print it beneath your signature?"

Angell took the pen and paper and glanced around himself for a solid surface. This, at least, he knew he could still do properly.

"You may use the book as a desktop," she pointed out.

"But—we're movin' so I—"

"I'll understand if it's messy, Mr. Angell." She smiled and nodded her head for him to begin.

Carefully, he arranged the paper so that its edges aligned neatly with the corners of the book. Then he took up the pen and gazed at it. He raised it up, about to speak, when she said smoothly, "It has ink inside of it."

"No kiddin'?" he asked, awed, and looked at the thing. After a moment, he realized they were staring at him, perhaps thinking he was stalling. He laid the pen to the paper and confidently scrawled his name. Then he printed it beneath in neat block letters, or as neat as could be achieved in a moving coach. He held it up, blew on it, and handed it across to her.

"Joshua Angell," she read. "Hmmm. That's an interesting spelling. Of what derivation is your name, Mr. Angell?" she asked.

Angell was so engrossed in the conversational tone of her voice he nearly forgot to pay attention to its meaning. She sounded as if she were talking to one of her own, which made him both suspicious and strangely flattered. Unfortunately, it wasn't until he'd been staring at her an unusual amount of time that he realized he could not recall what "derivation" meant.

"Huh?" popped out of his mouth before he could stop it.

"Oh, for *God's* sake, where does it come from?" the little professor burst. Then he ran a hand through his perfectly combed hair and turned apologetically to Miss Moreland. "I'm sorry, Ava, but this is going to be impossible. I told you before I had a bad feeling, and I'm just—I'm really starting to feel worried about this."

Miss Moreland stopped him with a gloved hand to his forearm. *"Harvey,"* she commanded quietly. "Hush. It's done now. And Mr. Angell is doing splendidly." She bestowed a warm smile on him. "Now, are your parents from this country, or did they emigrate from somewhere else?"

Angell was so irritated with himself for being charmed by her patience, and so annoyed at Winters' intolerance, that he decided to make a point of shocking them.

He sighed. "No, ma'am, they were both from right here in America. My mother, she called me Angell as a boy because when I was young I was real fair and blond. She said I looked just like a angel. Then, when I got older, she said I needed a proper name, so she picked Joshua from the Bible 'cause she liked the sound of it. From then on, I guess I was known as Joshua Angell, but most folks just call me Angell."

When he finished this speech, Winters closed his eyes and laid his head back against the seat. Miss Moreland sat stock still and looked at him with an expression that could only be described as *disturbed*.

"But what about your father's name?" she asked, her voice just a hair above a whisper. "Didn't you and your mother bear your father's name?"

Angell frowned and shook his head. After a moment, his eyes stole back to her anxious face and, thinking it would do no good to screw up the deal, he smiled ruefully. "Well, to begin with, yeah, of course we did. *Certainly,"* he added for good measure, thinking it sounded like something they'd say. "But me and my father, well, we had somethin' of a fallin' out, you might say, quite a few years ago, right before my mother died. I wouldn't never use his name now. *Never,"* he repeated vehemently, feeling the old anger rise up inside him.

But her next words confused him, drawing his thoughts away from old hurts, best-forgotten injuries. "Then why the unusual spelling?"

Caught off-guard, he could only respond, "What?"

"Angell, with two '1's, instead of just one?"

Angell felt his toes curl up in his boots with humiliation. His cheeks burned and his palms dampened. He clenched his teeth together so hard he thought they might split. The little professor lifted his head and sat looking at him with brows raised.

"Well," Angell forced out between stiff lips, "I figured it didn't much look like a name, you know, with just the one '1.' It more looked like a *word*, you know. So I stuck on another one just for the hell of it. You know."

He was lying, they knew he was lying, he was sure of it. But he forced himself to hold the gaze of the little professor until that man looked away. Then he turned a guarded look on Miss Moreland. She was looking at the paper with an open expression.

"Yes, I see," she said. "You're quite right. And you have a fine hand, Mr. Angell. Really, Harvey, look and see. A good strong hand." She held the paper out for Winters to look.

Angell was impressed with the generosity of her words, but his humiliation was so complete that he could not feel good about them. In her kindness, she was tossing him a crumb. Him, a man who could not even spell his own name right. For the first time, he wished he'd never seen them, never spoken to them. He wished they'd just left him in prison. At least he knew how he'd gotten there. At least there he knew who he was .

Or did he? Before this, he'd always considered that side of himself the act.

Winters glanced briefly at the paper and nodded once. "Fine," he repeated, solely for Miss Moreland's benefit, Angell knew.

"Now," she said with more confidence, "here is the plan. We're to travel on to St. Louis tonight, though we probably won't arrive until morning, and we'll stop there for the week. Harvey and I passed through on our way to Kansas City, and it was quite a bustling little city. We should—"

"Wait a second," Angell said. He may be giving them a few months, but he was not going to erase all consideration of what he'd gotten on his own. "Am I gonna be able to stop at Miss Howkam's and get my things? I got a coat cost me a bundle last winter and another change a clothes could make me a much better travelin' companion, if you know what I mean."

"Oh, we know what you mean," Winters said, just loud enough to be heard.

Miss Moreland wore a rueful expression. "I'm sorry, but I'm afraid you can't go back to Miss Howkam's. You see, everyone knows you've been arrested. You are supposed to be in prison. That's why we came so late."

"But I could just sneak in, quiet as a mouse—" Here, Winters snorted and Angell frowned at him. "I'd be back before anybody'd know I was there."

She shook her head. "Miss Howkam cleaned out your room as soon as she heard you were apprehended. I believe she planned to sell your things to pay for the room."

Angell swore softly under his breath, picturing the thick leather coat with the shearling lining. That coat would pay for the room for a year. He'd actually been looking forward to the cold this year, so warm and sharp-looking was the garment.

"Please don't worry," Miss Moreland said, her tone truly apologetic.

"It's not as if you could actually *use* any of that cowboy gear," Winters added. "Not in New York City."

To hear him say it, a body could of thought he was saying *the Kingdom of Heaven*, Angell thought. Hell, New York was just another town, just like Dallas, or Little Rock, or St. Louis for that matter.

"It's use it or walk around buck naked in *New York City*," Angell retorted.

"Gentlemen, *please*," Miss Moreland insisted. "Mr. Angell, let me finish. We intend to replace everything you've lost once we arrive in St. Louis. We shall outfit you as a well-bred man of means. There will be no place for your heavy boots, your broad-brimmed hat or your guns. Denim is not worn in the city, nor is such raw leather." She indicated his vest with a refined sweep of her hand. "You can keep those things, certainly, for your return. And we will replace what you lost when your time in New York is finished. But henceforth, you have agreed to become what we need you to be."

Angell thought of his leather saddlebags, threatening to rip at the seams. He thought of his threadbare bedroll and his old Sharp's rifle with the cracked lever. He thought of the two other shirts, patches at the cuff and elbow, and the one pair of pants with the mud-stained knees he'd left behind. And though he was thankful he'd dressed in his best that night to see Beauty, he didn't figure he had anything back there in that room worth missing except the coat.

"All right," he said, taking off his hat and pushing his hair back out of his face. He laid the hat next to him on the seat and gazed at its dusty brim a moment. "I guess I should just count on nothin' bein' the same, here on out," he added, more to himself than anyone else.

No one replied, so he folded his arms back over his chest. "What else we gonna be doin' in St. Louis, and how long before we leave for New York?"

Beauty got back down to business. "We shall stay in St. Louis for the time it takes to procure you something of a wardrobe. We can supplement that when we get to New York. We'll simply say your trunks were stolen." She pulled her cape more closely around her as cold seeped into the carriage. "We'll start work on your speech tomorrow. From now on, you must try to emulate either Mr. Winters or myself in our manner of address and deportment. Try to study us, Mr. Angell, and copy what we do. Surely you can hear the difference between your speech patterns and ours."

She looked as if she wanted an answer to that last statement, so he nodded.

"Where is it you are originally from? You have something of a drawl. From the South, perhaps?"

He nodded again, unwilling to elaborate.

"Well, a slight trace of the South should be acceptable, but strong local accents tend to brand one as ill-bred. No more idioms or colloquialisms please, Mr. Angell. Try to say exactly what you mean, unless the subject is a delicate one." Her brows knitted as she thought for a moment, no doubt remembering the privy conversations. "In which case I think it would be best if you kept silent entirely."

She continued on for what seemed like hours, enumerating all the pitfalls he should avoid, which was pretty much everything he did on a regular basis, and pointing out those things he should learn to do, which required a collection of talents he had not possessed for many, many years. She outlined a course of study, complete with textbooks and manuals of etiquette she had brought with her on behavior suitable for New York. People like Mr. Beadle, Henry Willis and Miss Leslie were to become his closest companions, she said, as they had all written "guides to good behavior for those who had neglected to avail themselves of refinements within their reach."

By the time Ava finished talking, Angell was exhausted, and not from lack of sleep. The whole prospect of what they were planning to do seemed suddenly enormous, and not a little intimidating. He wondered if any strength he'd achieved over the last twenty years would be required and tried to think of one thing he was good at that might be useful in New York.

He was good with guns—not likely.

He was physically strong and could travel long distances without much rest—other than tonight, no.

He could sit a horse tighter than a cinch on a peg pony—slight chance.

He knew how to treat a whore like a lady—definitely not.

He could lasso a steer, break a horse, skin a buffalo, spit ten yards and piss in a circle, but he *knew* none of that would come up.

Nope, as far as they were concerned, he was a babe. Green as the greenest tenderfoot this side of the Mississippi. As unbroken as any bangtail pony on the plains. And while that may not be true in the strictest sense, he reflected, it behooved him to have them believe it. Besides, it had been so long since he'd given a thought to his early training, it was becoming clear that it might be lost to him now anyway.

They arrived in St. Louis and checked into the Brown Hotel, an establishment the likes of which Angell hadn't seen in years. Dark polished wood shone with a richness he could practically see himself in, and massive chandeliers hung like great watchful birds from the ceiling. The furniture in the lobby alone surpassed anything he'd sat upon in recent memory, and the rugs were so clean and intricate they could have been hanging on the walls.

While he didn't want to overdo it, it was not hard to gape like an ignorant rube as they led him up a staircase that could have accommodated a trolley car. Beyond that stretched a hallway lined with oil paintings and spotless brass wall sconces. He couldn't even hear his own footfalls on the carpeted floor and thought, if nothing else, he was going to get the best night's sleep of his life in this place.

Angell watched the bellhop insert an ornate key into the brass door lock. As the door swung inward, he was assailed by a sudden brief memory, a dark shadowy moment from another life, unexpected and eerie . . . coffee-colored hands holding a snow-white cloth and slowly, with great care and practiced movements, stroking a round, gleaming knob of brass.

"Gots to go in the same direction, the same direction," the rich voice spoke in his mind as the polishing cloth caressed the metal. "But you won't never have to do dis kinda thing . . ."

The bellhop cleared his throat. "Mr. Angell? Is this suitable?"

Angell took a breath and looked at the man's face. "Yeah, fine." He shook his head free of the memory, unable to shake as easily the queer tingling up his spine.

"Miss Moreland has ordered you a bath, sir, so I'll

be sending the maid up directly. The barber should arrive shortly after that."

After that, Angell knew, he and Winters were to visit the local haberdashery to outfit him for travel to the Kingdom of Heaven.

"Thank you," he said, feeling in his pockets out of habit more than any hope that his money was still there.

The bellhop gave a brief bow. "That's all right, sir. The lady has taken care of everything. Thank you."

Angell laughed once and shook his head. The lady had taken care of everything.

He entered the room and was astonished to find that not only was there a bed the size of a stable, but just off the right-hand wall was his own personal water closet, the size of a bedroom and complete with running water.

Moments after he closed the door behind the bellboy, there was a knock at it. Angell opened it to find a pretty maid all dressed up in a neat black gown with an apron and cap.

"Good morning, sir," she said, "I'm here to draw your bath."

"Draw my—well, come on in." Angell stepped back to let her enter and watched as she efficiently drew the curtains, filled the tub with water and set up chair, scissors, blade and bowl in the washroom for the barber's imminent visit.

"Will there be anything else, sir?" she asked him.

He sat on the side of the huge bed, pulling off his boots. "For the life of me, I can't come up with a damn thing," he said, amazed that it was true.

"If you think of anything, just ring the bell." She indicated a long, velvet bell-pull. "Someone will be right up to help you." She issued a pert curtsy and disappeared through the door.

Angell looked around, bewildered. If this was the way Miss Moreland *traveled*, how well did she live? And, more to the point, if she lived this well, how well did her sister live?

Fingering the petal-soft bedspread, he wondered

again if he'd done the right thing. He'd avoided society for so long he wasn't at all sure that any of it would come back to him. Nor was he sure it was in his best interest to remember. Though they'd figured out he was from the South, they didn't know where, and they didn't know how it was he'd come to leave. What would they do if they knew? he wondered briefly, then frowned at the uncomfortable vision.

So they never would know, he vowed. New York City was a long way from Georgia. A long way and a lot of years from his past.

He'd done the right thing, he told himself. He'd needed to do something to get himself some decent cash, maybe to buy that old broken-down ranch he'd seen in Oklahoma. Maybe it was fate that he'd met them. It was certainly strange, he thought again. Hell, it was downright unbelievable that he and Miss Moreland should, at any time in their respective lives, have found themselves staying at the same boardinghouse. He supposed he owed it to the fact that Himey was such an ass-backward town that it didn't even have a hotel. But that Miss Moreland would even *appear* in a town like that *and* have this outlandish plan was beyond opportune—it was positively fateful. Maybe there was a reason he happened to be there and be thick-headed enough to get himself embroiled in another gunfight.

The barber had arrived and Angell had already bathed, donned the white robe that hung next to the tub and settled down in the chair in the washroom when someone knocked on the door. The barber, a small, balding man, slapped a hot towel over Angell's face and told him to sit still, that he'd get the door. A moment later, two sets of footsteps entered the washroom.

"Mr. Angell," the little professor's voice announced. "As soon as Mr. Isaacs is finished, I want you to get dressed and meet me in the lobby."

"Srrr fnnng," Angell mumbled.

He heard Winters sigh. "What?"

Angell pushed the damp towel up past his lips. "Sure thing," he repeated.

"Good."

"Hey, Winters?" he said, impulse getting the better of him. "Can I ask you somethin'?"

He heard Winters turn slowly. Then, *"Thing,"* the man said forcefully. "Some*thing*. You just said *thing* a minute ago; it's the same word. Some*thing*. Say it."

Angell pushed the towel off his face as the barber stropped his blade. He stared at Winters in concern. "Somethin' eatin' you, Winters?" he asked.

The man sighed and stared at the floor as if counting to ten before an explosion. The barber began slathering Angell's face with soap.

"Yes, some*thing* is eat*ing* me," he said finally. "You. This whole endeavor. We're doomed to failure because *you* are a hopeless idiot. We might as well build another Frankenstein's monster as clean you up and present you to society. We'll be laughingstocks, and Miss Priscilla will be shunned." He shoved his hands in his pockets and looked to Angell like he was about to cry.

Angell studied him while Mr. Isaacs shaved the right side of his face. "About that," Angell said finally. "I don't know any Frank Stein, but I wonder why you folks had to come all the way out here to a plug-ugly town like Himey to find this woman a husband. Ain't there nobody back home willin' to marry her?"

At this, Winters turned so swiftly that Angell thought he was going to get hit. He suffered a brief vision of the barber's blade slicing open his throat before he realized that Winters had stopped himself, though the little man looked angry enough to spit feathers.

"You don't understand," Winters ground out between clenched teeth. "New York is not like places *you're* used to. People there—they don't believe in people making mistakes. They don't understand when something is not exactly as they think it should be. Miss Priscilla would be completely ostracized if they were to find out about this scheme. She'd be humiliated, blacklisted—her whole family would be banished from all the best homes."

Angell watched the man try to get hold of himself and smiled lazily. "You make the places I'm used to sound downright friendly," he said. "And I know you don't mean to do that."

The words coaxed a tight smile from Winters's lips.

"I didn't mean to flatter you, you're right." He sat heavily on the side of the tub and, resting elbows on knees, put his head in his hands.

"You might still find some nice fella more suited who'd be willin' to keep the lady's secret," Angell offered. Mr. Isaacs wiped the remaining soap from Angell's face and turned him so that he could reach the long, unruly locks on his head with scissors. "Maybe I could help you do that instead," he offered. "I may not come up much in the ranks of gentlemen, but I'm a right good judge of character."

Winters didn't answer immediately. Angell watched him steadily. You didn't have to be a tree full of owls to know he was thinking someone like Joshua Angell had no business even being in the same room with someone related to Ava Moreland.

When Winters finally raised his head, he smiled ruefully. "No. You're the closest we're going to get to a nice fellow, I'm afraid. You see, it can't be anyone they know, anyone from New York, or they'll be ruined. Everyone will find out, and it'll spoil even Miss Ava's chances of getting married. We had to find someone completely unknown."

"Well, you done that." Angell shook his head, thinking of all the people he'd known and the chances of one of them ending up in New York City.

"And there's nobody *completely* unknown who's got money or the means of making any," Winters continued, his face lamenting the bleak circumstances more eloquently than his words. "Miss Priscilla had the chance to make a brilliant match. Both Richard Alden and Charles Montjoy were interested in her, and there was even a rumor the Duke of Suttercliff was making plans to come see her. She would have been set for life. Instead . . ." He let his hands drop open limply. "Nothing. She'll have nothing."

She'll have less than nothing, Angell thought, getting into the morose spirit of things. She'll have a husband with nothing, too, and that had to add up to a negative.

"Well, look," Angell said matter-of-factly. "I'll marry her, then I'll go off somewhere and you can tell everyone I died somehow. Then you can marry her off to the duke if he still wants her, see?"

Winters looked at him in astonishment. "That would be bigamy."

Angell smiled deprecatingly. "Hell, it'd be pretty big of me, too. But what the heck. You're buyin' me a new suit, right?"

Chapter Five

Ava stood on the front porch of the hotel in the sharp-angled glow of the evening sun. It was warm where she stood, though the fall air was cool as the sun sank rapidly. She scanned the faces of people passing by in search of Harvey and Mr. Angell. They were to have met her here at half past six and it was now a quarter to seven. She had made dinner reservations at seven to give them enough time, but apparently giving Mr. Angell the appearance of a gentleman was more involved than she'd thought. It wasn't like Harvey to be even five minutes late, let alone fifteen.

She looked as far up and down the street as she could, then scanned the chairs on the front porch. Could she possibly have missed them? She discreetly searched the collections of ladies taking the evening air and the men with cigars who populated the porch.

Sighing, she pushed the flap of her cape aside to look at the tiny diamond watch pinned to her bodice. Six-forty-seven, she read. With another glance up the street, she decided to avail herself of one of the rockers. She might as well look as though she were relax-

69

ing, she reasoned, so that no one would mistake her for a person in need of a hack.

As it happened, the Brown Hotel sat on the corner of two wide streets, and the amount of traffic made for a busy intersection. While the hotel had a crescent-shaped drive for coaches and cabriolets, at the moment it was completely jammed, with even more people being let off on the sidewalks by the roadside.

Ava kept her eyes on the crowds, occasionally noting a man who looked rather like Harvey, or another whose western mode of dress made her look twice for Mr. Angell. But none of them wore clothes with the stylish tailoring of Harvey's, and the cowboys were always too short or too gawky to match Mr. Angell's fluid physique.

It was amazing, really, she congratulated herself, that she'd found a man so physically gifted. Of all the rustic, unknown individuals she might have chosen, Mr. Angell was special. He was tall but not huge, broad but not bulky. He had fine, sculpted hands and thick, glossy hair, and best of all he carried himself like a lord. His movements were confident, his posture proud, without obstinacy. And somehow he was able to convey an impression of strength without behaving like a thug.

The very contemplation of it brought her pleasure. She could not imagine trying to alter a man's whole style of motion in such a short time, while also trying to realign his speech patterns. As it was, the physical area at least could not have been more perfect.

Yes, he might turn out to be quite presentable when all was said and done, Ava thought with satisfaction. If she could keep him from opening his mouth as often as he did, it could be even easier than she'd first imagined.

She watched a clean-cut blond gentleman in a passable suit help an overdressed woman out of a carriage. He stood by the step unobtrusively, offered just the right amount of support as the woman descended, bowed briefly with elegance and escorted the woman into the hotel.

Well done, Ava thought, mentally ticking off another item on her list of skills to impart to Mr. Angell. She must remember public gallantry. Perhaps a trip or two to the theater would be in order when they got home.

Her eyes fell on another cab, the farthest out, that could only pull a short way into the drive. A well-dressed man emerged and moved around the back of the carriage, evidently unloading a trunk or some other baggage. He reminded her of Mr. Angell in his movement, and Ava had the pleasure of thinking that, with a little work, perhaps he could be made as noticeably sharp as this man.

The traffic of the adjacent street was such that the long line of carriages in the drive had quite a wait before they could exit. Ava sighed and checked her watch again. Six-fifty-two! At this rate it was certain that taking a cab to the restaurant would not quicken the journey, unless they caught one at the front of the line. She wondered if she should send a messenger to postpone their reservation.

The gentleman from the far carriage headed her way, arms loaded not with baggage, but with packages. Though he was still a ways off, she could tell his clothes were exquisite. She wondered if he were from the East; his style was so much more sophisticated than the others she'd seen in town.

A second later she noticed Harvey rushing toward her. She rose instantly, ready to give him a proper dose of disdain for his untimely arrival, and noted that his arms, as well, were full of parcels. With an inward gasp, she swept her gaze to the man coming toward her. He saw her, and a breathtaking smile split his face.

As the blood departed from her head, Ava sat down heavily. It was unbelievable. She'd thought the man with the packages to be someone Mr. Angell could *emulate*—when all the while it *was* Mr. Angell.

She took a moment to catch her breath, then rose again on uncertain knees as he ascended the stairs.

"I'm real sorry we're so late, *Miz Moreland*," he said,

giving her a rueful smile. "We just got so tied up in what we was doin' that time run lickety-split."

She nearly laughed at the jarring speech, but she kept it to a smile and absorbed the transformation. His thick dark hair had been cut short in a style that showed off his high cheekbones and light eyes. He was immaculately clean-shaven, and the high white collar of his shirt contrasted pleasantly with his sun-darkened skin. He looked healthy and fit, and disastrously handsome.

"It's all right, Mr. Angell," she told him as Harvey puffed up the steps. "But you, Mr. Winters, should have known better." She arched an eyebrow at him.

He gave her an exasperated sigh. "The man's insatiable," he said, shooting a sour glance at Angell's back. "He wanted everything he saw. Bowlers and derbies, string ties and four-in-hands. I had to talk him out of the breeches and spats—the man says he wants to learn *tennis*, of all the ludicrous ideas."

She glanced at Angell and he shrugged. "Just tryin' to get in the mood of the thing."

Ava felt a chuckle bubble to her throat and could not stop it. Harvey gave her an appalled look.

"You may think," he said, "that shopping for a new wardrobe is some sort of picnic. But next time *you* can go with him and see how much fun it is. He actually wanted to buy a pair of striped stockings for *you*, but I refused to let him enter the shop."

"They'd'a looked real pretty, Miz Moreland," Angell said in a voice full of temptation.

She couldn't help it; she laughed at his boyishness. He gave Harvey a triumphant look.

"I cannot believe you're encouraging his effrontery," Harvey protested.

"Please relax, Harvey," she said, ignoring his astonished expression. "It was a kind notion. Now come, we're going to be late. Give the porter your parcels, and I'll secure us a cab. I don't know about you two, but I'm famished."

*   *   *

"Keep your mouth shut and do everything that I do," Harvey instructed Angell in the carriage. "And, for God's sake, remember your *ing*s."

Ava's face reflected confusion. "Remember his what?"

"His *ing*s," Harvey repeated. "He can say it; I've heard him. He's just too lazy to remember."

Angell took a deep breath and said to the ceiling, "I'd like to *sing* about every*thing*, but I forgot to *bring* my glasses. If I should *spring* and break my *wing*, it's because I'm slow as molasses." He turned a dry look on Harvey. "I get that right, Harvey?"

Ava looked from one to the other of them as if they'd both lost their minds. "What in the world was that?"

"Just a little some*thing* Harvey made up for me. Ain't it good?"

"I thought it might help," Harvey said. "It's an instructional limerick he can recite to himself in his spare time."

"Hmmm, yes," Ava said. "The vital words being 'to himself.' "

"I composed it for a specific audience. I never claimed to be a poet."

"Rightly so," Angell added, enjoying Harvey's irritation.

"And just what do you know about poetry?" Harvey demanded.

"I know I don't wear glasses."

Harvey pushed back in the seat and muttered, "Otherwise it's perfect."

"*Boys,*" Ava said, frowning. "Mr. Angell, I think it's a good idea for you to repeat the limerick as often as you think of it. And Harvey, perhaps you could put some more thought into future endeavors."

"I ain't interested in any more of his endeavors," Angell said.

"Perhaps something using various conjugations of the verb 'to be,' " Harvey suggested. "I *was* an imbecile, I *am* currently an imbecile, and I *shall always be* an imbecile," he recited loftily. "And I *am not* going to change."

73

Elaine Fox

"I *was* a jackass, I *am* a jackass, and I'll *always be* a jackass," Angell said. "How's that, Harvey?"

"You're both right," Ava snapped. "Now straighten up. I won't be embarrassed by the two of you bickering through dinner."

But Angell could tell she was amused, even if Harvey wasn't. In fact, the more Angell was able to make Miss Moreland laugh, the more ornery Winters became. It might have been a double bonus, if it weren't becoming so easy to get the little man's goat.

After they'd been seated, in a location conspicuously remote from other diners, Ava began to familiarize Angell with what she termed a "typically dressed table."

"The water glass is this one," she said, indicating a goblet just to the right of his knife, "this, for the wine. The implements are used in order. For example, the salad will arrive, and you will use the outside fork. When that is finished, the next fork in is for the entrée. If you were to have oysters as an appetizer, they would bring you an oyster fork and place it here. The same goes for the spoons—this one for consommé, this one for dinner, and these up here," she pointed to a spoon and fork above his plate, "for coffee and dessert."

Angell's eyes followed the movements of her hand, but he said nothing. It was all ridiculously overdone in his opinion, but there was no point in saying so.

"The napkin is placed in the lap . . ." She picked it up, flicked it open with a flash of her wrist and dropped it onto his lap, "which is where your hands stay when you are not using them to eat. Elbows are never on the table, and fingers are *never* used directly on the food. Is all of that clear?"

Angell nodded.

"One more thing. The knife is never used except for cutting. In polite society, people put only their forks in their mouths, never their knives. Any questions?"

He couldn't help it; he had to ask. "Peas?"

"Peas?" she repeated. He nodded. "What about them?"

Though his object was to goad her, the sudden vision he had of chasing down and spearing individual peas with the prongs of his fork was so far from what he would consider polite behavior that he really had to ask what to do in the event they turned up on his plate. "What if I order them? I mean, your average blade can hold a bunch of the little devils, while your average fork, on the other hand, takes a lot more balance. I can't use my knife for eatin'—eating peas?"

Ava's mouth twitched, but she maintained her sobriety. "I'm sorry, no."

Harvey began to snicker at the exchange.

"Well, it ain't as if I'm *real* fond of peas or nothin', but it strikes me the rule's a lot more work than it's worth. I mean, it's a little like eatin' your soup with a knittin' needle, don't you think?"

Harvey's snicker became an outright laugh, and Angell had to work to keep his face straight.

"A little," Ava admitted. "But you'll get used to it. And in any case, you won't find yourself dining where the old two-pronged forks are still employed."

"Well, that'll be a step up," Angell said and smiled at her.

She smiled back, and he thought again how easy as well as how profitable the next few months might be. Possibly even enjoyable to boot. For all her proper prickliness, there was something about Ava Moreland that intrigued him. Something beyond her obvious beauty. It was almost as if all that politeness and snobbery were trying to hide another side of her—a side that was real and alive, he thought. And Angell knew a lot about hiding things.

Dinner progressed rather well, he thought. If all her instructions were going to be as easy to remember as her advice about the silver, then he'd be fine in their hoity-toity little world. She only reprimanded him a few times, once for the perfectly understandable sin of pouring his own wine—servants should do that—and another time for the more heinous crime of propping his feet up on the chair opposite him.

He only caught Harvey rolling his eyes once, when he accidentally shot a clam into his own water glass with that stupid little fork. But the damn things were slippery as hell and the mistake perfectly excusable, in his opinion, particularly considering his accuracy. It wasn't as if he'd hit Miss Moreland's glass or anything. In any case, he decided he simply wouldn't order the little buggers again.

They finished dinner with a selection of cheeses, which, he learned, were also to be eaten with the blasted fork. He wasn't even allowed to *cut* it with the knife—only the fork—which meant the only acceptable use for the knife was wrestling whatever beast happened to be on the plate. Spoons were equally useless, being only admissible in the event that something arrived in a bowl and was liquid. So the fork reigned supreme, and its use was apparently monitored by huge numbers of people.

When they left the restaurant, the evening was cool and the sky filled with stars. Miss Moreland decided they should walk back to the hotel. Angell pounced on the opportunity to escort Miss Moreland and leave Winters the odd man out. He managed it by pointing out that he was the one who needed practice, and God only knew what trouble he could get into if he were made to stroll along behind the two of them—spitting, leering and generally acting savage.

He offered his arm to Miss Moreland, and she placed her hand lightly upon it, sending a strange, though not unpleasant, sensation through him. He inclined his head to her in what he thought was a genteel manner, and they proceeded.

"You know, I always hated cities," Angell said, gazing around at the carriages, wagons and drays that, despite the hour, still rumbled up and down the street. "They just don't give a man a chance to think, what with all the rushin' and pushin' goin' on all over the place."

"Rush*ing* and push*ing*," Harvey growled from behind them.

Angell glanced back at him, shot him an impudent grin and nodded. "That's right. I mean, it ain't as if *everyone's* got so all-fired much to do. They just rush around so's to get outa each other's way. You know what I mean, Miz Moreland?"

He looked down at her with suppressed amusement, taking in the soft wave of her hair beneath the hat with the feather she wore. She turned a quarter way toward him, enough for him to glimpse part of a milky-white cheek and see the sweep of her lashes as she surveyed him from the corner of her eye.

"On the contrary, I love the city, Mr. Angell," she said. "Nowhere else will you find such a concentration of cultured and fashionable people. Manners and civility abound in such locales because educated people tend to seek out others like themselves. And there are so many edifying things to do in a city. Museums, art galleries, theater. Once you experience these things from the level of *gentleman,* you will come to appreciate them, I'm sure."

Angell cocked his head and watched her watching the street in front of them. "I don't know about that, Miz Moreland." But he decided not to elaborate. "Myself, I always kinda liked the country. Some rollin' hills, a few trees, maybe some farmland. You got any idea how many stars you can see on a clear night in the country?"

As if to offer direct contrast, a fire truck rounded a corner in front of them and careened by, complete with thundering drafthorses and ringing bells, after which a woman emptied a bucket of wash water out of a second-story window across the street.

"There are great benefits to the country," Ava admitted after the commotion had passed, and she smiled wryly. "Quiet, for one. Fresh air, exercise. My family once owned a house in the foothills of Pennsylvania. I used to love to visit it as a child. I thought it was heaven on earth." She looked so pretty, remembering her childhood, that he wondered exactly what it was she remembered with such fondness. A time before etiquette ruled her life? A time when she scuffed up her shoes and soiled the hem of her dress without worrying about the consequences?

"What happened to it? You still got it?"

She waved a hand. "No, it was sold. We stopped going when I was about seven. It became much more fashionable to have a place near the ocean, so Father purchased a cottage in Newport."

"That don't sound too bad," he said politely.

"Oh, no. It's quite nice. I like the ocean, too." But her face was empty of its previous enthusiasm.

They turned a corner onto a quieter street. Here it was considerably darker and Angell paused, concerned. But Harvey insisted that since it was a shorter route back to the hotel, they should take it because Miss Moreland wasn't dressed for walking.

Angell shrugged. "What about your folks, Miz Moreland? They know what you're doin' out here, lookin' for a husband for your sister?"

She sighed and looked down at her hands. "Heavens, no. They believe Cilla and I have gone to visit friends in the Hamptons. Cilla is there, of course, because she couldn't possibly have made this trip in her—condition."

"Hmmm, no." Angell watched her. She was obviously uncomfortable with lying to her parents. It showed in her pink cheeks and the way she plucked at her purse strings.

"We'll meet her in Boston before we return to New York. I—I believe you'll like her. Most men do."

He laughed. "Apparently," he said, then wished he could take the joke back. She looked so stricken and embarrassed that he found himself laying his hand on top of hers and squeezing gently. "It ain't nothin' to feel bad about yourself, Miz Moreland. It happens all the time. And *you* didn't do nothin' wrong."

She pulled her chin up and sniffed. "It didn't happen the way you think it did."

He couldn't repress another smile at that. "It didn't?"

She flushed deeply this time. "That is, I believe that Priscilla was in love with the man. She was not simply—" she waved a gloved hand around in front of her in frustration, "*rolling around* in some *haystack* the way it may happen out here."

Angell frowned, concentrating. "A haystack . . . I never tried that."

She shot him a shocked look that tried to be scathing.

"You got any other brothers or sisters, other'n Miz Priscilla?" Angell asked then, not wanting to get her dander up too far.

Ava took a deep breath in an obvious effort to control her pique. "Yes, though you might have phrased that, 'Have you any *siblings* other than Miss Priscilla?'" she corrected. "In fact, I have an older brother. He was recently married, last summer. It was a *brilliant* match to Miss Dorcas Phibb, of the Rhode Island Phibbs."

He chuckled. "Sounds like a kind of fish. A Rhode Island dorcas phibb."

Ava's eyes snapped to his. "That is precisely the kind of humor that will no longer be acceptable. It's not polite to make fun at the expense of others."

Angell gave her an affronted look. "It ain't like they're here or anything. I wouldn't say nothin' like that to their faces." He reconsidered a moment. "Well, maybe not. Definitely not now."

He waited for the inevitable snicker from Harvey, behind them, but nothing came. He glanced back. Harvey was not there. In fact, he was nowhere to be seen. For one low moment, Angell debated not pointing this out to Miss Moreland, thinking how nice it was having her all to himself, but a lone dandy on a dark city street was a dangerous thing. His better nature won out.

"Uh, Miz Moreland?" he said, interrupting her daintily worded monologue on the evils of personal mockery. He stopped walking and she paused to look up at him. "Seems we lost Mr. Winters."

Ava whirled. Though there had been the occasional vehicle on the street, there were none now nor any pedestrians, so it was easy to see that Harvey was not simply lagging behind.

"What could have become of him?" she gasped. She

turned anxious eyes to Angell, her hands kneading her reticule.

Angell felt the heat of her gaze to the soles of his feet. "He prob'ly just wandered off somewhere. Maybe he stopped in for a drink at one of them waterin' holes we passed."

Ava grimaced and moved swiftly back down the way they'd come. "He would never just wander off. And you know as well as I do that he wouldn't stop for a drink without letting us know."

Angell followed her, knowing she was right and wondering how one went about calming a woman too smart to be lied to.

"You know, Miz Moreland, I think maybe you'd better wait somewhere safe while I go lookin' for Mr. Winters," he said finally, coming up with no gentle way of getting her out of the way.

Ava stopped and glared at him in alarm. "You think something's happened to him. You think he's in some sort of trouble, don't you?"

Angell took her arm and tried to steer her across the street, but she persisted in moving back the way they'd come. Somehow, while they were chatting, the part of town they were walking through had become nothing but closed shops and warehouses. During the day, it was probably safe and well-populated, but at this hour, with none of the establishments open, a sinister darkness abounded. For some reason, the traffic had thinned to an occasional closed carriage going far too fast to be of any help.

"Where should we go?" Ava asked, alternately looking at him and twisting around to look for Harvey.

Angell, too, looked around uneasily. "I'll tell you what we're gonna do. We're gonna find some nice restaurant or saloon where you can stand safe while I look for Harvey."

"Absolutely not." Ava stopped dead in her tracks. Angell's hand on her arm had about as much effect in moving her forward as it would have propelling her into the air. "I'm going to look with you. We must have only just lost him; if we hurry, we'll find him close by."

Angell shook his head. "Beggin' your pardon, but you don't know nothin' about this, Miz Moreland. Maybe things back east are more tame, but 'round here, there's people who'll just as soon shoot you for a dime as ask you for spare change." He glanced over his shoulder at the other side of the street. His hands automatically felt for his guns. "Damn," he muttered, feeling only the new broadcloth of his trousers.

Miss Moreland's hand clasped his arm tightly, and he turned back to her. "We must find him. We can't waste time looking for a suitable location for me."

Angell shook his head and muttered under his breath. He had no guns, and he was toting a fancy lady on his arm. How much more disadvantaged could he be?

"All right," he mumbled. He turned back the way they'd come, trepidation in every step, and felt her grab his hand. With a downward glance, he saw her press something cold and shiny into his palm. He stopped, raising it up to find a tiny silver derringer engraved with fancy scrollwork from handle to barrel. He stared at her in surprise, tempted to laugh but knowing it would be the wrong thing to do.

"I bought it before we left New York. I feared for just such a situation as this," she said intently. "Use it. We must save Harvey."

A skeptical look crossed Angell's face, but he refrained from saying that the best he could do with a toy like this was poke the scoundrel in the eye with it. The average Missouri ruffian was like as not to mistake a bullet from a lady's derringer for a chigger bite.

An unexpected shuffling from behind them drew both their attentions. Angell pushed Miss Moreland behind his back with a rough hand before he spotted the source of the noise. Across the street, a wiry man skulked along the shadowy wall. He appeared to be facing them, though he kept close to the storefront and dipped into the blackened doorway when he got to it. The hair on the back of Angell's neck rose.

Then he heard it, the stealthy *pssssst* of a thug trying to get someone's attention.

"Stay close," Angell whispered, clutching Ava's hand behind his back.

"What is it?" she hissed. "What does he want?"

"Miz Moreland, please shut up."

They crossed the street, Angell's stride deceptively casual, and neared the darkened doorway. When they were a dozen yards from it, he let go of her hand and motioned her to stop. His other hand held the tiny gun in his pocket.

"All right," he announced, "come on out and tell me what you're wantin'."

The figure emerged from the blackness and leaned against the store window, glancing first one way, then the other. "Y'all missin' somethin'?" his raspy voice asked.

Angell stared him down. "Nope. Why?"

The man rubbed his hand along his head, ruffling greasy hair. "Mebbe I should say, y'all missin' some-*one*?" He nodded pointedly. "Iffen you are, I might as can help you."

"I don't think we're interested in your help, mister," Angell said. Ava's finger poked him in the back.

"Maybe he really knows something," she prompted in a whisper loud enough to make the greasy man grin in the darkness.

"That's right, ma'am. I surely do know somethin'." He stepped out of the shadow toward them. Something in the man's movements arrested Angell's backward step.

At the same moment, a carriage turned the corner at the end of the block and clattered toward them. The three of them turned wary eyes to it. The reflector lamps cast jerking shadows down the street as the span of horses neared. Angell glanced back at their stealthy companion.

The light played strangely over his averted face, and the one narrowed eye Angell could see glittered in the lamplight. Perhaps feeling Angell's eyes on him, he took a step back to the shadowed doorway, but the coach was upon them, and the lamplight infiltrated even that.

Angell took a step nearer. Harvey, Ava, the derringer were all forgotten as the carriage overtook them. In the split second of illumination, Angell glimpsed what he half-expected and yet prayed was not there—the opaque cloudiness of the man's left eye.

A thousand images flashed through his mind the instant he beheld the face. "*Good Lord,*" Angell said under his breath. The blood seemed to stall in his veins.

The carriage passed, and they were plunged again into darkness.

Without a second thought, Angell descended on the man. The rogue was tall, but Angell was stronger. A swift fist to the man's gut bounced him back against the shop door. Taking advantage of surprise and the man's blind left eye, Angell hooked a right to the side of his head and watched as the lean body crumbled, unconscious, to the sidewalk.

"What did you *do*?" Ava wailed. "What's the matter with you? He was going to tell us where Harvey is!"

Shaken, Angell rubbed his fist with his other hand and looked up at her. What was she saying? He tried to think, but all he could see was a milky-blue eye on a sneering face. If he concentrated, he could see the man's fist, raised up, with the thick butt of a leather whip enclosed in it.

He shuddered. Impossible. It couldn't be who he thought it was. He turned the man over with the toe of his boot. There, all too clearly, was the face he once knew so well. Barrett Trace—overseer of his father's plantation what seemed a million years ago.

Beads of sweat broke out on Angell's forehead, and he closed his eyes against the onslaught of memories. He had to leave—had to get the hell out of there.

He had to disappear before the man woke up and had a chance to recognize *him*.

Chapter Six

"What are you doing? Where are we going?" Ava was suddenly afraid. Not of the muggers or, at this instant, of Harvey's possibly dire fate. No, at this instant she was afraid of Angell, of this stranger who had become abruptly unpredictable. He was possessed, wild-eyed, and he had hold of her hand in a punishing grip as he dragged her down the street.

He moved so quickly that she stumbled as she struggled to keep up, but keep up she did, realizing that she was still more afraid of the shadow dwellers than this suddenly alien Angell.

The dark hole of the doorway receded behind them, the villain broken and bleeding in its mouth; but Ava could not forget the image. Nor could she forget the brutality that had landed him there. Two blows. Two merciless swings of those sizeable fists and the man was down. Unconscious. Ava had never before seen such ruthlessness.

She wondered if Angell were crazy. Then she imagined the whole episode had been his plan from the beginning. That other man might have been his partner—maybe he killed Harvey!—and now this man, this *Angell*, was taking her away to ravage her. Panic screeched in her chest like a wild animal, but she could not force a sound from her throat.

She could not have misjudged him so thoroughly, she told herself. He was harmless. Even gentle. Good Lord, she'd even had a moment when she'd found him attractive.

Her head swam and her toe caught on a chink in the sidewalk. She stumbled. Angell maintained his grip on her hand and tried to hold her up, but one foot tangled in her skirts and the other followed. One more step and she sprawled to the ground, awash in cape, skirts and petticoats.

Angell immediately let go of her hand. Her dizziness abated, but an unreasoning fear coursed through her.

"Miss Moreland!" He swooped down beside her.

Her eyes swept up to his in fright, and she shrank from his madness, even as she longed for his protection. Involuntary tears dripped over her lashes.

He took her hands and she cried out, so paralyzed by uncertainty that she could not fight him. She could only avert her eyes and let the unchecked tears dampen her cape.

"Let me be," she pleaded.

He froze, his hands still holding hers. "Are you all right? I'm sorry."

"No, don't—let go of me. Please don't hurt me." She didn't absorb his tone, his words; she knew only that he still held her captive.

"Don't hurt you?" His hands opened and she pulled hers free. "Miss Moreland—hell—I'd never hurt you. *Never*."

She turned distrustful eyes to him. "B-but what about—about him? That man?" Her voice and her limbs trembled from excess emotion. "What about Harvey?"

The fierceness left his face and his eyes became un-utterably gentle. "We'll find him. I promise. Please, don't be scared." For the first time, she noticed that he'd reached out again and stroked her arm lightly.

85

Through the fabric of her sleeve it felt nice, even calming. "Miss Moreland, I'm sorry. We had to get away from that man. He might have woken up and then . . . Oh, shhhh, quiet now, I'm sorry."

She was still crying, weeks' worth of tension dissolving into salty tears as she realized the absurdity of the flight her imagination had taken. For just that moment, she wanted to let it all go, all the determination, the resolution, the *responsibility* for everything and everyone, and lay her head on his shoulder. The need for someone stronger than herself was overwhelming, and at this moment, Joshua Angell was most definitely the stronger.

But she didn't succumb to the temptation. She couldn't. Instead she sat motionless, letting her tears dry on her cheeks while he comforted her.

"I won't let anything happen to you." His voice was quiet, as tender as the hand that stroked her arm. As he spoke, he moved his hand upward to her shoulder. Then after a moment, he touched her face, and his thumb stroked her cheek, tracing the path of her tears.

She stared into his eyes, dark in the night, unfathomable, but trained on her in a way that would not let her look away. He comforted her, but there was something else, something in his posture or maybe just the intensity of his gaze. Her breath stopped in her throat.

As if he, too, noticed a shift, his hand moved slowly to her neck, the touch changing from consolation to caress. His fingers gently pushed beneath the collar of her cape until his hand met skin, his palm warm against her neck. Her lips opened; breath came rushing back, shallow and rapid. His fingers touched her hair; her hat fell to the ground.

"You're so soft," he whispered.

It felt good, so good to be touched this way. Ava was entranced, her body thrumming with emotion. He pulled her toward him and she let him, until they were so close she could not focus on his eyes.

Her lashes dropped. She could feel his breath on her mouth. His fingers tensed, curled in her hair, and she felt his lips touch hers.

A kiss. So gentle, but *oh,* how it made her heart thunder. He pulled a short way back after the contact and looked her in the eye. His face was calm, his eyes potent. Heaven help her, but he was beautiful.

Inexplicably, she leaned toward him. It was his strength she wanted to feel, his control. She wanted to kiss him, to touch him herself, but she couldn't make her hands move. Oh, she wanted *more.*

"Ava." His voice was a low chord that hummed in her brain.

She licked her suddenly dry lips. He groaned and his mouth descended again. But this time, instead of the soft touch of a moment ago, their lips met with a force that pushed her head back. His hand buried itself in her hair. His other arm shifted around her back and pulled her hard against his chest.

Of their own accord, her hands rose and took fistfuls of his jacket. His tongue drove into her mouth, and she was assaulted by both the shock of her own lips opening under his, and the tidal wave of desire that caused her to moan—*actually moan*—into the hot cavern of his mouth.

His arm around her back was a vise, his hand was hot on her waist. She could not keep her breath, but what she felt was craving, not fear. She pushed herself against him, and he broke away to kiss her jawbone, her neck, the bare skin of her collarbone where her dress was askew.

She held his head, her fingers laced through his hair. He did something tantalizing with his tongue on her neck that raised goose bumps all along her skin, and she threw her head back. Her breath came harshly. Some remote, objective part of her could not believe the extent to which she let herself go.

His tongue traced a path to her ear, and she tilted her head, her eyes barely open. This isn't happening, she chanted silently. It's a dream. A strange, glorious dream. Then she realized that the shadowy movement she saw through her lashes was a person—a *man*— and he was moving toward them.

She gasped and pushed against Angell's chest. He pulled back and looked into her face.

"What is it?"

She pointed. "Look."

Through the darkness, far enough away that they could barely make him out, a man shuffled along the sidewalk.

"What the devil?" Angell stood and pulled her up next to him, one hand still on her waist.

With the approach of the stranger, reality rapidly set in. It had probably been less than two minutes since she'd tripped, yet Ava's cheeks burned and the scrapes on her knees from the sidewalk were a sudden source of acute embarrassment, though nobody but herself could be aware of them. She pulled away from Angell's hand, and her fingers flew to her hair, pushing loose tendrils into the mass and trying to settle the topknot once again on top. Her bonnet had fallen off and her cape was wrapped sideways.

Ignoring the way she'd pushed him off, Angell took a step toward the man. Then another. And another. Then he was running down the sidewalk toward the stranger and leaving her alone.

That's when she realized it was Harvey. Harvey, wearing nothing but a cherry-red union suit, and wandering down the street with his head in his hand. She ran to catch them.

Angell arrived first, with Ava just behind. "Damn, man, what happened to *you*?" he burst out.

Harvey groaned and shook his head, one eye already bruised and swollen shut. "What do you think, you idiot? I was robbed."

"Hell," Angell said. "Here, lemme help you."

"They took everything, everything," Harvey moaned. Despite an obvious limp, he jerked away from Angell's solicitation.

Angell stopped and donned an ironic expression. Raising a brow, he eyed the red union suit. "Well, not *everything*."

Harvey turned an unamused sneer back. "Yes,

everything. You don't think I'd actually wear something like *this*, do you?"

"You mean they left you their *underwear*?" Ava asked, stunned.

Harvey shot her a look. "The fat one couldn't get my suit on over it, so it was the only thing left in the alley. And I couldn't exactly come looking for you two stark naked."

Angell sighed, still trying to suppress a smile. "You gotta admit, it was right nice a them to leave you *somethin'*. Even if it was somethin' a mite . . . festive for the occasion."

As he spoke, something niggled at the edge of Ava's consciousness, something about Angell and the way he'd calmed her fears, the things he'd said . . .

"Oh, good Lord," she said softly, the realization hitting her that while she and Angell had been caught up in that fervid embrace, Harvey had been beaten up in an alley somewhere. "We must get him home. Mr. Angell, could you please run to that street up there and get us a cabriolet?"

"Where the devil were you two anyway?" Harvey asked, clearly out of his head to be swearing in front of her.

Ava swallowed hard and tried to come up with something—*anything*—but her mind was empty of all but the illicit feel of Angell's lips on hers.

"We run into what you might call a *questionable* character back there," Angell said, casually enough. "And when we tried to get away from him, Miz Moreland here stumbled. I was just helpin' her up."

Angell gave her a look that was completely unreadable—blank even—but for the heat that burned in his eyes and scorched her cheeks.

"Yes. Yes, that's right," she agreed, acutely aware, and somehow ashamed, of her gratitude for the cover-up.

Fortunately, Harvey was too distracted by his own misery to notice her behavior. "I can't believe it." He shook his head and laid a palm gingerly to his swollen eye. "My father gave me that watch. Now it'll have no more value than how much hooch it'll get those thugs. Oh, it just doesn't bear thinking about."

"I'll just go and get that cab." Angell stepped away.

Ava couldn't help the way her eyes trailed after him. She hated herself for what they'd just done. Hated it and felt shame to her very bones. But, even still, as she watched him walk away with that lithe stride, she knew that her attraction had not been momentary. And that knowledge frightened her more than anything.

They brought Harvey back to the hotel, where he spoke to the police. Then a doctor was called in to give him a sleeping draught. He was unharmed except for the eye, a bump on the head and some other bruises to his body, and that left him steaming mad.

Ava cringed as she listened to him rant the following morning. The wretches had made off with his wallet, his watch, his *clothes*, for pity's sake, and with all of that, his dignity.

"That Angell fellow is probably laughing up his sleeve at me right now," Harvey blustered. He was ensconced in an overstuffed chair in the sitting room of his suite, on his lap a knitted afghan and beside him a large cup of tea, which Ava knew contained a healthy shot of whiskey. "A ruffian like Angell would have had no trouble putting his fist through their greasy faces. I'll tell you, Ava, there are times when it simply doesn't pay to be a gentleman. Last night was one of them. People just don't have any respect anymore."

Ava let him fume and watched from the second-story window the ever-present procession of cabs and carriages in front of the hotel. She *knew* Angell would have had no trouble putting a fist through someone's face because she'd seen him do just that.

But Harvey's other point frightened her. Suppose Angell was laughing up his sleeve at them? Harvey had proven himself ill-equipped to fight those Missouri street scoundrels, and she had proven herself to be as easy as any common trollop. Could he be the type to enjoy it? For all she knew, he'd gone to some saloon last night after it was over to whoop it up over how shocking, how vulgar, how utterly lewd her behavior had been.

She swallowed back nausea. No, he wasn't that type and she knew it. It was that knowledge that pained her more than anything. He was all that she feared most—plain spoken, honest, good-hearted—and meant for her sister.

She placed a fisted hand to her chest, against the ache blooming there. She'd wronged him and she'd wronged Priscilla. It would have been one thing for her to have *allowed* a kiss. That would have been mistake enough. But to have so actively *participated*—that was where the guilt truly lay. She could not act on her attraction. What in the world would he think? And Priscilla—to have kissed her own sister's husband-to-be in such a way . . .

She clenched her fists until her nails pinched the flesh and she felt her entire body burn with embarrassment. Would she be able to look her sister in the eye?

Her thoughts returned to Angell. She wondered where he was, what he was doing. What *was* he thinking? Did he hope he would have an opportunity to repeat the act? She closed her eyes and hated the trip of her heart when she thought he might have felt the same things she did. She *couldn't* feel that way about him. She simply could not. He was a cowboy, a ruffian, a *bumpkin*, she railed to herself. But the real fact was the consequences of her feelings were too horrible to contemplate.

The only way out was to find someone new, and they couldn't possibly do that now. It was far too late to replace Angell with another fiancé for her sister. Anger rose up in her at the futility of it all. Why? Why *now*, after years of insipid men who did not interest her, why should she be attracted to this one? Not only was he stupendously inappropriate, he was meant for someone else.

She closed her eyes. Oh, but why, she moaned inwardly, why did Priscilla get even *this* one?

How she wished that kiss had never happened. Until last night, she'd been able to keep her interest under control, distant, scholarly. She had known even if he were not to marry Priscilla she could never have him. He was explicitly unsuitable. But that kiss . . .

He shouldn't have done it, she thought desperately. It was beneath her to be in this situation. If he were truly a gentleman, he would never have—

But of course that was the point—he wasn't a gentleman. She'd drawn him into this scheme, and now she had to see it through. She could not let him get to her again. But the thought of having to look him in the eye in all the days to come, knowing what had passed between them, was unthinkable.

"And then there's the possibility of actually *seeing* someone wearing an article of my clothing," Harvey continued, one hand outstretched in indignation. "Imagine walking down the street and seeing a man in my waistcoat, say, or wearing my hat. What should I be expected to do? Ignore it? Impossible. Demand my garment back, only to become embroiled in some sordid fistfight in the middle of the road?" He scoffed and shook his head. "I tell you, there is no gentlemanly way to deal with such an infringement."

Ava curbed a smile at the notion of robbery being an infringement. "I suppose you would simply have to summon the police, Harvey. Surely they would know how to deal with someone wearing stolen garments."

Harvey sighed. "I'm sorry, Ava. I have been going on about it, I know. It's just that it makes me so angry. I can't tell you how helpless I felt."

"I know. I understand." And she did. She had felt the exact same way—helpless. Completely powerless. As if her whole character had been stolen away from her, not just her watch or her topcoat.

"And they were such *uncouth* fellows." He looked genuinely saddened by this.

"As if the circumstances would have been any better had they been men of manners," she murmured, thinking.

"No of course not. You're right." He took the tea

from the table next to him and blew across its hot surface.

"Harvey," she began uneasily. "I'm beginning to think you were right about Mr. Angell."

He looked at her over the rim of the cup, sipped, and brought it slowly to his lap. "What do you mean?"

Ava clasped her hands and paced toward the window. "I mean that perhaps he is too coarse for Priscilla."

She could not meet his eyes. It was a selfish thing to say, a selfish thing even to think about doing. But how could she watch him marry her sister?

Harvey's brows drew together, and he gazed down at the cup in his lap. "It's funny . . ."

Ava turned. "What?"

One side of his mouth lifted in a half-smile. "I was beginning to think *you* might be right about him."

Ava folded her arms across her chest and looked at Harvey's feet. "Perhaps I wasn't."

The tone of his voice changed subtly. "Why? Did something happen to make you change your mind?"

She forced her eyes to his face, then let them skitter away. "No! Nothing at all. I've just been thinking, that's all."

Harvey nodded. "You know, I still hate this idea of yours. But as far as the man himself goes, I think he's not an altogether bad sort. I mean, as you said, he has shown flashes of integrity."

And more than a small flash of opportunism, she thought sourly, then chastened herself for trying to blame him. If anyone was to blame, it was herself. She was the one with the mission to help her sister, the manners to keep improper things like that from happening and the unequivocal knowledge of what was right and what was wrong.

A moment later, their independent reveries were interrupted by a knock on the door.

Harvey called his permission to enter and turned back to Ava. "It's probably the maid. I asked her for more pillows this morning. The neck's a little stiff, you know."

The door opened tentatively. Ava knew before seeing his dark head who it would be.

The door widened and Angell stepped forward, stopping when he caught sight of Ava. "I'm sorry. Are y'all busy?" His hand rested on the knob, as if he might back out again.

Once again, something teased the back of Ava's mind. Something about Angell. As if she were forgetting something important she'd noticed about him.

"No, please come in." Harvey waved him forward. "We were just talking about you."

At this, Angell's brows shot up, and he looked at Ava. She stood stock still and pressed her lips into a line. The simple brush of his gaze sent her pulse racing.

He made her nervous, she realized with dismay. Before, he'd made her anxious—about her decision, his suitability, the task that lay ahead of them—but now he made her nervous, made her embarrassed, made her blush. She looked away as he entered the room.

Amazing what a few clothes could do, she thought as she stared out the window and her mind's eye saw nothing but his tall form in the impeccable suit. He was like the devil sent to taunt her. If God were going to send anyone to corrupt her, she thought grimly, it would be a man like Angell—beautiful, graceful, an honest work of nature with edges so rough she would never forget the sin she was committing.

"Maybe it's good you're both here," Angell began, rolling the brim of his hat ruthlessly in his hands. "I wanna tell both a you I'm sorry. I let you both down last night."

Ava turned back but could not meet his eyes, could not tear her gaze from his hands and the way they kneaded and curled the brim of his high-crowned hat.

"What on earth do you mean?" Harvey asked. "It's not as if *you* set the rogues on me." His brows drew together. "Is it?"

Ava cringed, knowing she'd believed that very thing as Angell had pulled her from the scene of the beating. She glanced up at his face and watched him beneath her lashes.

He laughed dryly. "Wouldn't do me no good, you bein' broke. Not to mention naked."

Harvey laughed outright at this. "Then don't be ridiculous. You kept Miss Moreland safe, that's the main thing."

Angell looked at her warily. Heat suffused her whole body as their eyes met.

Angell's eyes were somber. "I'm sorry if you didn't feel safe, Miz Moreland. I guess I—I just ain't a good one for knowin' what to do in—certain situations."

Breathe. She must breathe, she commanded herself. She inhaled deeply. "Neither am I," she said.

"Look, I—I'll understand if y'all wanna scrap me as your project. I mean, I know you're prob'ly thinkin' you can get somebody better for the job, and I won't blame you at all if that's what you decide. We can even return most a the clothes, I think. I've only worn just the one suit . . ." He looked down at his clothes and rubbed one hand along the side of his trousers.

"Don't be absurd," Harvey said, glancing from one to the other of them, his confusion evident. "Because I was mugged you think we'd want to get rid of you? Frankly, I can think of a lot better reasons than that, I assure you. But Miss Moreland has made up her mind, and I can tell you that she never goes back on a commitment."

Ava felt misery tug at her very soul. It was just what she wanted to do. She wanted to back out, to send Joshua Angell back to the obscurity from which he'd come. She wanted never to have met him. He was dangerous. Not because of anything he might do, but because of what he might compel *her* to do.

But it had been a commitment she'd given him. As much as he'd promised to work for them, to fulfill his share of the bargain, she had promised to employ him. She had broken him out of prison, in a manner of speaking, made him leave all of his belongings, and coerced him into a total alteration of himself. Granted, they were not far along in the process, but how could she back out on him now?

"Isn't that right, Ava?" Harvey insisted, as if he'd said it a time or two already.

Ava straightened her shoulders and gave Angell an impersonal look. "Mr. Angell, you and I have made an agreement out of which I have no intention of backing. If, however, you would prefer to . . ."

The look in Angell's eyes caused her to stop. It was not condemning, nor accusatory for her coldness after last night's heat. It was sad. Sad and flatly unsurprised.

Ava cleared her throat and moved to the table next to Harvey where her reticule lay.

"Come with me, Mr. Angell. I have a book I would like you to read." She did not look at him as she snatched up her bag. "Harvey, I'll be back momentarily. I think it would be beneficial for Mr. Angell to begin reading some noteworthy books. Then we can work further on his language."

"Good idea," Harvey said as she strode toward the door.

She swept by Angell without a glance and opened the door herself. "Follow me," she commanded, sounding to herself like her childhood governess.

She marched so steadily down the hall that by the time she reached her room, Angell had fallen behind, stopping as he had to wish Harvey a good day and close the door behind him.

She entered her sitting room and stepped aside for Angell to follow. She did not look at him; instead, she gazed at the ceiling. He entered uncertainly.

"Miz Moreland, if you brung me in here to fire me personal, I understand and we don't need to talk about it." He faced her, hat still in hand, his expression blank.

"Mr. Angell," she began in as steady a voice as she could muster, "I brought you here to give you a book which you should read. But before I do, I want to tell you that what happened last night was inexcusable." She walked to the table near the window and deposited her bag. This was going to take every ounce of strength she possessed. "And I would like to caution you that if it ever happens again, I will fire you without thinking twice." It was a crime, a lie and a sin to pretend it was all his fault, but if she admitted any guilt, it would not squelch the ideas that might be forming in his mind, she told herself.

She pulled a book from a pile by the wing chair. "This book is not only edifying, but it is beautifully written. Pay close attention to the language as you read, as well as the worthy sentiments expressed." She realized, almost too late, that by giving him this book she might actually have to hand it to him, and getting that close to him suddenly seemed like a very bad idea.

She placed it on the table and walked to the window several paces away. When he didn't move, she motioned him toward it. "Go on."

His expression was unreadable, but he moved forward and picked up the book off the table.

"*Nature,*" he read aloud. "Ralph Waldo Emerson."

"Yes. It's quite good. Quite contemplative."

He nodded, his eyes on her face. She looked out the window.

"*Nature,*" he repeated.

"That's right."

"Miz Moreland," he said quietly.

She felt her throat close and her stomach clench. "Yes?"

"Miz Moreland, please look at me."

She took a breath and tore her gaze from the street. Cool blue eyes regarded her steadily and she tried to do the same.

"I don't like the thought of you bein' angry with me," he said. "And I want you to know that I really am sorry about what happened. It won't happen again, I know that."

She nodded, sure her hair would go up in flames if her face got any hotter.

He continued. "But if you're gonna treat me like I'm invisible now that it happened, it ain't gonna be worth it to me. You see, you treated me with respect all along. Not like Mr. Winters, though I reckon I understand him good enough. So if I lost that from you, that trust you seemed to have in me, I think maybe we'd better call it quits now anyway."

Ava swallowed hard. His earnestness shamed her. "I trust you," she said, in a voice that wouldn't rise above a whisper. She cleared her throat and looked away. "I want nothing to change between us, Mr. Angell. I want everything to be the way it was, exactly."

She heard him shift his weight from one foot to the other. "Well. That's good then," he said. "All right."

From the corner of her vision, she saw him look at the book again.

"I'll just go read now, then," he said.

"All right."

"I'll see you at supper."

She straightened the front of her skirt, smoothing the pleats and studying the material. "And we have the opera tonight."

"Oh, yeah, right."

"Ask Harvey what to wear." She finished smoothing her skirt and began plucking at her gathered sleeve.

"I'll do that. Is he gonna feel good enough to come?"

She clasped her hands and settled them at her waist, looking back out the window. "He'll come."

Chapter Seven

Angell hated the opera. He hated the white stiff-bosomed shirt he was obliged to wear, and he hated the scratchy cuffs and high collar. He hated the way Miss Moreland would only talk to him in clipped sentences that only addressed the screeching performers waddling on stage.

He liked the opera glasses.

But he hated the hard, round-bottomed chairs and the sneering, pomaded men with their sneering, powdered wives who populated the boxes. He hated their formal calls and their obsequious efforts to please the aristocratic Miss Moreland and Mr. Winters. In short, he hated the false crimson lifestyle that existed within the amphitheater.

He also hated Ralph Waldo Emerson.

Try though he might, he could not get through even a page of the rambling monologue without dozing. And though he was anxious to find something in the book that would warrant Miss Moreland's high opinion of it, he could find nothing of interest in the minutiae rhapsodized in the text.

It bothered him. Angell loved nature. He loved looking down from the saddle at a meadow filled with wildflowers, looking out from the shore over a broad swollen river, looking up from a warm bedroll at night and seeing the stars. To him, nature was not something to sit in a chair and contemplate. It was something to walk through, swim in, sleep under. Nature was something to be *lived in*, not philosophized about. And Emerson's obscure statements of the obvious tired him to no end.

Miss Moreland told him to read passages of it out loud at night, so he would read a sentence or two aloud. Then another several to himself. Then he'd blink, only to open his eyes and find that it was two o'clock in the morning and he'd only gotten another page into the damn thing.

Still, he tried. Each night, he resolutely opened the deadly tome and forced his tired eyes to the page. And each night, he found himself, hours later, clutching the book with the lamp burning, and his neck stiff as a crowbar from the awkward angle his head had fallen onto the headboard.

The fact was, he admitted to himself time and again, he'd blown it. Kissing Miss Moreland had been a mistake of colossal proportions. It was obvious she didn't trust him anymore. And when he was honest with himself, he knew that the biggest reason he had accepted the assignment was because of her, because of that something he'd seen in her that she wouldn't let out. Of course, she was beautiful, too, and the most desirable woman he'd ever seen. But it was the unseen suspicion of depth that had him studying her so intently, the way a child looks for the strings on a puppet.

But he should not have touched her. Thinking about it afterward, as he did far too often, he knew he couldn't help himself that night. She'd been so supple and willing. Her passion had astounded him, and confirmed what he thought he'd seen in her eyes all along—a kind of heat and life that was not revealed in her movements and her speech.

But it didn't take genius to see that since that night, he made her uncomfortable. She closed up when he was near and skirted him as if she feared for her virtue. He couldn't blame her, really. After witnessing what he'd done to Barrett Trace, why wouldn't she be afraid of him? He couldn't explain to her why he'd beaten the man. He couldn't even tell her that he knew him—and had some damn good reasons for not wanting to be recognized by him. No, that was completely out of the question. She was curious about his past, his home, his family, and he would give her no clues to them. Rich people had ways of satisfying their curiosity that Angell had no intention of aiding.

To her credit, she hadn't asked any more about the incident, though that may have been from fear of the answer rather than trust that his actions were justified.

Angell was sitting on top of the bedcovers, fully clothed in an attempt to stay awake, with *Nature* propped in front of him, when someone knocked at his door. He called out to enter and watched as the doorway offered Harvey Winters, a stack of three books under one arm. At the sight of them, Angell groaned and dropped his head back against the headboard.

"Please, not more," he pleaded from behind closed eyes. Then he raised his head and fixed an ominous look on Harvey's amused face. "I'm afraid Ralph'll get jealous if I start sleeping with someone else."

Harvey tossed the books on the bed, where they bounced twice with heavy finality. "I think you'll find these a little easier to swallow than Mr. Emerson. He might be one of Ava's favorites, but I think it's pretty obvious he'll never be one of yours."

"Now there I gotta disagree with you. Any night I can't get to sleep, he'll be higher up on my list than warm milk." But he put the book down and leaned over the pile at the foot of the bed. "Have a seat." He waved Harvey to the chairs near the fire and dragged the books to his lap.

Harvey seated himself and folded his arms over his chest.

"*Moby-Dick,*" Angell read, then put the volume down and picked up the next. "*Twenty Thousand Legs Under the Sea.*"

"*Leagues,*" Harvey corrected.

"*Tales of the Grow—tess—Grotesque.*"

"That one I think you'll particularly like. That fellow Poe knows how to grip a reader. I looked for *Frankenstein,* but the shop here didn't have it. I'll get it for you in New York."

"Oh, yeah. You mentioned him before; I forget why."

Harvey raised a brow and didn't enlighten him. "Listen, Angell, I wanted to ask you a question."

Angell flipped open the "gross" tales and glanced at a page. "Shoot."

"Did anything odd happen between you and Ava the night I was robbed? She's skittish as a colt, and I can't figure out why."

Angell's eyes flicked up to Harvey's, his body motionless. "Nothin'. Nothin' at all," he answered quickly. Too quickly.

Harvey's eyes narrowed and he murmured, "Ah, ah, ah . . . Don't forget your *ings.*"

"*Nothing,*" Angell repeated, calmer. "She mighta lost some faith that I could protect her, or something. Why? She talkin' about ditchin' me?"

Harvey's brows raised again, expectantly.

"*Ditching?*" Angell enunciated. "Can't you just answer the damn question?"

"She mentioned it once," Harvey said mildly.

For some reason, this surprised Angell. After her assurance the day she'd given him the book, he'd believed she had no intention of backing out. He'd even hoped part of the reason might be because she had some feelings for him. That she'd actually said something to Harvey about getting rid of him was disconcerting.

"Right after the robbery," Harvey continued. "She mentioned second thoughts, but then she remembered her commitment to her sister. It's not like Ava to question herself, but she looked truly torn after that night."

Angell studied the tooled leather cover of the book in his hands. "I reckon—"

"*I think.*"

He issued a long-suffering sigh, his mind using the time to try to come up with something. "I think I scared her. That man, the character we run into on the street, I had a suspicion about him, so I knocked him out. It mighta seemed a bit savage to Miz Moreland."

Harvey nodded and watched him. "Why does that embarrass you?"

Angell's head jerked up. The man was far too astute. "It don't—"

"*Doesn't.*"

"Damn it, can't we just have a regular conversation here?"

Harvey blinked. "That's precisely what *I'm* trying to have." He leaned forward in his chair, his elbows on his knees. "Listen, Angell, you've got to remember when we get to New York that no matter what the topic, no matter how involved you get in the conversation, you must *never* forget your manner of expression. Those people will crucify you for a slip of the tongue. If even a trace of your origin shows, you'll be discovered. And they'll cut you like a hot knife through butter."

Angell wanted to laugh. Being cut by a bunch of prigs was nothing compared to the real dilemma at hand. "Nice bunch."

Harvey shook his head. "No. They're not. Not in the slightest. But they are *crucial* to your success. And if you don't succeed, you'll be out a lot of money."

"And you'll be out a bridegroom."

Harvey spread his palms out before him. "I won't pretend that we don't have as much—even more—riding on this as you do. So we've got to work together." He settled back in the chair. "Now then, why are you embarrassed about that night?"

Angell mentally cursed the man's persistence. "I ain't—"

"*I'm not.*"

Angell blew air out of his cheeks and laughed hopelessly. "I'm not embarrassed. Well, all right, maybe I am, a little bit. I guess I looked like a brute to Miz Moreland, and that embarrasses me."

Harvey thought about that, his eyes not straying from Angell's face. Then, just as Angell started to feel naked beneath the stare, Harvey said, "*Miss* Moreland. *Missssssss.* Say it."

Like a well-trained puppy, Angell thought, he obeyed. "Miss."

Harvey nodded. "Good. But if you're afraid that Ava has lost faith in your ability to protect her, why are you ashamed of striking a man who might well have done her harm?"

Angell laughed again and shook his head, looking away. "What are you, some kinda damn lawyer?"

"I just like to get to the bottom of things."

Angell turned back to him. "Well, there's some things you just can't get to the bottom of, Harvey. The things I do, the things I say, they might not always make sense even to me. So don't expect that I can explain 'em to you."

"Oh, I don't know, Angell," Harvey said quietly. "I think it all makes perfect sense to you."

Angell's gut clenched and he didn't answer. The silence ticked by with the mantle clock. The two eyed each other.

"All right." At last Harvey rose and walked to the door. "I believe in allowing a man his secrets—as long as they don't prove harmful to anyone else. They won't, will they, Angell?" With this he turned on him with a questioning expression.

Angell shrugged. "My secrets don't harm nobody but myself."

Harvey pursed his lips. "I guess that'll have to do. Good night, Angell."

"Good night, Harvey."

He was partway out the door when he poked his

head back in the room. "Oh, and Angell? Read those books aloud, would you? It'll help."

Before he could reply, Harvey was gone.

"When you invite a lady to dance, Mr. Angell," Ava pronounced, feeling distinctly uncomfortable knowing the lesson that was to follow, "you should use the phrase, 'Will you *honor* me with your hand for a waltz?' or whatever such dance as you would like. But you should not wait until the signal is given to take a partner. Nothing is more impolite than to invite a lady hastily."

The furniture in the large downstairs parlor had been pushed to the walls, and Ava stood at one end near the fireplace, as though lecturing to a class. Harvey and Angell stood at the opposite end, Angell with his hands in his pockets and Harvey perched on the arm of a chair, holding a walking cane from the lobby.

"Now. Harvey shall introduce us, we shall make polite small talk, then you shall ask for my hand in a dance. Do you remember all I've told you?" Ava kept her hands clasped at her waist to avoid the nervous fidgeting they longed for. In a matter of moments, Mr. Angell would touch her for the first time since he'd kissed her. The prospect was uncomfortably energizing.

"I do." Angell's eyes were hooded, his face inscrutable, but Ava could swear she saw a smile lurking at the corners of his mouth.

"Very well, then. Harvey . . ." Ava nodded to him to begin.

With great flourish, Harvey stood, deposited the cane against the chair and pressed his hand to his heart. "My dear friend, Mr. Joshua Angell, there is a woman of uncompromising brilliance to whom you must be introduced. I believe her acquaintance would improve you greatly. Would you join me?"

"I'd be delighted," Angell answered, in a perfect mimic of Harvey's theatrical tone.

The two of them started across the room together.

"Wait." Ava held up one hand. "Mr. Angell, take your

hands from your pockets, if you please. Move confidently but not too quickly. If you keep your hands tucked away and sidle over, we shall wonder if you've some sort of disfigurement to hide."

Harvey rolled his eyes and turned around. Angell pulled his hands from his pockets and held them up to her. "Nothing to hide."

Despite the innocuous nature of the jest, Ava felt her pulse quicken. Those hands, so well-shaped and capable, had held her close against his body, had pressed hotly at her waist and had ruthlessly felled a man in front of her. She was not sure which of these facts caused her the most uneasiness.

"My friend," Harvey began again, resigned. "Have you had the pleasure of meeting Miss Moreland? I'm sure that her feet could do with a flattening. Perhaps you'd care to dance with her?"

Angell executed a courtly bow. "Whatever the lady might desire."

The words were not pointed, but Ava felt her cheeks burn at the statement anyway. She had to get over this, she thought desperately. She felt like a young girl who suddenly becomes aware of the gardener as a young man.

They started across the room again, this time confidently. Despite her uneasiness, Ava was conscious of the irony of the sight. They looked for all the world like two gentlemen of the highest set. At this moment, neither one of them would have looked out of place in even the Aldens' palatial ballroom, even though, at this moment, neither of them would be invited.

She let her eyes rest on Angell as they approached. Steady now, steady, she told herself. His pale eyes on her were cool.

"Miss Moreland, may I present Mr. Angell, lately of St. Louis?" Harvey asked with decorum.

Angell held out his hand.

"Mr. Angell." She inclined her head. Then, as she might in an aside to the audience during a play, she explained, "In a ballroom a hand is rarely offered, Mr. Angell."

He withdrew it and held it behind his back. Silence reigned for a moment before Harvey elbowed Angell in the side.

"Ah." Angell cleared his throat and one corner of his mouth kicked up in a smile he clearly could not repress. "Might I have the pl—*honor* of the next waltz, Miss Moreland?"

In spite of herself, Ava found she wanted to smile in return. She controlled the urge and swept past him to the imaginary dance floor.

"So, we'll say that I've assented and the next waltz is imminent. You have approached me at the appropriate time and we are now on the floor. I curtsy to you, while you bow to me."

She dipped into a curtsy and watched as he executed a handsome bow. She allowed a small smile. "Fine."

He moved toward her; her heart accelerated. She stretched out one hand and took up her skirt in the other. His left hand took hers, firm and dry, while his right circled her waist. At the familiarity of the contact, her throat constricted and she could not raise her eyes above his cravat.

The sensation was—she could think of no other word—*delicious*. She stepped away from him and he let go.

"Do not *grasp* a lady's waist, Mr. Angell," she said, aware of the fire in her cheeks. "But place your palm lightly along it. Your left hand should remain open just a bit. The lady may hold it as she pleases." She moved toward him once again.

This time his touch was slight, his left hand almost a caress against her palm. She forced herself to look into his face.

So near, she thought she could feel his breath. He gazed down at her through lazy lashes, his eyes disconcertingly clear and close. His lips twitched once in what she interpreted as a private smile.

"How'm I doing?" he asked, and she noted, like an austere schoolmarm, that his *ing* was crisp and slightly emphasized.

She took a breath that was not what anyone would call robust and gazed at his shirtfront. "A little too close, Mr. Angell. You must remember that many of these women will be virtual strangers to you. Distance is the soul of decorum."

He took a step back.

"Fine. Proceed, Harvey," she commanded.

With the cane, Harvey took up the steady one-two-three beat of the waltz on the floor.

With an ease that shocked her, Angell swept Ava into the dance without hesitation. Around the room they went—windows, doors, lamps splashing past with the poetic rotation of the waltz. Breathless with surprise, and rushing to keep up with so broad a stride, it took Ava several minutes before she realized that Harvey's beat had stopped and they were dancing to nothing more than the rhythm of their bodies.

"Mr. Angell," she said breathlessly, stopping so abruptly that her skirts twirled around her legs. "That's fine. That's enough."

Angell stopped a step or two after her, letting go of her in the process.

Ava wiped her suddenly damp hands on her skirts. "That was very good. Really surprisingly good, Mr. Angell." She placed a hand to her chest as if to calm her heartbeat.

The look of satisfaction on Angell's face was erased with Harvey's next words. "I don't know," he remarked speculatively from the edge of the room. He stood up and strode ponderously with the cane to the center of the floor. "In dancing, it is generally the purpose of the man to be little more than a *foil* for the woman. Do you understand what I mean, Angell?"

Angell turned on him with a sigh and folded his arms over his chest.

Harvey continued to walk in a circle around them, the sound of the cane on the wood floor a sharp punctuation of his footsteps. "I mean, the man is out there to make the woman look good. Think of it as a way to show *her* off, not yourself."

Angell smiled. "I thought she looked good. You didn't think she looked good, Harvey?"

"Not," Harvey replied, "as good as you did."

Angell laughed. "You tryin' to tell me after all this time I finally did somethin' *too right*?" He laughed again, but Ava could detect an edge to it. "Damn, you're gettin' creative with your cuts." He turned abruptly and stalked to a chair, which he threw himself into, shaking his head. "You got me this time. You really got me."

Ava sent Harvey a look of reproach. "Mr. Angell, you did beautifully."

Angell bowed his head, on his lips a sarcastic smile. "Wish I could say the same of you, m'dear. But alack, our Mr. Winters thinks otherways." Angell's pale eyes glared at Harvey.

"You also failed to bow at the culmination," Harvey pressed.

Ava turned on him. "Harvey, what on earth are you being so critical for?"

To her surprise, Harvey turned a heated glare on her. "Ava, are you aware of how much time we have left? It would be nice to have months to polish this rock to a gem, but we have only weeks. And I'm afraid it's gone rather slowly. If you don't want to be called on the carpet by every Henderson, Smythe and Alden in New York, you'd best put a little starch in *your* manner."

Ava gasped. "I have been nothing but firm in our lessons." She bristled.

He gave another thump with the cane. "I must disagree. You've been entertained; I can see that. And maybe this project brings you some kind of pleasure that I don't understand, but I *don't* see you being firm and I *don't* see you being strict." Harvey's small brown eyes burned with emotion.

"Harvey!" she protested. "What on earth has come over you?"

His mouth thinned into a line. "I'm sorry to put it so bluntly, Ava. But I'm having serious premonitions of doom. Here we are, in the middle of the country, with no one and nothing we know to judge by, and it's all seeming like something of a lark, isn't it?" He ran a hand through his hair, causing it to spike up at the part. "I'll confess that even I have had a moment or two of enjoyment from the task. But the closer we get to returning home, the more nervous I become."

Ava felt anger well up inside her. "You forget, Harvey, that Mr. Angell will be brought into society by me and my family. He will be presumed to be of the highest class. People will not scrutinize him to the degree that you and I do."

Harvey scoffed and threw out a hand toward Angell, who was slouched in a chair watching them. "They won't need to!"

Angell's eyes narrowed, and Ava again saw in her mind the swift, deadly movements that felled the stranger on the street.

"He's been doing *well*," she insisted. "And I think you're forgetting something else, Harvey," she continued, tired of having to make this decision over and over again for all of them. "You're forgetting Priscilla. You're forgetting that we can't return empty-handed now. Ultimately, it doesn't matter a whit if Joshua Angell speaks with a Southern accent or eats his salad with an oyster fork. He can go to a ball barefoot and dance like a leprechaun; it will still be better than Priscilla having a child on her own. That *cannot* happen, do you understand me? I will *not* see my sister shamed."

She stood trembling with suppressed rage before him, her hands fisted by her sides.

Harvey turned on her, undaunted. "So instead you will see her shamed by marrying her to a *nobody*, someone so far below her station that if the truth were ever discovered, she would never be allowed back into decent society again."

"Maybe she shouldn't be!" Ava countered, her voice uncharacteristically shrill.

Harvey was aghast. "What are you saying?"

"I'm saying that she has already done the unthinkable. She has already secured herself a place outside of decent society. By marrying her to a nobody, as you so colorfully put it, I cannot drag her any further down than she's dragged herself. And it could help. In this situation, *any* husband is better than none at all."

Harvey straightened his back and puffed out his chest with a deep breath. "On the contrary, Ava. I've come to the conclusion that the degradation of marrying so far beneath her can only make her troubles worse."

"Worse? *Worse?*" Ava flung her hands out to her sides. "What could be worse than having an illegitimate child?"

"Being married to an outcast, a *drifter*, about whom we know nothing. Think about it, Ava. I asked you before, consider if it were yourself. Would *you* marry him?"

Ava's ire was brought to a screeching halt, and she became suddenly aware that Angell was still in the room. His silence in the face of their argument held the weight of accusation.

She couldn't answer. There was no way for her to answer and speak the truth, any sort of truth. But she knew her silence was more harmful than a lie.

She turned to Angell, intending to say something, to apologize for their rudeness, to make excuses for their viewpoints, but there were no words with which to do it. He stared at her enigmatically, and she was frozen.

Finally, he stood, his lean form unfolding from the chair with an almost feline grace. "I'm sorry, Miss Moreland, Mr. Winters." His voice was hard, his eyes pale switches that lashed first Ava, then Harvey. "But I don't understand you people at all. And I'm done bein' a puppet."

Ava watched him walk to the doorway, his back straight, his head up. Harvey's eyes also followed him.

"What?" Ava asked.

He didn't turn. "You heard me," he said.

When he reached the door, he flung it open so hard it clattered against the wooden chairs stacked nearby, knocking them back against the wall. Ava and Harvey both jumped as wood scraped wood and then crashed to the floor.

A long, guilty moment passed after he left while they stood watching the empty doorway. Remorse seeped through Ava's veins like the stinging heat of whiskey. She closed her eyes and pressed a fist to her lips. If only she could take it back. If only she could take back all that she'd said from the moment they'd stopped dancing.

"We treated him like an animal," she said, and heard Harvey's slow exhale.

With a short, dry laugh, she continued. "And *we're* teaching *him* manners." She looked up at Harvey and found him still watching the door. "The man's been nothing but kind to us, and we treat him like he's less than human."

A muscle worked in Harvey's jaw. "We've been kind to him. We bought him clothes."

Her look was incredulous. "He's treated us with *respect*, while we've barely condescended to him."

Harvey turned on her angrily. "We *deserve* respect. He doesn't. It's as simple as that."

Ava's mouth dropped open. "Why? Why do we deserve respect? Because we have the money?"

"Yes." Harvey leveled a hard look at her, his brown eyes barren. A muscle clenched in his cheek. "That's exactly why, Ava. Because we have the money."

Chapter Eight

Ava knocked lightly on Angell's door, trepidation thundering in her chest. From inside the room, she could detect only silence, and she wondered with a brief shot of panic if he'd packed up and left. She had wanted to come sooner, but despite a constant racking of her brain, she could not think of one thing to tell him that would excuse the ugly things she and Harvey had said. Instead, she had paced in her room and relived the argument, time and again, until its unpleasantness numbed her.

She knocked again and this time, with relief, she heard someone stir. Slow, measured steps approached, the knob turned and slowly the door opened.

Angell stood before her, tall and disheveled, his cravat and collar gone, his shirt open to reveal the dark skin of his throat. She could smell traces of whiskey, but his eyes were clear, his posture sober.

"Miss Moreland." He bowed and she noticed then that he held a small jigger in one hand, out of which he spilled not a drop with the motion. "To what do I owe the pleasure?"

As he raised back up she felt the heat of his gaze, the judgment of his look.

"I've come to apologize," she said. She raised her chin a fraction to dispel the suddenly weak image she had of herself looking like a recalcitrant child. "Harvey and I were dreadful today. You deserve better. I'm sorry."

Angell's eyes grew hooded, the dark-lashed lids lowering over cutting blue depths. "You've come to apologize." He bit the inside of one cheek pensively and nodded, moving to lean against the door frame and look at her.

She glanced nervously down the empty hallway. "May I come in?"

He feigned surprise but did not move. "You want to come in? You want to come, alone, into a man's bedroom? What would people think? What if I did something—*unseemly*?"

Ava took a breath and returned his steady look. This brittle banter was not something she'd counted on, and despite her feelings of guilt, it irritated her. "Are you apt to?"

He smiled slightly. "I don't know."

She managed a stern expression. "Let me come in, Mr. Angell. We must talk."

His eyes hardened, and he waited while the imperiousness of her words became obvious.

She swallowed. "Please."

He studied her a moment more, then stepped back into the dimness of the room. She followed, closing the door behind her, and saw him stroll casually to a chair by the fire. A solitary lamp was lit on a table next to his chair.

Ava stopped uncertainly behind the opposite chair and surveyed the scene. Also on the table was a bottle, its label proclaiming it to be a distinguished brand of scotch, and next to that were several books. One was open and lay face down atop the others.

"Oh, excuse me," Angell said, rising. "I forgot—

114

never sit when there's a lady standing. Must be tiring at the theater."

Ava frowned at the mocking tone and moved around the chair to sit, gingerly, on its edge. Angell plopped back into his seat.

"Now," he said, dangling the shot glass from languid fingers, "what did you come to apologize for?"

"I should think it would be obvious," she murmured, unsure of his flippant attitude. The last thing she wanted was to have her guilt thrown back in her face.

"Oh, so that's the tactic. A blanket apology for anything I might have felt wronged by." He nodded sagely. "A good decision."

Perhaps unjustly, his anger irked her. It smacked of self-pity, which she would have thought beneath him. "No," she said firmly. "I'll not apologize for trying to help you."

Angell sighed and looked into the fire, contemplatively taking a sip of scotch. "You know, it doesn't bother me, the fact that y'all are so—changeable. If I could see it coming, just once, I'd be happy, but it doesn't really bother me. In fact, you probably don't even notice it, the way you go along, being real nice, then *bam*. I'm just never prepared for it, I guess."

Ava sat still and stared at him. Firelight played over his features and gave them an enigmatic aspect, made shadows and contrasts, made him a stranger.

"I mean, it's not as if I don't know," he continued, his tone reasonable, detached, "how you all really feel about me, that I don't belong. But sometimes I forget . . . sometimes things are different." He turned his face to her, and with the lamp beside him, she could see directly through his transparent blue eyes. "Sometimes you're different."

She thought she could see the memory of their kiss in his eyes—the knowledge, the frustration, the desire. Fear made her speak harshly. "We agreed not to speak of that night—"

"I'm not speaking of *that night*," he said vehemently. With the sudden words, he stood so quickly that she grasped the arms of her chair, as if he might move violently in her direction.

Instead, he headed to the fireplace and tossed the remainder of his whiskey into the flames. A sharp hiss sounded, then a quick flame erupted and died. He placed his empty glass on the mantle and rested his arm along the polished wood.

"I'm talking, Miss Moreland, about you, and even Harvey. How nice you can seem, and then . . ." He gazed into the bottom of his empty shot glass. "I wouldn't have brought up that night. But since you have, I'll tell you something—I think about it. I think about it a lot." With that he turned a penetrating look on her. "Do you ever think about it, Miss Moreland? Do you ever think about it without *shame*?"

She gritted her teeth and swallowed. She didn't deserve this, not for coming to apologize. "I don't—I don't wish to talk about it."

He laughed dryly. "Ah. I guess not, then."

Ava felt humiliation sting her to the core. This conversation was only making things worse, and she had no idea how to turn it around.

"Tell me something else," Angell continued. She could feel his eyes on her, so she stared resolutely into the fire. "Why did you kiss me like that?"

Whipping angry eyes to him, she opened her mouth to speak.

"No, no." He held up his hands. "No anger. That's the only question. Then I'll drop it forever. Promise. I just need to know. Why did you kiss me?"

"*You* kissed *me*." Her voice was hard, unconvincing even to her own ears, but anger made her vow never to believe otherwise.

He watched her, an unpleasant smile on his lips and in his eyes. It wasn't a leer; it was something harder, more calculated than that. "Maybe I started it."

Panic assaulted her. How *dare* he taunt her like this. What sort of man was he, really? First kind, then threatening. "I thought I could trust you that night," she confessed, her voice snapping desperately. "For some reason I felt safe with you. But now I see that wasn't the case. Now I see I should have been more wary of you than of the rogues on the street."

She rose to leave, nerves trembling, but the hollowness in her center was staggering. Somewhere inside of her, she wanted him to deny it, to tell her that she could trust him, that he was not mocking her for her part in that kiss.

But he remained silent. She turned to the door, her limbs stiff, her heart painful in her chest. It was fear, she told herself, fear that he would expose her for her wantonness.

"Miss Moreland," he said when she'd moved only a step.

She looked back at him, a thin hope trying to blossom under the fear in her chest. "Yes?"

He raised a brow. "You're not the only one taking chances here."

"I know that," she said quickly. Then she wished she'd asked him what he meant. Was he talking about the task itself, or readying him for New York? Or did he speak of the danger of that kiss, of the need for trust, of all the hundred fears that lurked in her breast? But he couldn't know of those, she reminded herself. He couldn't know what lay buried inside her.

"I know that, Mr. Angell," she repeated in a stronger voice.

"Sit down a minute." The intimacy of his tone made her bristle. She raised her chin. He took a step toward her, and the lamplight again illuminated his eyes, intense, compelling. "Sit down, Miss Moreland."

She sat.

"You really don't know what's bothering me, do you?" he asked mildly.

She took a moment, made her expression blank. "Yes. I think I do, yes." There was another beat of silence. "I'm sorry."

He moved toward her, then turned at the last moment to the bottle on the table next to her. The splash and gurgle of whiskey emptied into glass struck her ears, loud in the quiet of the room. She glanced up at him through her lashes, and saw that his face was illuminated now that he stood over the lamp. A lock of dark hair fell over his forehead as he bent his head to his task.

He held the jigger out to her. "Care for a snort?" he asked quietly, on his lips a devil's smile.

At the coarse words, she felt another niggling of suspicion, something she couldn't put her finger on. She turned her gaze away, confused.

"You think I'm mad 'cause of how you talked about me. You think I walked out 'cause of the meanness of your words." He stood over her, looking down.

"Yes," she said quietly. "I don't blame you."

"Well, that's real nice of you, Miss Moreland," he said. She looked up quickly to see if he mocked her, but he turned away and she couldn't tell. "I did walk out 'cause of the meanness. You both really surprised me this time. But I ain't—" He stopped himself and turned to her with a small smile. "I'm *not* talking about myself."

Ava tried to follow him, tried to glean his meaning before he had to spell it all out for her, but she couldn't. And it made her angry that he was suddenly able to befuddle her. "Then what—?"

"You feel ashamed of that kiss, Miss Moreland, I know you do. And you'd like nothing better than that it never happened, isn't that right?"

Ava felt anger well up inside her again. Why couldn't he just drop it? He knew it pained her to think of that night, yet he continued to push her.

At her stubborn silence, he continued. "But you were swept up in something that night, Miss Moreland. You can deny it all you want to everybody else, but I was there. And I've had too much experience in these things not to know what happened." He sipped casually at his drink and watched her try to deal with her anger.

After a moment, he continued. "The fact is, that night never did happen." She swung surprised eyes to him. "As far as you, me, Harvey and the world's concerned, that night never happened because we won't admit it. But imagine for a second if there was some

118

kind of proof that it did happen. What would you do then, Miss Moreland? Would you marry me? Would you tie your life to mine so that you could sit in all them drawing rooms that seem so *damned* important to you?"

Ava started at his language, as well as his words, and gaped at him. "What are you *saying*? Are you implying—?"

Angell bent his head and squinted at her as though she were a slow child. "You still don't get it?"

A blush fanned her cheeks as she stared at him in confusion.

"Your *sister,* Ava," he said bluntly. "I'm talking about your sister. She doesn't want to marry me either, I'll bet. And *she* didn't even kiss me." He shook his head at her. "Now you and Harvey can stand in the middle of some ballroom and argue that Miss Priscilla'll be devastated if I step on someone's foot. Or you can even argue that it doesn't matter what I do, as long as I'm there, covering some other man's tracks. But you're missing the point."

"And I suppose you've grasped it unquestionably."

"The point is, who *is* the father? Doesn't he care about his child? And what about the child? Do you think he won't care who his real daddy is a whole helluva lot more than which sitting room his mama's allowed into, or what balls she can attend?"

"Of course he will," she protested. "But the father is not an option in any of this."

"Why not?"

Ava sighed. "Priscilla says he's dead." At his silence, she glanced up at him. "Oh, you can wipe that stricken look off your face. She's lying."

He exhaled heavily, then downed his drink. "He's probably some poor sap just like me," he scoffed, "undeserving of the *rich* lifestyle you all enjoy."

"I believe that's probably true. I think he is someone beneath her, and she's ashamed to admit it."

"*Hell,*" he spat. "You told me once you thought she loved him—the father of her baby. Why don't you try to polish him up for her, instead of some stranger she's never even met before?"

"Because the person with whom she dallied is somewhere in New York. Someone surely would know him. Don't you see? The child would be forever tainted in others' eyes."

"Ah ha." He nodded. "I do see. It makes no difference whether this man can be taught the high-falutin' ways of your 'society.' Or even that he can father a child with both your sister's glorious bloodlines and his own lowly ones. The fact is, he'd still be poor, he'd still be the butler, or the groom or whatever, and everyone would know it. He could never be snuck into the privileged, fairy-tale life you lead, where *shame* ranks higher than truth, and money beats love every time."

Ava dropped a fist onto the arm of the chair. "That's not true! You're deliberately misconstruing what I said."

"You don't think it's true?" He pinned her with a look. "I do. That's all I ever hear you talk about. The *shame* of this, the *embarrassment* of that. Harvey tells me my pronunciation is 'crucial.' You say my table manners must be 'irreproachable.' Do you ever think about what any of that really means? I'm telling you, it means nothing. Hell, I'm glad my stay in that carnival is gonna be temporary."

Ava sat dumbfounded in her chair and stared up at him. He wasn't right; he couldn't be right. She struggled for words to rebut him, but all she had was a tightness in her chest. "You don't understand," she said finally.

He scoffed lightly.

"No." She shook her head. "No, you have no idea what our life is like. I'm not worried about embarrassment, not the way you might feel it if you used a word incorrectly at the dinner table." She shook her head again, a feeling suspiciously like fear gnawing at her stomach. "I'm worried about humiliation on a grand scale, the loss of life as I and Priscilla know it, the casting out of my entire family from the social strata where we *live,* where we've *always* lived." Her words became more heated as she spoke, her frustration making her voice shake. "*You've* never lived anywhere, as far as I can tell. What do you know of society, of community, of the deep attachments of home, friends and family? You don't understand that everything can be lost with just one wrong step. Priscilla has made that wrong step, and now it's up to me to save her."

She stopped, hating the fact that she was losing control, hating how she sounded and the look of contempt that would not leave his face. She had to get back to the point. She needed him, misperceptions and all. Eventually, it wouldn't matter what he thought of their lifestyle. He would be the instrument of restoring its order, and then he would leave. "You don't understand," she said again, striving for calm.

He shrugged with a dry laugh. "No, I don't."

"You don't understand the—the *intricacies* of our life, our culture. We cannot leave it the way you leave towns through which you may pass. We love our home, and so we must do all we can to preserve our life there."

Angell gazed at her now, his contempt fading, but instead of concession to, or even comprehension of, the possible merits of her points, she saw pity in his eyes. The man felt sorry for her.

The notion galled her. She cleared her throat and stood. She had to leave. The point was best dropped. "Well, regardless. It appears obvious that we shall never see eye-to-eye on this issue." She turned and strode two steps toward the door, then turned back, her expression somewhat more in order. "Shall I see you at breakfast then? Or will your romantic scruples keep you away?"

In the dim, flickering lamplight, his eyes were black, his mouth brooding. He leaned against the mantle, but there was a wariness to the set of his shoulders, an aloofness in the tilt of his head.

"I'll be there," he said quietly.

Ava thought she heard derision in his tone. She

waited a moment for a wry chuckle or a flash of the self-deprecating warmth she'd grown accustomed to, but there was nothing. Only the dark stillness of his face.

"Good night, then" she said.

He responded by turning away.

It wasn't until she was halfway to her room, replaying the conversation line by line in her head, that she realized what had been nagging at the back of her mind.

Angell's English was good—quite good.

Perhaps too good.

The following days were business as usual, but the restraint that hung in the air was icy cold. Ava tried to ignore it, but it crept into her bones like a damp draft.

Angell was doing well, seemingly without much effort. He was concentrating hard and absorbing everything she and Harvey told him with a seriousness that had been absent up to then. He was also emulating their behavior remarkably well, sometimes to the point where she was not sure he wasn't subtly ridiculing her.

He read voraciously now that he'd found books that captivated his interest. Far from being disappointed in his not liking Emerson, Ava was happy that he found the works of Melville, Poe, Dickens and Verne to be riveting. She could hear him once in a while, when she passed his room at night, reading the stories aloud to himself, and she wondered if that was enough to account for the rapidity with which his speech was improving.

But when she thought about how things were even two weeks ago, she was dissatisfied. The fact was, she missed him—the old him. She missed his constant laughter and teasing. She missed the inventive mistakes he made. She missed the beginnings of the camaraderie she'd felt.

Oh, it wasn't all bad now, Ava told herself. He wasn't completely cold to her, and he did make a spirited and engaging gentleman. He would still make the occasional joke, mostly at Harvey's expense, and raise that assessing eyebrow whenever the rules of etiquette became too absurd for him. But the warmth in his gaze was missing. The hungry appraisal of her, which had formerly made her flush with nervousness, had cooled as well. Ava would never have thought she'd miss it, but she did.

Part of the reason was the underlying guilt she felt for its absence. She suspected the reason he no longer looked at her in the same way was due to something she had done wrong. Or something she had gotten wrong. He wasn't angry at her. He didn't resent her. It was more as if she'd disappointed him.

They made arrangements to leave St. Louis two-and-a-half weeks after arriving. Ava telegraphed Priscilla to inform her of their projected arrival in Boston and instructed her to meet them. They would stay for two nights in Boston, then the whole group would leave for New York.

The thought of going back to New York produced mixed feelings in Ava. She was more than ready to be home, in her own house with all of her things in closets instead of trunks. She yearned to reclaim her room with its daily vases of fresh flowers and her bed with its crisp linen sheets that always smelled of lilacs.

But she was afraid of returning, too. She was terrified of turning Angell loose to the lions who might discover their ruse and swallow him whole. She was nervous about Priscilla and her cutting tones, and what she might do to Angell's self-confidence with her sarcasm and apathy. Ava was most particularly afraid of her father's possible rejection of this unexpected guest, who would ask for his youngest daughter's hand so quickly—no more than a month after their return.

However, the feeling overwhelming all of these fears, positively dwarfing them with its forbidden potency, was the jealousy she was afraid would resurface when Angell proposed to Priscilla. It didn't matter that it was all arranged, that he was to do it no matter what his feelings for her sister were. What mattered was Ava would lose him. As soon as Angell was accepted by Priscilla, *she* would be cast out of his inner circle forever.

The desolation this evoked in Ava was something she could not ignore. He was her project, she told herself, like an artist's painting. Certainly it would be difficult to give him up after all of her hard work. But in the depths of her unhappiness, she knew it was more than that. Much, much more.

The express train would arrive in Boston approximately twenty-seven hours after they left St. Louis. Harvey booked them in Pullman sleepers, and the trip promised to be no great hardship. Ava said she remembered from the trip out that the food was good, and the berths and lounge were elegant, the latter complete with a piano, armchairs and tuxedoed waiters serving champagne. There was even a separate car for the men if they chose to smoke.

Disembarking at the depot in St. Louis, they found it teaming with people. They were dropped off just in front of the station by the hotel hackney, but it looked as though they might have trouble getting a porter, until Harvey charged off into the crowd and nabbed one heading in the other direction. With a fistful of cash, he persuaded the man to their carriage, where their trunks were unloaded.

Angell looked around at all the people and wondered what on earth he was doing here. He wore another new suit, this one with a cutaway jacket and pale gray pants, and a high silk hat. Though he was starting to feel a little more comfortable in his new finery, at times like this he still felt the discomfort of old memories and painful, unexpected reflections.

As they made their way through the thronging press of people, Angell kept his eye trained on Ava's rose-trimmed poke bonnet, a feminine thing that allowed just enough of her honey hair to show to remind him of how it felt in his hands. As usual, she looked immaculate—but her straight back and polished speech couldn't hide the haunted, wary look in her eyes.

Angell was perfectly aware that she was increasingly uncomfortable around him. While it wasn't something he necessarily wanted, he believed it was unavoidable. She was, he was convinced, denying herself, smothering with refinement the most potent part of herself. The lifestyle she clung to so tightly was the blanket that suffocated her spirit. If she could only see what he saw, he thought for the hundredth time; if she could only see the look in her own eyes.

He had flattered himself during the last few days that her loss of vitality was due in some part to what he'd said to her and to his detachment from her. But then reality set in, and he read her wan face as nervousness that their plot was about to be put into action with the strong possibility of failure. She was obviously anxious about his performance, and her nerves threatened to infect him.

He wondered at the sort of people he would meet. What were they like, these people who would "cut you," as Harvey had put it, if you forgot an "ing" or an "am"? Why had he agreed to return to a place with such a ruthless society? And was *Ava* as ruthless as she'd seemed that day arguing with Harvey? It had unnerved him, that heartlessness, and it made him angry.

He hadn't explained it very well to her, but her blindness to the real issue at hand was a shock to him. She'd always seemed so reasonable, so perceptive. But she couldn't see herself. She couldn't see the blatant way she was putting reputation above truth. The danger in that was obvious to Angell, but to Ava it seemed a matter of course, of self-preservation.

They pushed and squeezed through the crowds toward the platform.

"Oh, Harvey," Ava called. Harvey stopped in front of her, where he'd acted as something of a blocker, and turned. "There's a news butch—see if you can't get us a newspaper, will you?"

Harvey nodded and started after the boy.

"You got him trained pretty well, Miss Moreland,"

Angell said, staring after the man and wondering if he would be expected to jump at every command the way Harvey did.

Ava didn't answer. She glanced up at him with a stern look, then leaned on her slender umbrella and let her eyes follow Harvey.

Angell sighed and looked around. He'd brought it on himself, he guessed. He'd withdrawn from her. Even now he was hesitant about jesting with her, about returning to his old—albeit improper—familiarity. He had no right to try to get close to her. And he certainly didn't have the right to judge her. The distance between them was fitting; it was safe and it was necessary. The kiss had been an impulse, and it served him right if he couldn't forget about it once he'd done it.

As he glanced around the platform, his eye was caught by a movement, quick and sly amidst the slow and herdlike multitudes. He craned his neck for a better look. It was near the stairs, where people parted after descending to avoid the pillar situated at the base. He stared into the crowd, searching.

When he turned back, Harvey approached with a newspaper and a handful of hot pretzels. Irritation flickered across the man's face as he was jostled by someone in a business suit, and he very nearly dropped one of the snacks.

Angell tried to shake the stealthy image he thought he'd just detected, but a prickling along the back of his neck made him look again toward the stairs.

There—again. To the left. His eyes darted and just caught sight of it. A dodge and a swivel, a slim man in black garb disappearing around another pillar. Angell's palms dampened.

"Thought I'd grab us a bite," Harvey said, shoving a pretzel at him. "The attendant told me we're on the right platform anyway. Should be boarding any minute."

Angell glanced back to where the black-clad man had been, but he'd disappeared completely. Scanning the crowd for another fleet movement, or any sign whatsoever, he saw nothing. He'd have felt better to have seen him again before boarding—just to be sure—but the man was gone.

No doubt some common pickpocket, Angell told himself. But he couldn't shake the way his scalp prickled, and the area between his shoulder blades felt peculiarly exposed. Once again, he turned swiftly to look behind him, but there was nothing, and this time Ava looked up at him strangely.

At long last, the train doors opened, and the three of them made their way forward. Before stepping over the threshold, Angell paused and glanced back once more.

Nothing. The man was gone. Even so, Angell could not stop thinking about him and his slight resemblance to Barrett Trace.

Chapter Nine

Angell stepped out of his berth into the narrow passageway of the speeding train. Dark shapes hurled past the window, no sooner becoming perceptible than disappearing into the night. The car rocked over a rough joint, and he steadied himself against the windows. Carefully, he proceeded down the hallway toward the smoking car, or where he thought the smoking car was. For some reason, though his choices out the door were always left or right, he could never remember in which direction to go. The dining car was to the right, he was pretty sure, so he went left.

Because of the stuffy confines of the passenger cars, passing over the links between them was Angell's favorite part. Though it was cold, it was the only place fresh air could be found. The clatter of the couplings and the screech of steel wheels eating up miles of track were a refreshing change from the muted sounds of conversation in adjacent cabins or the occasional bump and curse of someone making his way down the passage.

Angell paused for a moment in the drafty spot, enjoying the whistle of the wind through the expandable doors that joined the cars. He liked the sense of movement the train gave him. Its effortless speed relaxed him, which was due in no small part to the fact that behind him, on the other side of the ever-widening gap, stayed Barrett Trace.

As soon as he'd felt the first jerky thrusts of the train, his whole body had relaxed. Whatever it had been, phantom or thief, that had caused him such trepidation in the station, faded as the train lumbered from the station.

He took a deep breath and pulled the new gold watch from the pocket of his waistcoat. Leaning into the light from the car behind him, he could see it was nearly nine. He pushed the heavy timepiece back into the small pocket with two fingers, the way he'd seen Harvey do it a hundred times, and shoved open the door to the next car.

Halfway through the second sleeping car, he knew he was near the lounge because he could hear the soft tinkle of a piano drifting out over the clap of the train's wheels. He entered and the door slammed shut behind him, effectively sucking out the noise of the track and replacing it with a muffled calm. The quiet was intensified by plush armchairs, thick carpeting and a long polished bar. Wall sconces lit the car with flickering light, softening the edges of the furniture and making the bottles behind the bar gleam like jewels.

There were five people in the car, including the piano player. On a loveseat in the corner an older couple, broad-beamed and well-dressed, sat stiffly and stared about themselves as warily as if waiting for a robbery. Angell was sure if he turned on them and said "Stick 'em up," they'd plunge their hands into the air and look relieved into the bargain.

A dark black fellow in a starched white tuxedo played the piano with a touch soft as a baby's coo. His eyes were closed, and he swayed with the melody, obviously somewhere far away from the opulence of the Pullman lounge.

Angell made his way to the bar. The only other people there were a thin mustachioed bartender and a respectably dressed gentleman of about fifty with a bald pate and a large whiskey.

"Good evening," Angell said, seating himself two chairs down from the gentleman.

"Good evening to you, sir," the man said in a jovial baritone that effectively ruptured the silence of the car.

The bartender appeared silently before him. "What can I get for you, sir?"

Angell glanced at the gentleman's glass and nodded slightly. "Whiskey'll do."

The gentleman watched him with genial interest. "This isn't any ordinary whiskey, son. This here is the finest Tennessee bourbon available. Couple of shots of this and you'll be seeing the world through a new set of glasses."

Angell smiled at the man's bluff good-humor. "Sounds good to me." He nodded again and the bartender moved off to retrieve it. "You from St. Louis?" Angell asked, feeling instinctively that the man's outspoken liveliness would rank somewhere around the low end of what Miss Moreland would consider "polished."

"No, sir, I'm from Tennessee originally."

Angell laughed as the bartender brought his drink. "I should have known." He lifted the drink in salute.

The man returned the gesture. "Glad you didn't. I've been out of there for years. Where are you from, Mr . . . ?"

"Angell. Joshua Angell." He straightened in the seat and held out his hand, ignoring the man's other question.

"My name's Weatherton. Chester Weatherton."

The two men clasped hands and released. Angell sipped his drink and gazed around the car. The train car had better furnishings than most homes he'd visited.

"Heading to New York, by any chance?" Weatherton asked, studying him through a narrowed eye.

Angell looked surprised. "Actually, yes. Boston first, then New York. Yourself?"

"New York, absolutely. I'm a businessman there. Handle investments, real estate, that sort of thing." The man puffed his chest out as he spoke. "I can always tell when a young man's heading for New York. They got a kind of *hunger* in the eye. I was just that way myself, years ago."

"You don't say. You doing pretty well now?" Angell asked. It crossed his mind to wonder if that came under the heading of "inappropriate conversation" in Miss Moreland's book, it being money related, but the man took no offense.

"Yes, prodigiously well. New York's definitely the place to be for a businessman. I was just out in St. Louie checking on a little farming investment I've got. Going well, going well. I'll be happy to report back to my clients on the status of this one. What about you? What kind of business you in?"

Angell paused, sipped his drink, and glanced over at the piano player. "Cattle," he said. "But I don't do much more than keep an eye on the place. You know, an occasional trip to St. Louis, make sure my boys aren't taking advantage of me."

Weatherton laughed and slapped him on the shoulder. "Know just what you mean, Mr. Angell, just what you mean. Precisely what I was doing. Do most of my business from New York, as you probably do. Yes, sir, that's the pulse of the business world, right there in New York."

Angell turned around in his seat to lean his back against the bar, sipping pensively. After a moment, he pulled out the cigarette case Harvey had insisted he buy—claiming no one, absolutely no one, carried cigarettes in the boxes in which they were purchased—and extended it to Weatherton.

The man looked dismayed and glanced around the car, putting his hand against the case. "Oh, no. Put it away, son. You can't smoke in here. This is where the ladies sit." He inclined his head toward the matron in the corner. "Smoking car's the other way. Next to the

131

dining car." He jerked a thumb back the way Angell had come.

Angell sighed and flipped the lid shut. Fifty-fifty shot and he'd blown it again. Well, at least he'd gotten some liquor.

"Tell me something, Mr. Angell," Weatherton said, leaning a little closer and scrutinizing him. "You done business long in New York?"

Angell gazed at him a moment and decided it would be best not to lie. For all he knew, he'd meet up with this man again, and pretending to be something that he wasn't already pretending to be struck him as stupid, entertaining as it might prove to pull this fellow's leg.

"Frankly, Mr. Weatherton, I've never been to New York before. This is my first time, and I'm hoping to stay."

Weatherton sat back, looking pleased at this statement. "Well," he said, drawing the word out dramatically and assuming an air of self-importance. "You've got quite a journey ahead of you." He chuckled and polished off his drink. He slapped the glass on the bar and gestured for the bartender to bring him another. "New York's a curious place. They've got a code all their own, and frankly it's damn hard to break. I've done it, but it took years of hard work and not a little know-how." He tapped a finger to his temple.

"Is that right?" Angell said mildly, wanting to hear the man's opinions but not wanting to appear too curious. Weatherton obviously had him pegged as an ignorant rube—not far off the mark—but Angell had him pegged as well. Weatherton was a hustler, a man with enough intelligence to know what he didn't have and not enough skill to actually be able to get it.

Weatherton sighed and hooked a thumb into the armhole of his waistcoat. "Yes, sir. Took me years to break into that game, but New York City's the only game around if you really want to get somewhere in the world. You see, there's *levels* of society there, and it doesn't just depend on money. No, sir. You could be rich as Croesus and some families would never look twice at you. Some would, of course, they got their share of the bourgeois, you know, but they're not the ones you need to get *in*, if you know what I mean."

Angell must have frowned because Weatherton elaborated. "I'm speaking of the *new* rich, you know. The kind that would sell their own grandmothers for a buck. But the *highest* level—the one most everyone would give their balls to be accepted by—*including* the women—" At this he laughed indulgently with himself. "Or I should say *especially* the women. *That* level you don't get to unless you got a pedigree a mile long and a ticket stub from the *Mayflower* itself."

Angell laughed. "Most of my relations came over on a ship, but I'm pretty sure it wasn't the *Mayflower*."

Weatherton shook his head and swilled half his new drink. "You can laugh, Mr. Angell, but I'm telling you the truth. And I ought to know. Unless you got some connections, you got a tough row to hoe ahead of you."

Angell watched the piano player, thinking about relations and the bizarre part they'd played in his life. In some ways he knew they would always play a part, despite the fact that they were mostly dead and buried.

"I've got a few connections," he said. He wondered what Weatherton would have to say about the Morelands. Maybe they weren't as affluent as they appeared. Maybe they were really members of this bourgeois group Weatherton mentioned. He was curious to hear an outsider's point of view, but decided he was better off not name dropping until he knew the facts.

Weatherton raised a brow skeptically. "Well, I hope they're the right kind. You've got to start out on the right foot in the big town. You put your money on the wrong horse and you'll never live it down. Might as well just pack up your tent and head home to St. Louie if you get in with the wrong set. They don't give a damn if you made an honest mistake."

Angell looked back at him. "How'd you get in? I mean, coming from Tennessee and all."

Weatherton took another gulp of Tennessee's finest, and Angell noticed that his cheeks were becoming rosy with the stuff. "Maybe you don't see it, but I've got something of a pedigree myself," he said with an air of injured pride that Angell should have to ask. "Just because I come from Tennessee doesn't mean I can't bargain with the best of them. I've a maiden aunt lives there, and she's second cousin to Mortimer Bristol. You may not know it now, but Mortimer Bristol is a *name* in New York City. Yes, sir. Old Mort's got some money, though he lives modestly on the West Side, and I was able to double some investments for him. That's right, double. 'Fore long, I was doing business with a bunch of his cronies, and Fifth Avenue was pricking up its ears. I got a couple of clients in the big bucks now. Took years, but it's starting to pay off."

Angell nodded. "I see."

"I hope you do. I don't mean to be discouraging, son, but unless you got a foot in the door, you've got nothing but failure ahead of you. I had my aunt, but I also had to rely quite heavily on my own God-given resources. Don't know as every man can claim the sort of resources I've got. But I wish you luck. Yes, sir, I surely do wish you luck."

Angell turned back to the bar and flagged the bartender. "Two more," he motioned to his and Weatherton's glasses. "And send something over to the piano player, would you? What's he drinking?"

The bartender looked down his long thin nose to the black man at the piano. "He isn't drinking, sir."

Angell paused, thinking he detected some condescension in the words. "Well, perhaps he'd like to."

Though the bartender didn't move, he looked uncomfortable. "I don't think so, sir."

Angell looked casually back at the piano player, the bartender's attitude distinct now and rankling. "He looks thirsty to me," he said. Then he reached into his pocket and pulled out a wad of bills. Peeling off a couple he laid them on the table. "Get him whatever he wants."

The bartender glanced down at the bills and his eyes

widened. Scooping them up in an abruptly fluid movement, he nodded and said, "Yes, sir."

"And keep 'em coming all night, if he wants."

"Yes, sir." The man scurried off to do his bidding.

Angell relaxed, satisfied. He was going to enjoy this, he thought with a fresh eye on the situation. He didn't much care about clothes and watches and top hats, but getting his way was a pretty satisfying thing. And how simple it was with money. No threats, no fists, no firearms.

He sighed with the pleasure it gave him and picked up his drink. Catching sight of Weatherton's scrutiny from the corner of his eye, he shrugged. "I like the music."

Weatherton watched him a moment, then glanced at the piano player. "Yeah, he's pretty good."

A second later, the bartender conveyed a drink to the musician. The black man opened surprised eyes and then, at the bartender's gesture, he nodded warily at Angell. Angell nodded back.

As Angell pocketed the rest of his cash, Weatherton asked in a cautious tone, "Who did you say your connections were in New York?"

At that moment, the door at the end of the car blew open, and with the attendant blast of noise and air, Ava Moreland and Harvey Winters filed into the room.

Angell smiled and let his eyes warm with the sight of her. She wore dark purple with white lace at the neck and cuffs. With her hair in a topknot and soft tendrils ringing her face, she looked the very picture of youth, wealth and beauty. Angell could practically feel Weatherton's jaw hit the floor when she entered.

"Jesus, Mary and Joseph," the man murmured, straightening in his seat and reaching a hand to his cravat. "What a sight."

"Ah," Angell said calmly, "here come my connections now."

This time he felt the force of Weatherton's stunned gaze on himself. He turned a benign smile on the man. "Would you like to meet them?" He asked, adding just a touch of the haughty inflection to his tone that Har-

vey used when he was feeling particularly self-
satisfied.

Weatherton could do little more than nod.

The two men stood up as Ava and Harvey approached.

"Mr. Angell," Ava said, bestowing on him a polite
smile that nonetheless warmed his blood. "We wondered where you'd gone off to after dinner."

"Let's sit over here, shall we?" Harvey asked, ignoring him and directing the question to Ava. He indicated several large armchairs grouped together near
the windows.

Angell noticed the older couple in the corner smiling stiffly in their direction. They were looking a little
looser, but whether that was due to the presence of a
lady or the presence of several empty glasses on the
table in front of them, he couldn't say. He nodded an
impersonal greeting at them. The old lady giggled and
smiled back while the old man touched his fingers to
a nonexistent hat.

"Yes, let's sit," Ava murmured, looking at Mr.
Weatherton, then passing the glance significantly to
Angell.

Angell glanced at Weatherton, too, then started as
if pinched. "Oh, yes. Sorry. Miss Moreland, permit me
to present to you Mr. Chester Weatherton. Mr. Weatherton, Miss Ava Moreland."

Weatherton, whose florid face had grown deep red
upon her entrance, now turned round eyes to Angell.
The color drained from his face like sand from an
hourglass. "M-Miss *Moreland*, did you say? Ava Moreland?"

Angell did nothing to stop the grin that presented
itself at the man's shock. This was gratifying. The
Morelands were obviously not hovering on the edge
of respectability.

"That's correct," Ava said, drawing the man's attention back to her perfectly composed face. "Is something the matter, Mr. Weatherton?"

"No, no. Oh, no," the man said, too loudly. His eyes
widened even more, if possible, as she offered her

hand. Angell could see the man desperately trying to remember if he'd treated Joshua Angell with enough respect. "I've just—it's just—it's such an *honor* to meet you, Miss Moreland. Yes, ma'am, an *honor*." He pumped her hand gracelessly until she pulled it back with a smile.

"The pleasure is mine," she answered demurely.

Weatherton's amazement pleased Angell enormously. For a moment, he verged on adopting the same pomposity the man had shown him. But after a period of outright pleasure at the man's discomfiture, he decided against it. It was actually more fun to play up his own ease with the obviously eminent Ava Moreland than it was to assume the energetic self-importance Weatherton had employed.

They reached the chairs, and Angell introduced Harvey Winters, who produced little effect on the dumbstruck man as he was having a hard time taking his eyes from Ava. They all sat down. It took a while for Weatherton to get over his shock, and Angell could tell when it happened because the man was able to turn his amazed look back to Angell.

At a moment when Harvey and Ava were conferring over what to order, Weatherton said quietly to him, "I have to say, Mr. Angell, you'll have no trouble whatsoever in New York City with a connection like this. I was about to offer you some help myself, but now I can see you don't need me a bit."

Angell smiled and inclined his head. "Thank you, Mr. Weatherton. That's good to know. It's nice to hear the truth from an outsider."

He could tell Weatherton did not like being referred to as an outsider, but Angell figured it served the man right. He hadn't been planning to offer his help to Angell. On the contrary, Angell knew Weatherton had been sizing him up from the beginning with the objective of deciding whether or not he should even acknowledge the acquaintance once they arrived in New York. But the man had not been above using the moment to aggrandize himself to a stranger.

Harvey ordered champagne for himself and Miss

Moreland while Weatherton and Angell had their bourbons freshened. As Weatherton's awe diluted with the copious amounts of alcohol he consumed, his survival instinct again flared to life. Finding himself in the midst of such an unexpected and golden opportunity, he could not stop himself from talking business, with the obvious hope of convincing a Moreland to take part in one of his money-making schemes.

Angell, after tiring of studying the man's ways and vowing never to be like him, leaned back in his chair and listened to the music. He couldn't identify any of the songs, but they were soothing, moody tunes, complex in their execution but simple in the emotions conveyed.

He wished he could light a cigarette. Watching Harvey and Ava respond politely to Weatherton's blousy prognostications on the future of real estate was interesting only from the point of view of the sheer endurance of their interested facades. But the man's words threatened to take the pleasantly numbing effects of the bourbon and turn them into a sedative if Angell didn't get some air soon.

At a momentary lull in the conversation, wherein Weatherton was no doubt only refueling himself with more oxygen, Angell rose and excused himself. Making his way to the back of the car, he opened the door to find himself on the short open platform at the end of the train. Over his head was a shallow roof, but around him stretched miles of dark empty farmland and cold bracing air.

He pulled the door shut behind him and inhaled deeply. The air smelled of damp earth, and his cheeks stung pleasantly with night mist. Yellow light from the train windows illuminated the scraggly brush that lined the tracks, its swift, blurred passage emphasizing the inexhaustible speed of the train.

He pulled from his pocket the gold cigarette case and extracted one. After putting the case back, he took a match, scraped it against the iron body of the car and held the flame to the cigarette. The bright flare so close to his face temporarily blinded him to the dark night. Squinting, he threw it to the side and leaned back against the cold metal, letting his eyes adjust to the darkness again by gazing up at the star-laden sky.

He drew deeply of the rich tobacco and marveled again at the quality of it. There were some things about wealth, he mused, so subtle that the enjoyment of them was beyond pleasure. He blew the smoke out in a stream that rallied into a tiny, momentary cloud before it was absorbed by distance.

It would be these pleasures, he believed, that would be the most gratifying of his stay in New York. After weeks of training at the hands of Ava Moreland and Harvey Winters, he had few illusions about the nature of the society to which he was journeying. They were a small nation of snobbish, superficial pretenders, terrified of being discovered for the fallible humans that they were.

To his own chagrin, he had to lump Miss Moreland in with the appraisal, for it was mainly from her that he had gleaned the opinion. In both Harvey and Ava he saw the same sort of superficiality, the same anxious protection of a facade they slaved to maintain, but it was in Ava that he saw its evil most clearly. Not because she was more snobby or superficial than Harvey, but because she was less, infinitely less so. And by having that real, passionate human side and denying it, she was committing the greater sin.

He gazed out over the open land around him and imagined being out in it, building a fire, unrolling his bedroll and sitting amidst the stars and crickets. For a moment he pictured Ava across the fire from him, clad in an old brown wool riding habit with a slouch hat pulled low over her shiny hair. He pictured her turning the spit with a rabbit on it and reveling in the night sounds and the solitary distance from the world. She would have no pressures, nothing to maintain. Her face would lose that tense paleness and the subtle line between her brows that showed so frequently.

He thought, with a clarity of insight so strong he knew it to be true, that she was the least *free* person he'd ever met.

He heard someone struggling with the door behind him, and he raised himself from his leaning repose to push it open.

Speak of the devil, he wanted to say, but he toned that down to an ironic smile as Ava peered into the darkness.

"Mr. Angell?" she asked, squinting at him.

"You got him," he said. "You coming out or is this a summons?"

She frowned at that, the line between her brows showing and destroying the image he had of her by his fire. "I merely wondered what had become of you."

"Well, come on out. You're not going to escape Weatherton's sermon standing there." He stepped back, took her gloved hand and helped her over the threshold, pulling the door shut behind her.

She shivered lightly. "It's chilly."

"Yes," he agreed. Then he placed the cigarette between his lips and pulled off his jacket.

"What are you doing?"

He turned her around and draped the huge garment over her slim shoulders. "Being chivalrous." He turned her back to face him and then leaned against the door. "Should I put out the smoke, too? I wouldn't want to ruin your lace." He knew at that moment they both remembered the way he'd sneered at the idea of separate sitting rooms for men and women because of the women's maternal shielding of their lace.

He smiled at the memory and saw her frown deepen.

"That's not necessary." After a moment of silence she asked, "Won't you be cold?"

He shook his head on the final pull of his cigarette, then flicked it off the train. "No. I like it." He noted the way her hair blew in the steady breeze as more locks escaped the loose control of her bun.

She shifted uncomfortably and gazed uneasily into the darkness that surrounded them. "Please don't stare at me."

"Why not?"

She sighed, exasperated. "It's not gentlemanly."

140

He laughed lightly. "I've decided that my gentlemanly ways should be for public consumption only. I don't want to waste any; the effort might undo me."

She didn't smile. "You did quite well with Mr. Weatherton. He's most impressed with you."

"That means a lot."

This time he saw her lips curve. "So, you took him for a charlatan."

"Miss Moreland, you supplied the manners. The brain I brought myself."

She lowered her head and drew his jacket close around her. He thought he saw her slowly inhale its scent, and he tried to see her expression. But the collar had been pulled close to her cheek.

"Mr. Angell," she began quietly, then stopped.

For a long moment there was nothing but the clatter of the railroad and bowing of dry cornstalks as they passed.

"Yes, Miss Moreland?" he asked quietly.

She took a breath and let it out slowly, raising her head. "You don't . . . like me anymore, do you?"

He felt a stab of guilt, a shard of remorse that he'd treated her so coolly for a fault she could not fathom—and hell, one that might not even exist outside his own private estimation.

At his silence, she turned a fraction and looked up at him obliquely, with a palpable air of uncertainty.

He met her diffident eyes. "I like you," he said in low tone, meaning it.

At that, he knew she blushed, because she flicked her head up with that efficiency of movement she affected when she was uncomfortable.

"Are you nervous?" she asked then.

He smiled. "Right now?"

She laughed quietly. "I know you're not nervous now. I meant about getting to Boston. About meeting Priscilla."

He thought about that a minute. "No, I'm not nervous. Are you?"

"A little."

He reached into his pocket and pulled out another

cigarette. After he lit it, he said, "I'll try not to let you down."

She turned and leaned one shoulder against the car so she faced him. Enveloped in his jacket, she looked small, a tiny presence in the diorama of farmland around them. He wondered why, despite that, she took up such a disproportionate expanse of his consciousness.

"I'm not worried that you'll disappoint me."

He blew smoke away from her. "Then what are you worried about?"

She laughed slightly. "I don't really know." She looked out the back of the train, watching the track disappear behind them. "That you'll do too well?"

He laughed then. "Like the dancing?"

Her face clouded at the memory, and he knew she remembered their talk, his anger, her inability to explain to him about Priscilla. "No, not like the dancing."

He took a breath and decided to let her off the hook. "Do you think Priscilla will like me?"

She looked up at him. "I don't know," she said pensively. "I don't know what Priscilla likes. I don't understand her."

He thought about this. Her sister's predicament bothered her, then, on more than one level. Stretching his imagination a little, he thought she might be intimidated by this sister, this person who had done the "unthinkable."

"I'll give it my best," he said, trying to be light, trying to keep the worry from her face.

She looked at him and said solemnly, "Then I don't know how she will resist."

Chapter Ten

She wanted him to touch her. She knew she should move, say something, go back inside to her berth, but she simply stood there, longing for his kiss. She pulled his jacket closer and willed the feeling away.

He looked so aloof, standing there with his cigarette. The darkness gave him that aura of mystery he seemed so frequently to possess lately. How strange to remember the way she'd thought of him when she'd first met him. It felt like ages ago now, but at that time she'd believed him to be an open book. A simple man. Predictable. Malleable.

But now he seemed so different. Now he practically oozed control, and she was the one who felt off balance, unsure. She hated it. And yet, she was fascinated by him.

"That's quite a compliment," he said, the timber of his voice warming her more than his coat.

For a moment she'd forgotten what she'd said. Then, upon remembering, she murmured, "It's only the truth." And it was. She didn't know how Priscilla

143

would resist him. Priscilla, who'd already shown herself to be incapable of resisting much.

Ava had the sudden disagreeable thought that soon Priscilla would not have reason to resist him. After all, in a few short months they would be married. She could do what she wished with him, take him to her bed if she so desired, legally, morally and without guilt. The thought caused an unpleasant bile to rise to the back of Ava's throat.

God in heaven, she was jealous already. She was jealous and they hadn't even met yet. She closed her eyes consumed by a foreboding sense of doom.

"Miss Moreland." His voice startled her, so real beside her mental picture of him embracing Priscilla. "Are you all right?" he asked. "Maybe we should go in now."

She swallowed and shook her head. She couldn't go in now. Her emotions were written all over her face, she knew, as she felt the uncontrollable intensity of the twisting of her stomach.

"I'm fine. I—I don't want to go in just yet."

He leaned back against the car and studied her. "All right."

From the corner of her eye, she could see the tiny orange glow of his cigarette as he put it to his lips.

She had to give him up. It was crazy. She could neither admit nor keep up this proprietary feeling she had for him. She'd worked long and hard with him for the express purpose of saving her sister. And save her sister she must. It was far too late now to do anything else. Though what else she might do, if her sister were suddenly not in need, she dared not contemplate.

She pictured Priscilla's pretty, sulky face and felt anger tumble inside her. No, she mustn't let it. She steeled herself against the ugly feeling. But still, the vexing fact was that Priscilla had gotten herself into this horrific state, and now she was to be not only saved, but practically *rewarded* with a man whom Ava had come to care too much about. The bitterness of it galled her. The sensation of being cheated appalled her.

"So, think you'll invest in Weatherton's boarding houses?" he asked conversationally.

Ava pulled her attention away from her pettiness and sighed. "No. And I believe it was an apartment building."

A puff of smoke, then, "Hmmm."

"You'll meet a lot of people like him. Entrepreneurial types without much to recommend them." Why could she not lose that schoolmarmish tone? Why did everything she say have to come out stiff and condescending?

"I don't doubt it," he answered.

He was bored out of his mind with her, she could tell. He was going to be swept off his feet by Priscilla. Pretty, charming, sexy Priscilla.

I like you. The words sprang into her head, in the exact, spine-tingling tone he'd used. But he didn't know, couldn't know, the tantalizing model of womanhood that awaited him. If he thought Ava was attractive enough to kiss, Priscilla would make him positively salivate with desire.

"Miss Moreland, I wish you'd lose that morbid expression," he said. "You don't have to worry. I'm sure Priscilla and I'll like each other just fine."

It was almost laughable, how he misjudged her fears. But what could she do? Set him straight?

The idea of it intrigued her. How would he react, she wondered, if she suddenly turned and kissed him? He would respond, she felt sure. What man wouldn't to a willing female? But the feeling she knew it would give *her* caused a heat and a melting inside that was delicious. To feel his hands again on her body, his lips on her face, on her neck, on her mouth. She wanted it. Oh, how she wanted it.

But the knowledge of the disappointment he'd feel in her when he laid eyes on Priscilla was too much to bear. She wouldn't be able to stand it, especially not if they were to repeat the folly of their attraction. Their last kiss was weeks behind them now. He'd probably even forgotten about it. But the feelings it awakened

145

in her every time she thought of it were as vital and alive as if it had happened yesterday.

"Yes, I'm sure you will," she said in a tiny voice.

He started. "What?"

She realized then how long it had been since he'd spoken. "I said I'm sure you and Priscilla will like each other." Too sure.

He blew out some smoke, then got rid of the cigarette. "Hmmm. As much as you and I like each other?" She could hear the teasing in his voice.

She looked up at him, glad of the darkness. "Perhaps."

"I wonder . . ." His voice trailed off.

"What is it you wonder?"

"No, nothing. It was impossible."

Curiosity insisted she pursue it. "What was impossible?"

"I only thought . . . We never would have met, except like this, because of these circumstances. Don't you think?" His voice was low.

"No. I don't expect we would have."

"But now, these circumstances . . ." He frowned, thinking.

Yes, she thought. That which had brought them together—these circumstances—were what stopped them from . . .

Her heartbeat accelerated. "Yes, the circumstances are . . ." Her voice was barely audible above the noise of the train and the whistling of the wind it created.

He shifted so that he faced her, both of them leaning one shoulder against the back of the car. Then the train hit a curve, and she lurched against him, her hand on his chest.

His hands caught her shoulders as the train steadied, but he did not loosen his grip. She felt her nerves melt beneath his touch, felt the barely concealed longing within her rise up and make her lean into his hands.

His eyes were on her; she could see them despite the darkness, now that they were so close. And they were so close. It was so dark. And they were so alone. On the back of a speeding train that raced through the coal-black midnight of Midwestern farmland. The knowledge of such privacy squelched the protesting voice inside her.

"What do you want, Ava?" he asked, his voice husky, his hands hot even through the jacket.

She was on the verge of saying it, of asking for what she'd wanted since she'd stepped out on this platform with him. Her breath came rapidly, and she parted her lips to speak.

"Say it," he said, his grip tightening. "You have to say it, Ava."

"Kiss me," she said on a hot, hoarse breath.

He didn't wait for her to repeat it. He drove forward, his arms enveloping her, his mouth covering hers. She slid into the warmth of his chest, indulged the long, slow, delectable merging of mouths and tongues, breaths and bodies. Her hands clutched his back, reveling in the expanse of hard muscle. Her breasts were crushed against his chest, her neck bent pliantly to his aggression. His tongue plunged into her mouth, and she yielded to it.

Some primal instinct beneath her consciousness made her pull closer, made her fit her hips against his. He groaned and lowered a hand to the small of her back, pulling their bodies close. Shifting, he turned her so her back lay against the cold metal car, and she could feel his hardness as he pressed his hips into hers.

Around them impenetrable darkness reigned, and the rhythmic clacking of the railroad ties merged with the hammering of her heart, the pulsing of their bodies and the gasping of their mingled breath.

Hot, fluid desire filled her, raged upward through her body from the point of his maleness. She knew what madness her senses craved. She knew that if they were not standing on the back of this moving train, she would have no defense against her own yearning.

But what could happen here? Where could it lead—even if they weren't on this platform? The questions threw themselves at her, regardless of her need to ignore them. Was this it, then? Was this the thing that had made Priscilla surrender herself to ruin?

Her defensive impulse was propelled by the horror of this new realization. With a suddenness that surprised both of them, Ava shoved him away. Angell backed abruptly into the iron railing that was the only thing between safety and the onrushing track. Clutching the metal bars, he glared at her, his hair blowing recklessly in the wind, his eyes on fire.

"Stop it," she said breathlessly, the words unnecessary in the face of his stunned and angry immobility. "We mustn't. You can't."

Angell's breathing was harsh, his lungs expelling brisk clouds of frustration.

She glanced fitfully at him through her own confusion—shooting wary eyes at him, then yanking them away to try to gather her thoughts. Why didn't he say something? What was he thinking?

"I'm sorry," she said. "I've led you on. It's my fault. My fault entirely, but it mustn't go on." She couldn't look at him now. She only knew she had to back out of this volatile situation as quickly as she could. Perhaps it wasn't too late to undo what she'd done. After all, they'd been able, for the most part, to ignore their last kiss.

"You're right, Ava," he said finally, and she couldn't help the startled jerk of her eyes to his. "It mustn't go on. But not for the reasons you think." His voice was charged with an emotion she could not name. "Not because it's wrong for you to want to kiss me, not because the feelings you have, the wanting—"

"No!" she protested, turning from the words. "Don't go on."

He stepped toward her and took her upper arm in his hand, turning her.

"Let me finish." His face was hard, his grip extreme. "You want me; don't kid yourself about that. And God knows I want you. But the reason I don't take you right here tonight—"

She gasped.

"—has nothing to do with your high-class morality

or your blue-blood superiority." He spat the words with venom. "God, there's nothing I'd like better than to show you what you are. What you can feel—to take that prim little spinster inside you and show you what a *real* woman feels like. 'Cause you've got it in you, Ava Moreland. You've got blood as hot as any three-dollar strumpet."

She gasped again and struggled to pull away. But he had her solidly by the shoulders, and she had no choice but to stare up at him. Aghast, she saw him smile.

"You think I've insulted you, don't you? And if I didn't have hold of your arms right now you'd slap me and disappear right back through that door. Wouldn't you?"

She clamped her lips shut and glared at him, breathless now from anger, her self-righteousness billowing with the onslaught of his words.

"Well, not before I have my say," he continued, his body so close to hers that she could feel the heat and energy he exuded. At this moment, it was hard to believe that seconds ago she'd been pulling him to her like a raft in a churning sea.

"You show yourself off as a lady; you're always in complete control. But from the moment I set eyes on you, I could see the passion in you. Someone should bring it out, Ava. Not for just a kiss or two, but for a lifetime. If there's one thing you should learn from me, Miss Moreland, and from this, it's that you're human. Yes, ma'am, though you can deny it all you want. You've got blood that needs stirring, and you damn well better find a man who can do it for you." He took a breath and expelled it slowly. "It won't be me," he continued. "You got that right. But not for the reasons you think. I've got reasons of my own or there wouldn't have been much to stop me from taking advantage of you here tonight, Ava."

At first, Ava could only gape. Then rage took hold of her, obliterating embarrassment and guilt. "There wouldn't have been much to stop you?" she asked in a voice quavering with wrath. "Then perhaps I should

149

know these reasons, Mr. Angell. If they are the only things that kept me from ruin, perhaps you should *enlighten* me." Her fury was blinding, so extreme that she could think of nothing scathing enough to say.

He looked down at her inscrutably. "You'll never know my reasons."

She scoffed. "No? No?" Her voice rose as her mind clouded with all the ruthless, hurtful things she wanted to say. How dare he believe that she wouldn't have stopped him. How dare he presume . . . Her thoughts sputtered as she could not pick anything both accurate and stinging enough to say to him, and the moment lengthened.

After a minute, he said, "No."

Trembling with outrage, she pushed against his chest and muttered a frustrated, *"Oh!"*

He let her go. She spun and grabbed at the door handle, pulling with all her might. The door didn't budge.

Angell reached a hand in front of her and she flinched, stepping away from him. With an ironic lift of his brows, he pushed the door open.

She glared at him, then snatched his jacket off and threw it at him. He caught it in one hand.

"Bastard," she hissed, and pushed past him through the door.

Angell stood motionless as the door slammed in front of him. Then he nodded and laughed derisively. "Truer than you think, Miss Moreland," he murmured to himself. "Truer than you think."

They arrived in Boston without Ava having to utter another word to Angell. Their last meeting hung palpably in the air between them, and she refused to meet his eyes or say anything that might make him think she forgave him. Her anger was a constant companion, alternately simmering and boiling, depending on whether her humiliation was foremost or subdued. When she thought about how he'd goaded her into asking for that kiss, then threw her desire back in her face, she thought she would explode with the frustration of her inability to set him to rights. For he had the upper hand now, and he knew it. She'd bared her soul by asking for that kiss, and he'd rejected it.

They were met at the station by Embrey, the Moreland driver, who procured enough porters to convey an army's luggage to the coach without Harvey or Angell having to lift a finger. Ava strode imperiously before them all, anxious to reach the coach that would take her to the hotel and a room where she could bury her head in a pillow and wish she were dead.

As they swept through the streets of Boston, Ava keep a surreptitious eye on Angell as he studied the city around them. Though he said nothing, his expression was intense, and she reluctantly found herself wondering what he thought about, if he thought about her at all.

"Miss Priscilla is already at the hotel?" Harvey inquired.

Ava nodded. "Yes. She's resting, according to Embrey. She said she'll meet us at dinner."

Harvey issued a quiet snort and hunched back in the seat.

"As you may or may not know, Harvey," Ava said, "the early stages of her predicament require her to get a good deal of rest." Unwillingly, she glanced at Angell, who was suddenly regarding her with amusement. Blood flooded her face, and she clenched her teeth. "Is something humorous, Mr. Angell?"

He folded his arms across his chest. "Nothing I could explain."

Ava pressed her lips together. For some reason, she wanted to cry, and she couldn't think of anything that would be more mortifying.

She mentally drew herself up. This was insane. At one point, she'd worried he might take it into his head to believe the role they'd created for him; but now it seemed it was *she* who had believed the role too thoroughly.

Moments later, they pulled up in front of the Saucerby Hotel. Embrey opened the carriage door and Harvey debarked, turning to offer Ava his hand.

Just behind her, Angell descended. "I suppose we're on the top floor of this place," he said, halting on the sidewalk and looking upward.

"Those are the best rooms," Ava said coolly, pulling a hat pin from her bonnet and repositioning it.

Harvey rounded to the back of the coach. A moment later, he emerged with his bag and entered the hotel.

Angell's eyes rested on her, hooded and shrewd. "I'm sorry you're still upset," he said quietly.

Ava shot him a hard look and brushed past him toward the door. "Don't be ridiculous."

It had been well over a month since Ava had seen her sister, and in that time Priscilla had grown slightly more plump and depressingly more beautiful. Though she'd always had a glow to her fine, porcelain skin, she now looked positively radiant. Her hair had a healthy sheen, and her sleepy-lidded cat's eyes shimmered with life.

Maybe it was her imagination, Ava thought, or perhaps it was that she hadn't seen Priscilla in so long, but Ava was sure Priscilla's beauty had matured. She hated herself for having to admit it, but before she'd left, she'd entertained the thought that pregnancy might not agree with Priscilla.

"Ava, darling," Priscilla said, her full lips curving into what looked like a genuine smile. She didn't rise from the sofa as Ava entered the suite, but held out her arms for Ava to come to her.

Ava bent and placed a kiss on her cheek. "Priscilla, dear, how are you feeling?"

"Like the very devil," Priscilla said with an exaggerated grimace. "Try though I might, I can't seem to get enough sleep. I'm constantly exhausted. And food! I eat everything in sight, only to be hungry again ten minutes later." She pushed herself up straighter on the couch. "But tell me about your trip. Where is my husband? Pray tell, is he handsome? And how is our Harvey? Still disgusted with me?"

Ava couldn't share Priscilla's amusement at the situation, and her sister's flip tone threatened to undo all

Ava's avowals that she would not lose her temper.

"I can't answer for Harvey," she said, pulling off her gloves with short movements, "but yes, we've found you a husband—as you already know from my telegram."

Priscilla frowned and waved an impatient hand in circles. " 'Found the man—stop—bringing him four-thirty train Boston November sixteen—stop—will marry you off as soon as you set eyes on each other—"

"I didn't say that," Ava said.

"Stop," Priscilla finished. "Just about. You didn't give me a clue about him, and I've been fairly *dying* of curiosity. Where did you find him? What's he like? I thought you'd at least send me *one* letter about him."

Ava tossed her gloves to the table and concentrated on removing her hat. "Yes, I apologize for that. We were very busy, you know. He needed a few lessons."

"Lessons?"

"Yes, he was a bit rough when we found him, but we've cleaned him up and taught him some manners."

"Heavens, he sounds like a stray dog," Priscilla mused. "Does he sit up and beg now? Or is that one of the things you had to teach him *not* to do?"

As Priscilla's laughter tinkled over her nerves, Ava clenched her teeth and sat carefully in the armchair across from her. Despite her anger at him, she felt a rush of protectiveness for Angell's quiet dignity, for his unaffected strength and the integrity that would matter to no one if it was discovered he was without means.

"He's not a dog, Cilla, he's a cowboy, though I daresay you won't recognize him as one now. He's quite handsome, actually." Ava looked down at her hands where they gripped each other in her lap. Priscilla's gaze on her face felt uncomfortable. With an effort, Ava separated her hands and placed them on the arms of the chair.

"He's been a very quick study," she continued, "but he is, obviously, a novice in the ways of New York. It shall be up to you and Harvey and me to protect him from harm. And I'll thank you to put rein to your sarcasm while you're with him." She fixed her sister with an authoritative look. "I don't want his confidence undermined."

Priscilla's expression was unreadable as she gazed through lazy eyes at her sister. In fact, the look was so inscrutable that it reminded Ava of Angell, and she felt the chill conviction that they really were, in many ways, perfect for each other.

"He doesn't sound like a cowboy," Priscilla said at last. "He sounds like a child who's done very well in mathematics."

Ava sighed. "I only mean—"

Priscilla laughed and held up a hand. "All right, Miss Ava, I'll be gentle with him. I won't give him any difficult equations, and I'll make sure he gets a good mark on the final exam."

"That's just the sort of banter I'm talking about."

Priscilla rolled her eyes. "Is he as delicate as all that? Where did you find him? In St. Louis? Is he a puke?"

Ava made a horrified grimace. "A what? What sort of disgusting term is that?"

"A puke—a Missourian. I read it in *Pride of the West*."

"Oh, Cilla, you haven't been reading those cheap westerns again, have you? I asked you to read *Nature*. I thought it would give you something to discuss with Mr. Angell."

"Angell? Did you say his name is Mr. Angel?" Peals of laughter bubbled from Priscilla's mouth. "How fiendishly appropriate. Mr. Angel, my guardian angel, protecting me from scorn."

"*Please*, don't tease him about it," Ava pleaded, horrified by her sister's rudeness, though Angell was not in the room. "He could be a little sensitive on the issue. And in any case, it's Angell with two l's, instead of one."

"What's his first name?"

"Joshua. And he's not a—a—"

"A what? A dog? A cowboy?"

"What you said—"

"A puke!"

154

"That's right. He's from Georgia originally."

Priscilla donned a thoughtful expression. "Joshua Angell of Georgia. Angell . . . Angell . . . Do we know any Angells in Georgia?"

Ava shifted in her seat. "I believe his family is—obscure."

Cilla nodded. "Of course. He would have to be obscure, wouldn't he, or he would never consent to marrying a soiled woman."

"Exactly."

This time Cilla looked away, her color high. After a moment of uncomfortable silence, she turned back to Ava with an overly bright expression. "So where is our Harvey? You know, I actually missed the old curmudgeon. I swear, he gets more like Father every year. Don't you think so, Ava?"

Ava forced a tight smile at the thought. "Yes, now that you mention it. I believe he even emulates him at times. On this trip, he frequently said and did things that were quite fatherly."

"Did he?" Cilla asked. "Did he have second thoughts about the endeavor? That's just like him, you know, to listen to his conscience only after it's too late to do anything about it."

Ava looked at her sister in surprise. It was one of the aptest observations of Harvey she'd ever heard. Coming from her silly, self-absorbed sister made it doubly astute.

"Well, he didn't renege on the project anyway," Ava said. "And he seems four-square behind it now. I believe he even likes Mr. Angell a little, though he was quite disapproving of him in the beginning."

"Joshua Angell," Cilla repeated. "You know, I think I like the sound of it, despite its religious overtone. Priscilla Angell. Why, that positively *rolls* off the tongue, don't you think?"

A sick feeling curled Ava's stomach, but she pasted a pleased expression on her face anyway. "Yes it does."

They regarded each other with equal degrees of trepidation and false optimism. Ava only hoped her own worry appeared to stem from the audacity of the venture and nothing else.

"Will he like me, do you think?" Priscilla asked then, in a small voice.

Ava looked quickly at her sister's troubled face, and her heart went out to her. She could see the fear in Priscilla's eyes and the uncertainty that marred her smile.

"Don't worry, Cilla," she said softly. "He'll like you and everything will be fine. He's an upstanding man, for all his humble descent, and he'll be good to you. And anyway, you'll only have to be with him a few short months, then he'll go away and you'll have your life back."

Thinking the words generously optimistic, Ava was surprised to see her sister's face crumple and tears drip heavily from her lashes.

"Oh, Ava," Priscilla said, burying her face in her hands.

Ava rose and moved to the sofa beside her. As her sister sobbed, she rested an arm around her shoulders, feeling Priscilla's trembling as if it were her own.

"Everything will be fine. Please don't cry, Cilla," she pleaded. "You'll like him. Even *I* like him, and you know how difficult I am to please."

Priscilla laughed through her tears and looked up through damp lashes at Ava. "You do? You really do?" she questioned.

"Yes. I really do," Ava said with a sincerity she did not, this time, try to hide. "I like him very much."

Priscilla sniffed and dabbed at her face with a hanky from her sleeve. The storm was over, like a tiny summer shower.

"Then I know I shall like him." Priscilla blew her nose. "Goodness, I just cry at the drop of a hat these days." She blew again, and Ava patted her shoulder.

"Don't worry," she murmured, wondering how she could utter the pointless words when all she wanted to do was sit down and cry like her sister. She swallowed hard over the lump in her own throat.

"Don't worry," she said again, wishing she herself could heed the advice, "everything will work itself out. Everything will be just fine."

Chapter Eleven

Angell and Harvey sat in the lounge of the Saucerby cradling brandies and acting like congenial gentlemen.

"So," Angell began, "tell me about your life in New York. You're obviously close to the Morelands. You a friend of the whole family's, or just Ava's?"

Harvey looked at him quizzically. "I work for them," he said, amused. "I'm Mr. Moreland's personal assistant."

"Oh." The news surprised Angell, and Harvey's enjoyment of the fact irritated him. Harvey was so polished, so snobbish, so strict and unrelenting about Angell's lessons, Angell had been sure that Harvey was some rich bastard helping Ava out of class loyalty, or some other unfathomable reason having to do with wealth.

Regardless of Harvey's thinking him a fool—nothing new and therefore not daunting—Angell pressed on. "You mean, you're not—how's it put?" He searched for Chester Weatherton's words on the train. "You're not *of the same set* as the Morelands?"

At this Harvey actually laughed, a condescending sound with a bitter edge. "God, no. And Julius Moreland would launch a fit just hearing you ask the question. Not to mention Cameron. *He'd* probably call you out for it."

Angell furrowed his brow. "Cameron's the brother, right?"

Harvey nodded with exaggeration.

"Julius is the father?"

Harvey scoffed. "And don't you ever forget it. Julius is a lion. Very fierce, very protective of his family. But he's fair, too. Just don't step out of line."

Angell sighed and raised a corner of his mouth wryly. "I imagine I'm already out of line. There isn't any way now to start square with him, things being the way they are."

Harvey shrugged. "If things go as they should, he'll never find out. And once you leave New York, he'll cease to be curious. It's just getting you past him in the meantime."

Angell thought about that. "If he's so protective of his family, what's to stop him from investigating me? I don't imagine it'd be all that hard to find out I'm not what you claim."

Harvey eyed him a moment, sipped his brandy, then looked past him. "He trusts me. He'll believe that I checked you out."

"And you're willing to risk that for me?"

Harvey raised a brow and focused his attention back on Angell. "Not for you, no. Of course not. For Miss Priscilla. Don't forget, Angell, this is *all* for Priscilla." His eyes darted past Angell again and then he stood up, his eyes on something beyond the lounge.

For a second, as he rose, Angell kept his eyes on Harvey, noting the man's extraordinary change of expression. A curious mix of pain and relief lighted his features, quickly overlaid by his usual ironic control. Interesting, but when Angell turned he was not at all surprised to see Ava and another woman—the fabled Priscilla, no doubt—descending the shallow staircase to the lounge.

Priscilla was shorter than Ava, blonder and more fair-skinned. She had a wispy, cloudlike quality to her that contrasted in a frothy way with Ava's slender, solemn strength. The familial resemblance was plain—the light, feline eyes, the high cheekbones—but without doubt the similarities ended there.

"So, *this* is my cowboy," Priscilla purred, floating toward him in a white chiffon dress that did much to foster the cloud image. Her tongue flitted out and wet her pink lips before she smiled up at him.

Angell's gut tightened involuntarily, and he glanced at Ava and Harvey to see if they'd noticed the gesture. Their identically glowering expressions told him they had.

Amusement tickled his lips; he let it out with a smile. "Joshua Angell, Miss Priscilla. It's a pleasure to finally meet you."

Priscilla's expression was delighted as he bowed over her hand. She tossed a smile over her shoulder at Ava. "Oh, you were so right, Ava. He's delicious."

Angell knew, with every ounce of his being, that Ava had never called him "delicious," but he did wonder what exactly she had said. Good things? Guarded things, most likely. He wondered if the two were close enough that she might have mentioned his kiss. He thought not.

Priscilla's fingers tightened when he would have let hers go, forcing his eyes to hers.

"Yes," she exclaimed, holding his gaze, her painted lips curved, "we're going to have fun, aren't we?"

Angell couldn't help the answering smile that broadened on his lips. She's a terror, he thought. No wonder Harvey and Ava had to go to such lengths to save her from herself.

"I believe that's up to you, Miss Priscilla," he answered. "It seems I'm here for your convenience."

She took her hand back and clapped it together with her other one. "Wonderful!" She turned to Harvey and Ava, who were both beet-red in the face. "I *like* him," she pronounced. "Let's go to dinner."

She curled her arm through Angell's and pulled so

it nestled against the side of her breast. "Tell me, Mr. Angell," she continued, drawing him forward past a smoldering Ava and a bullet-eyed Harvey, "tell me all about yourself. I want to know just what sort of husband my dear sister and my darling Harvey have picked out for me."

They were seated at a round table in the middle of the opulent hotel dining room. Angell held Priscilla's chair for her, exactly as instructed innumerable times in the weeks before, and waited for Harvey to seat Ava. The two men then sat simultaneously.

"Champagne!" Priscilla ordered with a flourish as the waiter appeared. "We must celebrate. I'm to be married, you know," she told the server in a sultry, confidential tone.

The man flushed. "Congratulations," he said with a short bow, his gaze fixed on her upturned eyes.

"Priscilla," Ava warned.

But she went on. "Yes, and my parents don't even know it yet. Isn't it too wicked? It's to be a dreadful surprise."

Her voice was honeyed, like Ava's, but consciously so. And it was obvious as far as the waiter was concerned that she might have been reciting the Gettysburg Address. She simply dripped sensuality.

Angell found himself marveling over the skill with which she wielded her charms. The waiter was helpless as a butterfly in her web and, though he may have been easy prey, Angell was sure her talents were not confined solely to the powerless.

"Miss Priscilla," Angell ventured, when the waiter had stumbled off to do her bidding, "I wonder if you'd tell me about your father."

Priscilla's porcelain brow furrowed momentarily. "Why? Hasn't Ava filled you in on the dregs of all that nonsense?"

"I'd like to hear your opinion." He reached into his coat pocket for a cigarette, saw Harvey's minuscule shake of the head, sighed and removed his hand.

"Oh, he's an ogre." Priscilla sighed. "But a manageable one."

Elaine Fox

Angell lifted a brow. "I'd like to meet the man you considered unmanageable."

She gave him a sharp look, then softened it with a slow smile. "I'm still looking for him," she said quietly.

Angell didn't answer, and Priscilla went on eyeing him. Harvey cleared his throat and picked up his water glass, hitting the empty wineglass next to it with a *clang*.

Angell continued. "What's he likely to say about an unexpected engagement, do you think?"

Priscilla leaned back in her chair and shrugged. "He'll be full of sound and fury, I'm sure," she said dramatically, "but ultimately, there'll be nothing for him to do about it, will there. I mean, I *am* marrying a *real* man, aren't I? You're not going to cower simply because the beast roars?"

"I reckon that depends on the size of the beast's teeth," Angell mused.

Priscilla snickered. "You *reckon*? Oh, that's charming."

"Cilla." Ava frowned at her sister, then passed the look to Angell.

"Excuse me. I *suppose*," Angell corrected, thinking it might be a good idea to assess how large Priscilla's teeth were.

"Oh no, don't change it." Priscilla leaned forward and put a warm hand on his arm. "It really is charming. So colorful. Tell me, can you shoot a gun?"

Angell looked at her dubiously. It was impossible to tell if she were serious or baiting. In either case, she was directing the conversation, indeed the whole mood of the table, according to her whim. "Of course."

She bit her bottom lip in a childlike gesture and gazed up at him. "Are you good?"

He chuckled cynically. She was so confident, she didn't even feel the need to be subtle. What she needed was a good taste of her own medicine. "I'm very good," he said, his tone low, his eyes penetrating.

She sat up abruptly, delighted, and clapped her hands together again. "Oh, you're *perfect*, simply perfect!"

162

"Miss Priscilla," Harvey interrupted in a tone as sobering as ice water. "I think we ought to concentrate on the business at hand. The two of you have been courting for the last month, ostensibly, so you should know a thing or two about Mr. Angell."

The waiter appeared with the champagne and began pouring all around.

"Oh, but I *do* know about Mr. Angell," Priscilla said. She turned on him with those bedroom eyes. "I know he's from Georgia originally, which accounts for that darling little drawl of his, and that he's heavily invested in cattle. *Filthy* rich, isn't that what they're all to believe?"

Angell smiled slightly, watching her.

"And he's just the most *perfect* gentleman," she continued, "well-read, as I understand it. Dickens, Poe, Melville . . . a veritable font of knowledge."

Angell raised a brow and glanced ironically at Ava. So she *had* briefed her sister. He wondered if it were possible the "delicious" conversation had taken place. Ava's look was unreadable, her eyes hard and cold as stones.

"And," Priscilla added, leaning toward him, "he kisses *divinely*."

At this, Angell's glance whipped to Priscilla, who smiled like the cat with the canary. He looked quickly back at Ava and searched her face. *Had she told, then?*

Ava's face was scarlet, her mouth open in shock and her clasped hands lifted from her lap as if she were praying.

He glanced back at Priscilla, whose expression was one of childlike delight as she gazed between Ava and Angell.

He willed himself to remain still. "And what would make you think that, Miss Priscilla?" he asked, unable to resist another glance at Ava. She'd lowered her hands and shut her mouth, but her flaming face said far more than it should have.

Priscilla watched him with a shrewdness that had hitherto been hidden by her baby-doll flippancy. "I can tell just by looking," she placed her hand on his arm once again, "at your lips." She ran a finger along his forearm.

Angell used his other hand to take up his wine and sip before answering. "You are," he said, "unusually astute."

She laughed lightly. "And you, so modest."

She leaned back, and Angell breathed a silent sigh of relief. The woman was outrageous. It was no wonder she was in the condition she was in, he thought. Even now she was begging for something—what, he wasn't yet sure. He didn't think it was the obvious, but there was only one way to find out.

It was a guess about the kiss; he knew that as soon as he'd looked at Ava. But it was clear Priscilla was uncertain no longer, and he wondered what had led her to suspect. He also wondered how she'd feel about marrying a man who had kissed her sister, even though it was to be nothing more than a marriage of convenience. She had to know her sister did not kiss men regularly—even Angell knew that. So what did she think? For that matter, what did he think?

He didn't. He wasn't being paid to think. He was a hired hand, an underling, someone outside of their social class. He wasn't going to matter to Ava Moreland any more than the clerk, or the butler or any other person in her employ.

Which was just as well, Angell reminded himself. For even if she were able to get over the unfortunate facts of his poverty and obscurity—which she wasn't—she would *never* get over his parentage.

She probably considered the sexual attraction unfortunate, but not insurmountable—no temptation was insurmountable for Ava. Not so, apparently, for Priscilla.

The waiter returned and set a plate of raw oysters in front of each of them. Angell stared down at them in distaste, then glanced at Priscilla as she picked up the tiny fork that had come with them. She looked up, caught him watching her and smiled as she dropped the slithering mass between her parted lips.

Angell briefly closed his eyes. When he opened

them, the six gooey fish still lay expectantly before him. He picked up the fork and poked one. It slid off the prongs and hung in a gray blob off the side of a shell. He speared it through the center, the fattest part, and noted the sensation was exactly that of stabbing the belly of a deer to gut it.

He glanced around the table and saw Harvey neatly insert the thing into his mouth and swallow. Ava dabbed some sort of sauce on hers, which Angell considered, but decided there was too much likelihood he'd end up wearing it, so he brought the thing up to his lips naked.

He thought he'd take it slowly, but as soon as the blob was in his mouth it dove straight for the back of his throat. He gagged, drawing the attention of his companions. Too late, the thing descended on its own to his stomach. He reached for his wineglass.

"Are you all right?" Priscilla asked. She drank some champagne and watched him.

Harvey rolled his eyes and slapped him—hard—on the back.

Angell swallowed, coughed and jerked away from Harvey, making a screech with his chair on the wood floor that startled even nearby diners.

"Hey, take it easy," he choked out as Harvey lifted his arm for another blow.

Harvey shrugged. "Just trying to help."

Angell coughed again, eyes watering, and reached for his napkin. Silverware clattered to the floor with the volume of orchestral cymbals.

"Sorry." He bent to pick up his fallen fork and nearly bumped heads with the waiter. They both backed off immediately, and Angell, realizing his error—attempting to do something for himself while there were servants around—waved his hand for the server to continue.

He pressed the napkin to his streaming eyes and drank again from the wineglass. God, it had been going so well up to this. He imagined he could feel the oyster squirming in his stomach and wished to God he were anywhere but at this table. Though he hadn't looked at her, he knew Ava's eyes were boring holes through him.

"I never understood why," Angell said in a weak voice, after swallowing some more wine, "when you're choking, people feel the need to beat the bejesus out of you."

He finally risked a look across the table at Ava. She watched him with just the expression he expected—tolerant disapproval. When he finally got his breath back and replaced his glass of wine, she asked mildly, "I take it you don't like the oysters, Mr. Angell?"

He frowned, looked down at his plate and willed the heat in his face to abate. When the silence at the table lengthened, he looked back up at her.

"Was it that obvious?" he asked, attempting levity but feeling like an idiot. She merely raised an eyebrow. He dropped his smile. "No, I guess I don't."

"Then, please," she said as she picked up her tiny fork, "eat no more."

Harvey cleared his throat. "I feel compelled," he said in an ostentatious tone, "to keep up with the subject at hand. Miss Priscilla, your engagement is not to be announced immediately. I don't think you should be speaking of it so casually."

"I know that, Harvey," she answered smugly. "But he's just a waiter."

"Waiters have mouths. Waiters can gossip. And how do you know there isn't someone we know nearby? These things get out, you know. Surely even you realize how imperative it is that your father be handled correctly. If he were to find out beforehand—"

"Oh, yes, all sorts of horrible things might happen," Priscilla proclaimed, a look of horror on her face. Then she flashed Angell a confidential smile and sipped her champagne.

"That's right." Harvey leaned forward in his chair. "Things so horrible I'm *sure* you can't even fathom what they might be. And I don't think you should be guzzling so much champagne. You're starting to resemble a rummy fishwife," he snapped.

"Harvey's right, Cilla," Ava said.

"Of course I'm right," Harvey spouted, frustration spilling out as Priscilla narrowed her eyes and took another sip.

"I mean about Father," Ava continued. "If he were to find out any part of our plan, even just the engagement, at the wrong time—it could prove disastrous."

Priscilla sighed and carefully placed her glass back on the table.

Harvey leaned back abruptly and threw his hands in the air. "Look at her. No idea of the danger she's in. I tell you, Miss Priscilla, this irresponsibility of yours has got to *stop*. You can no longer play around like the reckless girl you were. You're going to—" He stopped, gazed about himself uncomfortably and lowered his voice. "Your responsibilities are going to increase a thousandfold in a very short time. You should be preparing yourself for them."

Priscilla fixed him with a look that could char wood. She reached out a hand and placed it deliberately over Angell's on the arm of his chair. "I am doing just that, Mr. Winters," she said in a steely tone.

The image Angell had of the frothy cloud evaporated. In that instant, Priscilla was a force to be reckoned with. The nimbus had swirled into a tornado.

"And if I hear that odious word come out of your mouth one more time," Priscilla continued, "I shall scream and scream and not stop screaming until you have left my sight forever."

Harvey's anger abated slightly, but he did not relinquish her gaze. "And which word might that be?"

Priscilla's teeth gritted. "*Responsibility*. My responsibility to my family, my responsibility to my child, my responsibility to God, to man—"

"Miss Priscilla." Angell turned his hand over and grasped hers. Her eyes shot to his, and he wondered briefly what he was doing, stepping in front of the hurricane. "I think we all know the sacrifice you're making out of your own sense of duty. No one wants to marry just for responsibility's sake, and I ask your forgiveness for my part in that unhappy truth. But the fact is, you are doing it and for noble reasons. We aren't going to forget that. So please, don't upset yourself any more."

Priscilla gazed at him, her tirade tripped up by his sudden interference. He couldn't tell if she was angry at his interruption or just stumped by his tone—whether it was serious or not. In any case, the look she gave him initially was not a pretty one. He held her gaze.

At length she said, "Thank you, Mr. Angell, for that stirring speech." She sighed and shot Harvey a scathing look. "I'm glad *someone* here recognizes my sacrifice."

"This is ridiculous." Ava's voice pierced the tension with exasperation. "Cilla, I'm sick of your manipulations. Harvey has traveled halfway across the country to help you, and you show your thanks by abusing him. He's only trying to do what's best for you, as am I. The least you could do is show some respect for the seriousness of the situation."

Angell was amazed, but Priscilla actually looked moderately contrite after this speech, though she sent one last rebellious glance at Harvey.

"Very well," she said with a sniff, and raised her head with an air of injured pride. "*Thank* you, Harvey, for *all* you've done."

This time it was Harvey's turn to look abashed. "I just want you to be happy, Miss Priscilla."

Priscilla *harumphed* in a none-too-feminine way and picked up her champagne. "*Now* can we eat, Ava?"

Dinner progressed with considerably less tension but proportionately more boredom. Angell managed to get through the rest of the meal without gagging and, he noted, Ava was able to ignore him by concentrating on Priscilla. They were drilling into her head the course of their plan the same way they'd drilled it into his. Priscilla looked just about as excited about it as he had been. He wondered why she didn't just name the father of her child if she were so unhappy with the scheme.

After dinner, they strolled to the lifts to be taken to their rooms. The first lift was nearly full—a wedding party having just broken up—with room only for two. With great magnanimity and some obvious maneuvering, Angell managed to convince Harvey and Priscilla to go on, telling them he and Ava would take the next one.

The next one was empty except for the operator, and Ava wasted no time in pinning Angell to the spot.

"Well, Mr. Angell," she began in a patronizing tone, "what was it you wanted to talk about?"

"Talk about?" he repeated.

She laughed once, without humor. "It couldn't have been more obvious the way you got rid of Harvey and Priscilla. What's the matter? Are you having second thoughts?"

"No, no." He shook his head, then decided to forge ahead. "But she's something, your sister." He could feel Ava's eyes on him. He looked into her stony face.

"Don't you like her?"

He knew he was crazy, but he thought he heard hope in her voice, though it was probably only incredulity. He understood now what she'd meant when she'd said most men liked Priscilla.

He shook his head thoughtfully. "She's a charmer."

Ava sighed. "Yes."

The lift creaked to a halt at their floor, and the operator opened the doors, then the wrought-iron gates. Ava nodded her thanks and exited the car, Angell close behind.

"Tell me something," he said, placing a light, guiding hand on the small of her back as they walked down the deserted hallway. He felt her tense at the contact. "Did you tell Priscilla about us?"

Ava halted dead in her tracks and glared up at him. If he'd been looking for a reaction, he'd gotten it.

Her eyes sparked with fury. She didn't answer immediately, as if she debated whether to understand him right off or feign confusion. Her choice was clear when she spoke.

"I did no such thing. And I'm sure you know that." She did not relinquish his look. "Why is it, Mr. Angell, that we cannot go two days without some mention of that—that *aberration* in my behavior being brought up for conversation?"

Something about the contrast between her hostile eyes and petal-soft skin got to him, and his patience for her hard-wrought coldness evaporated. "Maybe because it wasn't an aberration."

Ava took a deep breath, nostrils flaring. "You don't even know what the word means. You don't know what *any* of this means. To you, that night on the train—"

"And in St. Louis," he reminded her, an edge to his voice.

She flushed furiously. "Either time. Oh, I don't know what *possessed* me. But to you it's just a—a lark—something amusing to tease me about."

"That's not true," he said, unexpected force charging the words.

"But it's disastrous to me. Can't you understand that?"

He seized on the words at the same time his hands clutched her arms. "What's disastrous? What?"

She looked at him as though he were demented. "You're to be *my sister's* husband. How can you even ask?"

"That's not it," he muttered. Frustrated, he dropped her arms. "Why doesn't Priscilla name the father of her baby?"

Ava's hostility stumbled at his sudden change in topic. "What? Why, I imagine she's ashamed."

"You said you thought she loved him, the father."

"Yes, I believed she did."

"Then why won't she name him? Wouldn't she have to marry him then? Wouldn't he have to marry her?"

Ava laughed weakly, apparently puzzled by his questions. "Of course, we've discussed this before. That's precisely why she won't name him. Yes, maybe she loved him, but that doesn't matter if it's someone—inappropriate. Even she knows that."

He laughed incredulously and looked up at the ceiling. "Ava, what am *I*, if not *inappropriate*?"

"But that's just it. No one knows that *you're* inappropriate." She gazed at him helplessly, waiting for him to see the light.

But the light he saw was not the one he knew she'd hoped. Nausea roiled up inside of him, and for a moment he thought of the oyster, heaving about like a whale in a pond.

"My God, Ava," he said quietly, his disgust surprising even him, and bewildering her. "You're worse than I thought."

"What do you mean?"

"You're a snob." The word was inadequate, but it was the only one he could think of.

She drew herself up. "I am *not* a snob."

He laughed. "You've got to be joking. You stand there and tell me your sister can't marry the father of her baby because he's 'inappropriate,' and in the next breath you say you're not a snob?"

She pressed her lips together. "If, by snob, you mean that because I was born into money, I think I am better than others, then you are wrong. What I am trying to convey to you, apparently with little success, is that because I was born into money, I am *different* than others. Priscilla is *different* than others. A marriage between classes would never work because of the enormous *differences* between classes, not because of any superiority or inferiority."

"Bull," Angell spat. He could feel himself growing angrier with every word she uttered.

She drew herself up with infuriating calm. "Mr. Angell, you saw how difficult it was to learn all of our lessons, to change your speech, your manners, your level of education, though I must say you've done remarkably well. And that is just the tip of the iceberg, as they say."

He shook his head. "But I did it. Why couldn't Priscilla's man do it? Aside from that pitiful excuse that everyone would *know* he was low-class. That, my dear, kills your argument right there."

Ava clenched her teeth and lowered her eyes to watch her fingers remove her gloves with practiced precision. "Fine, brush that off as unimportant if you wish. Think about this. We've groomed you to take up a place in society for a short, short time. But for you to take up a permanent place in it *everything* would have to change—your outlook, your attitude, even your pleasures and desires. You would not be able to remain *you*, Mr. Angell, and I think that would bother you much more than you may believe." With that, she fished her key out of her reticule, pushed her gloves into the bag and looked up at him.

"I don't believe you. You're making up excuses."

She threw up her hands and turned away, moving down the hall. "Then I give up. You will never understand."

He watched her go, her straight back and refined walk irritating him still further. "You're a bigger fake than I am, Miss Moreland," he called after her, frustrated anger knotting his gut.

Ava stopped at her door and turned back. "I don't know what you're talking about. And please keep your voice down."

Angell started down the hall after her, his eyes locked on her defensively closed face. "I may be here pretending to be someone else, but you, Miss Ava, you don't even know who you are. You're nothing but a balled-up bunch of rules and restrictions. Do you even know why you do what you do?"

Ava glanced uneasily down the hall. "Of course I do. And I don't appreciate—"

"Then why did you kiss me? Hmmm? Tell me why, and I'll let you alone."

Ava's face flushed and she lowered her head. "I don't care to discuss this in the middle of a public hallway."

"Fine. Give me your key."

"What?"

"Give me your key, and we'll get out of the public hallway."

She looked aghast. "You can't enter my room."

Angell took the key from her hand and opened the door, then followed the portal into the room without waiting for her to enter.

Ava stood in the hall and looked at him, nonplussed.

"What are you doing?"

He dropped the key on a table and turned. "Getting out of the public eye."

She clasped her hands in front of her and didn't budge. He lowered his head and said, "All right."

He strode toward her. She looked up at him with nervous eyes. When he got within a foot of her, he reached out, took her hands and pulled her into the room and into his arms.

She looked up at him belligerently. "Is this your solution to everything?"

He let his hands circle her waist and kicked the door shut. "No," he said, backing her against the door. "Just one thing."

He lowered his mouth to hers, expecting, hoping, willing her reaction to be the same as it was the two previous times. But though she did not push him away, she did not respond. Her hands were clasped at her waist, her knuckles pushed into his stomach. Her lips remained closed.

He pulled back. "Ava," he said quietly, "you know this is where you lose your argument." He kissed her again lightly, then moved his lips to her neck, just below her ear. He felt her shiver lightly.

"I don't," she began, then inhaled deeply. "I don't know what this is, but it is not an argument."

He laughed and pulled her hands apart, placing her arms limply around his waist. He leaned in and kissed her again, her cheek, her jaw. She shuddered and lay her head back against the door.

"Come on, Ava." His eyes searched her flushed face. Her eyes, half-closed, were dark and unfathomable. "Why can't you admit that you kiss me because you like to? Why can't you admit to even one damn human weakness?"

. She closed her eyes and he kissed her again. This time her lips opened. Her hands clutched the back of his jacket, and her breathing accelerated. Just as the kiss began to deepen, he pulled back.

"Now tell me about how what's between us is 'inappropriate,'" he said softly. "Tell me what you feel for me is 'different' than what other men and women feel."

She opened her eyes. "You're a devil," she snapped, pushing at his chest.

He took a step back, shocked at the anger he saw in her eyes. "And you're a hypocrite," he spat, instantly furious.

She looked up at him in amazement. "Me?" she countered, her voice incredulous. "*I'm* a hypocrite?"

"You allow yourself this—this *dalliance*, I suppose you'd call it—and at the same time you tell yourself how beneath you it is. How wrong it is. How wrong *I* am."

Her eyes narrowed. "Tell me something, Angell. If I'm the hypocrite, how is it that you even know the meaning of the word?"

"I—*what*?" His frustration soared, but his anger stalled at the strange question, and irritation was foremost in his tone.

"I mean," she continued in a hard voice, "how is it that your English is so good, when just weeks ago you were nothing but a country bumpkin. How is it that suddenly you're using words like 'aberration' and 'hypocrite' when just last month you didn't know what 'derivation' meant? I'm a good teacher, Angell, but I'm not that good. And I don't like being lied to."

He stepped back, gut clutching and muscles tensing as if he faced a mountain lion instead of this delicate, beautiful woman.

"I've never lied to you," he said quietly, thinking that in itself was most likely a lie. But he had no other choice, and he would die sooner than see his secrets revealed here and now.

"Then tell me who you really are," she said vehemently. "Tell me why you're pretending to be someone you're not." Her color was high, but her eyes were uncompromising.

He stared at her. Would she drop over in a dead faint if he told her the truth? he wondered silently. But he would never find out. "Same reason you are, Ava. Fear." He scoffed lightly. "But don't get your hopes up, sugar," he said derisively. "I'm no better than you originally thought. Just different. A little early schooling coming back to me, is all. You still kissed a cowboy."

Ava swallowed and her gaze dropped to the floor.

"Disappointed?" he asked softly, some strange emotion thrumming along his nerves. When she didn't answer, he added acerbically, "Or are you relieved that I'm still as wrong for you as ever?"

She looked up at him, her expression truly tortured. "*I* am wrong, too," she said sadly. "I am wrong for you. Why can't you understand?"

He took a deep breath and stepped farther away, studying her coldly. "But Priscilla's not," he said, his voice low. "Priscilla's perfect for me, don't you think?"

Ava made a slight choking sound and bowed her head. "In some ways, yes."

"Priscilla doesn't have ice water running through her veins," he charged. Ah, hell, what was he saying? He didn't want to push her but he couldn't help it. It was the only way he saw a piece of the real person.

Ava raised her head. "Priscilla doesn't need ice water."

He laughed slightly, hopelessly. "Neither do you, Ava." With that, he moved past her and out the door.

Chapter Twelve

Ava stood trembling against the wall, staring at the open doorway through which Angell had disappeared. She didn't move—she couldn't—not even to push the door shut, but she listened to his angry stride down the corridor and wished with every step he would turn around and come back. She wanted to be convinced he was right. Dear Lord, why didn't he come back and show her—with his words, with his hands, with his lips—that he was right and she was wrong and everything could be all right between them.

She closed her eyes and bit her knuckles, trying to imagine explaining to her father, with none of the elaborate lies and schemes she'd built for Priscilla, that she wanted to marry Joshua Angell, a nobody they'd plucked out of a jail cell in a backwoods Missouri town. She couldn't do it; she knew she couldn't do it. And the ruthless clutch of her stomach at the prospect told her it would be wrong to try.

She squeezed her hands to her middle and took a step toward the door. Her knees wobbled, and she wished she could let herself dissolve into tears on the floor. But if she allowed even that much emotion, she knew she would never regain control.

She reached for the doorknob at the same moment Harvey appeared, his hand raised as if to knock.

"Oh, Ava," he blustered, running the raised hand through his hair instead. "Thank God you're still up. May I come in?"

Without waiting for a reply, he swept past her. Ava stared after him.

"I simply don't know *what* to do with your sister." He paced to the window and pushed aside the drapes, speaking to the glass.

Ava used the moment of self-absorption to try to collect herself, wiping hastily at damp lashes, straightening her hair, collar, sleeves, skirt.

"She's completely indifferent to her problems," Harvey continued. "There is no sense of reality or responsibility or even *concern* for her own future." He dropped the curtain and paced to a chair, standing behind it to knead the cushioned back with agitated hands. "Honestly, Ava. She's acting like an obstinate, pig-headed, irresponsible—" He flung out a hand as he turned back to her and froze when he caught sight of her face. "Ava, what's the matter? What on earth has happened?"

Ava blinked. Then, noting the open door, she pushed it shut. "Nothing's happened," she said, her voice as steady as she could manage. Her hands fluttered to her hair again. She kept her eyes averted. "Go on. You were saying? She's a—an obstinate, irresponsible pig . . ."

Harvey was silent. Ava risked a look at him and saw him gazing thoughtfully at the door, his mouth open as if about to speak.

He paused. Then, "Was Angell just here?"

The mention of his name brought an uncomfortable feeling to the pit of her stomach—a longing so strong that she was sure it showed on her face. "What—why do you ask?" The words were pitifully weak.

Harvey's eyes shifted to hers. "Because I just passed him in the hall looking a bit put out. And now you . . ."

"Nothing's the matter with me." Ava moved past him, grateful that her legs still carried her. "Can I get you some sherry?"

She stopped at the sideboard and uncorked the crystal decanter. A moment before she intended, the stopper slipped from her fingers and clattered between the bottles. "Sorry," she murmured, dribbling the liquid into a glass with unsteady hands.

She turned to offer it to Harvey and jumped at finding him immediately behind her. The sherry jerked and splashed onto her fingers.

He took the glass from her hand and set it on the sideboard. His expression was intent, and had she been in a different frame of mind, Ava knew she would have been surprised, as opposed to mortified, at his level of concern.

He took her hands in his and led her to a chair. "Come sit down. You're in a state." Despite herself, she noted the softness of his palms and remembered with a flush the hard callouses on Angell's.

She let him seat her, sinking with fatigue into the chair.

"It's Angell, isn't it?" he said quietly.

Shame rose up and consumed her in a scorching heat. "I—" Her voice squeaked. "I'd rather not talk about it."

Harvey seated himself in the opposite chair with a long, low exhale. "Good Lord," he muttered.

Embarrassment made her straighten. "It's nothing I can't handle."

Harvey took off his glasses and rubbed the bridge of his nose. "I'm sorry, Ava." His voice was muffled behind his hand. "I'm so sorry. This is all my fault."

Ava sniffed and eyed him. "*Your* fault?"

He rubbed his whole face, then replaced his glasses. "Yes, I saw it coming. The man's been in love with you from the beginning. I . . ." He laughed incredulously. "I thought it didn't matter."

Tears pricked Ava's eyes and she blinked rapidly. How stupid they'd both been, thinking that what Angell did and thought and felt didn't matter. It wasn't until her own feelings had emerged that any of it *mattered*.

Lord, Angell was right. She was a snob. And so were Harvey and Priscilla and probably everyone else she knew. She buried her face in her hands.

"Ava, he didn't—he hasn't—" The dread in Harvey's voice caused her to stiffen. "He hasn't acted on his feelings, has he? I mean, he didn't *do* anything . . . ?"

She'd known the question was coming, but it was all she could do to keep the anger inside—anger mostly at herself. It was always what *Angell* had done, what problem *Angell* had caused. Nobody would ever ask what sort of trouble Ava had gotten herself into. Nobody would consider for a second that she might have asked for his kiss.

Tears dripped through her fingers. She shook her head.

"Well, thank God for that." He let out his breath and lay his handkerchief tactfully on her lap. "Then what, if I might ask . . . ?"

Silence descended as Ava tried to collect herself. Did Harvey know? Had he seen how she felt about Angell, the way he'd seen Angell's feelings? She thought briefly about inventing some story, some reason for her turmoil, but before she could muster the energy, her questions were answered.

Harvey uttered a low, incredulous, "Oh, God. Oh, no." Then he took her by the forearm and lowered one of her hands to expose her tear-stained face. "Ava. *You've* fallen for *him*?"

She wanted to laugh at the tragic tone of his voice, but she couldn't. The words made it all real. It was too stupid of her, too unthinkable that she, Ava Moreland, had fallen in love with a cowboy. Worse—a cowboy who was her sister's fiancé.

"Oh, Harvey." The words crested on a sob. "Please don't hate me for it. You—you know him—you *see*, don't you? I know it's impossible, completely—" She swiped at her eyes, then picked up the handkerchief and pressed it to her face. "Completely inappropriate. I *know*, I know all that. But—but he's a good man.

He's nothing like . . . anyone. No one else would understand and believe me; they won't have to. But surely *you* see, don't you, Harvey? You know him."

Through watery eyes she looked at him, pleading for understanding, for anything to lessen her terror at her own admission.

Harvey's stricken face did not reassure her. He stared at his shoes, hands clasped, white-knuckled between his knees.

Panic gripped her. She was making a fool of herself, not just in front of Harvey but in front of herself. She'd fallen for a man they'd unearthed out of nowhere. If Harvey didn't understand it, after all the time they'd spent together, her mistake must be beyond pernicious. Over the last months, she and Harvey had been so united in both purpose and mind, despite small disagreements, that for him to find her circumstances shocking was almost more than she could bear.

"I didn't mean for it to happen. And I know, I know, I know it's impossible. But Harvey, surely it isn't so abhorrent. Tell me you can understand it, just a little."

Harvey's face was a mask of astonished comprehension, his eyes focused inward as if putting all the pieces together. Finally, he bent his head and rubbed his hands on his thighs. "No, no," he said, almost absently. "I—Angell's a good man."

Relief for the simple statement undid her. A long, shuddering sob escaped her. "Thank you," she choked. "Thank you for that. I know you haven't liked him."

Harvey swallowed and shook his head, eyes still on the floor. "That's not true."

She glanced at him to see if he joked, then straightened her shoulders and attempted to wipe the traces of tears from her face. "We needn't speak of this again." She inhaled tremulously. "And we'll leave for New York tomorrow. The sooner we get this over with, the better."

Harvey looked at her but said nothing, his expression grave. Ava had a hard time meeting his eyes.

"I'll make the arrangements," he said.

She nodded and pressed her lips together to stop their quivering. "Thank you."

He rose and clasped his hands together. "You, ah . . ." He looked around the room distractedly. "You get some sleep. It'll be all right."

A weight descended in her chest at the words. There was only one way it would be all right, one very painful way—Angell would marry and she would never see him again. "Yes, I know. I'll be fine. I'm sorry to have burdened you."

"No burden." He turned back and gave her a strange look, intent, confused. "You can trust me, Ava."

"I know, Harvey." She stood slowly, wondering at his expression. "I never doubted it."

They took the train, a first-class car all to themselves, and bade Embrey to return with the coach. Returning via carriage would have taken far too long, and Ava was in no mood to be in company any longer than necessary.

Angell ignored her, concentrating on Priscilla, and a more willing audience he could not have found. Priscilla smiled or laughed at everything he said, teased him in return and generally acted the devoted betrothed.

Harvey and Ava sat forward in their seats, staring morosely out the window.

"I suppose it's a good thing they get along so well," Harvey said, after they'd been en route for some time.

"Oh, yes," Ava replied. Her eyes shifted to where the two sat a short distance away.

Priscilla held Angell's hand open on her lap. With one finger, she traced a line on his palm. Ava was not close enough to hear what she said, but the flirtatious curve of her mouth and the sidelong glances could not be mistaken.

"I hope she'll explain to him about Father," she murmured, unable to take her eyes from the two. There was something so—*kindred* about them.

Harvey answered in a surprisingly bitter tone. "I

wouldn't count on it. Nothing so practical as that is going to interrupt her game."

Ava turned to him. "What makes you think it's a game, Harvey? They're to be married. She's just trying to make the best of it."

Harvey picked up his book from his lap and frowned into it. "She's just trying to drive us mad."

Ava glanced back at Angell and Priscilla in time to see Priscilla's eyes dart away from Ava. Sudden dread descended on her. "What would make her think she could?"

Harvey didn't answer. When Ava looked back at him, he was reading intently, a muscle in his jaw flexing intermittently.

"Harvey," she said, "tell me. Why would Priscilla do that—unless . . . Does she know . . . That night at dinner—does she know . . . ?"

Harvey's lips pressed together tightly before answering. "She doesn't know anything, Ava. She's a spoiled little girl who's been pulled from her own fires too many times."

Ava stared at him. "Are you saying we should have left her on her own in this crisis?"

"She should have gone away."

"But she would have come back with the child. She said as much."

Harvey slammed the book shut with a resounding *clap*. Priscilla's voice was abruptly silenced. Ava chanced a glance at Angell and her sister and found them both staring at Harvey.

Harvey stood and gave Priscilla a withering glare, then turned to Ava and bowed. "My apologies. You're quite right, of course, but I can no longer talk about the situation with equanimity. I trust you'll forgive my need for solitude." With that, he stalked to the back of the car.

Angell watched him go and smiled. It was a grim smile, but still, he liked it when circumstances met his expectations.

"Miss Priscilla," he began, eyes still on Harvey, "may I ask you something personal?"

Priscilla's blue eyes narrowed, and her angelic features grew wary. "Not, I hope, the question on everyone's mind. I thought you were smarter than that."

He shifted his gaze to her, letting it linger a bit longer than might be comfortable. "I don't know about smarter. Maybe more careful. No, I want to know what you think of this marriage."

"Fishing for compliments?" One eyebrow raised. Clearly, she expected, and understood, manipulation.

He chuckled. "I don't think I want to know what you think of *me*, exactly. I'm curious about your participation in this scheme. It's been obvious to me all along that Ava cooked the whole thing up."

"Ava and *Harvey*," Priscilla said in a scathing tone. She flopped back against the seat and sank a few sullen inches. "They've got everything figured out. I positively couldn't argue with them."

"Did you try?"

She laughed. Ava's glance flicked over to them, then away.

Still smiling, Priscilla asked, "What do *you* think? Am I one to let others tell me what to do?" She fixed him with a gaze that dared him to say yes.

"I think . . ." He narrowed his eyes. "I think you didn't put up much of a fight at all."

Both brows shot up this time, and her mouth dropped open. "Is that right, Mr. Angell? You believe I stood idly by while others planned my future?"

"Oh, I didn't say that, Miss Priscilla."

"Yes, you did. You said that very thing."

"No. I said I don't think you put up much of a fight. But I don't for a second think you weren't getting your way."

She smiled, but her displeasure was obvious. "What a convenient point of view for yourself. You've concocted it so you can feel good about the wife you're getting, no doubt."

"Hmmm." Angell gazed at Harvey, who sat at the back of the car reading. Probably wasn't getting much out of it, Angell speculated, not the way his eyes kept straying to the moody child next to Angell.

"Why's Harvey so bent out of shape?" he asked.

"Who knows?" Priscilla muttered.

Angell shrugged. "I thought you might."

Priscilla expelled a disgusted breath and let that stand as her answer.

"What about your sister?"

She looked at him out of the corner of her eyes. "What about her?"

"You think she's happy with the way things are working out?"

Priscilla glanced at Ava, who looked out the window beside her, apparently lost in thought. "I don't know," she said carelessly. "Yes, probably. She'll be happy as a pig in—well, you know." She shot him a brief, challenging look. "As soon as everything's all sewn up and *appearances have been maintained,*" she intoned superciliously.

Angell looked at Ava. The blurred trees whipping by the window magnified her stillness. "She doesn't look very happy."

Priscilla looked at her sister again. "Of course not. She never does. It's undignified."

Her flippant tone angered him, but he was careful not to show it. "Maybe she's never happy. What about that?"

Priscilla looked up at him. "What does it matter to you? I believe your only job is to be concerned with *my* happiness."

He laughed carefully. "I don't believe I have much control over your happiness, one way *or* the other, Miss Priscilla."

"But you have control over Ava's?" Her lips curved in a smile that clearly anticipated a juicy morsel.

Angell took her hand in his, laying her palm flat along the broad expanse of his. It was small and white, and plumply soft. "No," he said finally. "But I understand you a whole hell of a lot better than you think."

She frowned, but left her hand on his. "You think so."

He nodded. "I think so."

"What is it you think you understand?"

He thought a moment.

"That I'm a confused and troubled young woman?" she prompted dramatically.

"You're not confused. You know just what you're doing." He traced a line down one of her fingers and up the next.

"But I'm troubled?" She sighed exaggeratedly. "Perhaps *deeply* disturbed?"

"In trouble, but maybe that was of your own choosing."

Priscilla gasped and started to jerk her hand away, but Angell quickly grasped it in his own. "Ah-ah-ah, not so fast," he murmured.

Priscilla glared at him, then glanced around and made a visible effort to calm herself. "That's a despicable thing to say," she said in hushed anger.

"Yes, I know."

"And it isn't true. What you think, it's not true."

He continued to trace the next finger. "No? Then I'm glad."

Priscilla glared at her captive hand. "You know, I thought I liked you," she said petulantly.

He smiled. "But now you don't?"

"I don't know."

After a moment's silence, her fingers curled through his. She leaned provocatively toward him, her elbow on the armrest between them. She drew close and gave him a slow kiss on the cheek. "You're a very strange man," she said so near to his ear he could feel her breath on it.

Angell stilled beneath the kiss but lifted his eyes to the other end of the car. Harvey glared so intently at Priscilla that he didn't notice Angell's gaze, his face red all the way down to his collar.

"And you," he turned his head so their faces were inches apart, "are a very predictable woman."

Her eyes narrowed, but she did not move away. "Are you trying to make me angry?" she asked quietly, her voice throaty.

"Do you want me to kiss you?" Uncompromising eyes punctuated his low-voiced words.

She dropped her gaze, and he noted that she looked sideways down the car.

"Would it help?" he added.

She looked up at him and smiled, sinking slowly back down into her seat. Comprehension dawned in her eyes. "Probably," she said. "But we'll save that for later."

Chapter Thirteen

"Do you see that tall white building, there?" Priscilla gestured with the sable muff on the end of one arm.

Angell nodded.

"That's Father's building. Actually, he owns the whole block, but that's his favorite, so he keeps his office there." She brought the muff back in and snuggled her other hand deeply into it with a shiver. "I simply *abhor* the cold, don't you?"

Angell studied the building. "You sure he's there today? Maybe he's waiting at home for you."

Priscilla pouted. "Good heavens, no. He's always at work. I'll bet he doesn't even know I was due home today, he's so wrapped up in his own little world."

Angell looked at the block of office buildings and believed that Mr. Moreland's world was probably anything but little. "He'd have found out eventually. Maybe we should just wait till he comes home for supper."

Priscilla smirked and gave him a narrow look from the corner of her eye. "Don't tell me you're *afraid* to meet him. Not my fearless cowboy. And after the way

I hear you stood up for Ava—a *gunfight,* after all—
well, I believe I should be insulted."

Angell pushed his hands into his pockets and didn't
laugh. In fact, he was afraid to meet Mr. Moreland.
This would be his first contact with someone who was
to believe the unbelievable tale of his success, and it
made him uneasy.

"Is Harvey's office there, too?"

"Of course, just next to Father's. But he won't be
there now. He's probably still helping Bennis unload
the coach."

Angell thought that he shouldn't be there either for
the same reason. Running off to introduce himself to
Priscilla's father the moment they stepped off the train
struck him as pushing things. But Priscilla had insisted, and Ava had agreed that perhaps it was best to
get the worst over with quickly.

Angell slowed his pace to match Priscilla's distracted ramble as they strolled along Fifth Avenue.
Every now and again, Angell was jostled by one of the
multitudes around them, a rushing businessman or
courier, or he had to stop and step around a child or
stationary adult, but Priscilla continued along unperturbed, one eye trained on the shop windows they
passed. Though he'd been often in St. Louis, Angell
marveled that the people were as thick here on a regular Tuesday as they were in St. Louis with the circus
in town.

"Oh! Look at this one." Priscilla grabbed his arm
and pulled him toward a window. "Isn't it just *divine?*"

On a platform inside the window, an ostentatiously
feathered hat on a false head presided over lesser bonnets like a great crimson swan over ducks.

Angell looked at it doubtfully. "Looks like the slow
turkey on Thanksgiving to me. Where'd they get red
feathers from anyway?"

"They dye them, silly." She bent close to the glass.
"And they're not red, they're *scarlet.* I *must* try it on, I
really must. I can't tell you how many times I've seen
something in a window and returned the next day only
to find it gone."

Angell gave the back of her head a skeptical glance. "Tragic."

"Yes, isn't it?" She tapped a finger against her teeth, then straightened. "I've just got to have it. Are you coming?" she asked, moving toward the door.

Angell stayed where he was. "What about your father?"

She flipped a hand out nonchalantly. "Oh, he can wait. I'll be right back." With that, she disappeared through the door.

Angell looked around, irritated. It was one thing to be on your way to an unpleasant assignation, quite another to have it delayed for the sake of a *hat*, and an ugly one at that.

As he stood on the sidewalk alone, parting people the way a boulder parts creek water, he felt suddenly very alone. Being the outcast in a crowd was not new to him, but alienation from himself was not. He looked down at the double-breasted wool coat he wore and tried to pinpoint the exact reason he was in New York. For a blank, restless moment, the logic of it eluded him, and his sense of displacement was so severe it made him dizzy.

A job, he thought to himself. He was here to do a job.

He backed up to lean against the storefront, clinging to the rough feel of the brick against his back and the comforting way it pulled at the fabric of his coat. A lady with a perambulator ran over his foot without so much as a glance in his direction, much less a "beg pardon," and he clung to that, too, the slight pain in his instep and the scuffed leather of his shoe. He watched her continue past, the feathers in her hat bobbing dispiritedly and looking even less fortunate than the turkey Priscilla was trying on.

Get hold of yourself, he chided, raking a hand through his hair. But the feeling was slow to ebb. Strangely, he thought of the bears he'd seen at the circus in St. Louis. How he'd laughed and applauded with everyone else when they stood on their hind legs and danced in those enormous, ridiculous pink skirts.

The memory brought none of the hilarity of the moment. What he recalled most clearly now was their halting, uncertain movements, and the way he could see the whites of their eyes as people closed in to watch.

He turned to look in the window for Priscilla and spotted her immediately, preening in front of a mirror with two sales clerks and several ladies standing nearby. There was no doubt in his mind they were all telling her she looked great in the thing. God knew, a sales clerk wasn't going to tell her she looked like an upended paintbrush. He contemplated going in and telling her to buy the damn thing and be done with it when he noticed an imperfect reflection in the glass just beside him.

For some reason, the hairs on the back of Angell's neck rose. It was a man and he moved not a muscle; he simply stood a little too close behind Angell, facing the window.

Angell told himself to stop behaving like a gritless pansy. Still, he remained frozen and prayed the person would continue on by. For a long moment, the two of them stood side by side watching Priscilla.

Then, in answer to his worst fears, an oily voice emerged from the reflected pattern beside him.

"Doin' pretty well fer yerself."

Angell's head jerked to the figure beside him. His right hand slid to his side, as if it might find a gun there, then fisted closed on itself.

Thin, dark hair slicked back over Barrett Trace's narrow head. His pointed smile showed stained, crooked teeth. "Yeah, I thought it was you. It's mighty good to see you, Angell."

Angell took a controlled breath and forced an ambiguous expression onto his face as he looked at the man who'd once had the power to make him fear for his life. Even now, confronted with this skeletal, worn-out version of the once ruthless man, it took Angell a minute to realize how much stronger he himself was than the object of his fear.

"Can't say the same for you, Trace," Angell managed in a low voice.

Trace cocked his head and fixed his one, pebble-hard eye on him while the other floated in its milky haze. "Well now, that's a fine welcome for someone coulda been yer kin."

Angell scoffed, a short, disgusted sound. "You were never my kin."

"You don't know that. I coulda been yer daddy." He cackled obscenely, drawing the startled attention of several passersby.

An old rage began climbing the back of Angell's throat. He had vowed to kill this man untold times as a child, and the urge was still strong within him. "You know perfectly well who my daddy is."

"Only 'cause he got there first. Besides, I know who he *was*, Mr. Fancypants." Trace cast a scathing glance at Angell's fine coat and grinned. "He dead these past two year. Reckon that makes you a orphan now, don't it, Angell?"

Angell measured his words, enunciated them slowly. "Better that than kin of yours."

Trace drew himself up and looked around. "You lose yer lady friend?"

Angell felt his insides clutch with the deep panic of one who discovers he's been watched. "Did you follow me here? From St. Louis?"

Trace coughed a little and spit off to the side, then he wiped his mouth with a threadbare glove. A gentleman passing by gave him a disgusted look and side-stepped the offense.

"What do you want?" Angell insisted, a desperate clamor inside him.

"Well . . ." Trace smiled, with far too much confidence. "I seen this here fancy man in St. Louis, a pretty young thing on his arm, an' I thought, man like that could help me in my troubles. Then I looked a little harder, you know, and that's when I said to myself, I said, Holy Christ in Heaven, that there's ole Angell from back home." He laughed, a sound that made Angell's skin crawl. "Yes sir," he continued, "there you were lookin' shiny as a new penny, and I realized right then that maybe like you could help me out with a few bucks . . . seein' as how yer doin' so well an' I done fallen on some hard times."

Angell kept his gaze hard, his words low. "And what did you think would make me help *you* out?"

Trace shrugged and looked casually around. "Well, I thought about that some. I thought, I know that boy always hated me. Reckon I hated him, too. And I got to wonderin'—that's when I hit on it—that pretty girl you got, she know about you?"

A chill swept Angell at the words, as if a thin layer of ice had frosted onto his skin. He managed to jerk his head up and down once.

Trace's black eyes narrowed. "*Everything?* Be honest now, Angell. Wouldn't tek me long to figger out otherwise."

For one long moment, Angell was sure he was going to be sick. With more strength than he knew he possessed, he forced himself to stand placidly in front of Trace.

"What do you want?" he repeated.

Trace cackled again. "That's what I thought. She don't know about you. You wouldn't never get a showy piece like that what with your—"

"So what do you think, Angell?" Priscilla's voice came over Angell's shoulder with the same unexpectedness a symphony orchestra might have produced striking up a tune on the street.

Angell whirled as Trace slunk back a step, eyeing her like a wary dog.

Priscilla stood before them like an exotic queen in full tribal array. Scarlet feathers swept upward from the crown of her head into the frosted air; a matching boa wound around her neck quivered nervously in the winter air. If he'd been in any other frame of mind, Angell would have burst out laughing. As it was, her outrageousness unnerved him. What in *hell* was he doing here?

"That's a hat, Miss Priscilla," he said blankly.

Her laugh bounced through the air and hurt his

ears. "Yes, it is, Angell. Who were you talking to?" she asked, peering around him.

Angell's spine tingled as he turned back toward Trace. A panhandler, he thought to himself. No, someone asking the time . . . Get rid of him and walk away. But when he turned, the emptiness beside him gave him a start. Trace was gone.

"Just a—someone—nobody," he said absently, looking around, unsure whether he hoped to find Trace or not, for while he longed for the man to disappear, it was insidiously frightening not knowing where he was, or what his next move might be.

"Probably just a beggar," she said with disgust. "An unusually creepy one, didn't you think so?"

Angell's eyes continued to rove around and ahead of him as Priscilla took his arm. "Yes, I did, Miss Priscilla. I surely did."

Ava sat in the parlor with her mother and tore at the ends of a knitted afghan with agitated fingers.

"I should have gone with her," Ava said. "Don't you think so? You know how Priscilla is with Father."

"Don't be silly, dear," Frances Moreland said, pouring tea into an eggshell-thin cup. "And stop mutilating that blanket. Why should you be there when you've already said that he's really a *special* friend of Cilla's? Isn't that what you said?"

Ava dropped the fringe she'd laced through her fingers and sat forward to receive the tea. Never had she wished more strongly that she could flounce off to her room and sulk. That's what Priscilla would have done . . . Priscilla who always got what she wanted.

But Ava *should* be there, she felt. It was in everyone's best interest. Priscilla barely knew Angell, and Father could be so intimidating, especially after Priscilla riled him into an overprotective huff.

"Now, tell me again about this man," her mother prompted, sitting erect in her straight-backed chair with a petit four balanced delicately between two fingers. "Where is he from? Has he got any references?"

Ava's nerves quivered at the question, knowing that

Angell was fielding inquiries just like it from her uncompromising father.

"He's very well-respected where he comes from," she said with attempted nonchalance. She was surprised at the trouble she had lying to her mother, even though they'd never been particularly close and they certainly never shared confidences. "He's well-off and a perfect gentleman. You'll love him, Mother. I know you will. Even Harvey approves of him, and you know how difficult he can be. Sometimes I think he's even more obstinate than Father."

Frances smiled. "Yes. You know, I always liked Harvey. Such a protector of the family's virtue."

Ava nearly laughed at that, a nervous, hysterical laugh that no doubt would have curled her mother's hair. The family's virtue was already a good deal beyond Harvey's saving. "He was such a help on the trip. I ought to talk to Father about giving him a bonus."

"But you haven't told me about this Mr. Angell. Such an unusual name . . ." She sipped her tea, a tiny frown of concentration on her face. Not a frown that anybody else would notice, of course, but just enough of an expression that Ava could tell she was thinking.

Her mother held the belief that facial expressions marred one's complexion, so she never allowed herself more than just the barest of movements to accompany her words. Ava could remember times as a child when she would watch her mother, usually when she was with company or at a party, in an effort to detect even one lift of the eyebrows. But she never saw anything other than the tight smile her mother allowed to express politeness. All during the time she was growing up, Ava would practice in front of the mirror, but she could never get her face to behave in so controlled a manner. She thought it must be the real mark of a lady to possess an expression that gave no indication of life.

Ava tried to smooth the worry from her face in preparation for the lie to come. "It is an unusual name. Unfortunately, it's a very sad story," she said with as much detachment as she could muster. "He's originally from somewhere in the South—Georgia, I believe—and his parents passed away when he was very young. During the war, you know."

Her mother hummed sympathetically and nodded.

"So he was left to his own resources and has made a great success of himself in cattle ranching."

One of Frances's fingers tapped the side of her cup thoughtfully, a gesture Ava used to believe was the consequence of all that facial control. "And how did you meet? Who introduced you?"

She took a breath. "It was a bit unorthodox. You most likely won't approve, but you know, they do things differently in the West. They're much more casual about such things."

"Good heavens, you didn't meet him on the street, did you? Oh, I positively *abhor* that sort of familiarity in a man. He sees a pretty girl on the street and simply takes it upon himself—"

"Mother," Ava interrupted. "Please let me finish before you leap to ugly conclusions. *Harvey* met him one evening at dinner. Cilla had a bit of a headache—you know how she'd been feeling a bit weak before we left—and I stayed to read to her. So Harvey was eating alone and was invited to Mr. Angell's table. Mr. Angell was sitting with quite a distinguished group of friends."

"Oh? Were they cattle ranchers as well?" Her finely arched brows, though they had not risen with the inquiry, appeared haughtier to Ava just the same. She used the words *cattle ranchers* in much the same way she might have used *cowboy*.

"I believe they were bankers."

Her mother nodded deeply and the tight smile appeared. "Very good."

Despite herself, Ava breathed a sigh of relief. If she ever found out the truth . . . "And he doesn't actually *live* on the ranch, or work it himself. He simply invests in them and lives off the earnings. More along the lines of a cattle *broker*, really." So you needn't expect him to smell of cows, she wanted to add, knowing the direction of her mother's thoughts.

195

"I see. And how serious is it between him and Priscilla?"

Ava forced the words out. "Well, I believe it's somewhat serious. They're—they're quite enchanted with each other." Ava shifted uncomfortably. It didn't help that this statement was the closest one to the truth in the whole conversation.

"Well." Frances sniffed and placed her cup on the table beside her. "We'll just see how enchanted your father is with him. You know how fussy he can be about his youngest."

Ava dropped her eyes. She was acutely aware of how fussy he was about his youngest. "Yes, I know. But he also respects Harvey's opinion, doesn't he? I mean, Harvey approves of him, as I said, and Harvey is there at the office with them."

"I don't know," Frances said dramatically, implying that even Harvey's good opinion couldn't lessen her husband's predisposition to dislike anyone after Priscilla's hand. "We both know how flighty Cilla can be, and no one knows that better than your father. What he wants to see is Cilla adopting a more mature attitude and taking her time about things. No rushing into anything that could prove disastrous."

Nothing could prove more disastrous than *not* rushing into this, Ava thought morosely.

A knocked sounded at the door. As a matter of course, Ava said nothing and Frances waited a good fifteen seconds before calling to the servant to enter. It had to be Bennis, the butler, for no one other than the family had access to the back parlor, and the family never knocked. It was her mother's policy to wait before allowing the servants entrance on the point that it didn't do to have them think she wasn't busy when the door was shut.

Sure enough, Bennis's studiously impassive face appeared around the edge of the door as it swung inward. With a short bow, he said in his deep, rich voice, "Mr. Cullum Henderson to see Miss Ava, ma'am."

Her mother turned back to her with the tight smile. "Oh, dear. He is so prompt, isn't he? He's been after

196

me for a month—practically since the day you left— about when you were planning to return."

Ava sighed and closed her eyes. "Must I see him now, Mother? I've only just arrived, and I'd like to take a nap before supper."

The barely detectable frown returned. "Ava, you should give him a minute. He's been so *anxious*, and he's come all the way over here. And you did rather shock us with this sudden adventure of yours. It's no wonder the boy's been heartsick over your absence."

"He's not a boy; he's thirty-seven years old. And he hasn't been heartsick. I'm sure he just hasn't had anyone else to talk to since I left. He's not exactly a scintillating conversationalist."

"Ava! I'm surprised at you, being so cruel."

"It's not cruel, Mother. It's true."

Frances set her cup down with a controlled *chink* of ire and stood. "Very well. Bennis, tell Mr. Henderson that Miss Ava is indisposed. Perhaps she'll think better of it tomorrow."

Ava sank under the weight of her mother's disapproval, and it occurred to her that this might be a golden opportunity to stop talking about Angell. "No, no, I'll see him now. I might as well. I'm sure I'll feel the same way tomorrow."

Frances shook her head. "I don't know what's gotten into you, Ava Moreland. I don't think this trip has been good for you."

Ava did laugh then, bitterly, and stood in order to avoid feeling the chastened child. "You're right, Mother. I don't think it has been either. Bennis, send him in."

"Yes ma'am," he said with another bow. After a quick look at Frances, who nodded, he disappeared.

"I thought you liked Cullum," her mother persisted. "You know, it's always been our hope that you and—"

Ava turned on her abruptly, fixing her mother with a look that stopped the dreadful sentence she was about to utter for the thousandth time. "I do like Cullum. I just see him for what he is."

The aggression in her mother's perfect posture was unmistakable. "And what is that?"

She sighed, giving up. "He's a bore, Mother. You can't deny that. He bores everyone, including you."

The door swung inward again and Bennis announced their guest.

Hat in hand, thinning hair combed straight back, Cullum Henderson made his stooped way into the room. He always looked as if he were about to be rapped across the knuckles for some minor misdemeanor, Ava thought. She wished she could infuse him with some life, some self-respect, some little spark of energy that might alter him from the gray, lifeless presence he was.

"Hello, Cullum," she said cordially, extending her hand. She would show her mother she could have independent thoughts and still behave like a lady.

"Miss Ava, I'm so pleased you've returned. How was your journey?" He took her hand with the softest of touches, lifted it toward his lips and kissed the air above it.

"It was very long and very tiring. I'm happy to be home." She removed her hand from his lingering grasp and moved to the sofa.

"No happier than everyone is to have you home, I'm sure," he murmured, glancing around as if afraid to come farther into the room.

"Would you have some tea, Cullum?" Frances asked, moving toward him, hand outstretched.

Cullum bent over it and nodded. "Thank you, madam," he said to her fingers.

Frances looked at his bowed head and glanced at her daughter. Ava raised her brows.

"Come along then, young man," Frances snapped. "Come sit next to Ava on the sofa."

Humility was not something her mother had much respect for, Ava knew. But in this instance, her mother's aggravation was more with Ava's being right than any ineptitude on Cullum's part. Ava was half-tempted to take advantage of the fact by asking about Cullum's pigeons, but she knew her mother would not forgive that. It had become something of a family joke how one night at a party Cullum had cornered her mother and regaled her with stories of his pet pigeons for over an hour after Frances had done nothing more than express admiration for a watercolor of a sparrow her hostess had painted.

Cullum perched on the edge of the sofa at the opposite end from Ava, so far that she had to rise to hand him his tea.

"Thank you, Miss Ava. Thank you so much." Carefully, he placed his hat on the arm of the couch.

"Why don't I get Bennis to take your hat," Frances offered.

Cullum looked up at her in alarm and placed a swift hand on the crown. "Oh, no. No, no. I'll keep it with me."

Ava gave her mother a significant look.

Frances sighed. "So, tell me. Cullum," she said with the tight smile, "how are your parents? Are they planning any interesting parties or anything?"

Something about the way her mother asked the question made Ava suspicious. Cullum's answer doubled it.

"Oh, yes. That's right. The party. Can you all come?" He looked expectantly from one to the other of them.

Ava nearly smiled because her mother looked so frustrated. "What party is that, Cullum?" she asked.

"Mother's dinner party. The day after tomorrow. We know it's dreadfully short notice," he recited as if by rote, "but we were hoping to catch you just as you arrived, before your busy schedule filled up." He smiled, pleased with himself.

"Of course, we'd be delighted to come," Frances said. She sat back in her chair and gazed smugly at him, hands folded at her waist.

Cullum smiled back, apparently more relaxed now that his task was completed.

"Blast it all, Angell." Priscilla's voice blew through the room as the door burst open. "I don't know *why* you're so concerned about *him*."

She was through the door, her bag tossed at a

nearby chair, before she noticed the stunned group around the tea table.

Ava gaped at her sister's shockingly red head and the array of feathers tall enough to graze the top of the doorjamb. Poor Cullum, she noted after a moment, was so enthralled with the vision that the hand holding his teacup dipped dangerously low.

"Oh. Hello," Priscilla halted and said with a quickly donned smile.

Angell stopped in the doorway, surveying the group with surprised, apprehensive eyes.

Though she tried to stop it, Ava's heart jumped to her throat at the sight of him. Perhaps it was the obvious comparison to Cullum, but Ava thought he'd never looked so handsome. It was as if she were seeing him for the first time all over again, only this time as a gentleman in her drawing room, impeccably dressed. He was, in that moment, a dream come to life.

"Pardon us," he said with a near-perfect bow. "We didn't realize anyone was home." He sent a sharp glance to Priscilla, who caught it and lobbed back an unconcerned grin.

The words were pure poetry, relatively speaking. In fact, the very juxtaposition of them with the unpolished speech from her memory was enough to make her smile a warm private smile.

"Mother," Priscilla cooed and strode toward her, arms outstretched.

Frances took her hands. "Priscilla, dear, whatever have you got on your head?" She pecked her daughter's cheek while maintaining a wary eye on the crimson bonnet.

"It's new. Isn't it divine?" Priscilla twirled once in front of them, then realized her oversight. "Oh, hello Cullum." She held out a hand, which he struggled to take while righting his teacup and standing.

"Hello, Miss Priscilla," he mumbled.

"It's quite a hat." Ava nodded, wryly.

Priscilla turned on her. "Why, that's just what Angell said. He said it looked like the slow turkey on Thanks-

giving." She turned a scandalized look on her mother.
"Now, is that anything for a gentleman to say about a
lady's hat?"

Ava cleared her throat and rose. "Mother, this is
Joshua Angell. Mr. Angell, this is our mother, Frances
Moreland."

Ava watched carefully as Frances turned her gaze
to Angell. To her amazement, a slow flush stole into
her mother's cheeks.

"Pleasure to meet you, ma'am," he said, bending low
over her hand. Though he'd tried to hide it at first, his
native drawl was evident with these words, but for
some reason it only deepened the sensual flutter of her
stomach. It's his voice, she thought, it's his voice that
unnerves me. Against her will, she heard it again in
her head, close in, just before his kiss. *What do you
want, Ava?*

Ava mentally shook herself and watched as her
mother's eyes took in Angell's dark, glossy hair, his
broad shoulders and the impeccable cut of his suit.

"How do you do?" Frances said.

"Frankly, Mrs. Moreland," Angell said, "I'd be doing
a bit better if I hadn't just been dragged up and down
Fifth Avenue by your daughter. When we couldn't find
Mr. Moreland, Miss Priscilla felt the need to wander
all over town showing off this," he glanced at the
feathers on Priscilla's head, "new article of clothing."

Ava closed her eyes. Coarse, that's what her mother
would call him. An amusing little speech like that, in
conjunction with the turkey comment Priscilla had
mentioned, would be more than enough to gall her
prim, proper mother.

"Poor Mr. Angell."

Ava's eyes popped open at the indulgence in her
mother's tone.

"It's so nice to meet someone who understands our
little Cilla so well." Frances's smile was positively fat-
uous, and she had not yet let go of his hand. "Ava's
been telling me you're something of a, well, a *special*
friend of our Priscilla's."

Angell's lips curved into a small smile that made

Ava's face hot, even though it was directed at her mother. Did she imagine it, or did he actually look pleased?

"I'd like to think so," he said. "And I'm real grateful for you letting me visit with her."

"We're happy to have you, truly. But please . . ." Frances turned fractionally toward Ava and Cullum. "Let me introduce you to Cullum Henderson. He's a *special* friend of Ava's."

Chapter Fourteen

Ava's mother was a formidably built matron with a high, corseted bosom and an impressive mount of silvering brown hair. She was, Angell could see at once, a woman of great control and little imagination.

Next to her, Ava's spirit glowed like a live coal. After her mother's comment about Cullum Henderson's desired role in the family, Ava's face glowed as well, red and hot as a blacksmith's iron. With every utterance the toad made, Angell was sure the hue deepened.

"Ava, why don't you walk Cullum to the door?" Mrs. Moreland suggested as Cullum lifted his sorry frame from the sofa and made a shuffling inclination toward the exit.

Ava glared at her mother. "Bennis can show him the door."

Mrs. Moreland looked down her nose at her daughter, clearly not happy with the breech of obedience. "But who," she insisted, "will show him to Bennis?"

Angell pressed his lips together to keep a smile from his face; for some reason, Ava's discomfort gratified him. Perhaps it was because he knew she was embarrassed by the toad, or perhaps it was because her conviction about marrying appropriately was so devilishly problematic in this instance. In any case, relief was his primary emotion upon learning of her parents' design that she marry such a dullard. If anything might force her to loosen up, the threat of marriage to Cullum Henderson was a good bet.

"Oh, very well," Ava capitulated, snatching up her skirts and moving hastily to Cullum. Despite his timid stride, he'd almost reached the door. "Thank you for coming, Cullum, and thank your mother for the kind invitation."

Cullum turned at the door and gazed vaguely back at the group. "Yes, and you all can come," he said, encompassing them with a weak sweep of his hat. "Thursday night. Seven-thirty. Are you interested in birds at all, Mr. Angell?" Cullum's watery eyes settled briefly upon him.

"Birds?" Angell repeated, with an involuntary glance at Priscilla's hat. "Sure, I like birds."

Cullum smiled. "Perhaps I could show you my birds, then. On Thursday."

Angell smiled back at the man, a modicum of pity surfacing in his heart. "All right," he said.

"If there's time," Ava said, hustling Cullum to the door and out into the foyer.

Priscilla and Angell took seats side-by-side on the couch, the crimson hat beside them, while Mrs. Moreland, sitting in a nearby chair, fixed a look of unmasked scrutiny on them.

"Mr. Angell, my eldest daughter tells me you were discovered in Missouri and introduced quite without references," she stated, taking his measure as she issued the challenge.

Angell half expected Priscilla to say something flippant to ward off the serious tone, as she did with Ava, but in this instance, she kept silent. He threw a glance her way only to find her staring out the window, as if resigned to an interrogation of her suitor.

"Of course, you know," Mrs. Moreland continued, "in ordinary circumstances her family would find this absolutely unacceptable." She took up her teacup and sipped, not taking her eyes from his face.

"Well," he began, then cleared his throat, "it was unusual, I have to say. But no disrespect was intended, or, you know, shown." He cleared his throat again. "Perhaps Miss Ava's already told you, but it was Mr. Winters I met first, and he introduced me to your daughters. But Mrs. Moreland, if there'd been any other way, any more suitable way, I want you to know I'd have preferred it myself."

The words were true, for the most part, and his conviction on the last sentence must have carried in his voice for she smiled. Kindly, he thought.

"From all I've heard of the West, I'm sure that your options were limited. It's just that we've been so careful all through the girls' lives. If we seem a tad suspicious, it's because of a commitment to maintain the quality of our family affiliations. It is not meant to be a personal reflection on you, you understand. The future of our daughters is of paramount importance to us, Mr. Angell, *paramount*."

Angell cleared his throat once more. "Yes, ma'am, and that's mighty commendable."

"Mr. Henderson, whom you've just met," she continued, acknowledging his words with just the barest of nods, "is from one of *the* most respectable families in New York, so we have no worries for Ava. Both families could not be happier about such an alliance, and I believe she'll come around in time."

The door opened. "What are you talking about, Mother?" Ava asked in a glacial voice that indicated she'd heard at least a portion of her mother's comment. She took the remaining armchair.

Unperturbed, Mrs. Moreland picked up her cup. "I was just educating Mr. Angell about the family. You know, we were all so happy when Cam got married—that's Priscilla's brother," she explained to Angell. "The next in line is naturally Ava, and it is just so *logical* for the Morelands and the Hendersons—"

"Mother," Ava warned. "I've explained to you many times—"

"Well, I don't care, Ava. You're going on twenty-five, and it's well past time for you to start thinking about these things. I will not have a spinster for a daughter."

Blood stormed Ava's face, and she obviously couldn't bring herself even to glance in Angell's direction. "Mother! Must we discuss this in front of our *guest*?"

"Now Ava, you said yourself Mr. Angell is practically family . . ." Mrs. Moreland bestowed a smile on Angell, which he returned with surprise.

Ava glanced at him. "Mother has always considered Cullum part of the family, too," she explained. "It's why she can't get it out of her head that he might someday become another son."

"No one could be more appropriate for you, dear," Mrs. Moreland said. "His family is as old as ours, and he's so proper, just as you are. The two of you really have quite a lot in common."

Angell couldn't resist. "So long as he's appropriate," he pitched in, watching Ava's discomfort intensify, "I can't see what argument you might have against it, Miss Ava."

If he'd said it to win Mrs. Moreland's regard, he would have been richly rewarded. But since he said it to taunt Ava, he was compensated in kind.

"You're absolutely right, Mr. Angell," she said firmly, her gray eyes fixed on him solemnly. "I applaud your sensibility. Such considerations should always be foremost. Though in this case—"

Mrs. Moreland leaned over and squeezed Ava's arm, beaming. "Oh, Ava, I'm so glad to hear you say so. I was just saying I *knew* you'd come around."

Ava opened her mouth to respond just as the door opened, and all heads swung to see who it was.

"Glad to hear her say what?" a slim white-haired man asked gruffly.

He wore a black broadcloth cutaway coat with the ease of a cowboy in leather, Angell thought, and his eyes—gray like Ava's—were steadfast and flinty as gunmetal. He wasn't a large man, in fact some might say small-boned, but his presence was enormous.

Everyone rose at once. Mrs. Moreland approached her husband with a subdued air of excitement and accepted his chaste peck on the cheek as she spoke. "Ava's just been telling Mr. Angell how the appropriateness of a marriage such as hers to Cullum Henderson should be of foremost consideration."

Angell saw the surprise on Mr. Moreland's face and immediately liked him for it. As well, beneath the man's bushy white moustache, Angell thought he detected a hint of amusement.

"My dear, has a few weeks out West altered you so severely, then?" He moved to take Ava's hands.

Ava smiled more genuinely than Angell had yet seen. "Not so severely, Father," she said, offering her cheek. "Mother didn't let me finish my sentence."

He chuckled. "No doubt. And no doubt as to how it would have ended, either." He turned to Priscilla. "And how is my youngest, eh?" He kissed her on the top of the head as she gave him a quick hug.

"Oh, Father, I'm just happy to be home. I missed you so." She hugged him again and wound her arm through his as she turned to Angell. "And Father, I want you to meet someone very special. This—" she splayed a hand proudly in Angell's direction—"is Mr. Joshua Angell. We all call him Angell, though, don't we, Ava? He's a *darling*, Father. I just know you'll love him."

Angell felt the gaze of the man as forcefully as the grip on his hand. "How d'you do?" he said with a nod. Though he met the man's eyes squarely, inside he fought a desire to squirm. Mr. Moreland had the expression of one who was never duped, and Angell didn't flatter himself that he would be the first.

"How do you do, Mr. Angell."

"We found Angell just in the nick of time, didn't we, Ava?" Priscilla fluttered like a pampered pet on her father's arm. "After that long, dreadful tour through those awful backward towns, we just *happened* on him, just like that." She beamed into her father's face. "Imagine, such a gem amongst all those rocks. We *had* to invite him back to stay."

"Oh? You'll be staying with us?" The hard eyes probed him again.

"With your permission, sir." Angell inclined his head, reluctant to say any more than was absolutely necessary. He had the uncomfortable feeling that the more he said, the more he would unintentionally reveal.

His fears were immediately confirmed.

"Georgia," Mr. Moreland said, one lean finger extended. "I'd know that drawl anywhere. Am I right?"

The man's delight was at once relieving and excruciating. Angell didn't have to worry about concealing his accent anymore; he just had to worry about the man's instincts and all the other secrets he could conceivably deduce.

Angell smiled politely. "That's correct, sir."

Mr. Moreland's bushy white brows drew together. "Whereabouts?"

"I grew up on the Altamaha, southeastern part of the state." The mere memory of it caused his gut to clench.

Mr. Moreland leaned back on his heels and looped a thumb in his vest pocket. "Ah, I know it well. Beautiful country. You're of plantation stock, then?"

Angell chuckled ironically; plantation stock, indeed. He tried to ignore the alarm in his head that sounded whenever the subject of home arose. "That's right. My father owned a few thousand acres on the river. Cotton, mostly. Some tobacco."

"You weren't of a mind to follow in his footsteps, I presume?"

Angell's face grew hot under the older man's scrutiny, but he forced himself to maintain eye contact.

"I wasn't given the choice, sir. I had a brother more suited to the job."

Mr. Moreland nodded. "So you took off to find your fortune out West, eh?"

He inclined his head once. "That I did."

"He's in cattle," Ava interjected. Angell could have kissed her for stepping in. "He invests in ranches. He's done quite well for himself."

"And am *I* glad of it," Priscilla bubbled with a laugh. "Can you see me living on a plantation?" She laughed again, oblivious to the sudden silence around her. "I mean, if he hadn't told me we could live in New York, I *never* would have agreed to marry him!"

Angell's mouth dropped open, and he heard Ava gasp. Mrs. Moreland froze into stone, while her husband's white brows drew together over darkening eyes.

"What did you say, Priscilla?" Mr. Moreland's tone was quiet, but it reverberated around the room as if he'd bellowed the words in a church.

Priscilla evidently realized her error and gasped, covering her mouth with both hands. Her eyes sought first Ava's, then Angell's.

"Oh, I'm *sorry*, Angell." She disentangled herself from Mr. Moreland and rushed to Angell. Her hands settled on his chest, and she turned simpering eyes up into his face. "I've ruined it now, haven't I. Oh God, I'm so *stupid*. Can you ever forgive me?"

Angell stared into her face, his own slack with shock, and saw through an astounded haze that she lied. It was clear in the laughing limpid pools of her eyes. She'd done it on purpose. The surprise he felt was immediately replaced with anger. Of course she lied. *He* was the stupid one. He should have seen it coming. She *wanted* the plan to fail.

Anger emerged as Priscilla's nonchalant abuse of her sister's efforts became clear. He circled Priscilla's waist with one hand and drew her around to his side. "It's all right, darling. We had to tell them. I'm just happy not to pretend anymore."

His eyes grazed Mrs. Moreland's white face and came to rest on Ava's. Her hands covered her mouth, just as Priscilla's had, but in her eyes was genuine fear. Priscilla played a game, but Ava's intentions were serious. She looked ill. In his mind, he saw himself going to her, holding her against him as he now held Priscilla, and making a plea to her father for *their* future. But that was impossible. On so many levels, impossible.

He met Mr. Moreland's hard eyes. "Sir, let me apologize for the, ah, haste of our decision and this *precipitous* announcement." He nearly tripped over the word, but his pride would not allow it. He concentrated on Ava, on the devastation he could see in her eyes. "But we agreed, didn't we, Priscilla," he squeezed her waist hard and heard a small, surprised intake of breath, "that our wishes would come second to your family's."

Priscilla started to speak, but Angell shot her a quelling glance and tightened his grip on her waist again. He looked at Ava, who lowered her hands and watched him with miserable eyes.

He let out a slow breath and looked down. "You see, Mr. Moreland, I love your daughter," he looked back up with the words. "I knew it the first moment I saw her, with a part of me I never knew I had. I only want the best for her, and I'll work hard, harder than anyone else, to keep her happy. So I ask, humbly, Mr. Moreland, you don't know how humbly, for your daughter's hand in marriage. I know you don't know me from Adam, but I'm a good man. And if you'd like to take some time before answering, I'd be more than happy to wait for your answer."

Priscilla cowered against his side, seemingly abashed by her gaffe, but Angell didn't doubt that her trembling had more to do with suppressed glee than fear of repercussion.

Mr. Moreland studied him a long, uncomfortable moment while the clock ticked loudly and the other occupants of the room waited, barely breathing.

"I do not approve of this," Mr. Moreland said finally, his voice deep and decisive. Angell could imagine him addressing Congress in such a voice. "However, because I dislike acting *precipitously* . . ." he fixed Angell with a condemning eye, "I shall wait before making a final decision."

"Talk to Harvey," Ava burst out.

Mr. Moreland's gaze snapped to her.

"Yes, by all means, talk to Harvey," Priscilla seconded.

Angell had half a mind to move his hand from her waist to her mouth.

"Harvey knows about this mess?" Mr. Moreland demanded. The ice in his tone was enough to make Angell pity Harvey, which might have been refreshing in other circumstances.

"He knows Mr. Angell. He met him first," Ava persevered. "He approves of him."

She was grasping, and it was as obvious to Mr. Moreland as it was to Angell.

"I cannot believe Harvey allowed this," Mr. Moreland said with disgust. "And you, my dear, I would have expected more of you," he continued to Ava. "I assume Priscilla will go off half-cocked at any given moment, but you've got a head on your shoulders, Ava. I'm disappointed in you."

Angell bit back a curse but could not stop the words that followed it. "Begging your pardon, sir, but Miss Ava couldn't be her sister's keeper. She tried to make us see reason, but we're of a similar stubborn mind, I guess, Priscilla and me, so Miss Ava was left with nothing to do but help us. Because she loves her sister, sir. She'd do anything for her family, I know."

Mr. Moreland turned back to him, an inscrutable expression in his eyes, and even Priscilla looked up at him with something other than duplicity in hers.

"You say you want the best for my daughter, Mr. Angell. Do you consider yourself to be the best?" Mr. Moreland asked.

The cynical laugh that rose to his lips was probably the wrong answer, but he let it go anyway. "I'm not anywhere near the best, sir, and that's why I can't do the noble thing and leave her. But for some reason, she's got a regard for me and, being the selfish man I am, I can't turn it away. But I'll try, sir, maybe harder than the fancy men you can find around here, to make sure she's happy."

Mr. Moreland's eyes narrowed thoughtfully. "Hmmm. We'll see, Mr. Angell. We'll see. Have a financial statement to me within the week." He turned away. "Frances? Come with me."

Mrs. Moreland hurried over, and the two disappeared through the door.

The second they were out of sight, Angell dropped his hand from Priscilla's waist and abruptly stalked to the window. *"Damn it,"* he exclaimed, stuffing his fists into his pockets.

"What on *earth* were you thinking?" Ava pounced. "Of all the *stupid*—"

Priscilla drew herself up. "Well, Ava, I'm *sorry*, but it just slipped out. I was getting so involved in my role that I just kept on talking, and before I knew it . . ."

"Before you knew it, you'd ruined months of work and planning and worry for your future." Ava's voice broke on the last word, and Angell turned to look at her.

Ava sank onto the sofa; Angell rested his weight on the windowsill.

"He'll never approve of it now," Ava said, her face tired, her tone blank. "Never. God help you, Priscilla, you're going to have to give that baby up."

Priscilla whirled on her sister, her face flaming and her hands fisted at her sides. "Don't you dare say that," she growled. "I don't care *what* happens to me. I'll *never* give this baby up."

Ava turned on her with fatigue and despair. "You won't have a choice. Do you have *any* idea what will happen if Father finds out about this? He'll have that baby shipped out the moment it's born, and *you* may never see the light of a New York day again."

Fear flitted across Priscilla's face, followed quickly by bravado. "It's *my* baby. He can't do anything to me. I'll run away. He won't find me—"

"Don't be a fool," Ava scoffed, her hopelessness as obvious as Priscilla's fear. "Don't underestimate what you're up against. You'll lose everything, Priscilla, believe me. If you leave, you'll have no place to come back to. And where would you go? What would you do for money? Do you know what it's like to bear a child? You can't simply pop in when the time is right and do it, you know. You'll be incapacitated for weeks, possibly months. How will you live?"

"Don't treat me like a child, Ava," Priscilla threatened, her voice quivering. "I know what it's like being pregnant, better than *you* do. I know what it's like to be sick every morning, to feel my body change in strange, scary ways. Yes, I know quite a bit more than you do about *a lot* of things." Tears streamed down her face.

"You know what it's like to be spoiled rotten," Ava spat, rising.

"I know what it's like to *love*. You—you have no idea. You're a cold, heartless fish, who's never felt passion about anything, much less a *man*. For you to presume to tell *me* what to do—it's—it's preposterous. You—why you're just going to grow so old and shriveled, you'll have no choice but to marry that old prude Cullum Henderson, who knows less about love than even you do. You'll lie in bed like death while he puts his clammy hands on you, and you'll never learn anything of what *I* know about love—about *desire*." Priscilla's eyes streamed, but she looked at her sister with pity. "And you'll lose, Ava. Because love is the only thing worthwhile. I don't care if they send me to Timbuktu. If I never see another ice angel or champagne fountain or chocolate truffle again in my life, it'll be worth it. Because *I* have known love. And this baby is the proof of it. Yes, proof. And I'm proud of it."

Ava trembled where she stood as they glared at one another. To Angell, Ava looked as if one touch would cause her to shatter into a thousand pieces, while Priscilla looked hard, like an unrepentant murderer on the way to the gallows.

Just when Angell thought Priscilla was about to relent, she drove in the last bitter nail. "Or maybe you'll just be a spinster after all."

Ava's eyes closed, and he could see her swallow hard.

Angell rose to his feet. "Tell me something about this great love of yours," he said to Priscilla from the window, his voice carrying through the room as if he'd opened the sash and let in a gust of frigid air. Both of

213

them turned in surprise, as if they'd forgotten he was there. "Where is he now? Why isn't this brilliant lover here trying to protect you, instead of leaving all that to your sister?"

Priscilla's eyes narrowed, and her lips curled into a sneer. "The cowboy speaks! Go on, Mr. Angell, tell us. Perhaps you know something of love—or isn't your experience *fit* conversation for the drawing room?"

He raised his brows and said coolly, "I never knocked anybody up and left her to deal with it alone, if that's what you're asking." He took slow, thoughtful steps toward the two of them.

"He has reasons," Priscilla defended, with a shade less than total conviction. "Reasons you two, of all people, would appreciate."

"Bull," Angell spat.

Priscilla's brows rose over condescending eyes. "You can dress them up . . ."

"There's no need for this," Ava said. "Angell, don't taunt her."

"Is that what I'm doing? Taunting her?" He looked at Ava, amazed that she could still defend this sister without a heart. "Seems to me I'm just speaking what's on everyone's mind."

"She's emotional," Ava said, bowing her head in the face of his vehemence. "Leave her be."

He laughed incredulously. "She's a liar," he countered. Then he turned on Priscilla. "Why did you do that—spill the beans to your father about the engagement? If you want to get out of this marriage, why don't just you name the father of that baby? Then you could stop dragging everyone all over hell and back trying to save you." Angell stepped close to Priscilla and spoke quietly. "Is it because he doesn't want to be named? Doesn't *he* want *you*, Priscilla?"

Priscilla's face suffused with color, and she stepped back away from him, chin high.

"He wants me," she ground out.

"Then tell us who he is. Come on, Priscilla. Is he ashamed, or are you?"

"Angell," Ava warned.

"You're talking yourself out of a job, aren't you, cowboy?" Priscilla asked. "Maybe you're not very bright after all."

"I think it's you, Priscilla. I think you're the one who's ashamed. What're you going to tell that little baby when he asks who his father is?"

"I'm not ashamed." She held his gaze for a tense moment, then let her eyes slip away.

"*Stop* it, Angell," Ava commanded, the tone of her voice demanding attention.

"Ah, the stalwart sister." Angell turned back to her. "Stepping in just in time to save her sister—again—from embarrassment. Or is it her own embarrassment? Is it *you*, Ava, who's so ashamed? Are you afraid he'll turn out to be someone so low that you can't even bear his name spoken?"

Ava glanced quickly at her sister, then back at Angell. "I have no such fears—"

"Oh, come on, Ava. You've admitted it to me before. Haven't you told Priscilla? Haven't you told her how bad *for the family* it would be to have her unsuitable lover be father to his own child? Lord, what if he turned out to be the gardener? Or the postman?"

Priscilla scoffed.

"You're being unreasonable," Ava protested.

"Am I? Tell me, Ava, tell us both. What's the real reason you've made no effort to discover who the father is?" Though he told himself he pushed her to admit it so they'd both know the kind of woman she really was, his tone had changed with the question. He didn't attack; he implored her for the real answer. He needed to know that it wasn't just shame that made her plan and go through with this charade.

Ava's mouth opened as if she might speak, but for a moment nothing emerged. Angell raised his brows.

She took a shaking, enraged breath, her eyes locked with his. "She wouldn't tell me."

"Did you really want to know?"

"Of course!"

"How hard did you try?"

She pressed her lips together and looked at the floor. "I couldn't try."

"Why not?"

She flared back at him. "Because she didn't want to tell me. Because it wouldn't have done any good even if she did."

"Wouldn't have done any good? You'd have ignored the facts even if you'd had them?" He felt his heart breaking.

She glared at him through welling eyes. "Because if he'd wanted to marry her, he'd have made a claim by now," she said angrily.

"Ava!" Priscilla gasped.

Ava's expression changed miserably. "I'm sorry."

Angell felt his insides nearly sing with relief. She thought her sister had been *jilted*. She'd rushed in to save Priscilla with this bizarre plan because she believed her sister had been used and dumped.

But Angell knew better.

Priscilla's voice rose, reedy and thin. "He *would* marry me, Ava." She turned angry eyes to Angell. "He *would*."

"Then say it," Angell pushed. "Say his name."

"No!" Priscilla pouted, her lips quivering. "I—he—I don't want to."

Angell enunciated slowly, "Tell your sister who he is, Priscilla." He waited a beat. "Or I will."

Ava gasped and spun to face him. *"What?"*

Priscilla's eyes widened, then shot quickly from one to the other of them. Her gaze finally came to rest on Angell, scared and haughty. "You don't know what you're talking about."

"Don't I?"

She sniffed and raised her chin. "You couldn't possibly know."

"Say it," he commanded. "And let's stop this stupid charade."

Priscilla turned away from him, smoothing the skirt of her dress with her palms. "I don't know what you're talking about."

A small commotion arose in the foyer, as if company had arrived, and the three of them stood motionless. A second later, the door opened and Harvey appeared, crossing the threshold before stopping in surprise at the agitated faces that greeted him.

"Hello," he said uncertainly.

"Hello, Harvey," Ava said quietly, turning her face away and lowering herself limply onto the sofa.

"Harvey," Priscilla said stiffly, not meeting his eyes.

Angell pushed his hands into his pockets with a grim smile and leaned back on the arm of a chair. "Harvey Winters," he said slowly. "Speak of the devil."

Chapter Fifteen

Priscilla spun so quickly that she lost her footing and grabbed the back of the chair for support.

Harvey took a step toward Priscilla, then stopped himself. He looked uncertainly from her to Angell.

Ava felt as if her whole body had been doused in ice water, then set on fire. She glared at Angell, who sat negligently on the arm of a chair, because she could not bring herself to look at Harvey.

Harvey. Of course. It all made perfect sense. As she stared at Angell's passive face, the pieces fell into place . . . The way Harvey initially agreed with her plan to find Priscilla a husband, then had such trouble carrying it out. In his estimation, no one had been good enough.

The way he constantly antagonized Angell and predicted failure for him over and over, even though he admitted to liking him.

The way he chastised and bullied Priscilla, then stared at her in bewilderment when he thought no one else was looking. Ava had thought it was disapproval.

But in light of this, his disapproval was clearly the self-condemnation of a guilty man.

It was all so clear to her now that she'd been practically slapped across the face with it. What a fool she'd been not to have seen it, when Angell had picked up on it right away. Her eyes focused again on Angell's face.

"What's the matter?" Harvey asked.

Ava envied him his temporary oblivion. For a moment, it struck her as almost cruel to lower the boom on him with this, the revelation of his most terrible, guilty secret. He was so clearly unprepared for it.

Angell didn't say anything, and Priscilla looked as if she were incapable of speech. She stood rooted to the spot, her hands knotted on the back of the chair, staring at Harvey as if he'd materialized out of thin air.

"Is something the matter?" Harvey asked again, trepidation spreading across his features.

"Don't tell me you didn't suspect," a bewildered Angell said to Ava.

She looked back up at him, feeling the same incredulity that he obviously did. "No, I didn't. I honestly didn't."

Harvey cleared his throat nervously. "Suspect what?"

Priscilla turned her back on them all and moved to sit in a straight-backed chair against the wall. "I didn't say anything," she whimpered, staring at the floor. "I didn't say anything, I swear."

At her words, Harvey blanched. "Good Lord," he said, stricken, and grabbed the back of a chair much the way Priscilla had a moment ago.

Priscilla looked up. "I swear, Harvey. I didn't say anything."

Ava was amazed at the dejected look on her sister's face. Did she fear his reaction so much? Had *Harvey* been the one who'd decided to leave her in this mess? At the thought, a towering rage erupted inside of her.

"So it's *you*!" Ava exploded, rising to her feet. "*You're* the one who did this—who wouldn't let her tell?"

Harvey gaped back at her.

"Harvey Winters," she said, her voice breathless and compelling, "on what's left of your honor as a gentleman and as a friend to this family, are you the man who defiled my sister?"

Priscilla let go a sob from her chair. Harvey glanced over at her, his expression torn between devotion and humiliation.

"I—" he began.

No one moved.

He tried to continue. "It's—she—"

"I *forced* him to do it," Priscilla blurted out. "He thought it *improper*, unseemly. Aren't you proud of him, Ava? He's so like you." She raised a shaking hand to her tear-wet face. "But I loved him. *I* wanted *him*. Then, after it happened, he couldn't live with himself—couldn't live with the *disgrace*." She buried her face in her hands.

Ava looked at him in disbelief. "You were ashamed of her?"

"No!" Harvey found his voice. "I wasn't ashamed of her—I was ashamed *for* her. Ava," he implored, "*you* must understand. She can't marry *me*. What would people think? What would they say? For God's sake, she's had a *duke* ask for her hand!"

"Harvey—" Ava began. Her insides quivered, and she could not escape the feeling that the moment was vital, more so even than was obvious, and somehow inevitable.

"She'd be miserable, and you know it," he continued, then threw a hand out toward Priscilla. "Look at her. Her shoes alone cost more than I make in a month. She'd grow to hate me." He shook his head as he stared at Priscilla, who could not even look at him. His face and neck were flaming red.

Ava turned to Priscilla, who sobbed dramatically, her face still to the wall. "Priscilla," she said. Then louder, to be heard over the din, "Priscilla, listen to me."

Priscilla raised her tear-stained face and pouted in Harvey's direction.

"Do you want to marry Harvey?" Ava asked. She was

acutely aware of Angell's eyes on her as she spoke, assessing every word, she was sure. "Be *honest*, Cilla. This is important."

Priscilla swallowed hard and nodded, like a child asked if a sugarplum would make it all better.

"Then you must marry her, Harvey," Ava said, turning back to him. "That's all there is to it."

Priscilla took light, slurping sips from the soup spoon as she lay in bed with a tray across her legs. Her sobbing had ceased the moment Ava had taken her from the room, and now all that was left of the scene were the red patches on Priscilla's cheeks from her tears.

At this moment, as Priscilla sat in bed, Ava thought she looked happy as a cat with a bowl of cream. She envied her sister that ability to discard her impassioned emotions once they were no longer necessary, just as a child stops throwing a tantrum the moment she gets what she wants.

"So . . ." Priscilla looked at her sister over the spoon and sipped before continuing, "do you really think Father will approve of Harvey?"

Ava felt her shoulders sag. "Of course he will. He thinks the world of Harvey."

"But—" She slurped again. "But the marriage would be so unequal . . ."

Ava smiled, sure of this position, at least. "Father will make sure he's successful."

Priscilla leaned back and pushed her tray to the side. With a satisfied sigh, she crossed her hands behind her head. "So it all works out after all. You see, Ava? Life is quite simple if you just know what you want."

Ava leveled a glare at her. "Simple," she repeated. "You think it was *simple* to go all the way out to Missouri, dig up some man to marry you, teach him manners—"

"Oh, give it up, Ava," Priscilla said, waving her off with a hand. "You can't tell me you didn't *enjoy* it."

"*Enjoy* it!" Ava stood with her outrage. "You think I

221

enjoyed chasing across the country to find a husband for you?"

"Well, no, maybe not at first. And you know I *do* appreciate that."

Ava scoffed in frustration.

"But you know, without that trip," she continued, "Harvey might never have realized how serious I was about waiting for him. He was so determined to help you with your plan, I don't think it occurred to him exactly what that meant until Angell made it real."

Ava felt tears sting her eyes and was not sure what to make of them. She was tired, that was probably all, she thought.

"In any case," Priscilla's voice chirped merrily, "it gave you the chance to meet Angell. And you can't tell me you don't think *that* was worth it."

Ava turned quickly away from her sister's prying eyes, her own filling with tears. She pulled the handkerchief from her sleeve and dabbed discreetly before turning halfway back to Priscilla.

"Of course I've enjoyed him. He turned into a charming gentleman." She walked sedately to the window, in which she could see nothing but her own wretched reflection. "And he'll be going back, I'm sure, as soon as Harvey can work things out with Father."

Priscilla was silent for so long that Ava chanced a glance over her shoulder. Her sister studied her intently, a slight smile on her lips.

"He'll stay if you ask him to," she said finally.

Ava's heart leapt in her chest at the same moment a voice in her head shouted *"forbidden."*

"What on earth are you talking about?" she asked, modulating her voice for the proper amount of astonishment, but she could not look again into her sister's knowing face.

"He's in love with you, Ava," she said, as if any idiot would have guessed it. "Frankly, it was that more than anything that convinced me to foil the plan as soon as possible."

Ava turned a disbelieving look on her sister. "So you did it for me," she stated dryly.

Priscilla chuckled and had the grace to look mildly abashed. "Well, it wouldn't have been as much fun, letting him squire me around, knowing that all he really wanted was you."

Ava sank back into the chair and let her fingers play with the handkerchief. "Why would he want me?" she asked tiredly. "He doesn't even like me."

"Don't be a fool, Ava. I told you he's in love with you," Priscilla repeated.

"No, he's not. He completely disapproves of me. Once in a while, he likes to tease me and goad me about my beliefs . . ." She thought of his kisses, of the raw passion he possessed and evoked in her—was that all just an effort to show that someone of her class could want someone of his?

If so, she conceded cynically, he'd proven his point on several occasions.

"You know, Ava, to you it might seem obvious that Father will accept Harvey. And I confess, after all this, to me it does, too. But it didn't in the beginning. It only looked impossible."

Ava raised her head. "What are you saying?"

"I'm saying that to me, it's obvious about you and Angell. And I think Father would let you do it."

Laughter rose to Ava's throat, and she looked at her sister sadly. "Oh, Priscilla. It's true what they say, isn't it, that people in love think the whole world should be in love."

"Don't make it sound silly."

"Trust me, Angell's *not* in love with me." She closed her eyes against the memory of his incredulous expression—*You're a snob*. "He thinks I'm a hypocrite—and he's right." *You're worse than I thought*. She opened her eyes and stared at her hands. "Everything I taught him, everything I said to him, was all in an effort to make *him* fit into *this* world. I didn't think at all about what he's like, about fitting this world into *his* life. And it wouldn't, Priscilla. He deserves something other than this. He'll hate it here."

Unbidden came the memory of a dim, lamplit evening in his hotel room, where darkness shadowed his face and intensity charged his words. *I'm tellin' you, I'm glad my stay is gonna be temporary.* For an acute moment, she missed him, the old him, the one who'd held her on the dangerous streets of St. Louis, the one who'd called her a snob, the one who'd challenged her devotion to this society at every turn.

Priscilla screwed up her face. "And do *you* like it here so much then?"

Ava looked at her sister and felt the question reverberate in her head. Did *she* like it here? Did she? The question had never arisen, and even now did not seem to have any possible answer but one. She could be no place else.

But when she thought of Angell, of his resolution to leave, of his social blasphemy and irreverence, she couldn't imagine staying—not without him.

"It's what I know," she answered vaguely. "It's all I know."

But the truth of the words felt hollow, and the answer did not fill the sudden void in her heart.

After Ava whisked Priscilla off, Harvey didn't waste a glance on Angell before doing the same. Perhaps he feared some sort of gloating from that quarter. In any case, he disappeared before any further confrontations could arise.

All of which left Angell alone, in more ways than one.

Bennis showed him to his room and offered to bring him a plate of dinner, but Angell declined. Somehow, the wild ride of the afternoon had stolen his appetite. Even the opulence of the bedroom failed to hold his attention beyond the initial, now habitual, disbelief that he resided even temporarily in such a place.

He took off his jacket and paused, fingering the fine material, hefting the quality weight of it twice before hanging it in the huge armoire. To his surprise, the rest of his clothes were already there, neatly pressed and arranged in the deep cedar depths.

It was a good thing that the truth had come out so

quickly, he decided, else he might have been spoiled by this life.

He uncuffed one sleeve and rolled the soft linen partially up one arm. Real gentlemen probably never wore their sleeves rolled up, he thought, but that wasn't something he needed to worry about now.

He rolled up his other sleeve and took off his tie, loosening the neck of his shirt.

They'd probably want him to leave fairly quickly, perhaps playing the part of the duped fiancé. At least, they ought to move fast. In his opinion, people tended to handle multiple shocks better when they happened all at once. That way, when the mess was over, they knew just what they were dealing with. From what he could tell of Ava's parents, they'd appreciate knowing exactly what cards were dealt them.

Maybe he should reveal his true past, throw his own secrets into the mess, he thought with a grim smile, then scowled as the thought brought Barrett Trace to mind. If he did that, it would at least help Harvey look like a prince in comparison. Hell, Harvey *was* a prince compared to him. The Morelands would snap him up and consider themselves lucky into the bargain.

Then Angell would leave and Barrett Trace could just go back to the devil or wherever it was he'd been the last twenty years, thwarted in his attempt to wield dirty secrets for profit. Despite the thought, a chill swept over Angell at the image of Trace pulling that ace out of his sleeve for Mr. Moreland. Moreland would probably call Angell out, and Angell, hating the enormity of his own lie, would have no choice but to let himself be shot.

He shook his head to clear it. Stupid to think about such things. All Angell had to do was leave this place, and Trace wouldn't get a damn thing out of it. Simple. And necessary. And yet so hard.

He sat on the deep feather bed and laughed dryly at the ridiculous comfort of it. He leaned back across the quilt and threw an arm across his forehead. He ought to sleep on the floor is what he ought to do, he thought

Elaine Fox

with brief, energetic bravado. Just so he won't get used to this kind of pampering.

Several hours later, he was awakened by a soft knock on the door. He sat up quickly, squinted away from where the lamp still burned, and looked at the clock on the mantle through sleep-stupored eyes. Twelve-thirty. Past midnight. A brief vision of Mr. Moreland with a shotgun entered his mind, then left it as he rubbed his face with his hands. That was Harvey's worry now, not his.

He eased off the bed and moved quietly to open the door.

In the glow of one hall gas lamp, Ava stood in a white dressing gown, her hands clasped together at her waist.

"I'm sorry to disturb you," she said, her low voice tingling up his spine. "But I . . . I couldn't sleep, and I saw your light. I thought we should talk a moment. May I come in?"

Angell felt his stomach drop to his knees and thought, *This is it*. She was going to get rid of him, and no doubt she'd be relieved about it come morning. She couldn't even sleep, she was in such a hurry to do it.

He nodded and backed up a step.

"So," he said with a forced laugh as she entered the room, filling his senses with a fresh-bathed, lilac scent as she passed. "Here we are again, alone in an unsuitable place."

She looked so pained at the words that Angell felt a pang of remorse. He added more gently, "I'm sorry. I didn't mean to needle you. I admire what you did tonight, Ava. It was the right thing to do."

She turned somber eyes on him. "I didn't do anything."

"You insisted on what was right." He closed the door behind him, uncomfortably aware of the heated direction of his thoughts as he shut out the world with a turn of his wrist. The latch did not even click in the deserted hallway.

The light was dim, the fire was dying and only the

one lamp burned on the other side of the room. Though Ava's hair was pulled back, it still glowed with a richness he knew it would have only in the dark, private recesses of his bedroom.

She sighed and unlocked her hands, letting them fall to her sides hopelessly. "But I didn't see it—I didn't see it at all. If it hadn't been for you . . ."

"Sometimes the closer things are, the harder they are to see." Her legs were a filmy outline through her robe, and he remembered clearly how firm that slim waist felt beneath his hands.

She smiled solemnly. "You're being kind."

He smiled back, appreciating her uncertainty. "Kindness isn't part of my makeup, Miss Ava. I just say it as I see it." He wished she'd get on with it. Any longer in this private situation and he might be inclined to take advantage of the fact that he'd never be back.

Both were silent a moment, Ava looking into the fireplace, Angell studying the curve of her cheek. He wanted to touch it, run one finger down her skin and see it bloom with that blush she got whenever he touched her. She would be wasted on a man who didn't know what to do with that passion.

He suffered a vision of Cullum Henderson's pasty fingers on a perfect, imagined breast and felt his chest tighten.

"Ava," he said urgently, before thinking.

She turned, her gray eyes luminous in the last flickering of the firelight.

He took a deep breath. "Do me a favor."

She looked at him with an unfathomable expression, one he could get lost in, so intimate it seemed. "Of course."

He forced himself to laugh. "Don't marry Cullum Henderson. He's the worst kind of fop, worse than Harvey even. And he doesn't deserve you."

Ava didn't return the laugh, and the heat in the room seemed to intensify. Her eyes studied his face, and he had the uncomfortable urge to look away, or say something stupid.

"I won't," she said finally. "I don't think I'll marry at all."

He nodded deeply and hated the pain the words gave him. He briefly imagined pulling her into his arms and demanding that she marry him.

Instead, he said, "That's kind of the way I look at things."

Her eyes dropped. He let out an unconsciously held breath.

"Rather a waste, isn't it?" she said quietly.

He wasn't sure which waste she meant—marriage or the lack of it—so he kept silent. He knew what *he* would have meant, but that didn't bear bringing up.

"So I guess you won't be needing me around anymore, huh," he said, a little too loudly.

She looked up quickly, then glanced at the door. "Oh, no," she said in a hushed voice. "That's just what I thought you'd be thinking. That's what I wanted to talk to you about. We need to keep this up a short while longer, until Harvey talks to Father, which can't be for at least a week. You see, he has to wire his grandmother in Pennsylvania. It's a long story, but he's due an inheritance, and if he gets it now, it might sway Father somewhat. It's not a lot, but he's not destitute. So you see, you're still needed. And you'll still be rewarded for your time and effort. And, of course, you can keep the clothes."

With that last added bit, Angell couldn't contain a bitter laugh. *As long as I get to keep the clothes*, he imagined saying sarcastically. But he kept it to himself, because this was the way it had to be. He could love Ava Moreland, but only from afar. For him to want or expect anything more was ludicrous.

He ran a hand through his hair and gave her half a smile. "Don't look so glum, Ava. I knew this was coming. Hell, I wanted it to come. This deal was too good to be true from the beginning." He paused, but couldn't bear the way the bitter tone of his voice hung in the air. "So . . . all's well that ends well, eh?" he finished lamely.

Ava put a fist to her mouth and looked away.

"Christ," he muttered, running a hand through his hair again. "Look, I know that sounds harsh. But I knew this would happen. It's good it did. Everything's much better this way."

Ava didn't move. She had turned so he couldn't see her face, but the trembling of her shoulders sent foreboding through his veins.

"Hey," he said softly, moving toward her. "You're not crying, are you?"

He reached the place where she stood before the fire and could not resist taking her arm. She turned easily toward him, lifting huge wet eyes to his face.

"But I don't—" She stopped herself, then forced the words out in a tortured voice. "I don't want you to go."

Angell felt the lump in his chest move upward to his throat. "Oh, Ava." He pulled her into his arms. His hands flattened on her back as hers clutched his shirt. He stroked the curve of her spine. There was little between his hands and her skin, and as his palms traveled the length of her back, he squeezed his eyes shut. The heat of her body through the silky material swallowed his senses, and he pressed his lips to her hair.

She trembled against him, her face pressed into his shoulder. "Please," she said, in a tiny voice.

He wondered if he'd misheard her. Please what—stay? She pulled back and looked up at him. She said nothing, but her eyes spoke volumes.

Angell groaned and captured her lips with his. She melted immediately into him, her arms moving up to his neck to pull him closer. The unexpected strength of her compliance sent a thunderbolt to his loins, and the desire that swept him was uncontrollable.

His hands moved up to her hair and tugged at the loose bun at the back of her neck. Hairpins clicked to the floor and the thick mass of hair cascaded over his hands.

"Ava, let me look at you," he said, pulling her back with his hands at the back of her head.

Thick, honey hair framed her flushed face. Her lips were wet and parted from his kiss, her eyes shadowed and pulsing with the same desire he felt throbbing in his blood.

"Ava . . . think. Is this what you want?"

She looked steadfastly up at him and said nothing.

He pulled her forward and kissed her hard, punishing her for the mistakes he was making, unable to contain the glorious pounding of his heart as she responded in kind. Her lips parted, her tongue sought his, her hands roved over his back with undisguised hunger.

Images entered his mind as he kissed her—the way her face had glowed pale from the hood of her cloak the night they'd left Himey; a demonstration she'd made of a courtly bow during one of their dancing lessons; the elegant, commanding way she'd entered the lounge car on the train where he'd sat with Weatherton. She was beautiful, she was quality, and she wanted him.

The danger of it struck him hard in the gut. With every ounce of strength he had, he moved his hands to her shoulders and gently pushed her back.

His pulse roared in his ears, and he could not meet her eyes. "*Damn it,*" he exclaimed. He dropped his hands from her shoulders and closed his eyes, his head bent. "Ava, I—we can't do this."

He glanced up to see her hands pressed to her mouth. For a long moment she was silent.

"It's wrong—for you, I mean—"

"I know. I'm sorry," she interrupted quickly, her voice breathy and muffled. She lowered her hands. "I only wanted to ask you to stay. I didn't intend . . ."

He swallowed. "I'll stay. I'll play the thing out—but then I'll go."

She nodded vigorously and looked at the floor. "I understand."

A short laugh escaped him. "You don't, not really. But I can't explain it."

She turned and moved quickly toward the door.

"Ava?"

She stopped.

"I'm sorry. I've—pushed you—made you do things maybe you didn't want to do. I'm sorry."

She looked back at him.

"And I'm sorry I called you a snob," he continued. "You're not. You're a good, decent person."

She smiled slightly. "No, Angell. You were right the first time. You were right about everything."

With that, she slipped out the door. Angell was left to wonder what it all meant, and how it was he had ended up in a position to take what he wanted, when he was so clearly not meant to have it.

Chapter Sixteen

Ava ran her hands down the front of her skirt and studied herself in the mirror. With thumb and forefinger, she pulled a few strands of hair loose along her hairline, then turned her head slowly from one side to the other, holding her own gaze. After a moment, she made a face, strode abruptly to the dressing table and snatched up her brush, roughly taming the ringlets back into place.

She plopped onto the seat at her dressing table and stared at herself. White lace encircled the throat of her gray merino gown, making her head, she thought glumly, look like the ham on a white platter at Christmas dinner. She'd always considered the gown elegant, its tailored fit subtle yet flattering. Yet at this moment, it made her feel like a maiden aunt.

She smiled grimly. It was exactly what she was—or would be soon—a maiden aunt.

She lay her elbows on the table and rested her face in one hand. With the other hand, she pinched color into her cheeks without much enthusiasm. She was plain. There was no getting around it. No wonder Angell had pushed her away last night.

Humiliation rose to her throat, and her cheeks pinkened without the aid of her fingers. Abruptly, she sat up straight in the chair, held her chin up high and refused to let the emotion overtake her.

She raised her brows and looked down her nose at the mirror. Immediately a look of horror replaced the expression and she covered her face with her hands. Her mother! The face in the mirror was *her mother's*. God help her, she was becoming just like her.

"Oh, it's no use. I'm as false and pretentious as she is," she wailed through her hands. "And Angell hates me. I've made him hate me." She wondered briefly if, when she smiled, it was the same little tight smile her mother used, but she was too afraid to try it to see.

A knock sounded on the door, and Ava lifted her head, her hands sliding down her face until they only covered her mouth. She looked at the door in the mirror, as if she could see through it that way.

"Who is it?" she called finally.

The door opened. "It's me," Priscilla said, flipping the door shut behind her and striding into the room. "Does this look all right?"

Ava turned in her chair and dropped her hands to her lap. "Oh, no." Dismay colored her tone.

Priscilla made a face. "A little tight?"

Ava looked from the straining purple fabric across her sister's middle to the voluptuous display of white flesh just above the daring neckline. She nodded. "A little, yes."

"Damn." Priscilla dropped onto the edge of the bed. "I suppose I'll have to wear that *tent* Carolyn laid out for me. God, I can't stand it. It makes me look like a battleship in full sail."

"The one with the white bodice?"

Priscilla nodded vaguely, then took a hard look at Ava and frowned. "You're *not* wearing that, Ava. Tell me you're not."

Ava looked down at her dress and moved a hand to her hair. "I thought maybe some ringlets . . . ?" She plucked at the strands of hair at her temple that she'd just brushed back.

"Ava!" Priscilla stood up and moved to the wardrobe, throwing open the door with both hands. "This is it. Tonight's the night. You've got to make your move or, believe me, he'll leave. He's dead set on it. And Harvey's going to talk to Father this weekend."

Ava's cheeks burned again, and she laid her palms along them. "This is silly. I'm not going to make any moves. Goodness knows, if he wants to leave he's going to, no matter what I do."

"Oh, stop it." Priscilla studied the contents of the wardrobe with a practiced eye. One hand pushed through the garments, then dove in and emerged with a handful of blue silk. "Peacock blue!" she crowed. "This is *your* color, Ava." She held the dress up to herself and laid an arm across the fabric at her waist. "Oh, yes. This is the one."

"I'm not going to wear that," Ava protested. "It's completely unsuitable. It's a ball gown."

"And this is a dinner party. What of it?" She tugged Ava's arm to make her rise from the chair. "Come on. This is your color, I'm telling you. Take that rag off. The only thing you're going to attract in that outfit is a parson."

Reluctantly, Ava rose. "There won't be any parsons there."

"Lucky thing. Who will be there?" She turned Ava around and began unbuttoning her dress.

"Well, the Hendersons, of course."

"Oh, goody. With the riotous Cullum."

"And the Aldens, the Smythburns, Mrs. Carruthers, Godfrey Baldini—"

"Godfrey Baldini! Oh, that'll be a hoot. I bet Angell will like him."

Ava's hands gripped each other. "He worries me. I hope he doesn't see right through Angell. He's the type to do it, and say so."

Priscilla pushed the sleeves of Ava's dress down her arms, forcing her anxious hands apart. "If he does, it'll be out of jealousy."

Ava turned. "What on earth do you mean?"

Priscilla pushed her dress over her petticoats, and Ava stepped out of it.

"I mean, he's always been interested in you. You know that."

"I know no such thing." She thought for a moment, while Priscilla tossed the gray dress onto the bed. "What a gruesome thought. Godfrey Baldini. He's such a . . . he's so . . . well, he just seems to hate everything."

"And everyone. Except you." Priscilla bunched the peacock dress up and pushed it over Ava's head. "Put your arms through here."

Ava did as she was told.

"Is that it? Nobody else?" Priscilla asked, yanking the dress into place.

Ava sighed. "Regina Van der Zee."

Priscilla stopped what she was doing. "No."

Ava grimaced. "Yes."

"Oh, God," Priscilla groaned. "The dullest people on earth under the eye of the dourest dowager."

"Angell doesn't stand a chance," Ava said softly. She could envision the whole fiasco. Angell's blunt speech, his broad laughter, his candidness, all of it would be like the screech of an unoiled hinge in an otherwise pristine household to Dame Van der Zee. He wasn't going to fit, and the universally acknowledged matriarch of good society would reject him.

Ava closed her eyes as Priscilla relaced her corset.

"Let your breath out," Priscilla ordered.

"It's too tight," Ava said. "I won't be able to eat."

Priscilla pulled anyway and Ava let out her breath in a whoosh. Priscilla knotted the strings, then buttoned the long row down her back. "It's perfect. And they'll only be having the same old roasts they always have. You can eat when you get home."

Ava started to move toward the mirror.

"Ah-ah-ah," Priscilla admonished. "Not yet." She stepped in front of her and pulled the cap sleeves down just off her shoulders. Then she loosened Ava's hair and gave a sharp pull downward on the bodice.

"Cilla!"

"There. Now look." She stepped back and Ava moved to the mirror.

There, in the cheval glass, was a much different woman than the maiden aunt who'd stood there minutes before. This woman was something else—someone else. Ava wasn't sure what it was. She'd worn the dress before, but this time . . . this time the woman in the mirror had dressed with someone in mind. This time, the flush in her cheeks was not rouge. And the pulse that quickened visibly at her throat was due to some very unmaidenly thoughts.

She stared at herself for a long moment.

"Ask him to stay," Priscilla said quietly behind her. "If he says no, I'll eat my hat."

Ava's lips curved. The woman in the mirror looked positively sultry. "Which one? The turkey bonnet?" she asked.

Priscilla laughed. "I won't even have to decide," she said. "He'll stay."

Ava exhaled. "Oh, God, Priscilla. And then what?"

"And then we worry about that later. Everything will work out. Just stop worrying. Father already loves him, for pity's sake. Just this afternoon, he took him to Wall Street."

Ava turned in surprise, looking into her sister's face instead of the reflection. "Father took Angell to Wall Street? What on earth for?"

Priscilla smiled. "Why, he's grooming him to be a son-in-law, of course. It would be a shame to waste his efforts, don't you think?"

Despite her skepticism, Ava felt her heart trip a beat. Angell as her husband. The idea made her blood sing. Father *did* like him, that was true. Ava could tell. Every meal, the two were engaged in conversation almost constantly, to the exclusion of everyone else, according to her peeved mother. Father would grill Angell with questions about cattle or horseflesh or life in the West; Angell would either deflect the question with his natural humor, or answer in what sounded to Ava like very convincing terms.

"So?" Priscilla interrupted her thoughts. "Are you going to ask him to stay?"

Ava swallowed. "I already did."

"You know what I mean. Not for a few days. Forever."

Anxiety twisted her stomach. "What if he says no?" she nearly whispered.

Priscilla sighed and gave her a look of exaggerated tolerance. "We already talked about the hat, remember?"

"But he thinks—I've just made it so *clear* how I felt about marriage, and marriage partners. That marriage is an *alliance,* that there are families to consider, class, society, appropriateness." As she said the words, they resounded like a death knell within her chest. The weight of her own faulty convictions threatened to crush her.

"Oh, *balderdash,*" Priscilla spat. "Keep talking like that and you'll end up with Cullum Henderson yet. So who cares what you said before? You were a different person then. God knows, *he* was a different person then. Things change. And you, Ava, have changed."

"Have I?" She turned questioning eyes on her sister. "Do you really think I have?"

Priscilla snickered and inclined her head. "Look at yourself in the mirror, if you don't believe me."

No one commented on Ava's dress when she finally descended the staircase. It wasn't, after all, so inappropriate to the occasion. It just wasn't quite Ava's customary style. She thought she noticed her father give her an unusually long appraisal, but he said nothing pointed and even murmured a quick, "You look lovely, my dear," before ushering his wife out the door.

But Angell looked at her so hard she thought her blush must have colored her crimson to the tips of her toes. Her insides turned molten with the boldness of his gaze, and she thought for a second that she might not catch her breath in the snugly laced corset.

Then he turned and offered Priscilla his arm.

The whole drive to the Hendersons', Ava felt Angell's

eyes on her. The carriage was tight with the five of them in it—Ava, her parents, Priscilla and Angell—and Ava envied her sister for sitting so close to Angell on the seat opposite her and her parents. It was getting ridiculously hard for Ava to maintain the pretense of their engagement. And trying to keep her eyes off of Angell in his evening finery was painful.

She looked down at her hands in the dim light of the carriage lamp. What *would* he do if she asked him to stay, really stay? If she confessed all the tumultuous feelings she had, if she gave in to the desire that coursed through her whenever she looked at him, if she told him the next time he sent her away from him that she didn't care about his past, that she loved him . . . What would he do then?

Love. The blatant thought made her inhale sharply and look up. All heads turned to her.

"What is it, dear?" her mother asked, leaning across her father to peer at her through the dimness.

"Nothing," Ava answered quickly. "I—I thought I'd forgotten something. I didn't."

"Well, no sense in panicking. We can always send Embrey back for whatever it is."

"No, no," Ava murmured, thoughts blooming inside her.

She *could* tell him all of that. She *could* tell him she loved him. The admission was so unexpected that she hardly believed she'd made it. But the more she thought about it, the more surely she knew it to be true. She was in love with the man. The idea terrified and exhilarated her.

They'd planned for Priscilla to marry him—why couldn't Ava? What was the worst that could happen? Her father could find out he was penniless, worse off even than Harvey. But would that be so bad? Well, yes, it would be awful. But somehow it didn't matter. She wanted him. She loved him. It was an amazing feeling.

They arrived at the Hendersons' exactly on time, at eight minutes late. Ava's mother was a stickler for *fashionably late*, and as such they were the last ones to arrive.

Introductions were made, sherries and whiskeys handed out, and before she knew it Ava was ensconced on the sofa next to Cullum and an enormous *Encyclopedia of American Birds*.

Across the room, Angell stood with her father, Mr. Henderson and Mr. Alden. They were situated so that Angell faced her, and the fact that his eyes strayed to her each time he leaned forward to listen to the soft-spoken Mr. Alden was not lost on her. Her own gaze fled to him more often than she could control. He was so completely handsome, she marveled. Could someone so striking, so dynamic, really want her? Though she'd always rejected the idea of Cullum, somehow he'd always been the one she pictured—unpleasantly—when she thought of marriage.

Angell's hair was just a shade past due for a haircut, but the threat of unruly waves only increased the rakish appeal he exuded. His tanned skin against the pure white of his shirt, his powerful shoulders under the impeccable cut of his jacket, the delicate cut crystal in his broad hand . . . all of the juxtapositions of refinery to ruggedness made her pulse beat a little faster.

To Ava, it was as if a spotlight shone directly on Angell and everyone else hovered in the shadows.

She sipped her sherry and dragged her eyes back to Cullum.

". . . And there are thirty-three pages on pigeons," he was saying, his quiet voice registering an awed amazement. *"Thirty-three pages."*

He turned the heavy paper reverently, smoothing a hand down each page before moving to the next one.

"It's a lovely book, Cullum," Ava murmured, sipping her sherry again and letting her eyes stray over the rim to where Angell stood.

His head was bent, but his eyes were directed upward at her in such a way that his gaze was not obvious to anyone but its object. A shiver ran through her, and she was conscious of the sweeping cut of her bodice. She laid a hand to her throat and looked back at Cullum's book.

"Homing pigeons, carrier pigeons . . . here's the

frillback, and the pouter and, oh, yes, the jacobin,"
Cullum continued, turning pages as he spoke. "All of
them breeds of the rock pigeon, of course. And here,
no, no . . . ah, yes, here is the passenger pigeon. You
know, this bird is quite a bit less common than it used
to be. I predict some possibility of extinction. I've even
written a paper on it for the New York Ornithological
Society. Mr. Crandall said they may publish it in their
newsletter, if nothing else comes along."

And he could send it to them via carrier pigeon, Ava
thought to amuse herself. She briefly wondered how
many birds such a paper would require. At least a
dozen, if she knew Cullum.

She swallowed the last of her sherry and placed the
glass on the table in front of her, careful not to let her
bodice gape as she leaned over, though she'd have to
be covered in feathers for Cullum to notice. She let
her eyes stray back to Angell, but he was looking at
Mr. Alden and laughing, saying something that caused
the whole group to smile. She could just barely hear
the timber of his voice over the chatter around her,
and the sound sent a tingling of energy along her
nerves. She smiled to herself to see him looking so
comfortable—so much more comfortable, in fact,
than she herself ever felt.

She shifted her eyes and noticed her father looking
at her with an intense, interested expression.
Abruptly, she straightened and wiped the smile from
her face.

Her father nodded to her, the tips of his moustache
turning upward before he turned his attention back to
Angell.

Ava looked away, then repositioned her body so she
more directly faced Cullum and tried to look interested in his book.

"More sherry, miss?" one of the servants inquired.

"Now, this one, the *Columba fasciata*, is common to
the western territories . . ." Cullum droned, his fingers
smoothing the page several times though it lay perfectly flat.

Ava handed the servant her empty glass. He exchanged it for a full one.

Sighing, she leaned back and sipped at the warming liquid, letting it soothe her agitation.

"And the *Columba flavirostris,* which resides in the southwestern territories—"

"That's an unusual one," Ava said, placing a hand on the page to stop Cullum from turning it. "Look at that red bill."

"Yes. It's slightly shorter than the *fasciata,* at fourteen inches—"

"Have you got any of those?" she interrupted, determined to find *something* of interest in what the man was saying—anything to keep her eyes off of Angell.

"Oh, no," Cullum said, looking genuinely put out. "As I said, they reside primarily in the southwestern territories, and—"

"What sorts have you got?" she inquired.

"Well, mostly variations of the rock pigeon, as I said." He began flipping back through the pages.

Yes, it was obvious she could not spend her life with Cullum Henderson. Ava took a deep breath and felt relaxation and a general sense of well-being suffuse her. Really, she owed it to herself to speak with Angell, to ask him to stay. What was the worst that could happen?

A jolt of foreboding flashed through her at the thought of him pushing her away again, and she took a generous gulp of the sherry. After a moment, the liquid seemed to meld her fraying nerves back into submission. What could happen, after all? Angell had made it clear on several occasions that he wanted her, at least physically. If she told him how she felt . . . She sipped again, then paused and looked at the glass. This one must not have been as full as the first, she thought; it was nearly empty already.

She looked at the people around her, feeling more relaxed than she had in a long time in such distinguished company. Cullum continued on about his birds, and Ava wondered if it were possible that anyone in the room was having an interesting conversation.

She glanced at Priscilla, who sat with Mrs. Van der Zee. It was certain *she* was not having one. As she watched, Priscilla's face contorted as she tried to swallow a yawn. Mrs. Van der Zee didn't notice, however, so busy was she pontificating loudly on some element of Greek architecture that contributed to the general degeneration of morals in those who lived within it.

Ava felt a giggle rise to her throat. If architecture could horrify Mrs. Van der Zee, imagine if she knew that the woman with whom she spoke was almost four months pregnant with the child of her father's secretary. The urge to laugh out loud at the thought was overwhelming, but she swallowed enough of it back that she only made a brief, choked sort of sound.

Cullum looked up. "Did you say something?"

Ava blinked rapidly and looked at him. "No, no . . . You were saying?"

"Yes, well, these pigeons can be trained to return to their home site from a distance of one thousand miles—"

The fact struck Ava as interesting—which struck her as astonishing—and she focused intently on Cullum. "Is that *true*?" she demanded, leaning toward him.

Cullum leaned back, uncertainty in his eyes. "Why, yes, of course. Birds of this breed are often matched in races—"

"*Pigeon* races?" she asked, laughter bubbling again at this new thought. She imagined tiny little jockeys and pigeon feet thundering on dusty turf. In an effort to suppress her unreasonable hilarity, she sipped at her glass, but it was empty.

"Yes, races," Cullum confirmed. "In the East Indies, where the *Goura* genus can be found . . ."

Ava leaned back and let his monotone wash over her, pondering the pigeon races and how one might set up a finish line for such a thing. Her eyes settled once again on Priscilla and Mrs. Van der Zee.

"Did you ever notice," she said quietly to Cullum

after a minute, "that Mrs. Van der Zee's hair is actually blue?"

Cullum stopped and looked at her, then looked at Mrs. Van der Zee.

"I'd always considered it silver," Ava continued, "but looking at it now, it's really *blue*. Don't you agree?"

Cullum's expression was clearly disconcerted. "Well, I suppose . . . I don't know. It looks gray to me," he said stiffly.

Ava frowned. "Oh no. It's blue." From there, her eyes roamed to Angell.

Her father was talking, and Angell watched him with apparent interest. In fact, it didn't seem to be costing Angell anything to maintain that expression of attention. No swallowed yawns, like Priscilla. Then Angell replied and the other three, including Mr. Henderson and Mr. Alden, listened attentively to him. Ava wondered what they'd do if they knew who Angell really was. If they could have seen him even two months ago . . .

She laughed to herself. What fools they all were, with their self-importance, their pomposity and discernment, their rules about who should be let into their drawing rooms and who shouldn't. Why, look at them, she thought, they're hanging on his words—him, an ignorant cowboy.

She didn't notice that Cullum had left the seat beside her until Priscilla landed next to her, nearly upsetting Ava's newest glass of sherry.

"What on earth's the matter with you?" Priscilla hissed.

"What do you mean?" Ava looked at her sister in surprise.

"You're sitting over her, all alone, smiling and laughing at nothing. Are you all right?"

Ava smiled and felt that marvelous cloud of well-being envelope her again. "I'm wonderful, Cilla, really. Did you ever notice," she leaned closer, "that Mrs. Van der Zee's hair is actually blue?"

"Ava! Don't *point*, for pity's sake." Priscilla's hand grasped her arm and brought it sharply to her lap.

Elaine Fox

"I wasn't pointing," Ava protested. "I was gesturing."

"Well, whatever. People are starting to look at you."

Ava straightened and looked around. "At me?" She caught Angell's eye and smiled, letting herself bask in his gaze for a moment. He gave her a concerned look in return.

At that moment, Mrs. Henderson announced dinner, and the entire company rose to its feet. Ava pushed herself upward and felt the room spin with the effort. Priscilla grabbed her arm.

"Good God in heaven," Priscilla marveled, "you're drunk!"

Ava spun to face her sister but had trouble locating her face for a moment. "I am not," she said to it, once she found it in the crowd.

Priscilla looked aghast.

Ava giggled. To think that Cilla was angry with *her* for drawing attention! The irony was too absurd not to laugh. "I'm not," she insisted, smiling.

"You are and it's—it's unseemly," Priscilla said sourly, which made Ava want to laugh again. "Come along. A little food will do you a world of good about now."

Ava was seated between Amos Alden and Godfrey Baldini. Priscilla left her with a hushed directive to finish *everything on her plate*. But as Ava studied the layers of meat, sweet potatoes, green beans and rolls, she could not imagine fitting anything into her stomach that was not liquid. She picked up her water glass.

"Doesn't the pheasant appeal to you?" Mr. Alden asked.

Ava smiled, half-expecting Cullum to rise heatedly to his feet and demand to know how he was expected to eat *bird*.

She pressed her lips together—this giddiness was becoming downright unseemly—and set the glass down, staring at the mountain of food. "It's this corset," she said truthfully, tugging at her waist. "My sister laced it so tightly I don't believe I can swallow a thing."

Mr. Alden colored profusely and turned his attention to his plate. "Heavens, child," he murmured, digging with renewed concentration into his sweet potatoes.

Ava picked up her fork and felt herself tipping to the left. She put her fingers discreetly on the table to stop the motion. Goodness, she might just be a little tipsy after all, she thought, carefully depositing her fork and reaching again for her water. Her fingers stumbled against another glass, nearly knocking it over, but she grasped it in time. It was the wine. To be on the safe side, she sipped from it rather than going for the water and risking disaster.

Ava sighed with the full-bodied warmth of the liquid and picked up her fork. She was thankful Mr. Baldini was engaged in conversation with Mrs. Henderson, so he did not notice her near miss with the glasses.

"Did I mention that the Sinclairs are coming to visit?" Mrs. Henderson was saying to him. "Lovely old friends of ours from the South."

Ava cleared her throat and turned to Mr. Alden before she could get roped into that conversation. She'd met the Sinclairs on several occasions, and a more stuffy and boring couple she couldn't imagine.

"Tell me something, Mr. Alden," she said in a carefully modulated voice, "what do you think of our houseguest?"

Mr. Alden looked up. "Mr. Angell? A delightful fellow. Really, quite entertaining."

"Oh, I'm so glad," Ava said sincerely. "We just think the world of him."

Mr. Alden nodded and poked a slab of bird. "So I understand. Your father spoke quite highly of him as well."

"Did he?" Ava asked.

"Of course. Said he was a veritable genius when it came to the market."

Silence descended between them as Ava thought about that. Angell was playing his part well, apparently. She attempted another bite of sweet potato, chewed it slowly and swallowed, feeling the lump land in her throat and stay there. It was like trying to force something into the neck of a knotted drawstring bag.

"Miss Moreland . . ." Godfrey Baldini's voice sounded close to her ear.

She jumped and turned to face him, actually glad of the opportunity to put down her fork. She smiled. "You startled me."

Some people said he was a handsome man, though he was only about the same height as Ava. He had dark, slicked-back hair and black smoldering eyes, and he spoke with a slight Italian accent. But something about him bothered her, some element of insincerity or impropriety, and she'd always kept her distance.

"I'm sorry," he said, his breath caressing the bare skin of her shoulder. "I merely wanted to tell you how stunning you look this evening."

She inclined her head, feeling some nervousness return. It was something about those black eyes, and the way they never seemed to look *at* her, but rather *through* her. She felt his gaze travel the length of her face, then graze the expanse of white skin above her bodice.

"Thank you, Mr. Baldini." She took up the closest glass—her wine—and sipped, blinking twice to regain her focus on his face. She thought she noticed a glittering near his earlobe and had a moment of thinking he wore an earring. How like a pirate, she thought, and yet how perfect for him. She leaned toward it for a better look. "What an unusual—" She broke off, realizing that it wasn't an earring, but a strange trick of the light, or her eyes. "Ah . . . unusual," her brain fumbled for a word, "evening this is." She brought the glass to her lips to disguise her flush of embarrassment.

Baldini smiled, and his heavy-lidded eyes descended to her cleavage. "Yes, I believe so, too," he cooed. "How do you find it unusual?"

Her eyes scanned the table and lit briefly on Angell, who sat next to Priscilla. The two leaned close as he spoke.

Ava frowned and picked up her napkin.

"Why, it's just so hot," she said, dabbing the cloth to the corner of her mouth, then moving it down to her neck in an effort to conceal herself from Baldini's brazen eyes.

Baldini took a deep breath and said lowly, "You drive me to distraction when you do that. Your skin . . . it is paler even than the whitest fabric." His fingers rose and barely touched a corner of the napkin, flipping it lightly where it hung near her breast.

Ava dropped her hand to her lap. "I—I beg your pardon?"

He leaned toward her. "You're lovely, Miss Moreland." His hand sought her thigh beneath the table and stroked it. "Perhaps we could get some air together, after the meal, while the men are smoking."

Shocked at the contact, Ava pushed back her chair, the legs screeching on the floor. "Unhand me!" she demanded, rising unsteadily to her feet. Crystal clanged in protest as she clutched the table for balance.

Silence swallowed the room, and all heads turned to look at her. Ava gazed at the stunned, curious faces around the table. She blinked, and they wavered before her eyes like pebbles at the bottom of a stream.

"I—" she began. Her eyes fell on Angell and Priscilla. "I'm afraid I don't feel at all well," she pronounced, speaking each word carefully. "I believe I should go home now."

Priscilla stood up. "I'll take her."

Angell rose beside her, and Ava could swear she saw amusement in his face. "Don't get up, Mr. Moreland. Please, you all finish your dinners. I'll escort the ladies home."

Chapter Seventeen

The cold night air ought to do Ava some good, Angell thought as the three of them left the brightly lit house. But as Embrey brought the coach around, Ava threw open the front of her cloak, exclaimed about the heat, and nearly tumbled down the front stoop.

Angell grabbed her by the waist with both hands and pulled her back to him. Fixing one arm around her shoulders, his other hand gathered the cloak together in front of her. "Ava, keep your clothes on," he coaxed, easing her down the first step.

She turned her head and looked at his face, her eyes obviously working hard to focus. "What?"

He smiled but bit back a laugh. No *I beg your pardon* this time, just *What?*

Priscilla trotted down the stairs ahead of them. "You needn't hold the door, Embrey," she said. "Mr. Angell will get it. Just get us home; Miss Ava is sick."

"Yes, miss," Embrey said with a bow. He turned and climbed back up to the driver's box.

"Come on! Do you want everyone to *see* you?" Priscilla hissed, waving Ava and Angell forward anxiously.

She hiked up her skirt and disappeared into the coach.

"Let's walk, Angell," Ava said, leaning into him. She extricated an arm from her cape and threw it back again. "It's so hot, I just can't bear the thought of going inside again."

"I don't think that's a good idea," Angell said. "We need to get you home and into bed. You're going to feel like hell tomorrow." He reached around her and retrieved the cape.

"But I feel so *wonderful* now, Angell. I don't think I've ever felt so wonderful." She tossed one hand out to the side, as if she could sail off down the street alone. Angell pulled her in close.

"I suppose I've had a bit too much to drink," she continued. "It's rather a nice feeling, isn't it?"

He laughed. "Can be. But trust me," he added, "you'll swear you'll never do it again after tomorrow."

Ava sighed. "Oh, tomorrow, tomorrow, to *hell* with tomorrow. I'm sick to death of worrying about tomorrow." She stopped abruptly and gazed up at him. "Are you worried about tomorrow, Angell?"

He looked down at her, at her wide, guileless eyes and flushed cheeks. Her expression was so youthful, he imagined she hadn't looked this carefree since she was a girl. His hands cradled her elbows to keep her from swaying.

"I'm just worried about tonight," he said softly. Oh, how he wanted to kiss her. "Come on, Priscilla's waiting."

"Oh, bother Priscilla. Who put the bee in her bonnet?" Ava groused, yet she turned obediently toward the carriage.

"Seems to me she's not used to someone else being the center of attention," Angell mused.

Ava looked up at him as she turned and let Angell help her into the carriage. He sat down beside her and placed an arm around her shoulders to keep her upright. She leaned against him, eyes closed.

"I can't *believe* the display you made of yourself in there," Priscilla said. "Whatever possessed you to continue drinking? I told you to eat something."

"Leave her be, Priscilla," Angell said. "She didn't do it on purpose."

Ava opened her eyes. "What difference would it make if I had? I'm a grown woman."

"If that means you're entitled to make a fool of yourself, then I suppose I've nothing more to say," Priscilla sniffed.

"Oh, good," Ava sighed. "Angell, what do you think of this dress?"

He gazed down at her. "It's real nice," he said, thinking, *God save me from the dress*. Or rather, God save her. She'd already had one close call on account of it.

Ava looked down and pushed her cape aside once again. "Do you think so? Priscilla made me wear it. I thought it was too much."

Angell grasped the cape and brought it back around to cover her. "Trust me, it's not too much."

"Then why do you keep covering it up?" Ava pushed the cape back, and this time it stayed there. "It's just so *hot*," she murmured, closing her eyes again.

Angell and Priscilla exchanged a look, Priscilla's full of amazement. "If I'd known she was going to get herself soused, I'd never have suggested she wear the stupid thing. What in the world has gotten into her?" she whispered to Angell.

"Half a bottle of sherry, I'd say," Angell replied.

"Why do you suppose it is," Ava mused, her voice soft and melodic, "that no one ever mentions Mrs. Van der Zee's hair?"

Priscilla rolled her eyes.

"I suppose because it wouldn't be polite," Angell said.

Ava sighed. "But, I mean, it's *blue*, and no one ever acknowledges that. It shouldn't be impolite to state a fact."

"Shouldn't be," Angell agreed.

Silence descended. Angell felt the deep even flow of Ava's breathing and thought she'd fallen asleep, until she broke the quiet with, "And Mr. Henderson's *flatulence!*"

"*Ava!*" Priscilla burst out.

Ava opened her eyes. "*You* know about it, Cilla. It's legendary, for heaven's sake. It'll positively *thunder* through a room, and no one will raise an eyebrow." She turned wondering eyes up to Angell. "They won't say anything. Isn't that odd?"

He tried to swallow his amusement. "That's probably for the best."

"Oh, but let on that *Angell*, here . . ." She leaned forward and flung out a hand; it struck him in the chest. "Let on that he doesn't have any *money*, and they'd clear the room faster than a stampeding herd." She gave them each an outraged look, then leaned back and giggled. "A stampeding herd, Angell. You know about that, that's western!"

"They did resemble a herd," Angell murmured. "In a few ways."

Ava pouted and snuggled into his side. "What a bunch of prigs."

Angell smirked at Priscilla. "Couldn't have said it better myself."

Priscilla frowned and looked out the window.

Ava sighed loudly.

"Oh, don't be so sore, Priscilla," Angell said. "You can make a spectacle of yourself at the next party."

"What on earth are you talking about?" she snapped.

"You're just mad because tonight, maybe for the first time, *Ava* was the center of attention."

"Ah, genius. You're a genius, did you know?" Ava murmured.

"Good God in heaven," Priscilla breathed.

"I'll bet you didn't think I was capable of it," Ava continued, eyes closed.

Angell felt a surge of indulgence as he held her close, reveling in the way she leaned into him, needed him. For just a moment, he could imagine what it might have been like with her . . . if he'd been lucky enough to be someone else.

"Capable of what, getting drunk?" he asked.

Ava shook her head. "Seeing through them. Seeing through all those *important families*. I bet you didn't think I knew that decent society was made up of . . ." She was thoughtful a moment.

"Prigs?" Angell supplied.

"They're all so scared," she said quietly and sighed. She lay her head on Angell's shoulder. "They're scared everyone else is going to find out they're who they should be . . . like we all should be . . ."

By the time they arrived home, Ava was asleep.

Angell jostled her gently. "Wake up, Ava. Come on."

"So tired," she murmured, sliding down his shoulder.

Embrey opened the door, and Priscilla descended haughtily. "I give up," she declared, stalking into the house.

Embrey held the door, silent and watchful after Priscilla's exit.

Angell rose in the cramped quarters and tried to pull Ava to her feet.

"No, no," she sighed, falling sideways onto the seat. "I'm quite . . . quite comfortable here"

"Oh, hell," Angell muttered. It would probably ruin her reputation with the servants forever, but Embrey be damned, he couldn't leave her there all night. He leaned over and bundled her into his arms.

The servants were discreet, though their curiosity was palpable. After all, it probably wasn't every day Miss Ava was brought home drunker than a wharf rat. Speculation was written all over their faces, particularly when she dismissed them for the evening with an imperious wave of her hand while Angell carried her past them upstairs.

Angell paused on the threshold of Ava's bedroom and looked around. One gas lamp was lit in the far corner where a large, canopied bed reigned. A frilly dressing table and a brocade-covered chaise were on the opposite wall. Books lined the wall near the fireplace, with more stacked on the tables beside her bed.

"Welcome to the sanctuary," Ava announced with a wide sweep of one arm. "Bet you never thought you'd see the inside of *this* room." She giggled, and Angell entered swiftly. The servants were downstairs, but giggling from the bedroom was not something to risk being heard. "You may put me down over there." She gestured toward the lace-covered bed.

He walked slowly toward it, in no hurry to give up his unusually affectionate burden. "Maybe you should call your maid—get undressed," Angell suggested.

Ava laughed. "Oh, don't worry about *that*. I've done it *hundreds* of times."

Angell deposited her gently on the covers.

"Probably wouldn't take much to get out of that dress, anyway," he murmured, rising.

Ava's eyes fluttered as he let go, and he watched her take a deep breath and stretch. She certainly was beautiful, he noted, telling himself he was just being objective. He liked the dark sweep of her lashes against her flushed cheeks.

"You'll probably be able to sleep whether you change clothes or not." Angell forced his gaze away and glanced around the room, wondering if he should leave her there, fully clothed and cloaked.

"Don't be silly," Ava said. "I'm not going to sleep in *this*." She flung back the cape, and her fingers fumbled with the clasp at her neck.

"Here," Angell said. "I can help you with that, anyway."

Ava pushed herself off the bed to a standing position in front of him. She swayed only slightly.

Somehow Angell managed to unclasp the cloak. It slid off her bare shoulders to the floor.

Her gray, somber eyes gazed up at him. "Just a minute," she said, holding one finger aloft. Then she turned and walked, with exaggerated precision, toward the door. When she reached it, she turned her face back to Angell. "You don't mind, do you?" she asked quietly. Without waiting for an answer, she pushed it slowly shut.

The gentle click of the closing door was loud with innuendo. Ava held his gaze steadily.

A thrill shot through him.

The servants were gone. Priscilla had left them alone. Ava was awake and without inhibition. To his fevered senses, it was as if that discreetly closed door was permission of some sort.

Angell took a breath to calm the sudden tingling in his veins. He cocked his head and smiled slightly. "How does this keep happening, us ending up in some bedroom all alone?"

She smiled back. "I plan it."

His senses thrummed with excitement, possibility and not a little chagrin, as if she read his mind and toyed with him.

She moved back to the bed and sat on the edge. "Why don't you sit down, Angell?"

"Ava, this might not be the best time to tell you," he started desperately, then stopped and laughed wryly, looking up at the canopy's fringe. "Or maybe it is the best time." He paused, then sighed. "I'm going to have to go soon. I mean, leave this place. It's got nothing to do with you. It's, well, I got—"

"Angell."

He looked down. Her gaze, remarkably lucid, was trained on him.

"Would you kiss me, Angell, the way you did that night on the train?"

He opened his mouth to reply, but what could he say? No?

It wasn't right. The truth was, that night on the train he'd felt safe, taunting her, knowing she would never fall for a ruffian like himself. The truth was, they were separated by more than class, more than attitude, more than anything she could imagine. But he couldn't get the words out.

"Please," she said quietly. Her eyes were dark and decidedly sultry. "Pretend you still have some feelings for me."

He expelled a breath and moved toward her. Taking one of her hands in his, he tried to explain. "Ava, my feelings—I can't—you don't completely understand."

"Then tell me," she offered.

He wanted to, God how he wanted to. But the explanation was too awful, and he wouldn't be able to stand seeing her turn away in disgust. Not now, not while she looked up at him with those liquid eyes, not while she invited him to those perfect lips, that creamy skin . . .

"Ah hell," he muttered and leaned forward to capture her mouth with his.

He meant to keep it light, pure, but her hand curled around his neck, and her lips opened under his. He hesitated just a second before his tongue dove into the sweetness of her mouth, finding her tongue and twining with it as she pulled him lower.

He leaned closer, and she lay back on the bed. He lay his arms on either side of her; her pliant body molded itself against his.

Just another minute, he told himself, losing himself in her mouth and letting one hand run down her side. His thumb traced the underside of one breast. It was just too cruel to have in his hands something he knew he'd have to give up.

In an effort to stop the momentum of the kiss, Angell tore his lips away, but the effect of seeing her, her hair tousled and coming undone, the shoulders of her gown draped low off her shoulders, the bodice barely covering the generous swell of her breasts, was enough to undo him. He bent his head to her cheek, then down her neck to the creamy expanse of skin. His tongue traced the edge of her bodice.

Ava's fingers twined in his hair. Her breath was rapid and so deep that it seemed her breasts strained up to meet his lips. He raised a hand and pulled the fabric down to reveal the tawny peak of one pale, perfect globe.

His mouth closed over it. She let out a breath and her hands halted, holding his head to her breast.

"Oh," she said with a sigh.

He teased the nipple with his tongue. He would pleasure her, he thought through the thickening haze of desire in his head. He would show her that outlet of passion without actually ruining her. But as her hands began to move again, his resolution faltered.

"Ava," he called out her name, hoping some semblance of sanity would return with the word.

"I know," she whispered.

He rolled onto his side, and Ava rolled to face him. Her hands found the buttons of his shirt, and he felt the light, fluttering motions of her fingers baring his chest.

His hand cupped her breast, and he placed a kiss on the corner of her mouth, then moved his tongue along her jaw and down her neck.

Soft intakes of breath rocked her, and her fingers clutched his shirt. His tongue teased her neck, and his hand pushed down the other side of her gown. He rolled her onto her back and pushed the material to her waist. Her pale breasts shone perfect in the lamplight. He dipped his head to taste of one taut nipple, his desire spiraling out of control.

He would just pleasure her, he repeated to himself. But at the same time, his body moved to cover her and his hips pushed forward. She responded in kind.

He ran one hand down her thigh and pulled her gown up almost ruthlessly. His fingers fumbled over her underclothes, finally pulling the pantalettes down and cupping her buttocks to pull her closer.

At the same moment, her hand descended to the bulge of his pants. He inhaled sharply. "Ava," he began.

"No," she said. "Let me."

As she stroked him through his pants, waves of decadent pleasure swept through him, threatening to undo all his resolve.

Pleasure her, he thought again.

His hand found the soft nest of hair between her legs, and his fingers probed its recesses. She was hot, wet and pulsing. He searched for her pleasure point with one last hope that if she climaxed, he'd be able to stop himself from going that last step too far.

She thrust her hips up as his fingers dove inside of her. Soft, rhythmic sighs accompanied her movements, and before he knew it, instinct took over. He rose over her and looked down at the wild mass of her hair spread on the pillow. Her body was bared to his gaze, the top of her gown pushed low and the bottom gathered at her waist. She looked at him with fevered eyes as he pushed his fingers inside her, feeling himself throb with every thrust.

She licked her lips and arched her back, her nipples thrusting upward. He leaned forward and took one in his mouth. She moaned aloud. He moved his left hand to her mouth, conscious of the quiet house.

Take her, part of his mind said. *Take her; she wants you. You can't deny yourself everything, all you ever wanted, because of something that wasn't even your fault . . .*

He looked down into her face, into the trusting eyes that gazed up at him with fervent, wholehearted desire.

With every ounce of strength he possessed, he pulled back.

"There's something you don't know about me," he whispered.

"I love you," she whispered back.

His mouth dropped open in shock. "No—"

"I want you to stay, Angell. Please stay with me. Don't go back."

The words were whispered but strong. She did not look tipsy now.

"You don't know what you're saying." He couldn't believe it himself. Her words dropped like stones into a lake, quiet, irrevocable, rippling outward until his mind was consumed by them.

"Oh, I do, Angell. I know exactly what I'm saying. I want you to make love to me. And then I want you to stay here with me."

For a moment, he imagined believing it. He pictured himself letting go, agreeing to stay, to marry her. He imagined pushing into her right now and claiming her forever, letting the devil take the consequences.

But he couldn't. No, no, he couldn't. Not children, his children, her children . . . He couldn't do that—not knowing what he knew, not without telling her about himself.

A knock sounded on the door.

Angell sprang off the bed. Frantically, he pushed his

shirt into his pants and buttoned it clumsily.

Ava pushed her skirts down and looked at the door in alarm. She pulled the bodice up just as the knock sounded again.

"Miss Ava?" One of the downstairs housemaids, Angell realized. He looked rapidly around. Lord, he couldn't actually hide behind the drapes, could he?

The door cracked open, spilling an apron of light onto the floor. Angell stepped behind the bedcurtain, hoping to God the maid didn't come any further into the room.

"I did not bid you to enter." Ava's voice rang authoritatively through the room.

Angell saw the light narrow to a sliver on the floor as the hapless maid apparently backed out.

"I'm sorry, Miss Ava." The maid spoke through the crack in the door. "There's—there's someone here," she said, her voice quivering with uncertainty. "He threatened to make a scene, to do something awful, if I didn't come get you."

Angell glanced at Ava, who was once again clothed, but so flushed and tumbled that no one would ever believe they'd been caught uncompromised.

"Tell whoever it is I've gone to bed." Her hands were clasped composedly in her lap, her eyes were unwavering on his.

"I did, ma'am." The maid sniffed and her voice rose reedily. "Then he asked to see Mr. Angell, but I can't find him."

Angell felt hope shatter within him. He lay his head back against the bed poster and closed his eyes. It couldn't be. Not here, in this house.

"I'll be right down," Ava said.

The sliver of light disappeared, and the maid's footsteps faded down the hall.

Ava stood up and tried to push her hair back into place.

"I'll go down," Angell said.

"No. I'm sure it's Baldini. They mustn't know you were in here." She straightened her dress with cool efficiency.

Baldini. Angell hadn't considered that. Of course, it had to be. He finished buttoning his shirt. "They don't have to know. And it could be dangerous. I'll go."

She looked up at him with a half-smile. "Mr. Baldini is many things," she said, "but dangerous is not one of them. I'll have no trouble getting rid of him."

Ava moved toward the door. Once there, she turned back to him with a sad expression. "You won't be here when I return, will you."

Angell hesitated. "Ava—" He stopped, torn. "Not like this, Ava. You deserve better than this."

Her lashes dropped and she smiled slightly. "Or you do." She turned swiftly and disappeared through the door.

Angell threw his head back and let out a deep breath. Baldini. Why would he have followed Ava here? Well, the answer to that was obvious. But what excuse could he have made for leaving the party? And he knew Ava was not alone. Everyone there had seen her leave with both her sister and himself.

An unconscious tightening began in his gut.

Ava was drunk. Granted, she'd looked better leaving this room than she had coming into it, but she was still without all of her faculties.

Angell ran his hand through his hair and moved to the door. It wasn't Baldini down there; he could feel it in his bones. Every nerve prickled, and every hair seemed to rise.

Why would Baldini have asked for Angell?

His fingers closed around the knob before he gave a thought to how it would look, his barging out of Ava's bedroom. He paused, the door partially open. Slowly, with nervous patience, he leaned out.

The hall was quiet, empty. He slipped out and pulled the door shut behind him. Then he strode swiftly down the hall to the stairs.

The moment he reached the foyer, his fears were confirmed. The first words he heard were Ava's.

"What is it you want with him?" Her tone was determined, with an undercurrent of fear.

"Well, missy, it might be as I can tell you that later.

259

Dependin' on how things go, with yer *Mister* Angell."
The crackle of Barrett Trace's laugh stumbled up Angell's spine.

With a burst of adrenaline and a muttered expletive, he barged into the room.

Ava whirled in surprise, her pulse thundering in her ears. The oily character to her left straightened slowly.

The look on Angell's face was one she'd never before seen. His eyes were fierce, his mouth and jaw hard. With his ruffled hair he looked wild, like some warrior from another time suddenly dropped into her drawing room. Was this really the man who'd just held her in his arms?

An uncomfortable niggling at her brain made her pause. She'd seen him this way one other time . . . one other dark, terrifying night . . . in St. Louis—

She turned incredulous eyes to the man in the shabby suit. He wore dirty, scratched spectacles, but she could easily see the milky, sightless eye. She just hadn't put the detail together with that awful memory until now.

"You're the man from St. Louis," she said. "I remember your eye. You're the one who tried to rob us." She turned to Angell for confirmation.

Angell didn't look at her. His hard, hooded eyes bored into the other man.

"I thought you'd be smart enough to stay away from here," he said in a feral voice that caused Ava to shiver.

He frightened her, this Angell did. She'd never known a man in whose violence she had such complete confidence. It didn't seem to matter that she knew, without doubt, that his violence would never be directed at her. The mere fact of its existence intimidated her.

"Well, now, we gots a thing or two to talk about," the man said. "And I didn't count on you comin' lookin' fer me." He laughed again, showing rotting teeth.

Angell turned his eyes to Ava, their depths tortured and angry. "You can leave us now, Miss Ava," he said. "I'll take care of this."

Ava felt the tension in the room like a magnetic current. She couldn't possibly leave. She knew instinctively that she was the only reason the two men kept their distances. If she were to go, there was no reason this man wouldn't try to take revenge on Angell.

"No, I'll stay," she said firmly, her eyes steady on Angell. Her heart pounded furiously, and she no longer felt any vestige of the alcohol she'd consumed. How strange that she should suddenly feel so attuned, so painfully awake.

"Now, I don't think that's such a good idear. Do you, *Mister* Angell?" the disgusting man drawled.

"I haven't the least interest in what you think of it," Ava declared, mastering her fear for the instant it took her to cast him a withering glance.

She turned back to Angell, who smiled grimly. "It's all right," he said calmly.

She searched his eyes for the truth of those words. "I—I'd like to stay, Angell," she said.

His expression softened minutely. "Actually, I don't think you would like it. Mr. Trace and I've got a little business to discuss." He threw a hard glance at the other man. "It won't take long."

She kneaded her hands at her waist, uncertain now whether her presence really would make things better. Without her there, maybe Angell could get rid of him more quickly. Maybe he knew how to treat such ruffians, in a way he could not use in the presence of a lady.

She bowed her head once. "All right. But I'll be right out there if you need me."

"Ain't that nice," the man cooed. "She'll be right out there iffen you need her, Ange. She'll come runnin' to save you from the bad, ugly man."

Angell turned a chilling glare on him. "You'll shut up now, Trace."

The man looked taken aback. "Is that any way to treat a guest, right here in this here parlor?"

But he was quiet after that, as Angell walked with Ava to the door, his hand on her elbow.

"Angell, who is he?" she whispered as he opened the door.

He shook his head. "Just an old acquaintance. Nothing to worry about. Go on, now."

Ava stopped on the other side of the door and glared at him. "You needn't treat me like a child. I know something is wrong."

"Nothing that hasn't been wrong for a long time," he said wearily. He gave her a ghost of a smile. "It's just life, catching up to me." He raised a hand and traced a finger down her cheek, then bent it and chucked her lightly under the chin. "Don't worry about me, Ava. This kind of scene scares you, I know, but I been living with it all my life." He stepped back and rested a hand on the knob.

"Let me know when he's gone. All right?" she asked. "I'll be in the back parlor."

He nodded and slowly closed the door.

She was about to walk away when she heard the man's distinctive voice and high-pitched laugh. "Blackmail! 'S that all you think this is?"

The next moment, the front door opened and her parents clattered into the hall.

Chapter Eighteen

All Ava could think about was getting her parents to the back parlor. They couldn't see Angell's grubby companion—for Angell's sake. It was all too obvious the man had come with dishonorable intentions, most likely to reveal Angell's poverty, or at least threaten to reveal it.

"They would have left in a week and nobody would have thought a thing about it," her father said, as he and Frances unbuttoned their cloaks and peeled off their gloves. "Now we're going to have to entertain the bores and risk having them respond in kind the next time we're in Atlanta."

"I couldn't possibly ignore the broad hints Regina was dropping," her mother rejoined testily. "Apparently no one has asked them anyplace since they arrived."

"Which ought to tell you something. You know how I feel about them, and yet you insist—Ava," her father said in surprise when he caught sight of her. "How are you feeling, dear?" He draped his coat over the bannister and muttered, "Where the dickens are all the servants?"

"I told them to retire," Ava answered, wincing at the memory and hoping the quick patch job she'd done to her hair was enough to make her look respectable. "And I'm feeling quite a bit better, thank you. I apologize for leaving so abruptly."

The words were as clear as she could make them, and she hoped the fuzziness that lingered in her brain didn't show in her demeanor.

"Perhaps it was something you ate, dear," her mother said briskly. "It'll be all right by morning."

Ava took a deep breath and closed her eyes against the slight dizziness that remained. "Yes, I'm quite sure it was something I ate." *Or drank,* she amended wryly. Though for all of that, she felt remarkably sober, a state entirely attributable to the uncertain factor of Barrett Trace, she knew.

Ava continued, "I'd love to hear how the rest of the party was. Why don't we go into the back parlor, and you can tell me all about it?"

Her father's white brows drew close, and he gave her an inscrutable look. "The drawing room is right here." He moved toward the door. "And I'd like a cigar. Henderson's cigars are inevitably the worst quality."

"No!" Ava glanced quickly at her mother and smiled. "There's no fire in there. Cold as ice; I was in there earlier. And you don't need another cigar, Father. Think of Mother's lace."

"Goodness, yes, Julius," her mother objected, brushing absently at the profusion of lace at her neck. "If you insist on polluting yourself, you can at least do it alone. Ava and I shall go to the back parlor."

Mr. Moreland turned back, frowning.

"I think there's a fire in the back parlor," Ava insisted. "Please come with us, Father. I'm just dying to hear what atrocities Mr. Alden has invested in now, and you know Mother likes to hear anything that takes Mrs. Alden down a peg or two." She looped her arm through her father's, then turned to reach an arm out to her mother with what she hoped looked like an inviting smile. "Now, who is it who hasn't been asked anyplace?"

"Ask your mother," Mr. Moreland growled, reluctantly changing course for the back room.

Mrs. Moreland joined them. "Perhaps you weren't well enough to notice, Ava," she said, "but Regina Henderson told me the Sinclairs are in town and that no one has asked them to dinner yet."

They crossed the threshold into the parlor, where Ava was finally able to draw a normal breath. "Why didn't the Hendersons invite them tonight?" she inquired, gently leading them toward the sofa.

No fire burned in the grate.

"My point exactly," her father crowed. "If they're so dashed anxious to have those bores entertained, why didn't they do it themselves?"

"But you heard Regina yourself, dear," her mother chided. "Her table only seats twelve. The Sinclairs would have made fourteen."

"Another leaf would have solved the whole problem," he groused, extricating his arm from Ava's and turning toward an armchair that faced the fireplace. But he didn't sit. Instead, he moved toward the mantle and turned on the gas lamp above it.

"And you would have been sitting on the sideboard," Mrs. Moreland rejoined. "The room simply isn't big enough."

"Then I'd have volunteered to stay home," her father muttered. "Anything to keep from having that pompous bigot Sinclair in my own home."

"You're just angry because of what he called you in the papers," Mrs. Moreland stated, "*twenty years ago!*"

"I could have done without Mr. Baldini's presence," Ava offered with a laugh, eyeing her father and hoping no one would notice the room's chill air. She'd heard the story of Sinclair's slander more times than she could count and did not want to get into it again now. It was the one subject likely to cause her father to storm out and head straight for the drawing room. Besides, as loathe as she was to adopt any attitude of her mother's, it was, after all, twenty years in the past.

"And I'm sure Cullum would have been happier with his birds," she persisted.

"Oh, poor Cullum." Her mother sighed, absently straightening the bouquet of silk flowers on the mantle. "He was devastated when you left."

Ava couldn't contain the doubtful scoff that issued forth from her. Then, appalled at the outward show of disrespect, she whipped up a hand to cover her lips. "I'm sorry, Mother. It's just that he's no more interested in me than he would be in—in sewing lessons."

Her mother turned toward her. "Ava, that's just not so. Regina's constantly telling me how much he thinks of you and talks about you." She laid a hand on Ava's arm.

Ava covered the hand with her own. "And what do you tell her about me?" she asked gently. "The same thing?"

Mrs. Moreland drew herself up. "Well, I—you know I do like to make her feel . . ." she began, then stopped, irritably. "You know it's not as if either of you have any other prospects!"

"Mother!" Ava snatched her hand away, a lump of humiliation forming in her throat.

"I'm afraid I have to disagree with you there, dear," Mr. Moreland injected, flipping his tails up to sit, finally, in the armchair.

The two women stared at him.

He leaned back. "A little chilly in here, isn't it?" he asked mildly.

Ava took a step forward. "What do you mean, you disagree?"

"Yes, what do you mean?" her mother asked, facing him stiffly.

Mr. Moreland curled one end of his moustache with two fingers. "I mean that I have reason to believe Ava has another admirer. One she might appreciate a little more than 'poor Cullum,' as everyone seems compelled to call him."

Despite herself, Ava's stomach fluttered. She edged closer to her mother in order to face her father more directly. "Who do you mean?"

His eyes crinkled and he gave her a smile that was positively bedeviled. "Who do you think I mean?"

Ava expelled a breath. "Father, please don't taunt me."

"Ava," her mother commanded, "if your father wants to taunt, we must go along." She turned back to him and inclined her head. "I think he means Mr. Baldini."

Ava felt her heart deflate. "Oh, Mr. Baldini. Cilla said the same thing. I hope you're not right about that," she said wearily, plopping with fatigue onto the sofa across from her father.

"Don't be so quick to dismiss," her mother said archly. "He's got a *fortune* according to Millicent Alden, and villas all over Italy. Why, she'd be positively green with envy if you were to snare him. She had him in mind for little Lucy."

"But Mother, he's a—"

"Now, ladies," her father said with a tolerant smile, the tips of his moustache curling upward toward shrewd eyes. "I did not refer to Mr. Baldini who, to be blunt, Frances, is a buffoon of the first order."

Ava tried to suppress a smile.

Her father continued, "Would you be happier if I said I thought it was Mr. Angell who admires you, Ava?"

"Mr. Angell!" her mother gasped.

Ava's mirth disappeared and her eyes widened. She felt suddenly weightless and very aware of her disheveled appearance.

He laughed. "Ah. I can see you would."

Ava stammered, "B-but he's Priscilla's—"

"Quite right!" her mother seconded.

"Priscilla can find another beau," her father commented with a wave of his hand. "She always does. Besides, it seems to take more to capture your heart than it does hers. Circumstances have led me to believe *he's* found himself engaged to the wrong sister."

Wild thoughts and turbulent emotions braided together in Ava's still-fogged brain. "He hasn't said anything to you . . ." she began dubiously.

"Not in words, no. But I know people, Ava. And Mr. Angell's a man who's found himself on the wrong side of the fence, I can tell you."

Ava's glance jumped from one parent to the other; her mother's expression was outraged, her father's pleased. But she knew which one mattered most. Eyes on her father, she steeled herself for the most important question she'd ever asked him. "And what—well, how—what would you think of that?" she stumbled, though she knew not where could it lead. Angell had made it more than clear he intended to leave.

"To be honest, I like the man," her father stated. "I'd have approved of him for Priscilla, but I'd be happier if he chose you."

Ava's glance slid to her mother, elation and fear dancing in the corners of her heart.

"Well," Mrs. Moreland said in a tone that conveyed obvious displeasure, "he's an interesting sort of fellow, I'll give you that. But I'm not inclined to let him change his mind too quickly. After all, if he made a poor decision to begin with, rushing into another engagement with Ava isn't likely to be any wiser."

"Nonsense," Mr. Moreland snapped. "It just took him a little longer to see Ava's worth beside Priscilla's flash."

Despite its backhandedness, the compliment brought a wave of emotion to Ava's chest. "Well," she said, issuing a nervous laugh. "Well."

The strange events of the evening, not to mention the wine, all combined to make her insides quiver. Her father was virtually offering his approval of a match that had so far only existed in her head. Could he possibly be right? Did Angell want her after all? Would he stay if he knew he had her father's approval?

But even as they spoke, Ava knew that in the other room, Angell was being blackmailed for something he would not share with her, and that knowledge weighed heavily. He had wanted her out of the room— was it because he considered the man dangerous? Did Trace know he was no cattle investor? Or was there something more, something *worse*, in Angell's past that he did not want her to know about?

"Would he make you happy, Ava?" her father asked gently.

Ava turned to him, her eyes welling with unexpected tears. She swiped at them with impatient hands. She would *never*, she vowed, never touch alcohol again.

"I think," she began, "I think . . ." But the words didn't come. There was something wrong. Something terribly, terribly wrong. She knew the decision would not be hers to make.

"I'm gonna *ruin* you, boy," Trace sneered. "I got no interest in keepin' you in this fancy life. And this ain't no *threat*."

Angell slowed his breathing with an effort, leaned against the back of a chair and folded his arms over his chest. "Then why don't you do it? Right now. What're you talking to me for?"

Trace shrugged and meandered toward the desk, several paces away. Opening the lid of the humidor, he said, "Wanted to give you a warning shot, Ange. For old times' sake." His grimy, gnarled fingers picked up a cigar and held it to his nose. His scrappy brows raised approvingly. "Yer livin' good."

Angell unfolded his arms, strode to the desk and slammed the humidor shut with a sharp *crack*. "You want money, Trace? I don't have any. I'm here on Moreland money, and they don't give a plug nickel what happens to me."

Trace laughed and nipped off the end of the cigar with his teeth. He spat it to the floor and pulled a match from the box. "I think that Miss Ava might give a nickel. An' I bet she got a few of 'em. Maybe I should be talkin' to her." He lit the cigar, blowing bursts of smoke out in little clouds.

Angell's mouth went dry. "She wouldn't believe you," he said. The statement rang true to him as the words left his lips. She *wouldn't* believe him, but she should.

Trace drew on the cigar and squinted at him through the smoke. "No?" he asked finally. "You don't

269

think she'd believe some desperado she picked up out West got *tainted* blood? 'Cause I been talkin' around, Angell. I know folks is wonderin' where in tarnation you come from, who in hell you are. Even if she don't, there's more'n a few people out there'd believe your sorry story."

"It's not the story," Angell said, more quietly. "It's *you* nobody'd believe."

Trace laughed, spewing forth a fountain of smoke. "Hell, Angell, don't you never look at yourself?" he wheezed through a gruesome smile. "I can see it from here."

"I don't want to hear it," Angell said, disgusted. He turned around and started for the door. "And I don't have time for what you're trying to pull."

"I'm talkin' about yer *black blood*, Angell," Trace trumpeted to his back.

Angell stopped but did not turn.

"Lookit you," the man continued venomously. "Yer hair's black as crow even if it ain't coarse. And yer skin. You look like a damn Injun."

Angell turned, his heart pounding with an intense desire to kill the beast before him.

Trace shook his head and flicked ash on the carpet. "Yer mama warn't nothin' but a piss-poor, black-assed slave wench, an' there's people all over Georgia can testify to that."

Angell winced at the words and looked down, his blood searing his veins. The truth had been unspoken for so many years, it seemed almost unreal now.

With a tight rein on his anger, Angell raised a scathing, hate-filled glare at the gloating man. "My mother was more respected than you were, Trace."

Trace snorted. "Yeah, right, an' whiter even, to the nekked eye—don't forget that, Ange. But everone knowed she was black inside, black as any cotton-pickin' slave in the South. She had it in her blood—enough to keep her at your daddy's beck an' call. Think if she'd a been white enough she wouldn't a beat all hell to git outta there? You thinkin' she liked it there, *liked* your daddy humpin' her whenever he damn well pleased?" A laughed squeezed out of his throat. "Don't kid yourself, Angell. She knew her place. She was the massah's whore. It was *you* was spoiled." His look turned ugly. "Mary's little angel, everone said. The bastard lord, trottin' through the manor house like you was gonna own the damn place someday. *Hah*. Happiest day a my life was the day Cord was born."

Angell shook his head, memories tumbling out of long-dead oblivion to cripple any possible response. His hands clenched painfully. He remembered so clearly the day Cord was born, his half-brother, son of the so-called "delicate" mistress of the house. The truth was, she was insane, and everyone knew it.

Angell was ten, and until that day he'd been treated as a master's son should be. He was educated, favored, promised, in deed if not word, a future. He was to inherit all. Until Cord was born.

The very same day, he and his mother were moved from the white frame farmhouse by the towering oaks to one of the slave huts behind the stables. They were hated there—hated, he remembered all too clearly—by everyone. The whites hated them for their black blood and their brazen aspirations. And the blacks hated them for their denial of who they were, for their "efforts to be white."

But was it brazen to want freedom? Was it wrong to take the only course that could lead to emancipation? Perhaps it was. These were the questions that had plagued him for more than twenty years.

For when it came down to it, both his mother, one-eighth black, and himself, one-sixteenth, were slaves. Neither of them were any darker complexioned than the master, and there were other slaves almost as white. But they were born into slavery, brought up in it, stained forever by the curse of the institution. There was no real freedom for any of them.

Angell swallowed hard and ran a hand through his hair, turning his back on Trace.

"They won't believe you," he repeated hoarsely,

clinging to the belief. But what did it matter? It was true.

He had to leave. He had to leave now, tonight.

"Maybe they won't," Trace conceded, too easily.

Angell turned slowly back.

"But sure as shootin' they'd believe the Sinclairs, don't you think?" Trace seated himself in the large leather desk chair and puffed his cigar with smug satisfaction.

Angell said nothing, but narrowed his eyes as he pulled more pieces from his shattered memories. The Sinclairs, neighbors to the east, fifteen hundred acres, two daughters, ninety-five slaves . . .

"Yep. I thought so, too," Trace continued. "They're here. I saw 'em. Now, it may be as they don't know *yer* here, and maybe I could keep 'em from findin' out. If, that is, I was offered the right kinda *reason*, you know, some kinda reward to keep quiet."

Angell took a deep breath. Time, just a little bit of time was what he needed. "I thought you said this wasn't about blackmail."

Trace gave an exaggerated frown. "It wasn't, at first. Mostly I just wanted to see the bastard angel fall. Seems you got more'n yer fair share a good luck—back then and now. More'n yer kind deserves." For a second, loathing flickered in the man's one good eye. "But now we had this chat, I reckon I'm feelin' a mite better about it. I'm thinkin' a little a that luck might oughta come my way—I'm thinkin' you *owe* me, Angell."

The two glared at each other, each, Angell knew, mentally reliving the scene in the farmhouse when Trace, scant hours after Cord was born, came looking for Angell's mother. He was supposed to kick them out of the house. But Angell's mother was beautiful. And the opportunity to take advantage of her now that her circumstances had turned so drastically was too much for Trace to resist.

The ten-year-old Angell had entered the house to find Trace and his mother on the kitchen floor, Trace on top of her, her body bloodied and broken. A boiling

272

kettle of water was on the stove, Angell remembered, filling the tiny room with a dank fog of steam. Trace looked up to see who had entered, spotted the boy and rose violently toward him. Angell, in his rage, had hurled the scalding water in the man's face. It was that that had blinded his left eye.

That's when Angell had left, running through the mud of a chill March downpour, only to keep running the rest of his life.

"You paid me back for that," Angell said lowly. "You killed her—wasn't that enough?"

"I didn't pay you back for *nuthin'*," Trace spat. "I'd a killed *you* if you'd stuck around."

Angell mastered the humming of his nerves and managed a tight smile. "Glad I didn't, then."

Hatred twisted Trace's features. "Damn straight," he growled, rising to his feet in sudden, unmanageable rage. "And now I aim to get somethin' back. You *owe* me, Angell, and I want it *now*. I want my due."

"*What* do you want?" Angell snapped. "I told you I don't have anything. What could I possibly give you now, except the satisfaction of seeing me run?"

"You ain't gonna run, Angell. You in here too thick." Trace dropped the cigar on the desk, where its tip immediately melted the finish. "You git me somethin', you make it *good*. I'll be back tomorrow—"

"*No.*" Angell's thoughts churned. "I can't get anything by tomorrow. Give me till Friday."

"Hah!" Trace snorted. "The day after tomorrow, then. But mind as I might not be feelin' so generous by then, get my meanin'?"

Angell felt his hopes rise fractionally. Day after tomorrow. That gave Priscilla time to talk to her father, and himself time to tell Ava—something. Time to say good-bye, at any rate.

It was enough. It would have to be.

He looked at Trace through hooded eyes. "I get it."

Ava found him in the drawing room after her parents went to bed. Angell sat in an armchair before the empty grate, elbows on knees, his head in his hands.

She stood for a moment in the doorway and gazed at him, at the way his hair draped over his fingers in pitch-black waves, at the straight line of his nose in profile, at the broad expanse of his back and the way his white shirt pulled slightly across the shoulders.

"What is it, Angell?"

Her words were quiet, but he started as if she'd slammed the door. He rose swiftly and pushed his hair back out of his eyes with one hand.

She took a step into the room, marveling again at the poise with which he moved. When his clear eyes met hers, they revealed an expression of vulnerability so startling that she stopped and raised a hand to her chest.

"Angell, what is it?" she asked again, this time with more intensity.

His gaze skittered away, causing her more trepidation than anything he could have said. He never had trouble meeting her eyes. He could always look into her face, her eyes, her very soul, and say anything. He always had.

"It's nothing," he said, his voice strong, decisive, belying the furtive slip of his gaze. "Trace is—an unpleasant character."

Ava felt fear rise up within her, fear of his fear, of whatever Trace had said to him that defeated him so.

Before she could think, she moved toward him and took his hands, squeezing them in hers. "Tell me," she said, grabbing his gaze with her own and not relinquishing it. "Tell me what he knows, how he's blackmailing you."

Angell looked at her for a moment in shock, then shook his head vehemently as if to clear it and turned away from her. One hand raked through his already disheveled hair.

He laughed shortly and turned back from a safe distance. "He doesn't know anything you haven't known all along," he said. In his eyes was a strange light, a sort of over-brightness with traces of anger, fear and outrage. "Basically."

"What do you mean?" she asked, her voice devoid of intonation.

"I mean, it's as you said from the beginning, Ava. We're different. You and I. Hell, me and everyone. *I'm* different. And I don't belong here."

She felt as if she were walking on glass, as if one misstep and she would stumble and bleed forever for it.

"I was wrong. You fit in well," she said cautiously. "My father thinks the world of you."

At that, his lashes dropped, dark smudges against the fine planes of his cheeks. He frowned and shook his head. "No, Ava. You were right. It's nothing to do with money, or clothes or speech . . . *manners*." He scoffed with the word and threw out a hand helplessly. "I am not good enough." His eyes met hers. "I am not good enough for you," he repeated, his voice a dry rasp.

Ava held his gaze, sensing the fragility behind his words. Her need to comfort him was crushing, her ineffectiveness debilitating. She wanted to go to him, but she knew he would not respond. There was a hardness to him that she never sensed before, a resolution.

"You don't mean that," she said finally. "It was you—you were right all along. It's not about money or clothes or manners. It's about character, Angell, and you've got that . . . impeccably."

He smiled, a sweet, sad acknowledgment of the compliment. His eyes rested on hers. "Ava," he said lowly, in a tone that made her nerves ripple, "what did I ever do to deserve that?"

A lump grew in her throat, and tears stung her eyes. She shook her head, unsure if she could speak.

"Everything," she said finally, but it emerged only a whisper.

He took a deep breath and looked at the floor between them.

"Please tell me," she said, her voice slightly stronger. "Please trust me. I can help you."

His mouth lifted up on one side. "No," he said at length and looked back up at her. "I don't think you can. And I don't think you'd want to, if you knew."

She swallowed hard and took a few steps toward him. His expression darkened, and she stopped.

"Knew what? What does Trace know?" she pleaded, desperation causing her voice to rise. "Tell me. Are you in debt? Did you steal?" At his successive head shaking, she clenched her fingers in her skirts. "Have you killed someone?"

He expelled a breath of air and looked at the ceiling. "No, but I should have," he said. "A long time ago."

She couldn't help her relief. Murder was the one thing she'd feared most, but even that she knew she would have forgiven.

Then another disturbing thought struck her. That man, he could be some girl's father. He followed Angell here from St. Louis. Could Angell have compromised some poor Missouri girl? Could the man be after Angell to do the right thing?

"Listen, it's nothing you can fix—"

"Is it a woman?" she asked abruptly.

"A what?"

"A woman?" she asked again. "Someone—someone you maybe—before . . ." She felt her face flame with embarrassment.

Angell looked at her long and hard, so long, in fact, that she averted her eyes.

"Yes," he said finally.

Ava's stomach dropped to the floor. She closed her eyes.

"I have to leave, as soon as possible," he said gently.

Ava swallowed and looked away at the door, blinking rapidly to stave off tears. "We could help her, you know, we could—find someone for her, support her." She stopped, ashamed, and fat hot tears dripped onto her cheeks.

"No. I'm the only one who can help her," he said, with such finality in his tone that she knew it would be useless to continue.

He wanted to go. She racked her brain for something to add, something to say that would help her leave this room, but she could think of nothing. She was rooted to the spot, immobilized by pain, dread and an overpowering love for him.

"Do you see now?" he asked. "Do you see that I'm not good enough for you?"

She could not look up. If she moved a muscle, she would crumple to the floor.

"But I do love you," he said quietly. "You should know that."

He turned and left the room.

Chapter Nineteen

Angell found his way to Harvey's flat with little trouble. Amazing how simple things were when one had money, a coach and a liveried driver at one's disposal. Embrey knew where Harvey lived and took Angell there before breakfast.

Moments after Angell's knock, Harvey opened the door. In shirtsleeves, with his hair damp and a towel around his neck, it was apparent Harvey had just finished shaving.

After a second's shock, Harvey's eyes took in the coach in the background, Embrey's patient figure atop the box and Angell's perfectly pressed suit.

He grimaced sourly. "World's a pretty good place for you these days, isn't it?"

Angell squelched the memory of Trace's similar words by shouldering his way brusquely into the room. In obvious surprise, Harvey let him pass.

"We need to talk," Angell said.

For a moment, Harvey didn't move. Slowly, he closed the door.

The entry opened into a small parlor, and Angell

turned when he reached the center of the sparsely furnished room, his expression hard. "I'm leaving in the morning. I'm going to be appalled to find out that my intended is in love with another man, and it'll be up to you to make clear that it's you. That means you talk to Moreland today. Got it?"

Harvey looked at him pensively, then took the towel from around his neck and wiped it slowly across the lower half of his face. "What about Ava?" he asked finally.

If the man had gut-punched him, Angell couldn't have felt more sick. But he kept his face expressionless. "What about her?"

Harvey laughed shortly. "For one thing, she's in love with you. For another, I believe you have feelings for her."

Angell didn't answer, and in fact felt powerless to move.

Harvey gazed at him, perplexed, as if trying to interpret his stony silence and unable to do it. "For pity's sake, Angell, if you were looking for a chance, this is it," he said, tossing the towel onto the back of a chair and rolling down his shirtsleeves. "We've built you up so much already, I believe Moreland's ready to let you marry her. I don't understand what the problem is."

"No, you don't." Angell glanced down for a second, wondering how much to say, what to confide, and decided to say as little as possible. "I would never marry her for her money."

"No, of course not," Harvey rejoined with just a trace of sarcasm. "If I honestly believed you would, I'd be helping you onto the next train west. But you'd get the money no matter why you married her. And from what I hear, Mr. Moreland's all but endorsed the match."

Angell's eyes narrowed. "What do you mean?"

"I mean, I heard from Priscilla this morning that her father practically offered you to Ava on a silver platter last night. And we're talking the finest of silver platters, Angell." He smiled wryly.

"But he thinks I'm engaged to Priscilla—"

Harvey scoffed. "Let's face it, an actor you're not. I plan to speak with him tonight. I've been invited for dinner. It seems an old rival of Mr. Moreland's will be there, along with the Hendersons and the Aldens, and Moreland wants to make sure there are also a few people he can stand. That's how Priscilla put it in her note, anyway."

"Good," Angell said, thinking. "Good, you talk to him. Then maybe you can volunteer to break the bad news to me, and I can head out first thing."

Harvey's look was incredulous. "What are you talking about? Don't you see? I talk to Mr. Moreland, then you tell him you were really interested in Ava all along, and that's it. You're happy, Ava's happy. There's nothing to stand in your way."

Temptation burned a hole in Angell's chest. He could pay off Trace. There was a chance no one would find out. "No." He shook his head. Trace would keep coming back, keep wanting more. Angell would be a slave to him once again. "*No.*"

"Do you deny that you're in love with her?" Harvey asked, exasperation in his tone.

Angell struggled with his answer. "I wouldn't—I would not marry her falsely—"

"*She* knows the truth!" Harvey flung out a hand. "For pity's sake, *she* knows you're penniless. And if you were ready to live off Moreland money before, what's the difference now?"

Angell continued to shake his head, holding off demons with waning strength. "None of them deserves to be lied to," he muttered.

"Well, that's just fine," Harvey scoffed. "Where did this eleventh-hour conscience come from? A couple of months ago, this looked like a pretty good deal to you, as I recall."

Angell ran a hand through his hair. "A couple of months ago, it was temporary."

"Ah." Harvey raised his head and looked disdainfully down his nose at Angell. "I see. The drifter can't give up his freedom, is that it?"

Angell laughed, a short, guttural sound. "Freedom,"

he repeated. "Freedom." He shook his head. The word brought it all back, the unbalanced ledger of his life, the inevitable, irrevocable truth.

He picked up his hat and placed it carefully on his head. "Harvey, you couldn't be more wrong." He started for the door, his steps heavy. "Trust me, it's not freedom I'm returning to."

"Then what is it? I don't understand," Harvey persisted, irritation clearly on his face. "Why back out *now*, when Ava's feelings are involved? She deserves better than this, you know."

At the threshold, Angell turned back, thinking he might say more. But after a moment's pause, he only added, "I know. But she also deserves better than me."

Angell asked Embrey to drop him off on Wall Street and then dismissed the coachman, opting to walk the rest of the way. It was nearly noon, and the street was teeming with people, women dressed in fine silks with fancy bonnets, men in dark suits and bowlers. Angell reflected how, if someone were to glance at him, he probably looked just like the rest of them. A working man.

The thought brought him a small measure of comfort. He *could* have been one of them. In fact, the few times he had come here with Mr. Moreland, to Moreland's office, he'd felt an energy, an excitement, he'd never felt before.

Trader's fever, Moreland had called it when Angell described it to him. It had seemed like an elaborate game to him, with astronomical payoffs. And Angell had been good at it; he had an instinct, Moreland said.

He stopped and leaned against a shop front, watching the people hurry by. It was sunny but cold, so people bunched themselves into their coats and rushed. Occasionally, he'd follow someone with his eyes, wondering if the man were married, if he had children, if he went home every night to a beautiful wife and a life he could count on.

But after a while, the envy wore on him. He would never be one of them; it was stupid to think about it.

He wasn't sure he even wanted to be. He just wanted something they had—stability, or respectability. Something like that.

Angell pushed off the storefront and continued down the street, looking up at the buildings and around at the elegant shops. He'd remember this day, this walk, for a long time, he thought. He imagined himself sitting by a campfire on the empty plains somewhere, safe in his anonymity, remembering the granite buildings, the clamor of the windy streets, the push and sway of a bustling crowd.

He imagined himself remembering Ava, remembering her fine somber eyes, her graceful hands, the honey-wheat color of her hair and how incredibly soft it felt in his hands—in his coarse, calloused hands. He would remember her tears, too, and it would pain him forever to see them in his mind's eye, knowing he was the cause of them.

But if he were to stay, the voice in his head murmured, if he were smart enough to figure out a way . . . If Barrett Trace were to die—

Angell stopped in his tracks, vaguely aware of the momentary congestion this caused on the sidewalk behind him.

Uneasily, he allowed himself the thought. If Barrett Trace died, no one could discover the story of his birth. Angell had no other enemies like Trace—none who knew the story of his birth anyway. And who would possibly care if Trace disappeared?

Have you killed someone?

Angell closed his eyes. How fragile Ava had looked when she'd asked him that, as if she would shatter like glass if he'd said that he had.

No, he wouldn't kill Trace. He couldn't do it, he admitted to himself, for many reasons, not the least of which was that he couldn't imagine the act would improve his lot any.

He paused. If killing Trace wouldn't improve his lot, what would? He stood, suspended in thought. That was it, he thought. Suddenly it all clicked in his brain.

It wasn't Barrett Trace who kept him from staying

and asking for Ava's hand. It wasn't even Trace's threat to expose his secret. It was the secret itself. It was the knowledge that if he were to aspire to marry Ava Moreland, a woman descended from the *Mayflower* crowd itself, his secret would have to eat him alive forever. He could never own up to what he was—he could never tell her he was the son of a slave.

As he stood there on the sidewalk in the middle of New York City, he realized for the first time what was wrong with his life. For all the years he'd wandered—drifting, as Harvey had put it—from one town to the next, he'd believed it was the *secret* that kept him from settling down. Fear of discovery had become a lifelong companion, and he was on guard from morning to night. Watchful and wary, he'd kept himself apart from everyone, so no one would know, no one could tell.

But he didn't realize until this moment that it was burden of *having* the secret that did the most damage. He was not ashamed of his mother—no, certainly not that woman who had single-handedly made sure he was educated and cared for in ways that far surpassed the care given any other child of similar descent. If anything, he should be ashamed of his father, that man who had used and abandoned his mother and then callously stopped caring for his son.

No, it was not the accident of his birth, not his mixed blood, that made him less than the man he should be. It was the falseness—the *fraud* he had made of himself because of it.

For too long he had subjugated *himself* to constant scrutiny, to an unrelenting prejudice against what he was—who he was. No one else had done it to him; he had done it to himself, despising himself first and more intensely than anyone else could. His own brutal judgment had protected him from the world's, he'd thought. Or had it? When had it stopped protecting and started separating? When had his safety turned into exile?

The quickening of his pulse started his feet moving again. His thoughts churned forward. He knew what he had to do. Perhaps he'd known it when he'd asked Embrey to let him out of the coach to walk.

It was time to face his fears. He'd been a coward for far too long.

Ava hadn't seen Angell all day. She had agonized in the morning over what to wear, what to say when she saw him, how to act as if her heart were not breaking. And then she had not seen him.

He'd gone out early, Bennis told her at breakfast, and he was certain Mr. Angell knew to be back for the dinner engagement at eight. In fact, he'd just retrieved Mr. Angell's dinner jacket from the cleaning woman, freshly pressed.

But Ava's fears had not abated with this news. It would be just like him, she thought angrily, just to disappear, to leave them all in the lurch—

She stopped herself. No, it wouldn't be like him at all. But it was just like her to fear it, to attribute the crime to him before he committed it. Lately, it seemed all she did was loath herself for all the wicked, self-serving judgments she made about people from what she used to consider her virtuous perch.

But the longer she knew Angell, and the better he knew her, the more layers of falseness he stripped from her carefully shellacked life. It was terrifying— and exhilarating. He was so *real*, he made her feel honest in a way she never had before. When he looked at her, he really looked. He listened to her, and it made her feel vital. Her feelings for him were like an animal living in her chest, feeding on her heart, living, breathing and growing larger by the day.

She didn't believe him about the other woman. There was something in the story that simply could not be true. The first time Angell had seen Barrett Trace, on that dark, deserted street in St. Louis, he'd knocked him out cold, before the man had barely time to say anything. That was not the action of a man who would now own up to such a responsibility. That was the action of a man afraid.

The Joshua Angell she knew would never leave a girl

in trouble. Of that she was certain, if for no other reason than that they'd discussed the very situation too many times for her to misunderstand his feelings about the matter.

Angell was afraid of something Trace knew or could do, and he was lying to Ava to protect her, to save her somehow from what Trace threatened. But what it was she could not fathom. And without knowing what it was, she had no way of showing Angell she wasn't afraid, didn't need his protection—and could perhaps offer some of her own to him.

While consumed by her thoughts, Ava had rattled around the house all day, jumping at each sound of a coach and looking up anxiously each time a door opened. But it was never him. Perhaps it never would be.

About an hour before the dinner guests were to arrive, the front door opened, and she scrambled to her feet from the sofa in the front parlor. After racing to the parlor door, she slowed to exit unhurriedly as the front door slammed shut.

In the hall, her father stomped his feet free of icy slush and shook white flakes from the brim of his hat. The marble floor beneath him glistened with melting snow. Ava stopped in the doorway as Bennis appeared and took the hat, brushing off snow with expert fingers.

"I see it's started to snow, sir," he said, helping her father off with his coat.

"Yes, blast it. Do you suppose there's any hope of it falling fast enough to waylay those wretched Sinclairs?"

Bennis smiled politely. "I think not, sir. They are due here within the hour," he replied, folding the coat over his arm and floating away.

Mr. Moreland pulled his watch from his pocket and scowled at it.

"You're late, Father," Ava said.

He looked up in surprise, obviously not having noticed her presence. "I'm well aware of that, Miss Ava," he said, his eyes steely, "and it's a lucky thing for you, or I'd sit you down right now."

"Pardon me?" she asked, taken aback.

"We've got a thing or two to talk about, and I think you know what I mean," he said.

Ava's heart thumped ominously in her chest. "But I don't, Father. What is it?" *Had Barrett Trace gotten to him already? Hadn't Angell been able to stave him off?*

Mr. Moreland arched an eyebrow and headed for the stairs. "Think about it," he said, his footsteps ponderous on the stairs. "And we'll talk about it tonight, after those damned people leave."

Ava moved to the bottom of the steps, gazing anxiously after him. "You're making me nervous," she said, attempting levity and failing.

"And well you should be, Ava Moreland," he said, reaching the top. He turned back and gave her a stern eye. "Well you should be."

He disappeared around the corner, leaving Ava in a knot of apprehension. Seconds after her father left her sight, Priscilla rounded the corner to the stairs. She wore a dark green velvet gown that strained noticeably across her middle.

"I feel sick," she announced, taking the steps slowly with a sour look on her face. "And what in God's name has gotten into Father? He positively growled at me as I passed."

Ava frowned, looking with dismay at Priscilla's gown. "I don't know. He just told me we needed to have a talk after the guests leave. You don't suppose he's found out, do you?"

"Found out?" Priscilla repeated. "How in the world would he have found out? Besides, he didn't look angry enough for that."

Ava chewed her bottom lip, a habit she thought she'd gotten rid of as a child. "No, he didn't. At least, he didn't look angry enough to know the whole story. What if he only found out about Angell?"

Priscilla grabbed the base of her corset through the gown and squirmed uncomfortably. "This thing is so tight, I know I'm going to throw up," she muttered, working at the cloth.

"Haven't you got anything larger to wear?" Ava asked.

Priscilla shot her a sour look. "If I had, don't you think I'd be wearing it? I used to positively *swim* in this gown. Anyway, Harvey's planning to talk to him tonight, so that ought to put off your interview. Oh, God, now I *am* going to be sick. Harvey's going to talk to him, and Father's in a foul mood."

Ava took her arm and led her into the parlor. "Don't fret, Cilla," she said absently. "Everything always turns out for the best." But she couldn't shake the feeling that something momentous was in the air. Harvey planned to talk to Father tonight, she thought. That meant that Angell could be gone by morning. The sickness Priscilla had claimed to feel took over Ava's stomach.

"I've never understood what that meant," Priscilla grumbled, sinking onto the sofa with a dramatic hand to her forehead. " 'Everything always turns out for the best.' What if Father says no? What if the best thing is for me to be miserable? Suppose he sends me away? Suppose I'm meant to take my life in some lonely Italian villa, with only a housekeeper and some ancient gardener for company?"

"Don't be silly," Ava said, forcing her gaze to her sister. "And I wish you'd stop reading those silly novels. Father's never been able to deny you anything. Why in the world would he start now?" This line of reasoning almost always worked with her sister, but not this time.

Priscilla's face began to crumble. "Oh, I don't know, I don't know," she mewled, her voice unusually high. "This is different." Her eyes filled with tears. "Oh, Ava, if he denies me this . . ." A sob caught in her throat, and she buried her face in her hands.

Ava sank down onto the sofa next to her and put an arm around her shoulders. For all the theatrics, the underlying fear was real, she could see. "Cilla, it'll be all right." She was sure that it would be, at least for

Priscilla. Her father really *hadn't* ever denied her anything; and knowing how he felt about Harvey, despite his economic status, Ava was sure he would approve of the match. Besides, she thought, casting another glance at Priscilla's ill-fitting gown, it wasn't as if he would have a great many choices.

"Oh, but this is selfish of me," Priscilla sniffed after a moment. She dabbed at her nose with a handkerchief pulled from her sleeve. "You have your own troubles. What about Angell? Did you tell him what Father said?"

Ava shifted on the seat and began fooling with the lace at her cuffs. "No, I, ah, didn't get a chance. He's decided he must leave, and it didn't sound as if Father's words would make a difference to him at all."

Priscilla expelled an exasperated breath. "Not make a difference to him? Why, how absurd! And how do you know until you tell him? His whole problem might be that he doesn't believe he'll be accepted—"

The front door opened, and the two women froze. Ava turned to look out the parlor door but could see nothing save the hall table. Bennis swept by, the door opened and heavy feet stomped the marble floor, just as her father's had done.

"Mr. Winters," Bennis' mellow voice said, "the ladies are in the parlor."

Priscilla was off the sofa like a shot. She met Harvey at the door and flung herself into his arms even though Bennis was barely out of sight. "Oh, Harvey," she cried, "I've been beside myself with worry. Are you nervous about tonight?"

"Priscilla, please," he protested, prying her hands from his shoulders.

Harvey looked mortified and gazed uncomfortably down the hall as if Bennis might magically reappear wielding a shotgun. When his gaze returned to Priscilla, his expression of concern changed immediately to horror.

His eyes trailed the length of her, stopping at her middle. "What on earth have you got on?" he demanded of her belly,

"Oh, Harvey!" Priscilla wailed with a stomp of her foot. "Just the largest thing I own!"

"I'm sorry, dear, it's just—it's so—you might consider . . ." His eyes flicked back to her face, which was perilously close to tears. "You look fine," he finished desperately. "Fine—is—is how you look."

Priscilla sniffed. "Are you sure?"

"Sure?" He glanced at Ava, who nodded with fatigue. "Sure! Yes, absolutely. Fine, yes."

"Harvey, you haven't seen Angell today, have you?" Ava asked.

Harvey turned toward her, but after an initial glance did not meet her eyes. Instead, he stepped away from Priscilla, straightened his shirt cuffs beneath his sleeves and cleared his throat.

"Ah, actually, yes. I did see him this morning. Early." He straightened his waistcoat and glanced at her. "I was shaving."

Ava's brows rose expectantly. "And? Did he say anything about where he might be all day?"

Harvey looked at her in concern. "Do you mean he hasn't been back?"

Ava's stomach dropped at the expression on his face. "No, he hasn't. What did he say to you this morning?" She stood slowly, as if she'd be strong enough to hear the news that he was gone if she were upright.

"Well, ah . . ." Harvey searched the ceiling, as if looking for a transcript of the conversation.

"Harvey," Priscilla said indignantly, sniffing away the last of her threatened tears, "just tell her what he said. She's been a mess all day wondering where he is. For God's sake, he hasn't *left* yet, has he?"

"No," Harvey said quickly.

Ava took a deep, relieved breath.

"That is, I don't think he has."

"Oh, my God," Ava muttered, and sank once again onto the sofa.

"He was talking about leaving tomorrow. Morning. I believe that's what he came by to tell me. I told him I would be speaking with your father this evening." Harvey moved to the sideboard and poured himself a drink. "I suppose I should tell you, too, that he, ah, he seemed relieved that it was to occur so soon. There seemed to be some reason he couldn't stay." He looked at Ava quizzically, as if she might know the reason.

"I hope you told him it wasn't so. I hope you told him all I told you this morning," Priscilla insisted.

"What did you tell him this morning?" Ava demanded.

Priscilla waved an airy hand in her direction. "Oh, you know, just all that stuff that Father said to you. Did you tell him that, Harvey?"

He looked uncomfortably at the floor. "Basically, yes."

"Oh, no." Ava moaned and covered her face with her hands.

"I tried everything I could think of, Ava," Harvey said, coming to sit beside her on the couch. "I don't know what's wrong with him."

Ava dropped her hands and looked at him fiercely. "I'll tell you what's wrong with him. He doesn't love me. He—"

"Excuse me, Miss Moreland?" Bennis stepped discretely into the room and everyone froze. Into the silence, he continued imperturbably, "I thought you would wish to know the Hendersons' coach is pulling up."

Ava looked quickly to the window, then back at Bennis. "Damnation!" she swore, rising. "They're early. Bennis, get my parents, *quickly*."

With a swift nod, he disappeared.

"Harvey, check with the kitchen to be sure they'll be ready early." She smoothed the front of her gown with nervous fingers and turned to her sister. "Priscilla, you sit here, by the fire. And place this afghan over your lap. We'll tell them you've got a touch of a migraine. Whatever you do, don't get up—that dress doesn't look like it'll hold much longer."

They both turned toward the door as they heard their parents descend the stairs. "Blasted people not only insist on coming, they insist on coming early," their father said. "Probably stay late, too."

Priscilla rushed to the chair and flung herself into it, quickly covering herself from the waist down with the blanket.

Bennis opened the door, and voices filled the hall. Ava stood motionless in the center of the parlor, for some reason unable to move. It was, she thought, as if the arrival of these guests put something terrifying in motion. She consciously forced herself to breathe and turned her head to look at her sister.

"What?" Priscilla asked, a shrill edge to her voice. "Doesn't this look all right?"

The words barely sank in as Ava gazed at her, her mind a tumult of unvoiceable confusion. Then, slowly, out of the mental chaos, one thought emerged.

"Angell's not coming," she said softly. "He's not coming."

Chapter Twenty

She'd heard the name countless times as she was growing up and never in anything but the most hostile terms. Robert Sinclair—scourge of the South. Her father would never reveal the whole story—it didn't warrant the credence of repetition, he'd always say—but Ava had gotten the gist of it from bits and pieces he'd drop when he was on a rampage with the memory of it.

Apparently, Robert Sinclair had repeatedly slandered her father in the newspapers in the years before the war. It had been mild at first, accusing him of being part of some radical political group in the fifties that he had never been a part of; then, when that failed to get a rise out of him, the man had resorted to worse fictions. He'd finally accused him of illegal and subversive activities that could have landed her father in jail.

It was only after her father had retained a lawyer and begun proceedings to take him to court that Sinclair had made his apologies and run a despicably thin retraction in the back sections of his conservative

Southern newspaper, *The Georgia Planter*.

Apparently, he and her father had met because of their political differences when her father had traveled to Georgia to make one of a series of lectures with a man named Lewis Tappan, who died years ago. Ava couldn't remember exactly what the vendetta had been about, nor even why Sinclair had done it, but she knew it had something to do with Sinclair's political aspirations, some desire he had to run for president, she thought.

In any case, Robert Sinclair in the flesh—and there was a considerable amount of it—was not nearly the ogre that years of storytelling had created of him in Ava's mind. He was short, shorter than she was, and extremely round, with a red-hued face that actually looked quite merry, particularly in contrast with his emerald-green waistcoat. Dark, thinning hair was combed back over his shiny pate, and he smelled strongly of cologne.

He and his plump wife entered the room like a German biermeister and his hausfrau, with the tall, lanky Hendersons trailing in their wake like a series of exclamation points. The ogre was even wearing a smile on his face, revealing a broad set of tobacco-stained teeth.

"Well, well, well," he boomed as he entered the parlor, "so these are your daughters, eh, Julius?"

"Ava, Priscilla," her father said without enthusiasm, "this is Mr. Sinclair and his wife. From Atlanta."

"How do you do?" Ava said, moving swiftly to them. "Please excuse my sister from rising. She has a bit of a headache."

"Hello, how do you do?" Priscilla called from her chair with a wave.

Mrs. Moreland moved quietly to her younger daughter's side with a tight frown.

Ava greeted the Hendersons, allowed Cullum to kiss the air over her hand and tried to keep her eyes from straying to the front door. *He's left,* she couldn't help thinking, *Angell's gone, you'll never see him again and it serves you right.*

"Lovely, just lovely, Julius," Sinclair said, eyeing first Ava and then Priscilla, but directing his words to their father. "Married either of them off yet?"

"*Mother*, I'll be fine," Priscilla whispered loudly in obvious irritation. "Leave me alone."

Mr. Moreland glowered at Priscilla. "Not yet, no."

Sinclair smacked his lips together and let his eyes trail Ava's figure. "Shouldn't wait too long, you know. They're pretty now, but you know what a few years can do. Have to pay someone to take them off your hands once they're past childbearing years."

Ava's mouth dropped open and she looked at him anew—the jolly biermeister turned troll, she thought with distaste. How she despised being talked about like a piece of horseflesh.

On the heels of that thought, she remembered what the row had been about between Sinclair and her father. Her father had been invited to lecture on the moral imperative of emancipation of the slaves to a congregation of possible sympathizers in Georgia. He'd made several speeches and was garnering significant praise for his efforts, until Sinclair accused him of failing to obey the Fugitive Slave law. Sinclair followed this up by declaring her father had actually *stolen* Southern slaves to set them free in the North—a punishable crime at that time no matter what your point of view.

The slander had cost her father what influence he might have had in the South, even though the charges were eventually dropped.

In any case, the man's actions explained a lot, she thought sourly, about his attitude toward women. Anybody who could buy and sell human beings would have no compunction about selling off a daughter or two to the highest bidder.

On the heels of Sinclair's tasteless remark about his daughters, Ava's father introduced Harvey and somehow got everyone settled with drinks and conversation.

Ava placed herself on the piano bench well out of range of the Sinclairs' perusal and sank at once into a miserable reverie of all she'd done wrong with Angell. As the conversation ebbed and flowed around her, she felt as if she were sitting under water, her thoughts slow and sunken in despair. She didn't want to be there. She wanted to be out searching for Angell, figuring out a way to make him come back—and stay. Instead, she sat obediently in the parlor, entertaining bores from Georgia, because that stupid prim voice in her head insisted it was the right thing to do.

But was it the right thing? Or was it the easy thing, the lazy thing—the *frightened* thing to do?

Why didn't anyone else think it strange that Angell was not there? she wondered suddenly. Why hadn't her mother commented on his absence? Had he already told them he was leaving? Had she missed something momentous—like a good-bye?

Sudden panic and a fury at herself for sitting idle while the best thing to have ever entered her life slipped away drove her to her feet. She couldn't just sit there and let Angell disappear forever. *She had to find him.*

The piano bench screeched on the wood floor as she rose and her skirts pushed it backward. All eyes turned to Ava. She opened her mouth to speak when the front door opened.

"Ah, here's our last guest now," her father said, strolling to the door with the first genuine smile of the evening on his face. "Let me apologize on his behalf for his tardiness. He had an important errand to run, for which he begged to be excused in advance."

Ava turned anxiously to the door, her heart in her throat.

Angell entered the room, large and breathtakingly handsome, exuding the night cold like an aura of power. His hair was ruffled, and his pale eyes stood out starkly against wind-stroked cheeks as he surveyed the company.

Ava dropped to her seat in relief. While the rest of the company rose with his entrance, she sat still on the bench, letting her eyes drink in the sight of him.

She was vaguely aware of the dumb smile spreading across her face.

He was *here*, her mind rejoiced. He hadn't left. And if he hadn't left, perhaps that meant he intended to stay. Suddenly all her worries—about their future, her father, the lies they had to undo or live with—all paled beside her profound relief at his return. She would not let him go now. No matter what he said, she would make him stay.

His eyes immediately sought her out of the group, and though she still wore a smile, the look on his face was so intense it caused her heart to stumble. He did not look happy, nor did he look away for a long moment. Fear tripped along her veins.

"Good evening," he said with a short bow. "I'm sorry to be so late. I had something I needed to do." He turned back to Mr. Moreland. "Thank you for your help, sir."

Ava watched her father smile and clap him on the back with one hand. "No trouble. Let me introduce you to our guests, Angell."

Angell turned back to the crowd, nodding a greeting to Harvey and bowing his acquaintance to the Hendersons, but when his eyes lit on Mr. Sinclair, he froze. The movement was so abrupt it drew the attention of the guests, and Sinclair lifted a brow with an injured air.

If her father noticed the strange reaction, he ignored it, pulling Angell forward with a subtle yet insistent hand and proceeding with the introduction.

Ava's gaze shifted from Angell to Sinclair, who stood with his portly stomach thrust outward and a shrewd look in his eyes.

"Robert Sinclair, Joshua Angell," her father said. "I believe you two might know each other. You're from the same part of the country. You did say you grew up on the Altamaha, didn't you, Angell?"

Angell cautiously extended his hand. "That's right," he said levely, holding Sinclair's gaze.

Mr. Sinclair started to proffer his hand, then hesitated. "Angell . . ." he said speculatively. His extended hand clasped slowly into a fist and withdrew. "Joshua Angell, is it?" Sinclair's eyes narrowed, all but disappearing in his rotund face. "From the Matheson place?"

Angell drew a long, deep breath. He dropped his hand before answering. "That's right," he said again, in that same curiously blank tone.

Something was happening, Ava thought, as she watched Sinclair's face grow redder than it had been when he came in from the cold. How she could ever have thought him merry she did not know. Looking at him now, he looked downright evil.

"Is this some kind of a joke, Julius?" he asked in a hard voice, looking more like the ogre Ava had imagined all those years with each passing moment.

"I don't know what you mean, Robert," her father said mildly. But he didn't sound surprised, and he didn't look away.

"I mean," Sinclair replied, all traces of civility gone from his tone, "is this some kind of damn *joke*, Moreland?"

"Robert," Mrs. Sinclair gasped.

Sinclair turned to her, and Ava saw the anger in his face full force.

"Don't you know who this is, Elberta?" he roared. "This is that Angell kid from Matheson's place. The one who ran off after trying to kill the overseer."

Mrs. Sinclair gasped again and brought a plump hand to her breast. "The poor man who lost his eye?"

He turned his livid face back to Mr. Moreland. "What the hell are you trying to pull, Julius? Is this some sick evolution of your damned abolitionist leanings? Is this your idea of revenge?"

"Mr. Sinclair," Ava's mother stated imperiously, "I'll thank you to watch your language in my house."

"I don't know why I should," the little man snarled, "when it's obvious you feed dogs at your table." He threw an indignant hand toward Angell.

"Mr. Sinclair!" Ava burst. "What on earth are you talking about? Mr. Angell is our guest, and no disrespect shall be tolerated from anyone, least of all *you*."

She glanced anxiously at her father, who observed the scene as if he'd choreographed it himself, a strangely smug look on his face.

"Father, have you nothing to say?" she demanded, her voice rising. "This man's manner is reprehensible!"

"It's all right, Ava," Angell said quietly. "The man has his reasons."

"Damn right I do," Sinclair crowed. "Expecting me to eat with a damn—"

"*No!*" Angell's back straightened, and he held up a warning hand in Sinclair's direction. His eyes glittered with fury, and the little man was momentarily silenced.

Angell turned to her father. "Mr. Moreland, perhaps I should—"

"No, hold on a moment, son," her father said and moved forward calmly. Pushing his hands casually into his pockets, he directed a mild gaze at Sinclair. "Would you care to tell us what you find so objectionable about Mr. Angell, Robert?"

"I'm not sure you want to do this, sir," Angell said, his voice low but determined. "Not here, not now. Your other guests . . ." His eyes moved to the Hendersons, frozen in a startled cluster by the couch.

"They'll be all right," her father said serenely. "What is it, Robert?"

Mr. Sinclair scoffed and looked at the sea of confused faces around him. "What, has he pulled the wool over all your eyes?" he sneered and looped his thumbs into the armholes of his bean-green vest. "Then it'll be my *pleasure* to expose him for what he really is. You see, I've known this boy since he was born, and a fine strapping lad he was." He laughed caustically.

Ava tore her eyes from the man's twisted face and looked to Angell. To her surprise, his gaze was pinned not on Sinclair, but on herself.

She searched his face. "Angell—" she started, but Sinclair talked over her.

"That's right. He was a healthy young buck, and he'd have fetched quite a sum on the open market. But Matheson, *huh*, he was a sentimental old fool. It happened he had a certain fondness for the boy's mother, seeing as how he'd paid *extra* for her because of her pale skin."

Ava heard her mother gasp, but still her eyes held Angell's. His tortured gaze studied her, while his face remained hard and expressionless. It was as if part of him looked inward and hated what he saw.

"I don't understand," she said quietly to him, wanting nothing but to hear his voice, to see his face without that dangerously blank look.

But Sinclair heard her.

"You don't understand?" he repeated, his disgust palpable. "Which part didn't you get, missy? Let me spell it out for you, then."

Angell shifted his eyes to Sinclair, resignation clear in the sadness of his gaze.

Reluctantly, Ava's eyes followed his.

"This boy's father might have been a planter," Sinclair began with obvious relish, "but his mother was a *slave*—a *black* woman. Which makes him a black man. You all been entertaining a Negro in your home, and you were about to serve him dinner at your table. How does that set with your old abolitionist views, Moreland? That Anti-Slavery Society you belonged to make you enlightened enough to have one of *them* at your table?"

A thump sounded behind them, and all heads turned to see Mrs. Henderson slumped on the floor in a faint. Ava's mother moved swiftly to the bellpull while Mr. Henderson knelt beside his wife, fanning her weakly with his handkerchief.

Cullum wandered backward toward the window, muttering, "Oh, dear, oh, dear me."

Ava glanced at Priscilla and Harvey behind her, and they shared equally stunned looks before Ava turned back to Angell. For some reason, she could not seem to draw a complete breath.

"Angell?" she managed, over the lump in her throat. Why didn't he say anything? Why didn't he defend himself?

Angell looked around the room, his eyes strangely empty. "I should leave now," he said, as simply as if the weather had just turned inclement.

Ava's thoughts churned slowly. He did not deny it. Was it that he didn't want to give credence to the accusation, as her father had always done with Sinclair's defamation? She moved her gaze to her father, who stood imperturbably watching Sinclair.

"No need for that," her father said.

And then it struck her. "Trace," she said suddenly. "That's what he knew, isn't it?" She stared at Angell, willing him to meet her eyes, to tell her something—anything—but to look her in the eye and talk to her.

"Trace!" Mrs. Sinclair repeated shrilly. "*That's* the man he tried to kill! He's the one who lost his eye, isn't he, Robert?"

"That's right. Barrett Trace," Sinclair said, nodding with great satisfaction.

Barrett Trace, Ava repeated, mentally recalling the sinister face with the milky-blue eye. The ugly secret he was using to blackmail Angell was not exposure of his poverty, Ava thought. The mystery Angell was determined to keep from her was not another woman. The horrible thing he meant to keep from her—the tragic secret he thought must keep them apart—was simply *this*, the providence of his birth.

Ava's heart thundered, and she glanced quickly at her mother, who knelt next to Mrs. Henderson, slapping her wrist. Her mother did not look up.

Her eyes slid to Priscilla, who held a corner of the afghan in both fists under her chin. Behind her, Harvey stood holding Priscilla's shoulders as if she might drop over if he let go.

"I have nothing to say about Barrett Trace," Angell said, his voice hollow in the silence, "except that *he* is guilty of murder, not I. Mrs. Moreland, I apologize to you for this—probably shocking revelation. I'm sorry for any dishonor I've brought on your family."

Ava watched as her mother continued to slap Mrs. Henderson's wrist with metronomic precision.

"And you, Mr. and Mrs. Henderson. Cullum. I apologize to you as well," Angell continued, his shoulders square, his voice strong and his eyes as vacant as a dead man's. "Priscilla . . ." He smiled slightly, and her lips curved in automatic response before she looked quickly away. Angell's face sobered. "Harvey. You knew all along something bad would come of me, I'm sure."

Ava watched in horror as Harvey looked down without replying.

Angell turned to her, the strangely pale depths of his eyes unutterably sad. *Do you see now?* he had asked her that day after Trace had left. *Do you see that I'm not good enough for you?*

"And Ava. I'm sorry," he said quietly, his chin raising fractionally with what vestige of pride he had left. "I apologize to you, most of all. I never meant it to be a lie."

She opened her mouth to speak, but nothing emerged. Meanings, questions, rebuttals crowded her mind, but before she could choose the right one, Angell turned and moved to the door. One thought sprang to the forefront.

"Where are you going?" she blurted, taking two steps forward, then stopping as he turned on her, his eyes hard.

"I'm going to get my things," he said. "Good-bye, Ava."

She stood stock still as he left the room, her feet planted to the floor, her heart stalled. Desperation rang like a bell in her chest. *Move, you idiot,* her mind screamed. But she remained still, staring at the empty hallway.

Had she been so weak all her life, she thought suddenly, that now when action was required she was powerless to provide it? *She* had to stop him. She and she alone.

Behind her, Mr. Henderson cleared his throat. "Under the circumstances, I think we'd best be going," he said stiffly.

His words caused her to turn slowly on the crowd behind her.

Mrs. Henderson, coming to, swirled a fish-eyed look around the room and wailed, "Is he still here?"

Cullum rushed forward, his hands clasped nervously together, his face pale. "It's all right, Mother, we're leaving," he said, his voice unnaturally high.

At that moment, she knew what she had to do. She was not weak, and she was not powerless. She was right and she was determined, and she was going to seize what she wanted.

"My God," Ava said, watching her mother and Mr. Henderson help Mrs. Henderson to her feet. She glanced again at Harvey and Priscilla, at Mr. and Mrs. Sinclair who stood triumphantly in the wake of their fleeing prey.

"You all make me ashamed," she said, her furious eyes landing on the Hendersons' censorious faces.

"We're leaving," Mr. Henderson said, looking down his long thin nose at her. "Do ring for our coach."

Ava shook her head. "No," she said. Then, as her mother rose to summon Bennis, she repeated more belligerently, "*No*, Mother. I have a few things to say before they go." She could barely believe what she was doing, but the feelings were so strong within her, she could not hold them back. "I defended you all, all along," she said incredulously. "And now, looking at you, I feel ashamed. I've been so blind. All my life, I believed we strived to do what was right and to shun what was wrong. I believed what society taught me— what you taught me, Mr. Henderson—that there were good people and bad people, and that both got what they deserved through the choices they made. I thought," here she issued a disbelieving laugh, "we chose who we associated with based on those choices, on morals and decency, not bigotry and pride."

"There is nothing *moral* about illegitimacy," Mr. Henderson spat.

"Or decent about miscegenation," Sinclair chimed in.

"But none of that is Angell's *fault*! He's lived a decent, moral life. He's a good man. Does that mean nothing? Good heavens, if he'd *killed* someone, or debauched someone's daughter, perhaps then he would warrant this repudiation, this—this shameful renunciation. But you, Mr. Henderson, an hour ago you respected him. And just last week, Mr. Alden called him a—a *genius* is what he called him. And Mrs. Henderson, I recall your wanting to introduce him to your niece. Such a fine man, you said. What's the difference now? He's still the same man."

Mrs. Henderson's face grew red. "Well, I never *dreamed* . . ." she muttered, with a fluttering hand.

Ava shook her head in an effort to break the spell of revulsion that surrounded her. Who were these wretched people?

"Harvey," she said, "Even *you* couldn't look him in the eye."

Harvey looked up. "I—that's not so," he said weakly, and glanced away.

Priscilla lifted one corner of her mouth in a feeble half-smile. "It was just a shock. Just a little shock, that's all."

"This is outrageous. We have done nothing wrong," Mr. Henderson said, gathering up his wife and edging toward the door. "I've lost my appetite."

"Don't be hasty," Sinclair said, surprising everyone. "I think we should stay for dinner. Now that *he's* left, that should satisfy those among us big enough to forgive an honest mistake. Miss Ava is obviously misguided, but she can be made to see reason. And Moreland, you've obviously been taken in by an imposter."

"Mr. Sinclair," her father said slowly, "I was aware of Mr. Angell's parentage before you arrived. I'm just not clear what bearing it should have had on dinner."

All eyes swung to him in shock.

"*You knew?*" Ava gasped.

Her father turned to her and smiled slightly. "If you want him, Ava, you'd best go get him."

Ava gaped at him a moment. He knew *and* he wanted her to stop him. Gratitude swelled in her heart, and she beamed at him, tears in her eyes.

"Thank you," she whispered, then gathered up her skirts and raced for the door.

As she exited the room and rounded the corner to the stairs, she heard Priscilla's voice rise behind her to announce to the stunned group, "Daddy, I want Harvey. Can I have him?"

Angell looked around the room and threw out his hands in disgust. Not a thing there he could call his own. His guns and the clothing he'd worn when Ava and Harvey had sprung him from jail were in a bag at the bottom of the armoire. He supposed he could put them on, but why add insult to injury. Leaving the Moreland house looking like a cowpoke wouldn't do any of them any favors. Hell, he probably wouldn't even be able to get a cab.

There was nothing for it, he thought blankly, he was going to have to take at least the suit on his back. He glanced at himself in the mirrors on the armoire door.

Joshua Angell, gentleman.

He felt himself suspended for a moment as he looked at the reflection, a vision of what he might have been, a vision of what never was.

Abruptly, he moved to the armoire and took the bag from the floor of it. He supposed he should wait until the assembled company departed before he left. Even though he wanted more than anything else to leave that house, to leave those drawing-room people and all they represented, there was no sense in giving them another opportunity to humiliate him.

On an impulse, he tossed the bag onto the bed and dug through the clothes within to pull out one of his guns.

The metal felt cool and heavy in his hand, familiar in a disconcerting way.

He should have known it was coming, he thought as he flicked open the cylinder and glanced at the empty chambers. No secret was safe forever. After revealing his parentage to Moreland that afternoon, he'd been naive enough to think it might end there, that it would be up to him to decide who should know and who should not. He scoffed to himself. Blindsided again. And not just by Sinclair.

He closed his eyes and again saw Ava's silent face—the disbelief, the confusion—it was only a matter of time before it became horror.

He shook his head to clear it. Despite the ugliness, there was some relief in coming clean, he told himself, especially to Moreland. Keeping the secret to himself had become more than he could stand.

The man had been surprised, but not shocked, when Angell had shown up at his office that afternoon. Apparently, he'd suspected something was amiss, though he'd obviously imagined nothing like what Angell had revealed. After Angell told him about his past and assured him that Ava knew nothing—except that he was a penniless nobody—Moreland wasted no time getting to the crux of the matter: Why had the plot been hatched to begin with?

Angell smiled to himself as he remembered Moreland's face when he'd refused to disclose the whole plot. He could only make his own confessions, he'd said, though he'd added that Priscilla might help him fill in the rest of the story.

Moreland was astonishingly nonjudgmental, Angell marveled again. He wasn't pleased, that was clear, but he'd seemed to understand. Plus, he'd helped get rid of Trace, and for that Angell would be forever grateful. He could still see Trace's face as he disappeared with the guards, his shock at being confronted by Moreland himself evident in his battered expression. Blackmailing Angell was not only illegal; it was no longer an option, and the news was obviously devastating.

After that, Moreland had asked Angell—actually *asked* him—at least to show up for dinner. That's all he wanted in return for his help. And though Angell had been desperate to leave, right away, without ever having to face Ava and tell her of his past, how could he have refused after the help Moreland had given him? He couldn't have, and Angell wondered again if Moreland had somehow guessed Sinclair would know him.

Angell spun the gun's cylinder shut and hefted the weapon in his hand, twirling it once around his finger. Perhaps Moreland had wanted the truth exposed to Ava. Perhaps he suspected she had feelings for him and knew they would be obliterated by the news of his tainted birth. That made some sense. Wouldn't do to have a Moreland daughter mooning about over a mixed-blood drifter, now, would it? he thought sourly. And the bonus was they could now use Angell as a tool with which to convince Ava to marry Cullum Henderson, Pride of the Upper Crust.

Angell sighted the gun on a sculpture of Cupid sitting on the mantle and imagined the bullet shattering the smug marble head.

He didn't know what he had expected. That Ava would turn on her whole family and their closest friends to stand up for him? That she'd renounce her precious society and publicly declare love for him? He scoffed at himself and lowered the gun.

He was a fool. He was worse than a fool—he was a dreamer. After all, he'd known all along exactly what *she* was. As proper a blueblood as ever walked Fifth Avenue. Cream for the alley cat. He'd seen it on her face as the news had sunk in and she'd realized what he really was. Disgust. If she'd hated what she thought he was before, she loathed him now.

He closed his eyes again and tried not to think about how she'd looked just two nights ago, her hair loose and her eyes heavy with desire. *I want you to make love to me. And then I want you to stay, here, with me.*

Angell whipped the gun up from an imaginary holster and leveled it at his reflection in the mirror. The imposter stared back at him impassively. Slowly, he squeezed the trigger, the hammer falling on an empty chamber.

"Bang," he whispered to the hard eyes in the mirror.

Someone rapped on the door.

Angell straightened and stared at it. After a second, he tossed the gun back into the bag, strode resolutely to the door and opened it.

Ava stood there, her face a study in composure. Her

gilded hair gleamed in the light from the hall lamp, subtly perfect. She was like living artwork.

"Ava Moreland," he said wryly, stepping back to widen the opening. "I don't suppose you came to help me with my luggage." He attempted to ignore the wrench of his heart at the sight of her. He moved toward the bed. She had come to reprimand him, he knew, to tell him what a low-class, uncouth scoundrel he was to have deceived them all so.

She watched him carefully as she closed the door behind her. "No."

He scoffed and snatched up his bag. "Well, if you've come to point out further flaws in my character, namely dishonesty and illegitimacy," he said, "you missed your chance. The news is out. I'm no longer in your employ. And I'm through bettering myself." He bowed slightly, his teeth gritted against an emotion he thought might overwhelm him—an emotion he could not identify. He decided it was anger. Anger at himself for denial of who he was, and anger at her for making him wish he could continue the charade.

"I didn't come to point out flaws in your character," she said slowly.

His mouth twisted. "To slap my face, then? To berate me for the bastard I am? Tell me, Ava, which was more horrifying, to discover that you'd kissed a black man or the son of a whore?" He dropped his bag on the floor and moved toward her, taking her upper arms in his hands so she had to look up at him. "Which was it, Ava? Or was it the public humiliation that upset you the most?" For a long moment he held her, their gazes locked as he fought the urge to kiss her, to join his lips with hers and compel the impassioned response he'd gotten before. But he didn't. He couldn't. He wouldn't have been able to stand the revulsion he might find in her eyes.

"I didn't come to slap your face," she said quietly, with great deliberation.

"No," he growled, letting go of her and backing away. She leaned back against the door. "No, I suppose you wouldn't. You wouldn't allow yourself to lose control, would you, not even in anger. Well, don't worry, Miss Ava. I won't upset you any longer. I'm leaving. You can marry Cullum for all I care, a man of *breeding* and *stature* who'll never make you think of anything outside of your own ordered existence."

Indignation sparked in her eyes. "I'm not going to marry Cullum," she said evenly. "And despite your low opinion, I have no trouble thinking of things beyond my own existence."

"You know what?" he said, barely absorbing her words through his anger. "I don't give a damn what you think. You or anyone else for that matter." He laughed to himself and grabbed his bag from the floor. "All this time, I've been so damned afraid of what everyone else thought of me and my unfortunate parentage, and you know I'm just too damn tired to worry about it anymore. You didn't kiss a black man, Ava. And you didn't kiss a white man, either. You kissed me. *Me*, Ava. Joshua Angell. And do you know why?" He glared at her. "Do you?"

Her breathing was rapid, as if anger dwelt just beneath the surface of those somber eyes. "What did you mean when you said Trace was guilty of murder?" she asked suddenly.

Angell jerked as if she'd slapped him. She didn't want to answer his question. His teeth clenched against an immediate—and unutterable—retort. Such a simple question, such a simple answer. "He killed my mother."

She flinched. A long moment passed. "He was the overseer on the plantation where your mother was a slave."

Angell eyed her, unable to read her expression, his body frozen. Was it pain there in her eyes? Or compassion. She looked—serene, almost. Well, he could fix that. Into the breach he leapt. "That's right. Trace raped her. Then he killed her." He swallowed hard as anguished emotion sprang unexpectedly within him. He'd never said the words aloud before.

"So you tried to kill him," she continued. Her voice was soft, her eyes bright with what could have been tears.

He took a deep breath. His hand gripped the handle of his bag. "I was ten years old. I did what I could. It wasn't enough."

"And your father—?"

"Was a *bastard*," he spat. Then he laughed. Anger at his father was the embodiment of futility. "Oh, not literally. Owen Matheson was as pedigreed as they come. But he used my mother like a whore, then tossed both of us aside when his legitimate son was born." He raked a hand through his hair and ground his teeth against twenty years of unspent anger built up inside. "Is this what you came up here to hear? The morbid details?"

"I just needed to know the truth," she said.

They exchanged a long look.

Finally, his voice low and raw, he said, "And I thought you'd just come to see me off."

She swallowed and glanced down at her hands.

"What is it? Talk to me, *damnit*," Angell demanded.

She raised her head slowly and met his eyes. She had reached a conclusion. He could see it in the set of her jaw, in the delicate cords of her neck.

Apprehension filled him.

"I know why I kissed you," she said, her voice stronger than he'd anticipated. She looked at him with the flinty eyes of her father. His heart hammered in his chest.

Silence quivered between them.

"I kissed you, Joshua Angell," she said firmly, "because I am in love with you."

He felt the ground dip beneath his feet.

"And I came up here tonight . . ." She paused, her eyes suddenly uncertain. Then she swallowed and raised her chin. "I came up here because Father told me if I wanted you, I'd best come get you. So I came up here," she swallowed again, "to ask you to marry me."

Angell's mouth dropped open. His bag slid from nerveless fingers. *"What?"* The word was a whisper.

She took a step toward him and stopped, her gaze steady. "Angell, will you marry me?"

Epilogue

The gunshot echoed through the valley, bouncing off hills quilted with trees of magenta and flame. A flock of birds exploded from the nearby brush, wings battering the air in sudden alarm. A squirrel froze, then dashed for the closest tree. The dog leapt up from his sunlit patch of grass behind the farmhouse and skittered toward the porch.

The five tin cans, however, stood undisturbed on the fence post.

Angell sighed.

Ava cocked her head and lowered the arm holding the gun.

"I think," she said finally, "that if I were to be accosted by something as small as that can, I wouldn't need a gun to defend myself anyway."

Angell suppressed a smile and shook his head, running a tired hand over his face. When he looked back at her, she was regarding him innocently, a small, mischievous smile on her lips.

"Let me explain this again. The can is not the accoster. The can represents the spot where the bullet

310

would have the best chance of *stopping* the accoster."
He rose from his seat and came toward her.

She frowned. "Is accoster a word?"

"I don't know, Ava. That's your department." He
took her shoulders in his hands and turned her back
toward the fence. She leaned back against him, and
he circled one arm around her waist. "Now," he said,
his cheek against her hair, "the accoster is in your
yard—"

"I don't think accoster is a word," she said.

"Fine." He raised her hand with the gun in it to the
level of her shoulder. "It's a bear. Big teeth, bad dis-
position. It's in our yard—"

"Here? In *our* yard? There aren't any bears in Pennsylvania."

"Like hell. Who told you that?" He couldn't resist
taking a speculative nip at her ear.

"Harvey did," she said, bending her neck to avoid
him, but he could hear the smile in her voice.

He laughed. "Yeah, Harvey would know." He tapped
the underside of her arm with a fist, urging the gun
higher when it dipped. "When are they getting here
anyway?"

Ava squinted her eyes and directed the gun. "Tonight. I've already had Jenny make up the rooms."

Angell craned his neck to look at the side of her face.
"Close one eye completely, Ava, not both of them partway."

Ava pressed her lips together. "Which one?"

From behind her he looked down the sights of the
gun. "I don't care. The left one."

She squeezed the trigger. The gun exploded. Her
arm jerked upward. The dog slithered under the
porch.

The cans stood steadfast.

She sighed and sagged against him. He rested his
chin on her head.

"There aren't *many* bears in Pennsylvania," he said
after a minute. "And I suppose the noise might bother
them some."

"Enough to make them change their mind about accosting me?"

He took a deep breath. "Probably not."

"Priscilla said Harvey's hired a new nanny. This one's put the fear of God into little Zelda, she says."

"Then she ought to scare the pants off the rest of us, too," Angell said wryly. "That child doesn't fear mere mortals."

"Just because she walks all over you, Angell," Ava said dryly, "doesn't mean she can't be disciplined."

"I can't help it," he said, moving his right hand to her ribcage to caress the side of her breast. "There's something about a mean blonde I can't resist."

"Be careful," Ava said. "This mean blonde is holding a gun."

He laughed. "I've seen this blonde shoot."

She raised the pistol and closed one eye while Angell continued to explore her body with one hand, holding her tightly around the middle with the other. "Stop it," she said, without much conviction. "You're distracting me."

"You're too tense. Relax into it. Let me help you." He traced the underside of one breast with his thumb.

Ava melted against him, her arm lowering slowly as her eyes closed. "Oh, who cares about bears?"

"I do. Now, come on. I can't be here all the time— not with all those damn cows to look after." He straightened and pulled her up tightly against him, her gun hand in his. His face next to hers, he said, "Line up the sights. Let your body relax, but keep your focus on the one thing, the one spot. Exhale, slowly."

They both exhaled, slowly.

"Pick your moment," he said, "and . . ."

His hand around hers, he squeezed the trigger. Once, twice, three times. Sound reverberated off the hills. The smoke cleared, and only one can remained standing.

"How did you do that?" Ava demanded. "You fired three times and hit four cans!"

"Magic."

"Those cows are all on paper," she said, turning in

his arms and looking up at him, her eyes narrowed.

"On paper in an office in Philadelphia," he said, his lips curving at the devilment on her face. "And your father expects great things of me. I can't let him down."

Ava closed her eyes and rubbed her temple against his cheek. "Hmmm. You know what else he wants."

Angell reveled in the feel of her arms around him, her free hand uninhibitedly exploring his back. "What's that?"

She turned her head into his neck and kissed him near the collarbone. "Grandchildren."

He raised his brows. "More than cows?"

"I think so."

He leaned down and captured her lips in his, his eyes open. Their gazes met, and they smiled with the kiss.

"Then come with your husband, Miss Ava," he said, kissing her softly, "and we'll continue our marksmanship in a more enjoyable location."

NO ANGEL'S GRACE

LINDA WINSTEAD

From the moment Dillon feasts his eyes on the raven-haired beauty, Grace Cavanaugh, he knows she is trouble. Sharp-tongued and stubborn, with a flawless complexion and a priceless wardrobe, Grace certainly doesn't belong on a Western ranch. But that's what Dillon calls home, and as long as the lovely orphan is his charge, that's where they'll stay.

But Grace Cavanaugh has learned the hard way that men can't be trusted. Not for all the diamonds and rubies in England will she give herself to any man. But when Dillon walks into her life he changes all the rules. Suddenly the unapproachable ice princess finds herself melting at his simplest touch, and wondering what she'll have to do to convince him that their love is the most precious gem of all.

_4223-1 $5.50 US/$6.50 CAN

Desperado's Gold
Linda Jones

Jilted at the altar and stranded in the Arizona desert by a blown gasket in her Mustang convertible, Catalina Lane hopes only for a tow truck and a lift to the nearest gas station. She certainly doesn't expect a real live desperado. But suddenly, catapulted back in time to the days of the Old West, Catalina is transported into a world of blazing six-guns and ladies of the evening.

When Jackson Cady, the infamous gunslinger known as "Kid Creede," returns to Baxter, it's to kill a man and earn a reward, not to use his gold to rescue a naive librarian from the clutches of a greedy madam. He never would have dreamed that the beauty who babbled so incoherently about the twentieth century would have such an impact on him. But the longer he spends time with her, the more he finds himself captivated by her tender touch and luscious body—and when he looks deep into her amber eyes, he knows that the passion that smolders between them is a treasure more precious than any desperado's gold.

_52140-7 $5.50 US/$6.50 CAN

DANGEROUS VIRTUES:

ELAINE BARBIERI *Honesty*

Honesty, Purity, Chastity—three sisters, very different women, all three possessed of an alluring beauty that made them...DANGEROUS VIRTUES

When the covered wagon that is taking her family west capsizes in a flood-swollen river, Honesty Buchanan's life is forever changed. Raised in a bawdy Abilene saloon by its flamboyant mistress, Honesty learns to earn her keep as a card sharp, and a crooked one at that. Continually searching for her missing sisters, the raven-haired temptress finds instead the last person in the world she needs: a devastatingly handsome Texas ranger, Sinclair Archer, who is sworn to put cheats and thieves like herself behind bars. Nestled in his protective embrace, Honesty finds the love she's been desperately seeking ever since she lost her family—a love that will finally make an honest woman out of her.

_4080-8 $5.99 US/$6.99 CAN

DANCE of the FLAME

ELAINE BARBIERI

**Elaine Barbieri's romances are
"powerful...fascinating...storytelling at its best!"**
—Romantic Times

Exiled to a barren wasteland, Sera will do anything to regain the kingdom that is her birthright. But the hard-eyed warrior she saves from death is the last companion she wants for the long journey to her homeland.

To the world he is known as Death's Shadow—as much a beast of battle as the mighty warhorse he rides. But to the flame-haired healer, his forceful arms offer a warm haven, and he swears his throbbing strength will bring her nothing but pleasure.

Sera and Tolin hold in their hands the fate of two feuding houses with an ancient history of bloodshed and betrayal. But no matter what the age-old prophecy foretells, the sparks between them will not be denied, even if their fiery union consumes them both.

_3793-9 $5.99 US/$6.99 CAN